BULL RIVER
House Creek
Marsh
Beach Hammock
Marsh
WILLIAMSON ISLAND
BILL'S REST
S A W
U N D
OLDFORT
N
MW00459563

Wassaw Sound

Wassaw Sound

William Charles Harris, Jr.

To: Bob Steed
A True Southern
Gentleman!
God Bless,
Bill [illegible]

FBC
Frederic C. Beil
Savannah

Copyright © 2008 by William Charles Harris, Jr.

First published in the United States by
Frederic C. Beil, Publisher, LLC
609 Whitaker Street
Savannah, Georgia 31401
www.beil.com

All rights reserved, including the right of reproduction
in whole or in part in any form.

Library of Congress Cataloging-in-Publication Data
Harris, William Charles, 1947–
Wassaw Sound : a novel / by William C. Harris, Jr.
p. cm.
ISBN-13: 978-1-929490-37-0 (alk. paper)
1. Hydrogen bomb—Fiction. 2. Accidents—Fiction.
3. United States—History—1953–1961—Fiction.
4. Wassaw Sound (Ga.)—Fiction.
1. Title.
PS3558.A662W37 2008
813'.54—dc22
2007043156

Endpaper map of Wassaw Sound by Torrey Stifel

This book is set in Galliard, composed by the Nangle Type Shop,
Meriden, Connecticut; printed on acid-free paper;
and sewn in signatures.

Printed in the United States of America

In memory of

Wesley L. ("Bud") Lewis
March 28, 1946–September 21, 1997

The Thousandth Man

Contents

Prologue

Savannah, Georgia, is arguably the most beautiful and charming city in the United States. I was born and raised in Savannah, and with the exception of the time I was away at school, I have lived my entire life here. Perhaps the most enchanting parts of the Savannah area are the marshes and rivers that lie east of the city and lead to the Atlantic Ocean. A great deal of the action in this tale takes place in these areas, and I have tried to correctly evoke the feeling of what it is like to experience these unique surroundings.

Although it is fiction, *Wassaw Sound* is historically and technically correct; the locations in the story are all real and accessible. Most of the characters are, at least to some degree, based on actual people I have known. With some of the lesser characters, I have used their real names.

William C. Harris, Jr.

Acknowledgments

I am happy to have had the help of many people with the writing of this book. There are a few who stand out among those who helped.

In the area of the diagnosis and treatment of brain tumors, Dr. John West was most helpful as was Kim Hodge, R.Ph., in the science of pharmacology. With a lifetime in the seafood business and in sailing the local waters, Buddy Nelson provided insight and information on shrimping and shrimp boats. Rabbi Arnold Mark Belzer of Congregation Mickve Israel and the Right Reverend Monsignor William O. O'Neill, rector of the Cathedral of St. John the Baptist, offered valuable information on religion and spirituality. I am most grateful for my wife, Pam, the most wonderful person I've ever known, and for her support during the writing of all of my novels.

And I thank the people of Savannah, who have always been there for me through my trials and tribulations as well as my triumphs. You are all so wonderful.

I

ADVISER TO THE PRESIDENT

The Return

Then shall the dust return to the
earth as it was: and the spirit shall
return unto God who gave it.
—Ecclesiastes 12:7

Present Day

JUDAH BENJAMIN knew he had had enough. He had grown tired of his work, his friends, even his pricey three-story in Georgetown. He was fed up with deadlines, reporters, lobbyists, and, most of all, the hard-looking, too-chic, and gluttonously ambitious women who seemed somehow to force their way into his life.

Judah had had a stomach full of the two cell phones clipped to his belt and the wad of cash he needed to carry just to maneuver the streets of Washington by day and its trendy clubs at night. He was burned out, finished, and heading out of the capital for home. He didn't even start to relax until he had reached Richmond.

When Judah passed the Philip Morris complex next to I-95, it reminded him of the thousands of Marlboros he had inhaled until he had quit twenty-five years earlier. This made him think about how he and his best friend, Billy Aprillia, would share a smoke as they drove along the Tybee Road in his father's car while passing a quart bottle of Pabst Blue Ribbon back and forth between them in the summer of sixty-three. They were on their way to Tybee Island, that huge hormone-magnet that attracted every teenager in Savannah to the sound of waves and the thrill of making out in the dunes. "That was so long ago," said Judah to himself, "and I loved it so much. I used to believe it would last forever."

In the seat next to him sat Moshe Dayan, his Doberman, who began to get restless. Judah knew the dog needed to relieve himself, so he turned off at a Stuckey's somewhere south of Petersburg. Judah had named his dog after the great Israeli general he admired so much, the hero of the 1967 Arab-Israeli war.

While Moshe sniffed a light pole, then left his mark, Judah admired his car. As a child he had been attracted to automobiles and could name every make and model. Later, as his fortunes improved, he was able to amuse himself with expensive sports cars. He took it as a sign of ageing, when he lost his interest in sports cars and started driving sedans. His latest indulgence was a 390-horsepower, pewter-colored Jaguar XJR. It was magnificent, and it pleased him—but not the way cars used to. Nothing seemed to please him much anymore. Maybe that was why he had just pulled up stakes and left.

A lot of people were angry with him for leaving so abruptly, but they'd just have to get over it. There were plenty of good, eager young bucks and broads who would be happy to scratch and claw one another for his position. He hadn't exactly just up and quit on a moment's notice. It had been more like a month's notice. He had visited all of his clients and pleaded his case with skill and grace. All had said they understood.

Nevertheless, Judah knew he was "the best," and all these people wanted was the best, no matter what toll was inflicted on the best. When he had met with POTUS (President of the United States), the boss couldn't have been nicer. Judah had thought that he had really understood; it was the chief of staff who was boiling.

Mac McClellan's words were still ringing in his ears when he crossed over the South Carolina state line. "Goddamn it, Judah, you're responsible for the TV ads and now you're quitting on me! I can't friggin' believe you're going back to Savannah, Georgia, just because you can't sleep at night! The president is in a tight one and he needs you and I'm not accepting your resignation. So see a doctor and get some damn sleeping pills."

That day, in spite of a jackhammer hangover, Judah remained

calm, forced a smile, said "Bye, Mac," and then walked out the office of the chief of staff of the president of the United States. McClellan later phoned him at home, blew off some more steam, and called him a chickenshit coward; but finally he was placated with Judah's promise that he would play a limited consulting role from Savannah—though only by phone. "Fuck this," he said to himself as he hung up the phone, poured another shot of Kettle One over ice, and resumed packing for his trip home the next morning.

When Judah saw the sign on I-95 that said Ridgeland/US-17-South, he knew he was less than an hour from Savannah. That exit would lead him down Highway 17 past a half-dozen fireworks stands and into the deep, thick green of the Lowcountry forest, then over the Savannah River into Georgia and on to his roots and home.

That stretch of Highway 17 had remained pretty much as Judah remembered it from his childhood. He had an ache in his stomach as he recalled a trip he had once taken with his father. They had driven that exact road to Charleston almost forty years prior on a visit to Fort Sumter. It was one of the most memorable days of his life. Colonel Benjamin was a Civil War historian who brought the entire battle to life for Judah as they stood together on the ramparts of Fort Sumter and looked back to the Battery at Charleston.

Tears started to well in Judah's eyes. A few moments later he began to sob; his eyes were so filled with tears that he had trouble seeing. Moshe sensed his distress and placed his great head in Judah's lap.

"Damn, Moshe," said Judah as he gently stroked the dog, "I didn't know this was going to happen. I'm supposed to be coming down here to feel better, not worse." Judah thought for a few moments. "Maybe this is what I needed, a release. Maybe letting go of some of the bullshit I've had wrapped inside for so long will make me feel better." Moshe whined a little, then licked Judah's hand.

Judah had taken Highway 17 because he wanted to cross over the Savannah River on the new bridge. It was a graceful suspension bridge and much taller than the old steel-truss Talmadge Bridge that Judah and his friends used to take on forays during their high school days to the beer joints on the Carolina side of the river.

The May sun was just beginning to set as he reached the crest of the bridge and looked over the skyline of Savannah. It was an urban forest that allowed its buildings to peak though the treetops. Judah was awed as the façades of downtown Savannah glowed in the last pink lights of the day. It was all still there—and Judah felt a smile begin.

With the exception of last St. Patrick's Day, it had been more than four years since he had been home. His work had kept him close to the New York–D.C. corridor, and both of his parents had been dead for years. The only relative he had left in Savannah was his cousin Bubba Silverman, and he hadn't talked to him since Yom Kippur two years ago. Judah chuckled as he remembered what hell-raisers they had been growing up.

As he steered his big Jag along Oglethorpe Avenue, Judah put all the windows down and sniffed the air. The smell of the paper mill was what he was searching for, but that had long ago been cleaned up, and only the light scent of oak leaves wafted through the air. When he got to the red light at Abercorn Street, he used his cell phone to call Billy Aprillia.

"I'm here, Bubba," was all he said when Billy answered. Billy laughed and told him his room was ready and that he had made reservations for dinner.

Billy Aprillia was the son of Charlie Aprillia, the Emperor of Thunderbolt, the Lord of Shrimp. "That was a long time ago, too," thought Judah as he pulled onto Victory Drive and ran his eyes down the double rows of tall palmettos that filled the median as far as he could see.

"Billy's had a hard time," said Judah to Moshe, who sat straight up in the front seat, head out the widow, sniffing scents he had never known before. "He's still a little screwed up, been married and divorced, but hey, Moshe, I've been married three times, so who am I to be talking?"

Moshe barked at a chocolate lab walking with an attractive blonde thirty-something in Daffin Park. She looked up and smiled. Judah smiled back, then said, "Good work, general, I'll catch her later."

When Judah turned onto River Drive in Thunderbolt, he didn't like what he saw. The grand and open vista of the Wilmington River that had once been the hallmark of the little fishing village was gone, blocked by a dry-storage barn for boats. This was followed by one set of condos after another, each one towering two stories above the bluff. Judah was shocked. "How could this happen?" he asked himself.

The last set of condos belonged to Billy. The only redeeming thing about them was that they were the best-looking of the lot. "Well, hell," Judah muttered as he and Moshe climbed the stairs to Billy's unit. He promised himself he would keep his mouth shut.

When the door to number six opened, Judah had an even greater shock. Standing before him was Hannah Meldrim. He hadn't seen her in maybe thirty, thirty-five years.

"Hannah," was all Judah could manage to say.

Hannah knew Judah would be surprised, confused, maybe even hurt—though she hoped it wouldn't be. It had been too long for that, she thought.

Smiling her sweet, precious, wonderful smile, Hannah came to Judah and hugged him. "You look wonderful. I can't believe you're with the president's reelection campaign." She stepped back, smiled again, then ran her fingers through her hair. "I'm truly glad to see you, please come in."

Judah searched for something to say, then looked down at his side and spluttered, "This is my dog, Moshe. He won't bite. I've had him for three years now, he's really well behaved and gentle, I promise."

Laughing, Hannah replied, "I love dogs, I've got two," as she took Judah by the arm and led him inside.

"Billy," she called, "Judah's here, sweetheart." Then she turned to Judah and said, "He's not ready yet. Always a slowpoke. You know that better than anybody."

Judah shook his head. "Yeah, Billy never got anywhere on time." His eyes wandered around the large great room, filled with all things nautical.

"Can I fix you something to drink?" Hannah walked toward an elaborate wet bar at the far end of the room. Just behind the bar was a wall-length window that afforded a splendid view of the Wilmington River, one denied to those on the street.

Still in a state of shock, Judah was a little slow to answer, but eventualy he shook out the cobwebs. "Uh yeah, that'd be just fine. It's been a long trip, I drove straight through. A vodka on the rocks if you've got it."

Hannah went behind the bar, found a bottle of Absolut, and held it up as Judah took a seat across from her.

"Will this be all right?"

Judah placed his elbows on the cold, polished surface of the bar and answered, "I think that'll do just fine."

As Hannah let the vodka spill over the ice, she glanced up at Judah with smile. "I guess you were surprised to see me here."

"A little." Judah gave a shrug as Hannah pushed his drink toward him. With no hesitation he put the glass to his lips, tilted it up, took a long pull, then returned his glass to the bar. "How long have y'all been seeing each other?" he inquired as he waited for the alcohol to do its work.

"Since a little after this past St. Patrick's Day."

"Well, the last time I talked with Billy was St. Patrick's Day, so I guess that's why I didn't know." Judah drained the rest of the vodka from his glass. "How did y'all start dating?"

"I ran into Billy after Mass one morning."

Judah's eyebrows went up. "You saw him at church?"

"That's right, one Sunday down at the Cathedral." Hannah poured him another drink without being asked. "We've been going to Mass together ever since."

"You mean Billy's got religion again? I remember when he quit going to church. That was back in high school. He'd tell his mother he was going to church and then meet me at the Triple X drive-in. I always thought it had a lot to do with his parents, especially his mother. She just kind of wore him out with religion. It was twenty-four-seven at the Aprillia house. They had more crucifixes than the Vatican."

"I didn't really know Billy very well back then. After I got married and had Matthew, I guess I was kind of cut off from all my old friends. You know, a different life."

Pain briefly slashed across Hannah's face as she talked, and Judah looked down at his glass to avoid her eyes. He couldn't believe she could still affect him the way she did after so long. He had admitted to himself years ago that he would probably always be in love with her. That was why his first marriage failed, and it was probably a factor in at least one other.

After a moment Judah looked up suddenly with a quizzical expression. "Wait a minute, I thought you were a Methodist. What are you doing in a Catholic church?"

Hannah ruefully smiled. "I was a Methodist, but after my divorce I just kind of drifted. I wasn't interested in religion, I'd been through too much and was generally angry. Then one day out of nothing but idle curiosity, I went into the Cathedral, just to see what it was like. Lloyd Bryan was saying Mass. You remember Lloyd, don't you?"

"Sure I do. We were at Benedictine together."

"Well, he gave the most beautiful sermon and I spoke with him after Mass. We got to be friends, and I just kept coming back. After a while I joined the Catholic Church. My mother probably rolled over in her grave. She didn't think too much of Catholics." Hannah paused for a moment and thought about adding "or Jews," but she didn't.

Judah was about to speak when he heard a door open and turned to see Billy coming down the hall. He had gotten just a little heavier over the years, had fought it, won some and lost some—but he was still the Billy Judah had always known.

"Jude, my man," cried Billy as he came across the room to embrace him. "How ya' been, Bubba?" Billy lifted Judah up in a bear hug. He still had his arm around him as he turned to Hannah and announced, "This is my best friend. We've been through some shit together, haven't we, Bubba?"

Judah shook his head and laughed. "We sure as hell have."

There was just something about Billy that attracted people to him. He always seemed to be in a good mood. His mother had been Irish and when he smiled, which was often, there was a distinct twinkle in his eye. He also had an Irish tongue, so the gift of gab came naturally. It had served Billy well for years.

"We're gonna have dinner at one of your old spots, Judah," said Billy as he turned to Hannah and asked, "Would you mind fixin' me a drink, sugar?"

"Where's that?" asked Judah.

"The 1790. Hannah's son Matt is going to meet us there."

Judah was watching Hannah; he caught her eye when Billy mentioned her son's name. For a moment he thought she was going to say something, but she didn't. When her eyes unexpectedly grew moist, she shifted away from Judah and smiled at Billy as she handed him his single malt and soda.

The 17Hundred90 Restaurant and Inn is located on the corner of President and Lincoln Streets in Savannah's historic district. During the 1980s, when Judah was running Congressman Will McQueen's successful campaigns, the ground-floor lounge was always Judah's last stop. It was a popular five-o'clock spot for many of the local politicians, and also where Judah had met his second wife, Cynthia. That marriage lasted less than two years.

Waiting for Hannah at the bar was her son, Matthew Davenport. He was thirty-seven and married, with a solid two hundred and five pounds carried on a six-foot frame. Everyone said he looked like Hannah, which was fine with Matt because he cared little for his father, Dr. Clark Davenport, a local orthopedic surgeon.

Dinner that night proved to be a delight for everyone. Matt always enjoyed Billy's company and was happy that his mother had found someone who so openly adored her. He was also drawn to Judah, and the two of them seemed to form an instant bond. Judah was a famous son of Savannah; his name was instantly recognized and Matt was flattered by the attention Judah lavished on his thoughts about politics . . . which was Matthew's secret ambition.

When the evening ended Hannah returned to her home in Kensington Park, telling Billy she wanted Judah and him to have some time together all to themselves. In actuality, with Judah there, she wasn't comfortable spending the night at Billy's. Sleeping with Billy outside of marriage was against the laws of the Catholic Church, but she and Billy were truly in love and committed to each other. They were both in their late fifties and had talked about marriage; and at her age Hannah just didn't think it was sinful to have sex with the man she loved, married or not. Judah's presence, however, was a delicate complication.

A little after midnight Billy and Judah were alone, sitting at the bar in the condo and watching the moon rise over the Wilmington River. Billy was feeling the effects of his single malt and was moved to pontificate on the virtues and failings of the women he had known. He finally summed up his present state of mind when he announced, "I got a real sweetheart in Hannah, don't I, Bubba? I hope I don't manage to fuck up this relationship, too."

"You're a lucky boy, asshole. You don't deserve her." Judah hoped that Billy wouldn't notice the twitch in his left eye, which always returned when he was stressed. He threw back one more vodka, rested his elbows on the bar, put his hands under his chin, and blew out a sigh. "I wish I had a decent relationship that I could worry about fucking up."

"Aw, man, give it some time. I'm tellin' ya', there are some really sweet things here in Savannah. They aren't like that bunch of hard-lookin', nasal-talkin', know-it-all Yankee broads you seem to go for. Hannah can fix you up, no problem."

"Not right now, Billy. I've got too much on my mind to be much fun for anybody."

"Yeah, well, next time you come back, maybe you'll be feelin' better and ready for a shot at a doll baby like Hannah."

Judah looked out over the river. "I'm here to stay, Billy. I'm burned out with the whole damn program, and I'm not going back."

Billy smiled and put his arm around Judah's shoulder. "I'm glad you're stayin', I've missed you." A moment passed; then Billy turned on his stool to face his friend. "I've got something to show you, but you've got to promise me you won't say a word about this to anybody. I was gonna show you tomorrow, but shit, this is just as good a time as any, so come on, let's go down to the garage."

As they walked down the steps to the garage under his unit, Billy started explaining. "I've only got one boat left now, the *St. Patrick*. You remember her, don't you."

On a shrimp boat deckhands are called strikers, and when Billy asked him if he remembered the *St. Patrick*, Judah chuckled and replied, "How could I ever forget! You and I were strikers on her for three summers."

Billy smiled. "Well, I don't do it very often, but sometimes I take her out just to give my skipper a little break on the weekends. Two weeks ago I'm draggin' the channel just outside Wassaw Sound. All of a sudden I can feel one of the nets has snagged on something. So I stop, put her in neutral, and winch myself back to whatever's got a hold of me. I thought I'd caught that damned old anchor that everybody bitches about. So I think, if I can, maybe I'll pull that sucker up, take her in, and be the hero of the shrimping fleet for a day or so."

At the bottom of the steps, Billy hit the light switch. His Ford F-150 pickup stood on one side of the garage. The other side was almost empty, but in one corner a paint-spattered tarpaulin covered an object that appeared to be about five feet tall and three feet wide. As they walked over to it, Billy continued his story.

"My boat can lift eight thousand pounds in the nets, so I wasn't too worried about bending a boom or anything. What I was worried about was that if that anchor had me it would rip through my net when I was hauling it up and I'd lose it, so when my lines were pointing straight down in the water and I knew my stern was right over it, I went and hit the GPS so I could know to keep the hell away from that area."

Judah's curiosity had been pricked. He watched intently as Billy went and stood next to whatever was under the tarp.

"Well," said Billy as he prepared to remove the tarp, "when I got this thing here on my deck, it was the surprise of my life." Then he ceremoniously pulled off the cover. Billy stood back proudly from his prize. "Know what this is?"

"Looks like the stabilizer fins to an awfully big bomb," said Judah as he moved in for a closer look.

"You damn right it is, Bubba. It was hooked to one of the biggest bombs ever made. These are the fins from that A-bomb that was lost in the sound back in the fifties. Remember that?"

Judah slowly nodded, then said quietly, "Zero-thirty-five

hours, five February, 1958, to be exact. My father was vice-commander here at Hunter Air Base the night this thing got lost. Holy shit, have you called anybody yet?"

"Nope. Not yet." Billy placed the tarp back over his find. "Because I hit my GPS, and saved the position in my unit, I know within thirty feet where the rest of that baby is, and I'm not tellin' anybody a damn thing for free. If they can throw away all the money they do on six-hundred-dollar toilet seats, welfare queens, and millions on all kinds of other bullshit, they can sure as hell afford to come up with a little reward for a guy who leads them to a damn atomic bomb they lost." Billy stopped for a moment, then said, "That's where you come in, Judah."

"What do you mean?"

Billy gave Judah the I-can't-believe-you're-that-dumb look. "You're the one with all the connections up in Washington. You can make discreet inquiries with the right people about me leading them to where the business end of this thing is sitting. I figure we start the bidding at two million. No money, no bomb. But if I'm right and they get that bomb back, I want to be paid."

The Bomb

I am become death,
the destroyer of worlds.
—Vishnu
From the *Bhagavad Gita*, and the words
murmured by J. Robert Oppenheimer
when he witnessed the first atomic
bomb detonation on July 16, 1945

Savannah, Georgia
00:35 hours, February 5, 1958

"COLONEL BENJAMIN here."

"Sir, this is Captain Ogilvie in the tower."

"I hear you, captain, what's the problem."

"Colonel, we've got a situation here that demands your presence."

"What kind of situation, Ogilvie?"

The captain hesitated briefly then said, "Uh, sir, for security reasons, I can't say over the phone."

Colonel Benjamin growled. "All right, captain, send me a car while I get dressed." The colonel pulled himself into a sitting position on the edge of his bed and reached for the lamp on the night stand.

"I've already done that, sir," said the captain in a nervous voice. "Your car should be pulling up in front of your quarters in about five minutes."

"Has General McBride been notified?" asked Colonel Benjamin as he stood and looked at his wife in the bed next to him.

"No, sir. He's not back from Washington yet. He got delayed. You're ranking officer on base, sir."

Colonel Paul Benjamin wouldn't have time to shave, just put on his uniform. It was chilly that night, so he purposely left off his regulation tunic, grabbing instead the old leather flying jacket he had worn while piloting B-17s over Germany during World War II.

He loved the jacket and would have worn it every day on the flight line if it had been regulation gear for a B-47 pilot.

"What's going on, Paul?" asked Arlene as she rolled over to face her husband.

"Can't say, sweetheart," replied the Colonel as he quickly checked his appearance in the mirror, then carefully placed his officer's hat on his head and cocked it slightly to the left. This was what Paul Benjamin called his "kiss-my-ass tilt."

"How long will you be gone?" asked Arlene as she checked the clock on the night table.

"I don't know. Might be an all nighter by the sound of Captain Ogilvie's voice." Then he leaned over and kissed his wife fondly, "See ya."

As he trotted down the sidewalk to the waiting staff car, Colonel Benjamin looked up at the Savannah sky. It was a cold, clear, star filled-night. On the ride to Hunter, the colonel produced a fine Cuban cigar from the top pocket of his flight jacket and went through his ritual of preparation and lighting. By the time he reached the top of the Hunter control tower, Colonel Benjamin had his cigar firmly placed in the left side of his mouth, game face on and ready for action.

"Okay, Ogilvie, what the hell is going on?" he barked as the young captain, who had been studying the radar screen, came to attention.

"Sir, there's been a midair collision over Sylvania about thirty minutes ago between an F-86 out of Charleston and a B-47 out of Homestead. The fighter went down, sir, and the B-47 is badly damaged but still flying. The pilot says he's got to put down pronto or he'll crash. He's headed our way right now."

"Have you got the crash trucks out on the tarmac, captain?"

"Yes, sir."

"Have you got him spotted on our radar yet?" Colonel Benjamin looked intently at the scope.

"Yes, sir. That's him right there." Captain Ogilvie pointed to a blip on the radar screen. "He's about thirty miles east of here, out over the Atlantic and making his turn for final approach."

"Well, it looks like you've got the situation under control, captain. All we can do is wait and hope he makes it."

Captain Ogilvie stood back from the radar screen, took a deep breath, and said, "Sir, there's something else."

"What else, captain?"

"Sir, the pilot reports he's carrying a nuclear device and that it is his intention to jettison it just offshore as he makes his approach. When I told him about the construction at the beginning of our runway and how high the tarmac was, he said he was afraid he'd come in short and hit the end of it. The bomb would tear through the fuselage like a bullet down the barrel of a gun."

Colonel Benjamin's eyes closely followed the moving blip across the radar screen. "Has SAC cleared this?" he finally inquired.

"Sir, I notified SAC just after I spoke to you and brought them up to speed. They didn't give permission for the jettisoning. They didn't deny it, either. Watch officer said he didn't have authority to okay something like that and he would get back to me. It was my impression from speaking with the pilot that he was going to drop his payload with or without permission. He says he's got one shot at landing and doesn't want the extra weight. Things have been moving awfully fast for that crew in the last half-hour."

Colonel Benjamin kept his eye on the radar screen while he spoke. "You've done a good job, captain." Then he turned to his driver and said, "We're going out on the field. I want to be with those crash trucks when this baby comes in."

Standing by his Jeep, which was parked next to one of the foam trucks alongside the main runway, Colonel Benjamin picked up the microphone on his radio. "Captain Ogilvie, how far out is our bird now?"

"Colonel, looks like about seven minutes from touchdown. He should be about five miles from the coastline."

Colonel Benjamin had just said, "Roger that," when the pilot of the B-47 came on the air and said, "Hunter Control, we have just jettisoned our payload. We estimate one mile east of Wassaw Sound. No problems encountered. We are now on final approach."

"Roger that," replied Hunter. "We've got you on the screen and followed your payload with our radar as it fell."

Only minutes later Colonel Benjamin could see the landing lights of the B-47 out in the distance as it made its way at 210 knots over the sleeping residential eastside islands of Savannah. He held his breath as the heavily damaged bomber came hurtling over the fence at the beginning of the runway, only a hundred feet in the air, its approach chute billowing from the tail like a giant mushroom. The colonel braced himself as he watched the plane shoot down the runway, its landing gear reaching out for the safety of Earth. Then there was the loud squeal of tires smacking concrete and a plume of black smoke from the burned rubber that followed. The plane bounced once, then settled in.

As the bomber rolled down the runway, the crash trucks raced behind it with Colonel Benjamin in the vanguard, listening as the pilot applied his brakes. Finally, after more than a mile, the B-47 came to a stop, surrounded by emergency equipment. In seconds the escape hatches opened and three frightened but safe men scrambled out. After they inspected their aircraft, all three knelt and kissed the tarmac.

B-47 #349 had sustained more substantial damage than the crew had originally assumed. On the right wing the number six engine was hanging at a forty-five-degree angle, about to fall off. There was an empty space on the wing pylon where the right fuel tank should have been. Also sustaining damage was the right aileron, which had a gash four feet long and twenty inches deep. Both the vertical and horizontal stabilizers had multiple holes cut by flying debris. Worst of all, the right wing's main spar, the structural support that bears the weight of the aircraft, was broken. There was no doubt that the plane's commander had made the right decision; his plane would never have made it back to Homestead.

The first hint the people of Savannah had about the jettisoned bomb was an article that appeared in the *Savannah Morning News* on February 6, 1958. The headline read: "Plane's Survival After Crash Amazes Airmen." There was also a photo of the B-47 with its damage clearly visible. The text described the midair collision and the plane's emergency landing at Hunter Air Force Base. No mention was made of the jettisoned bomb.

The public knew nothing else until it awakened to the headlines in the *Morning News* of Thursday, February 13. "Jettisoning Of Nuclear Weapon Here Disclosed After Air Collision." In the article staff writer Wallace Davis said, "A release from the Hunter Air Force Base public information office said the weapon was in the 'transportable configuration' (unassembled) when dropped and incapable of detonation."

The next day the headlines read, "Secrecy-Shrouded Hunt For 'Weapon' Continues." The article gave a sketchy description of the search operations and again stated that the bomb could not explode. From the 14th of February until the 22nd, six more articles appeared in the paper concerning the search for the bomb. After that, coverage began to fall off. On April 16th, 1958, the *Morning News* announced that the Navy had called off the search for the bomb in Wassaw Sound and deemed it "irretrievably lost." What the people of Savannah were never told was that the bomb was a 7,500-pound Mark-15, three-megaton hydrogen bomb, serial number 47782, built to wipe out cities the size of Moscow.

The Fire

We didn't start the fire
It was always burning
Since the world's been turning.
We didn't start the fire
No we didn't light it
But we tried to fight it.
—Lyrics by Billy Joel,
from "We Didn't Start the Fire"

8:30 P.M., October 22, 1962

OVER FOUR YEARS had passed since Judah had seen his father so concerned. The last time was when the bomb was lost in Wassaw Sound. Only this time the situation was much more serious.

"Is everything going to be okay, Daddy?" asked Judah as he watched his father hurriedly pack his flight bag.

Colonel Benjamin hardly looked up at his son as he responded. "Everything's going to be just fine." He then reached for the phone next to his bed and called the flight line at Hunter.

"This is Colonel Benjamin. How many of my birds are set and ready?"

Judah watched his father squeeze his eyes shut and rub his brow with the three middle fingers of his left hand. He also saw his mouth tighten just a little harder on his cigar, and waited nervously as his father listened to his executive officer give him the rundown on how many in his wing's fifty-five B-47s were ready for takeoff.

"All right, that's fine, Dick. I'll be there in less than fifteen minutes."

After his call Colonel Benjamin puffed up his cheeks as he blew out a sigh, and stood still for a moment. Then he was moving again. Judah's mother came into the bedroom with a bag full of sandwiches and a thermos of coffee. As Judah moved to her side, she put her arm around him.

No words had to be exchanged. The colonel stowed the food in his flight bag, then handed the bag to his son. "How about putting this in the car for your old man?"

"Yes, sir," replied Judah as he strained to carry the heavy bag from the room. When he was out of earshot, Colonel Benjamin turned to his wife. "This is the real thing. I don't know how long I'll be gone or what I'll get into. Just say your prayers, my love." Then he took his wife into his arms, told her he loved her, and kissed her. It wasn't a long good-bye. Arlene and Paul had long ago discovered that prolonged good-byes seemed to heighten the pain of separation.

Only two hours earlier the Benjamins had gathered around their twenty-one-inch Zenith in the den to hear President Kennedy's address to the nation concerning the Soviet missiles in Cuba and the naval blockade of the island by the United States. When the president announced the blockade, the colonel shot straight up in his chair and began making mental preparations for his command, the 308th Bomber Wing stationed at Hunter Air Force Base. Less than an hour later, the phone rang. It was Hunter's commanding general, placing the 308th on full airborne alert. That night Colonel Benjamin and the rest of his wing would be flying an orbit somewhere off the borders of the Soviet Union, ready to attack if the order came.

Back in '58, when the bomb had been lost, Judah had paid close attention to the news and listened carefully whenever his father spoke of the event—which wasn't often. He had turned eleven the day the government proclaimed the bomb irretrievably lost and called off its search. Judah hadn't been frightened then because of his father's assurances that everything was safe. This was different; Judah could sense his father's tension. He had never seen him like this, and it scared him. His older brother Jacob hadn't done anything to lessen those fears.

"This is real serious shit," said Jacob after the boys had said good-bye to their father and watched him drive down Althea Parkway towards Hunter.

"What do you mean?" asked Judah, looking up at his brother.

"I mean we could have a war with the Russians over this, and our father might have to bomb them. He could be shot down and killed. That's what I mean."

Jacob was four years older than Judah, already a sophomore at the University of Georgia, and a keen student of history and current events. He had had long discussions with his father about the world situation, then known as the Cold War, and realized how serious the unfolding events actually were.

"You mean he might not come back?" asked Judah in a trembling voice.

Jacob immediately regretted what he said and tried to repair the damage. "Ah, the old man's tough as nails. He completed thirty-five missions over Germany with the bastards shooting at him all the time. Don't worry about Dad, he'll come back okay."

Later that night, alone in his room, Judah began to prepare for school the next day. The events of the evening had so shaken him that he didn't even try to study. Instead he kept busy by getting his uniform in order.

Judah was a sophomore at Benedictine Military School, where four years earlier his brother had been a company commander. While he was polishing his brass, he glanced up at the officer's sword hanging over his bed. It was Jacob's, hanging there in wait for the day Judah received his commission at Benedictine.

Judah had never really considered what the price of war actually was. Not until this night. Everything about his life was steeped in God, country, honor, and military service. On both sides of his family men had served during wartime, starting with his namesake and great-great grandfather, Judah P. Benjamin. He had served the Confederacy as secretary of war, attorney general, and secretary of state. His mother's side had also been in the Confederate Army, and it was Judah's ambition to become an Air Force pilot, just like his father. But as he put the finishing touches on his cadet grey uniform and laid it out for the next day, he began to think about what might happen to his father and even what might happen to him if he were called up to serve. Those thoughts scared him; and because of this fear, he began to doubt that he could follow in those footsteps.

The next day at school, there were whispers in morning formation about how many B-47's had been heard taking off from Hunter during the night and whose father's national guard unit had been activated. Even the priests seemed to heighten the tension when they announced special prayers would be said that day for world peace. Judah had a knot in his stomach and couldn't eat his lunch. Instead he gave it to his best friend, Billy Aprillia.

Billy wasn't concerned about the situation. "We can kick the shit out of the Russians and they know it. If they don't pull those missiles outta Cuba, we'll make a parkin' lot outta the damn place. The commies aren't gonna do a thing, Judah." Six days later Nikita Khrushchev proved Billy right, and Judah's father was flying back to Savannah. When the tension subsided all that was left for Judah was the shame he had felt at being afraid. The remainder of 1962 consisted of the Benedictine football schedule, his interest in Lynn Victor, and his selection for the school color guard.

Although Judah didn't play on the football team, he went to every game, just like the rest of the student body, and attended all of the postgame dances. Lynn was always at those functions, and midway through the season Judah found the courage to ask her for a dance, even though he was terribly shy. Lynn was also Jewish and went to Benedictine's counterpart, St. Vincent's Academy for girls. She had noticed Judah earlier in the school year and had found him attractive, but she was even shyer than he was. Their relationship took root that night as they held each other and moved to the sounds of "Sherry," "Do You Love Me," "He's a Rebel," and "I Remember You."

Somehow both Judah and Billy Aprillia had been selected to serve on the school's color guard. It was a plum assignment that relieved them of many of the drudgeries of morning formation and drill. The four members of the color guard practiced by themselves in the gym; and it was there that the bond between Judah and Billy, one that would last a lifetime, was formed and solidified.

There were no storms in Judah's life for the next year. He had done well in school and had gotten his driver's license the following April, which put his romance with Lynn on the fast track. In the summer of '63 he went to work for Charlie Aprillia as a deckhand on one of his shrimp boats along with Billy. Judah had money in his pocket, a cute Jewish girlfriend, and the 1952 Ford his parents had given him on his birthday. He was safe and happy in a well-ordered world, living in a place he loved. That feeling lasted until 1:00 P.M. on November 22nd, 1963.

The assassination of President Kennedy left Judah in a daze. He had admired the president and had been as dazzled by the aura of Camelot as anyone. Everything that followed, from the killing of Lee Harvey Oswald to the president's funeral and beyond, turned his world on its head. He sensed, but was unable to see clearly at the time, that a new and violent world was emerging.

The River

I do not know much about gods; but I think that the river
Is a strong brown god—sullen, untamed and intractable.
—T. S. Eliot, "The Dry Salvages"

5:30 A.M., June 1, 1964

THE EASTERN SKY was just starting to turn a delicate pink when Judah and his father pulled up to the Aprillia docks on River Drive in Thunderbolt. It was the beginning of shrimping season, and Judah was excited about working on a shrimp boat again. He wore a pair of old khaki cutoffs and a T-shirt and carried a duffel bag with five changes of clothes in it.

The previous summer Judah had worked on the boat Charlie Aprillia captained. Colonel Benjamin knew Charlie and trusted him with his son. This season Judah and Billy would be working under a different captain.

Charlie had three boats in his fleet: *St. Joseph*, *St. Anthony*, and *St. Patrick*. The *St. Joseph* was named for the patron saint of Italy, the *St. Anthony* for another Italian saint: Anthony of Padua, patron saint of lost articles. The *St. Patrick* was named after the patron saint of Ireland, an acknowledgment of Mrs. Aprillia's Irish heritage.

For many years the captain of the *St. Patrick* had been Elijah Deveraux, the uncle and surrogate father of Lloyd Bryan, the first black student at Benedictine. Charlie trusted and admired the skills of Captain Deveraux more than those of any shrimper he had ever known. He believed Elijah had a sixth sense when it came to catching shrimp and reading the winds and waves. It was because of this that he assigned Billy and Judah to Elijah's boat.

Even though Charile had assured Judah's father of Elijah's competence, Colonel Benjamin, a real stickler for details, decided to see for himself before he entrusted his son to a stranger. Now the colonel, dressed in his summer uniform, hat sitting at the proper rakish angle, walked with Judah down the dock to meet Captain Deveraux. The bill of his hat was covered with silver oak leaves, a sign of his rank; and on each shoulder a silver eagle perched, wings spread in flight. He was an impressive man who could live up to the impression.

"I'm Colonel Paul Benjamin," he said as he approached the only black man on the dock. "You must be Captain Deveraux," he continued as he approached with his right hand extended.

Elijah squinted as he caught the reflection of early sunlight from the eagles on the colonel's shoulders. He reached into his back pocket, pulled out a wipe rag, cleaned off his right hand, then took the colonel's hand in his. Both men felt that a person could tell a lot about a man by the feel of his handshake. The sky over the Wilmington River was beginning its slow burn to orange when Elijah looked into Paul Benjamin's eyes and said, "Yes, sir, colonel, I'm Captain Elijah Deveraux, master of the *St. Patrick*." Then he looked over at Judah with a smile and said, "Billy's in the wheelhouse waitin' for ya'. Hop on aboard and get situated while I talk to your daddy."

Elijah dropped his head a little as if in thought, then looked up again at Colonel Benjamin. "I'll take good care of your boy, just like he was mine. I ain't never lost a hand in all the years I been on the river, and I give you my word on that."

A slight smile creased the colonel's lips. "That's all I wanted to know. His mother's a little worried, and I promised her he was with the best there is. I just wanted to see for myself—and I'm satisfied. I know you've got lots of work to do before you shove off, so I'll leave you now."

For a man like Colonel Benjamin, prior military service was one of the ways he judged a man's character. Just before he turned to leave he asked, "Captain Deveraux, were you in the war?"

Elijah was of the same mind. He proudly answered, "Yes, sir, colonel. I was in Europe with the Red Ball Express. Got out with sergeant's stripes."

"The Red Ball Express. You kept Patton rolling, didn't you?"

"Yes, sir, colonel, we did just that."

"All-colored outfit, wasn't it?"

"All-colored and all proud to do our part, colonel."

Colonel Benjamin drew himself straight and saluted. "Thank you for your service to our country, Captain Deveraux. Now I'll take my leave."

Elijah returned the salute and watched as the colonel climbed the ramp to his car on the bluff. Then he boarded the *St. Patrick* and entered the wheelhouse, where Judah and Billy were waiting. He busied himself for a few moments with charts and switches before he turned to Judah and said, "That's some daddy you got there, young fella. I'll bet he don't take nothin' offa nobody!"

Judah shook his head. "Yes, sir, Captain Deveraux, he's nobody to mess with."

With a smile Captain Deveraux said, "Call me Elijah, okay?" Then he extended his hand. "Welcome aboard, Judah Benjamin." After a meditative moment Elijah continued. "Now ain't that just somethin', a boy with a name like that. Judah and Benjamin, the only two tribes of Israel that ain't been lost, ain't that right?"

"Yes, sir," Judah smartly replied.

"Boy, you got a handshake just like your daddy! Now let's get hoppin' and get the *St. Patrick* movin' down the river."

The *St. Patrick* was a sixty-five-foot wooden boat weighing one hundred tons and powered by a pair of 350-horsepower Cummins diesels. Her keel had been laid in Thunderbolt in 1960 and she was the newest of Charlie's boats. He thought she was the prettiest, too: white-hulled with Kelly green trim along the gunnels and the outriggers. She could make a steady eight to ten knots at 1600 RPMs and two-and-a-half to three knots when dragging her nets. The name *St. Patrick* was on her bows and stern. On the stern, just below her name, were the letters of her home port, Thunderbolt. Two large shamrocks festooned the stern on either side of the town's name.

The *St. Patrick* had a pair of outriggers that lifted and swung her four nets out into the water. Each outrigger could lift a net filled with as much as eight thousand pounds of shrimp; and she could carry twenty thousand pounds in her hold. As with almost all shrimp boats of her day, the bow of the *St. Patrick* was sharply turned up, like the chin of a proud man. There was little angle to the cut of the bow, and the deckhouse stopped amidships.

After taking on five thousand pounds of crushed ice to preserve their catch, Elijah gave the order to cast off lines, and the *St. Patrick* slowly moved away from its berth at Aprillia's Seafood Co-op.

Elijah stood at the ship's wheel, with Billy and Judah by his side. A slight breeze from the south dusted the inside of the wheelhouse with the sweet smell of marsh grass and salt air as Elijah steered his boat past twenty others along the bluff.

The Wilmington River widened as it passed the Savannah Yacht Club and spread itself in a slow turn to the south. As the *St. Patrick* pushed her way down the river and pointed her bow at Priest Landing on Skidaway Island, the sun was spilling over the treetops on Wilmington Island and it burnished the faces of Elijah and his crew.

Judah had butterflies in his stomach as the thought of spending five days aboard the boat ran through his mind. Billy was excited, too. He nudged Judah with his elbow. "We're gonna work, but we're gonna have a good time too, Bubba."

Elijah chuckled at Billy's remark. "Mr. Billy here, I done heard he's an expert at having a good time, but he's right. St. Pat, she's a happy boat. After we finish our work today, I know a really fine spot to anchor back behind Wassaw Island. We got a perfect view of the sunset there and a cool breeze from Ossabaw Sound. We'll cook up a fine supper and you boys will sleep like babies tonight."

At that time the only aids to navigation a shrimp boat had were her charts, her compass, and her radio. Radar had been around since World War II, but it was provided only on warships and large commercial vessels. Global positioning systems wouldn't appear for another twenty-five years, and sonar wasn't commercially available; so knowledge of the water's depth came from charts and experience.

"We gonna' drag off Wassaw today, Elijah?" asked Billy. "We did pretty well there last year."

"I think we'll drag there first. The tide and the moon seem to be just right and the wind 'spose to stay down 'till late afternoon."

As the *St. Patrick* pushed its way through the olive-colored water of the Wilmington River, large mats of dead marsh grass floated past the boat. A spring tide the night before had lifted last season's dead grass and carried it out and away from the new marsh. A pod of dolphins swam just off the port bow, riding the pressure wave formed by the hull. A dozen or so seagulls perched along the boat's outriggers to catch a free trip to their hunting grounds on Little Tybee Island.

The bottom of the sun was just lifting away from the crest of the Atlantic and beginning to make its climb through a cloudless sky when the *St. Patrick* slowed and Elijah's eyes searched the surface of the water for signs of shrimp.

"Elijah," asked Judah, "how do you know where the shrimp are?"

Elijah squinted through the glass of the wheelhouse and never took his eyes off the water as he replied, "I look for muddy water. The swells stir up the bottom mud and the shrimps go down there. I don't think they like the daylight, and the mud makes it even harder for the sun to get through. I believe that, 'cause when I used to shrimp down in the Florida Keys, the water was clear as a bell. You could see bottom twenty feet below. Ain't murky like it is here. Anyway, you couldn't catch a thing in the daytime, but when the sun went down, Mr. Shrimp, he come out and we really catch'em."

Billy went out on the bow, shaded his eyes, and studied the water in front of the boat. After a few moments he turned, pointed to an area about twenty degrees to starboard, and shouted, "I think I see some mud in the water about a hundred feet out."

Elijah looked hard and long, then said, "I think I do, too. Come on, let's put the nets out."

Judah worked the portside winch, Billy the starboard as the two thirty-foot long outriggers pivoted slowly away from the side of the boat. Soon they were positioned at right angles to the hull. At the end of each outrigger hung a heavy, flat, wooden structure ten feet long and four feet wide. This "door," as it was called, pulled the net to the bottom and held it there. They acted like wings under the water and glided only inches from the bottom.

A shrimp net is like a giant funnel. The wide end scoops up the shrimp, and the water pushes them through to the small end. They would pass right through if the end of the funnel wasn't tied shut to catch the shrimp in what shrimpers call "the bag." When the full nets are hauled back in, the knots are loosened and the shrimp fall out on to the deck to be sorted, placed in the hold, and iced. The process is repeated many times over, all day long.

When the nets had been properly laid and all was in order, Billy and Judah went back to the wheelhouse. Elijah then advanced the throttles, and without complaint the engines moved the *St. Patrick* across the shrimping grounds just outside Wassaw Sound at two knots. Settling back in his chair, Elijah surveyed the waters of the sound. Then he turned to Judah.

"Back in fifty-eight, the Air Force went and lost an A-bomb right where we draggin'. Did ya' know that, Judah?"

Elijah had brought the *St. Patrick* into the Odingsell River behind the south end of Wassaw Island, where she swung gently on her bow anchor as the setting sun painted her hull a peach color. On the way to their anchorage, Billy and Judah separated the shrimp from what was referred to as "trash fish," which were dumped overboard. While they worked, a cloud of gulls followed closely behind the *St. Patrick*, swooping down to snatch the discarded fish as half a dozen dolphins grabbed their fair share. Now the gulls and dolphins were gone and the boys were in the hold shoveling ice over their catch. They wore rubber boots and shorts with no shirts, and the coolness of the hold was delightful. Both boys were sunburned; when they had finished, they sat on the ice and talked about the day, sometimes lying back and letting the ice cool their stinging skin.

"What if we caught that bomb in our nets," asked Billy, "do ya' think it might go off or something?"

"My father was a big part of the search for it, and he says that's not a problem because it's not armed. "He says the Defense Department just decided to let well enough alone since nothing's gonna happen."

"What about radiation leakin' out?" Billy asked as he rubbed some ice across his burning chest. "Isn't that dangerous too?"

Following Billy's lead, Judah rubbed a handful of ice over his forearms. "My father says it's buried in more than twenty feet of sand and mud and the bomb housing was built strong enough to withstand an incident like that."

Billy thought for a moment and then shrugged his shoulders. "If your old man isn't worried, I don't see why I should be."

Judah was about to say something when Elijah peered into the hold. "You two boys about ready for some supper?"

Elijah had prepared batter-fried shrimp from the catch of the day and served it with Savannah red rice and cole slaw. The batter and shrimp sauce were both recipes from Elijah's wife, Sally. She had been raised in the small town of Sandfly, and the recipe had been handed from one generation to the next in the tightly knit community. Both Judah and Billy swore they never tasted better.

When the meal was over, Elijah took the boys out on to the deck, hosed them down with fresh water, and then turned the hose on his own naked body. Judah thought about how wonderful the shower had been as he slipped into a clean pair of shorts and then went back to the cabin and stretched out on his bunk.

Billy followed a short time later. Looking around to make sure Elijah wasn't within earshot, he quietly said, "Elijah hits the sack early. After he falls asleep we can go down into the hold and listen to the Big Ape on the radio. I hid us some beer down there. It should be good and cold by now."

A few days before the trip, Billy had told Judah he was going to bring some beer, but Judah hadn't believed him. Now he sat straight up in his bunk.

"You got some beer down there, no shit?"

"No shit," answered Billy, feeling quite satisfied with himself.

Both boys had turned seventeen only months before and had only tasted alcohol by sneaking sips from glasses at their parents' parties. Neither had ever been under the influence.

The anchor light was all that was burning when Judah and Billy finally heard the first sounds of snoring from Elijah's cabin. "Let him get goin' real good before we leave," whispered Billy as they lay in the dark. Minutes later Elijah's snoring was loud and regular. A deep sleep settled over him in the coolness of the night.

Billy retrieved eight bottles of Pabst Blue Ribbon from their hiding place under the ice. The boys sat on the deck and rested their backs against the gunnels. Neither would admit to not liking the taste, and by the second bottle they were forcing them down—but they did like the way the beer made them feel. Soon they were engaged in conversation about all sorts of things, most of which made them laugh. It wasn't long before they were in a moonlight bottle-throwing contest as they pitched their mounting empties off the stern and into the lazy Odingsell.

The eastern sky was a dark blue dotted with a crowd of stars, and in the west the sunset lingered long enough to light the horizon with hues of darkening orange. There was no wind, and it wouldn't be long before the dew would settle on the decks when Billy and Judah started on their fourth beer. They were now boisterous and loud, talking about this girl or that in language punctuated by profanities, when Captain Deveraux was awakened by the noise.

Elijah slipped from his bunk and quietly slid out the portside hatch. He eased along the walkway in silence as Judah and Billy pulled themselves to their feet, hung their heads over the railing, and vomited. The next day Elijah said nothing about what he had seen. He considered the hangovers the boys had to be punishment enough. For the rest of the trip there was no more beer drinking.

That summer on the *St. Patrick*, Judah fell in love. He fell in love with the marshes and the skies, the rivers and the sounds, the smell of salt air and the caress of a summer wind. He also fell in love with shrimp boats and the sight of a full net being emptied onto a waiting deck and the way thousands of glistening, wiggling shrimp looked in the morning sun.

Judah also learned to love the feel of the *St. Patrick* as her bow crashed through waves when the weather was rough and the sweet sting of wind-driven rain drops on a hot day. But more than that, he came to love his two shipmates the way one brother loves another.

Elijah was easy to get along with, and Judah came to respect his knowledge of shrimp and the waters where they found them. He was patient in teaching the skills of the trade, and quick and generous with praise for good work. He also knew a lot about important everyday things; and Judah would long remember the conversations he and Elijah had in the wheelhouse as they dragged their nets across the Atlantic floor.

Judah and Billy were already friends, but working together on the *St. Patrick* only served to strengthen their bond. Billy never shrugged off work and would always help Judah if he finished before him. Whatever Billy had was Judah's, too, and Judah felt the same way. There was no jealously between them, only respect and admiration.

On the *St. Patrick* the boys developed a symbiotic relationship. Billy was bigger, stronger, faster, and perhaps a little impulsive in thought and behavior. Above all else he was kind and generous. Judah was slighter, more intuitive, and quick to see a better way to get things done; and, like Billy, he didn't have a mean bone in his body.

Billy was the athlete and Judah the scholar, but Billy had a love of history because his mother's ancestors had fought with the Irish Jasper Greens during the Civil War. At night they would lie in their bunks and talk about the war.

During the day Judah admired the way Billy handled himself on deck. During the evening hours it was Billy who admired Judah and his knowledge of history and politics.

Perhaps the thing that most impressed Judah that summer on the water was the feeling he got from working hard with good people, and the satisfaction it brought. He enjoyed the teamwork, the way the boat functioned, the power of the winches, and the way it all came together. He didn't want to think about the fall and his return to Benedictine; but when the time came and he left Elijah and the *St. Patrick*, Judah was maturing into a man.

The Gathering Storm

> Some men are killed in a war and some men are wounded and some men never leave the country. Life is unfair.
>
> —John F. Kennedy

April 8, 1965

THE FEDERAL COURT HOUSE on Wright Square was as beautiful as it was imposing. It had been designed to be that way, reflecting both the power and the majesty of the United States of America. In its basement was the local draft board.

In 1965 every American male in good health who was eighteen years or older was classified by the draft board as "1-A" and subject to military call-up. If selected the draftee was obliged to serve at least two years of active duty. There were, however, deferments of various types that could delay for as long as four years, and sometimes more, nonvoluntary entry into the military. The most common deferment granted by the draft boards was the "2-S" classification or the student deferment. This was given to those individuals who, after graduation from high school, became full-time college students. The deferment, however, had to be maintained. This required the young men involved to carry a full scholastic load each year and maintain an overall C average.

"Have a seat, young man," said the middle-aged woman on the other side of the gray metal desk. "I'll need you to fill these forms out completely," she added as she pushed a sheaf of papers and a pencil across the desk to Judah. "I'll also need some I.D. that shows your current address. A driver's license will do just fine."

Judah fumbled through his wallet and produced his license; then he started filling out the forms. The woman was busy typing on her IBM Selectric. When he had finished and pushed the papers back toward her, she stopped, examined them carefully, then inserted a new form into her typewriter and began copying some of the information. In no time she was finished.

"This is your draft card," she announced. "Sign on this line and carry it with you at all times. It's the law."

Judah scrawled his name on the bottom of the card—but then he looked at the woman in surprise. "This says I'm 1-A. That's wrong, I'm going to college in the fall."

"When you're enrolled, your school will notify us and you will be issued a new card. The 1-A status is a technicality. We're not drafting anybody the summer after they graduate, so don't worry."

On February 7, 1965, nine Americans were killed and 108 were wounded when the Vietcong attacked United States advisory forces and the headquarters of the U.S. Army's 52nd Aviation Battalion near Pleiku in central Vietnam. Three days later the V.C. struck again against a U.S. barracks near Qui Nhon. In response the United States Air Force, under the code name "Rolling Thunder," began a series of bombing raids deep within North Vietnam on March 2, 1965. The situation quickly escalated; and by the end the year, there would be fifty-thousand American troops fighting in Southeast Asia.

Judah's brother Jacob had accepted a commission from the Air Force upon his graduation from the University of Georgia in May. It was his intention to become a fighter pilot. Colonel Benjamin was proud of Jacob's ambitions and had encouraged him to pursue a career in the Air Force just as he had done. Jacob's mother, however, harbored mixed feelings. She knew it was time for her son to fulfill his military obligation, but she feared that he would be sent to Vietnam and placed in harm's way. It was because of this that she made a decision about Judah's college education.

Judah had his heart set on going to the University of Georgia in the fall of 1965. His brother had filled him in on what a great place Athens was, how many pretty girls were there, and how much fun he'd have at the football games. He had the grades to get in, and the application form was sitting on his desk. Judah had complete confidence in his ability to maintain his student deferment for the full four years he would be at Georgia. "Shoot," he said to himself, "by the time I graduate in '69, that war will be over and done with."

It was four in the afternoon when Judah returned home from the draft board. His mother and father were in the den watching TV when Judah entered the room, draft card in hand.

"They got me listed as 1-A until I start college," he said as he showed the card to his father. "Then I'll go to a 2-S deferment." Colonel Benjamin looked at the card then passed it to Judah's mother, who glanced at it for only a moment.

"Judah, sit down. There's something your father and I have to talk with you about." His mother's serious tone surprised him, and Judah obediently sat. "You know that Jacob is going into the Air Force when he graduates. He wants to fly fighters."

"Yes, ma'am," replied Judah, "that's been his plan all along."

"Well," said Arlene, "President Johnson has just told the country that he's sending fifty thousand troops over to Vietnam right away."

Then Colonel Benjamin spoke.

"It looks like this is going to be a much bigger action than we thought a year ago. I can't help remembering what General MacArthur said about getting involved in a land war in Asia."

"What was that?"

"Don't do it," replied the colonel, "there's just an unending number of those little bastards and we can't kill 'em all.

"Just what are y'all trying to say?"

"Judah, your mother is worried that Jacob will be over there as soon as he finishes his flight training. I kind of have to agree with her. She's afraid something will happen to him."

"I'm afraid, too," said Judah, "but what's that got to do with me?"

"Judah," said Arlene, "I don't want you getting drafted and

sent to Vietnam. If something happened to you and Jacob, I don't think I'd want to go on living."

"But, Momma, I've got a deferment for the next four years. I can't be drafted. Anyway, that thing'll be over with by then."

"You've got a deferment," replied his mother with a sharper tongue, "only if you can keep it."

"I can keep it!"

"It's your first year in college, Judah," explained his father, "and college is a whole lot harder than high school. Your mother is afraid you might get up there, and maybe get distracted or something, fail a course or two, and then wind up getting drafted and sent to Vietnam."

"No, I won't, Dad, and you know it, too," replied Judah angrily.

"Judah, you're not going to Georgia this year. You're going to be here in Savannah over at Armstrong College."

"What?"

"You heard me."

An argument ensued that lasted another fifteen minutes. It was finally settled by Judah's mother when she said, with tears streaming down her face, "Now you listen to me, young man. Jacob will be going to Vietnam by the end of the year and he'll be flying attack planes. My insides are in a knot already about that, and I couldn't take it if you got drafted and wound up there too. You're not so perfect that you're completely immune to all the hell-raising that goes on up at Georgia. I know you too well, and it wouldn't surprise me one bit if you got up there, started drinking beer, got a girlfriend, and slacked off from your studies. It happens all the time. Exactly the same thing happened to Mickey Polefsky last year, and now he's in the Army on his way to Vietnam!"

At this point Judah had tears in his eyes. He blurted out, "But, Momma—"yet before he could finish, his mother put up her hand like a traffic cop and shot back:

"That's enough from you, mister! You'll be going to Armstrong in the fall and living right here with us where I can keep an eye on you. I picked up an application yesterday and it's sitting on your desk. I want you to fill it out tonight."

Judah dropped his head and wiped the tears from his eyes, knowing he had been defeated. Then he shrugged, and without another word he turned and retreated to his room.

Sitting on the edge of his bed, Judah tried to digest what had just transpired. He must have muttered "shit" to himself twenty-five times during the next half hour, and "son of a bitch" at least twenty-five more. Finally he decided to accept his fate and make the best of it. Maybe Armstrong wouldn't be all that bad. After all, Billy would be there, too.

Miss Savannah

A pity beyond all telling
Is hid in the heart of love.
—W. B. Yeats, "The Pity of Love"

MISS SAVANNAH lived across the street from Judah. Her name was Hannah Meldrim, and she was truly as beautiful as her title implied. Her hair was a stunning shade of auburn, her large brown eyes possessed an almost perpetual twinkle, her lips were full and sensuous. She and Judah were the same age and had been casual friends from the time Judah had moved into the neighborhood. Judah had always admired Hannah, but by the time he was old enough to date, she was so pretty that Judah was intimidated by her good looks. Besides, she had a stream of boyfriends who were always older and bigger than Judah. More than that, Hannah was a Christian.

Hannah's father was a banker from a well established Savannah family and had served as a B-17 ball-turret gunner during the war. This was the basis for an immediate friendship between Art Meldrim and Colonel Benjamin. Hannah's mother, Joyce, was an attractive brunette from Lyons, a small town about sixty miles southwest of Savannah, in the center of onion-growing country. Art had met Joyce just after the close of the war while doing some loan work for her father's vast Vidalia onion farm. They were married a year later.

Arthur Meldrim's mother hadn't exactly been keen on the marriage. She had preferred Agnes Arnold, a Savannah debutante with an impeccable lineage—and Joyce knew it. As the years went by, the marriage became increasingly strained—as did Joyce's relations with her in-laws. This may have been the reason for what seemed to be Joyce's incessant need to be at the forefront of Savannah society. She belonged to almost everything, from the board of directors at the Telfair Museum to the presidency of the Junior League. She also pushed Hannah to excel, in order to prove to her mother-in-law that both she herself and her lovely daughter were good enough for the Meldrims of Savannah. She heartily encouraged Hannah to enter the Miss Savannah competition of 1965.

For Hannah the Miss Savannah contest had been a cakewalk. Her voice was stirring, and she could play the piano to perfection. When she sang "Hard Hearted Hannah, the Vamp of Savannah" while accompanying herself on the piano, she brought the house down. There were other pretty and talented girls in the hunt too, but Hannah steamrolled them all with the swimsuit and evening-gown competition.

Hannah, like Judah, had harbored dreams of going to the University of Georgia, but her social calendar demanded that she remain in Savannah. Her father was a member of the Cotillion Club, and she would be making her debut in the fall. In addition to that she would be representing Savannah in the Miss Georgia contest.

Her mother insisted that Hannah could easily become the next Miss Georgia, and perhaps the next Miss America, if only she stayed with her voice and piano lessons. Along with Judah from across the street, therefore, Miss Savannah would be a freshman at Armstrong College.

Armstrong had been founded as a junior college in 1935, but in 1964 the state elevated it to a four-year school. The college was scheduled to move to a new campus on Savannah's south side in the winter of 1966, but for the time being classes were still held at the old campus downtown. Armstrong's "campus" was actually a collection of elegant historic buildings located along Bull and Gaston streets and adjacent to Monterey Square and Forsyth Park.

The jewel in the campus crown was the Armstrong building, an Italian Renaissance mansion constructed in 1916 for the wealthy shipping magnate George Ferguson Armstrong. The house was later given to the city and incorporated into the campus. It was an exquisite structure that presided over an absolutely charming campus.

The first college lecture Judah ever attended was an English composition class held on the third and top floor of the Armstrong building. The room was actually a large sun porch; three of its four walls consisted of glass doors. Those doors opened to a veranda that overlooked moss-filled oaks and lovely Forsyth Park. All of the glass doors had been opened as the cool morning air of fall settled over the room.

Judah, the second person to enter the room, took a seat overlooking the tops of the big oaks lining Gaston Street. As the room filled he was surprised to see Hannah walk through the door and delighted when she took the seat next to him.

"Hey, Judah," said Hannah as she slipped into her seat. He didn't know what kind of perfume she was wearing, but its delicate scent drifted over him as Hannah's eyes caught his. Often had Judah dreamed of simply looking into those gorgeous dark brown eyes for as long as he wished.

"Hey, Hannah," he replied as he glanced at her lips for an instant and wondered what they were like. "How's the first day of college goin' for ya'?"

"Ugh," said Hannah as she made a desperate face—which immediately transformed into another brilliant smile. "I can't believe they think we can do this much work and still have time to breathe. You were always so smart, you'll breeze right through this mess. I might even get you to help me some with my algebra homework or something. Can you believe that Mr. Laffer, my algebra instructor, gave us a whole pile of homework on our very first day!"

This was the sort of opportunity Judah had been looking for, and he wasted no time in seizing it. "Hey, listen, if you need some help with anything, I live right across the street, remember? Just call me, I'll be glad to help."

"Oh, God, thank you, Judah," said Hannah with a heavy sigh of relief, "'cause I know I'm gonna need all the help I can get. Could you help me with this math junk for a few minutes tonight? Not very long, I'll come over to your house if you want me to."

Judah was ecstatic, but he had poise enough not to show his

glee as he casually responded, "Yeah, no problem. Sometime after dinner, okay? I'll call before I come over."

Judah's hand was resting on the desk top, so Hannah reached over and touched it. She sweetly cooed, "Oh, Judah, you are so sweet and such a doll, thank you so much. After dinner will be just fine."

A moment later their instructor entered the room, and Hannah removed her hand. It had been there for only a second, but she had touched him. When Judah was sure she couldn't see, he moved his hand to his nose and sniffed. Her scent was there, and for the rest of the day he thought of nothing but Hannah and the coming evening.

Judah was as good a teacher as he was a student, and that night in the den at Hannah's he taught her how to solve the math problems she regarded as impossible. After the tutoring they chatted for over an hour. It was the longest conversation he had ever had with her.

The next day in English class, Hannah took the same seat next to him and began talking about the previous night's conversation. She said she couldn't get over the fact that he was a Johnny Mercer fan because she really enjoyed singing the songs he had written, and if it wasn't too much trouble he could help her for a few minutes again. Soon Judah would be a regular presence at the Meldrim house. It wasn't long before this arrangement became the gossip du jour on the corner of Bull and Gaston.

When questioned by her friends about her relationship with Judah, Hannah would tell them how much she liked him. "But we're just friends," she would add, "I'm in love with Clark, Judah knows that. Anyway, he already has a girlfriend."

Judah had been dating Diane Alpern since the beginning of summer. She was attractive, which Judah liked, and she was Jewish. This pleased his parents, but it didn't matter much to Judah one way or the other.

Diane was also a student at Armstrong. She had been Judah's date for all of the school's social functions, and their friends considered them to be going steady. There had been numerous sessions of heavy petting with Diane and verbal exchanges of devotion, but it had gone no farther. Judah's inexperience and Diane's concern for her reputation were largely responsible for this potent abstinence.

When Diane questioned Judah about Hannah, he gave her the same response as Hannah had given her friends. "Besides," he added, "Hannah's a shikse. It can't go anywhere, you know that."

Diane accepted this explanation at first, but as the weeks went by, she began to sense a growing distance between them. Judah denied it, knowing full well she was right. He was at Hannah's two or three times a week, and thought about her every day. He looked forward to climbing the stairs to his English class, taking his same seat and waiting for her to sit next to him. Never did she disappoint.

By the beginning of November, the sessions in Hannah's den had come to be more social than academic. Judah had evolved into Hannah's confidant, her best friend. She grew to trust him, needed him to listen, and knew that he would not betray her. Slowly Hannah revealed the troubled life she lived.

The Debut

Never speak disrespectfully of Society, Algernon. Only people who can't get into it do that.
—Oscar Wilde, *The Importance of Being Earnest*, Act III

HANNAH had been dating Clark Davenport from the start of her junior year at Jenkins High School. He was handsome, smart, came from a good family. He had also been an outstanding football player at Jenkins. Hannah's favorable opinion of Clark was exceeded only by his own.

From the beginning of their relationship, Joyce Meldrim had decided that Clark was the boy for Hannah and had taken every opportunity to reinforce his standing with her daughter. Hannah's father was of the same persuasion, albeit to a lesser degree. Before Clark, Hannah had had many suitors but no steady boyfriend. After word hit the street that they were an item, no boy in Savannah had the courage to ask her for a date and risk the pain of rejection.

Clark, a year ahead of Hannah, was attending Georgia Tech up in Atlanta on a football scholarship. He had done well, and several articles in the sports section of the *Savannah Morning News* had favorably discussed his exploits. Joyce always had the articles clipped from the paper and placed in a scrapbook about Clark even before Hannah could read them.

For whatever reason, Joyce enjoyed living her daughter's life in this vicarious manner. Indeed she tended to dominate her daughter in almost all decisions, large and small. When Hannah was young and naive she accepted this behavior. As she matured, however, she began to resent the intrusion into her life.

These were only some of the things that began to bubble slowly to the surface in Hannah's intimate conversations with Judah. At first her frustrations were vague, and Judah didn't give them much thought; but as October cooled and became November, Hannah began to open up more and more. She revealed her feelings to Judah as she had never done to anyone else. The biggest surprise came at ten o'clock one Tuesday evening in the Meldrim's pine-paneled den. Hannah's parents had retired early for the evening, and to Judah she seemed unusually quiet. He could not help inquiring, "Is everything okay, Hannah?"

Without saying a word Hannah rose from the sofa where she and Judah were sitting and quietly closed the door to the den. Then she returned to her seat, looked down at the hands folded neatly in her lap, and began to speak.

"My mother and I had a fight before you came over."

"What about?"

"About the Miss Georgia contest. I don't want to do that kind of stuff anymore. Honestly, it's embarrassing for me. I think it's tacky."

"Well, what happened?"

"Judah, there's something you don't know. My parents like to drink a little too much sometimes and when my mother has had too much, she gets mean. She had had too much by the time dinner was over."

Judah looked down at the floor in embarrassment.

"I told her tonight that I didn't want to do another pageant ever again, and she just started screaming at me about how much she had sacrificed to get me where I was and what a selfish bitch I was being." Tears filled Hannah's eyes. Judah looked up in surprise.

"You mean she actually called you a bitch?"

"Yes, she actually called me a bitch."

"Was your father there? I mean, what did he say?"

"It was at the dining room table while we were eating. He had had a few too many, like he does every night, and he just sort of sloughed it off and told us both to calm down." She began to sob.

"I'm sorry," stammered Judah, trying to think of something to say.

Hannah turned quickly to face him. "Oh, no, I'm the one who's sorry. I'm sorry I've put this on you, but I just had to tell somebody. I could never tell Clark a thing like this, or any of my friends. It's a family secret, but it hurts, it really does. I'm getting to the point where I can't stand my own mother, and that's horrible."

"Why can't you tell Clark?"

"Because he thinks my parents hung the moon. He'd probably find some way to blame me, too."

In Savannah, when a girl wishes to make her social debut, she must be invited to do so by the Cotillion Club, a male-only organization whose founding predates the Civil War. Its membership is by virtue of familial lineage, and it is a closely guarded bastion of Southern gentility and manners. Only Richmond has a cotillion club older than Savannah's.

Upon a vote of the members, girls of acceptable social standing would be invited to make their debut at the club's annual debutante ball on the last Saturday before Christmas. Selection of the debutante candidates takes place the preceding spring, however, and therefore the summer and fall months of the Savannah social calendar are filled with scores of parties thrown by the parents and friends of the fortunate young ladies.

Because her father was a member of the Cotillion Club, Hannah was selected as one of the debutantes for the 1965 season. She had been escorted to all of the summer parties by Clark, but the height of the season took place during the fall football schedule. To make matters worse, Tech had landed a bowl bid on the other side of the country. Clark would not be able to take Hannah to the climax of the season in December.

The young ladies would be formally presented to Savannah on the Saturday before the Christmas debutante ball, and it was imperative that each have a male escort. When Hannah learned three weeks before the ball that Clark could not be with her that night, she panicked at first, then quickly hit upon the perfect solution.

"Colonel Benjamin," said the voice on the phone. Although Judah's father had retired from the Air Force a year before, he would never be able to break the habit of answering the phone in that manner.

"Colonel, this is Hannah Meldrim."

"What a pleasure to hear your voice, sweetheart. How is the loveliest girl in Savannah?"

"Just fine."

"What can I do for you?"

"May I speak with Judah?"

"Sure, I'll get him." A few seconds later Judah's voice came over the phone.

"Hello."

"Judah, will you do me the biggest favor in the whole world? I'm in kind of a pickle."

"Sure, what is it?"

"Clark can't be here for my debut, and I need an escort. Would you please be my escort for that night?"

Judah was so dumbfounded he had to take a seat on the little chair next to the phone stand in the hall. He took a deep breath. "Yeah, I'd be honored. Is it okay with Clark?"

"Oh, yeah, I already talked with him about it and he understands that I've just got to have an escort for these parties and he's fine with you, I promise."

"What about your parents? Have you talked with them about this?"

"Already done. They're fine, too."

For the next thirty minutes Hannah went down the list of social functions they'd be attending on the run-up to the big night. When the conversation ended, Judah went into his room, turned off the lights, opened the blinds, and looked across the street at Hannah's house. For a long time he sat on the edge of his bed just staring at the big picture window at the front of the Meldrim den.

Paul Benjamin and his wife came from a line of Southern aristocrats that could rival that of any member of the Cotillion Club—but the colonel would never be a member. There simply had never been a Jew in that club, and there probably never would. The Benjamins did not resent that: They understood and accepted the vagaries of the social structure not only in Savannah, but throughout most of the United States. Nevertheless the idea that their son would be escorting Hannah Meldrim to her debut came as a bit of an odd surprise.

"Can you imagine that?" said Arlene to her husband as she folded back the covers on their bed. "Our son will be at the Cotillion Club's debutante ball."

"I'm sure no Jewish girl has ever made her debut there," replied the colonel. "I just wonder if a Jewish boy has ever been an escort before."

"I doubt it," said Arlene, standing in front of the mirror and brushing out her hair. "I doubt any Jews have ever attended that affair in any capacity."

"Well, they're gonna have a member of the tribe this year!"

The big parties started the Friday after Thanksgiving, and there would be at least one party every weekend until the actual debut. Clark had been home for two days over the Thanksgiving holiday and was able to see Hannah briefly; but because of the annual Georgia–Georgia Tech football game on the Saturday after Thanksgiving, he was forced to return to Atlanta Thanksgiving night and wouldn't be back until Christmas.

The 1965 Cotillion Club debutante ball was held in the main ballroom of the Hotel DeSoto, which was scheduled for demolition the next year. It would be this grand old lady's last hurrah.

Three great crystal chandeliers hung from the ceiling of the ballroom, and mirrored walls reflected the light on the members of the Cotillion's board of directors, who were lined up at the far end of the room. In front of them stood their wives. Parents and guests lined the other three walls; and a twenty-piece orchestra was tucked into one of the corners. The club president was at the microphone; on his command the young men serving as escorts entered the room from two separate doors. Sixteen girls were making their debut that year, and as the orchestra played Johnny Mercer's "Moon River," one line of eight escorts in white tie and tails entered the ballroom. Another line of eight entered at the same time from the opposite side. They walked toward the board of directors, turned, crossed lines, and walked out the opposite door.

Then came the individual debutantes in white evening gowns

with long white gloves, escorted by their fathers, who presented them to the club's board of directors. Each girl was allowed to select the music to be played as she entered the room, and Hannah had chosen her favorite. When the orchestra started with "Hard Hearted Hannah, the Vamp of Savannah," she appeared at the entrance with her father. As the spotlight followed her across the room, Hannah sent the crowd buzzing. She was spectacular that night. Judah thought she had never looked better, and as they slowly danced to "Lovin' You," he told her so.

"You're just stunning tonight, Hannah." He was whispering into her ear.

"You're so sweet," she replied, in an affectionate tone that he had never quite heard before. Her left hand was resting on his shoulder and when she spoke she pulled him in closer. Hannah looked into his eyes and murmured enticingly, "You're one sweet boy, Judah. I'll always remember this."

By ten-thirty the whole affair was winding down, but for the debs and their dates there would be another party, absent their fancy gowns and parents. One girl's family owned a large house on Officers' Row at Fort Screven on Tybee Island.

Fort Screven had been deactivated at the end of World War II; the land and buildings were sold as surplus. Officers' Row faced the ocean: almost a dozen very large and imposing frame houses sitting along a berm with an unencumbered view of the Atlantic. The debutante class of 1965 gathered in the house of the former commanding general of Fort Screven for a spend-the-night party. Their parents knew, and everything was aboveboard. There was even a chaperon, an older sister of one of the girls, who managed to make herself scarce. The large living room had been cleared of furniture, and a jukebox was installed. The only light came from a large fireplace that filled the room with warm colors and shadows. By eleven-thirty Chubby Checker was in charge of the party as ten couples twisted the night away in front of the fireplace. The rest stood on the porch, arm-in-arm, watching a pale December moon rise over a restless Atlantic.

There was alcohol, as there always was. Some would drink in moderation and some wouldn't; and by one in the morning, half of the boys and almost all of the girls were ready for sleep. At this time the chaperon appeared, announced that the party was over, and disappeared again. By one-thirty the jukebox was silent, all the boys had gone, and all the girls were fast asleep in the cavernous rooms above. All except Judah and Hannah. "Don't go yet," said Hannah, "I'd like to stay up a little while longer and watch the fire."

Judah pushed the overstuffed sofa back into the room and positioned it in front of the fireplace.

The two sat silently together and watched the fire lick and dance around the logs. It was cold that night and the warmth was intoxicating. Hannah rubbed her hands together, then slid herself next to Judah. "Burr, it's cold in here," she said.

"But you're nice and warm." Judah was surprised. He instinctively placed his arm around her and she let her head fall to his shoulder. They had never been like this before, and Judah tried to control his emotions as his imagination roared to life. Finally he decided to just wait and see.

After a few moments Hannah turned her head up, looked at him fondly, and asked, "Did you have a good time tonight?" Her voice was almost husky, as sometimes happens with female singers, but it was delicate and full at the same time. Her aristocratic Savannah accent was also delectable; and the way she looked in the light from the fire gave Judah a thrilling and exalted feeling. Looking into her eyes, Judah knew. "I had a wonderful time." He also knew that Hannah wanted to kiss him.

The old house was still, and the only sounds were the crackle of the fire and the wind blowing in from the ocean. Judah held his gaze for a few seconds more, then moved his face towards Hannah's as she lifted her chin. She closed her eyes just before their lips met.

At first the kiss was soft and careful, but it quickly evolved into something deep and passionate as they threw their arms tightly around each other. From time to time their lips would part, and each would gaze into the other's eyes. Judah would take his hand and brush back Hannah's hair or caress her cheeks, astounded by the smoothness of her skin and the fullness of her lips. As the minutes passed the intensity of the embrace increased, until finally Judah was lying on top of her, pressing himself against her as she wrapped her arms around him and pulled him closer. Their breathing by now was heavy and loud; and just before Hannah felt she would explode with desire, she pulled away hotly.

"We can't go on like this. Somebody will hear us and come down here. We've got to stop."

The last thing Judah wanted to do was stop, but he knew she was right. He rolled off her, sat up on the sofa, and stared into the fire. Hannah moved next to him and kissed him on the neck and cheek. "It would be horrible if someone caught us."

"I know," said Judah. Then he lifted his head as if struck by a thought, and continued. "You know, I'm spending the night right next door, in my Uncle David's house. There's nobody there but me. Maybe we could slip out and go over there."

Hannah moved her lips to Judah's, and just before she kissed him she whispered, "I'd love to."

David Silverman's beach house was built in the 1890s as the quarters for a lieutenant colonel and his family. Slightly less imposing than its neighbor, it nevertheless had large rooms with high ceilings and ornate crown molding; and Judah's uncle had furnished the old quarters comfortably. With Hannah's hand in his, Judah guided her to a room with tall windows that overlooked the ocean. A wicker love seat with large cushions faced the water; and when Judah led her to it, the pale light from a full moon over the Atlantic bathed Hannah in mother-of-pearl. Without a word they both sat down and faced each other while leaning deeply into the cushions.

The clandestine walk through the wind and oleanders had served to cool Judah's immediate passion; and as they had climbed the brick steps to his uncle's door, questions had entered Judah's mind.

"Why has this happened, Hannah?" he asked, as he drank in her exhilarating beauty.

"Because I've fallen in love with you, Judah."

"But what about Clark? I thought you were in love with him?" Judah, whispering, was almost afraid to hear her answer.

She sat up straight, gazed at Judah for a very lengthy moment, then stood and went to the windows. Hannah's eyes fell upon the waves as she sought the right words.

"I thought I loved him, and maybe for a period of time I did. But now I know it was more what my mother wanted than what I thought. She pushed me to him, Judah. My mother wants me to be with him not for me, but for herself. Her main concern is what people will think. She wants people to think she's so perfect and wonderful because her daughter is so pretty and talented and, just look, she even has the perfect boyfriend. You know, Clark Davenport, handsome football star up at Tech. The one who comes from one of Savannah's finest families. The one who's family name even adorns the finest example of Georgian architecture in Savannah."

Now she turned to face him with tears in her eyes and sarcasm in her voice. "You know him, don't you, Judah? Everybody knows Mr. Wonderful." Then she sobbed and wrapped her arms tightly around herself. Hannah pulled her sweater against the cold.

Judah was astonished by what he heard, but also elated. It was clear that Hannah was finished with Clark.

"But why me?"

"Because you're the most wonderful person I've ever known. Because you're good and kind and generous and I can tell you anything and because you're sweet and handsome. And because you touched my heart like no one ever has in my entire life." Hannah came back to the sofa and took Judah's face in her hands. "I love you, Judah," she purred.

"Hannah, I've been in love with you since last September. I never thought this would happen, but I did wish for it. I dreamed about it." Then in a seamless movement they fell across the sofa. In a few swift moments, tenderness gave way to raw emotion; and suddenly the night was filled with bright stars and winds of passion and pleasure.

Hannah didn't protest when Judah moved his hands to her breasts. She said nothing as he opened her blouse and bra, exposing to his eyes and the moonlight what he had only dreamed of. When Judah touched her Hannah began to moan. When he pressed his loins against hers, she returned the movement. Judah was sure they would make love . . . then something strange happened that upset and puzzled him. At the peak of foreplay, Hannah began to weep.

Judah fell to his knees and wiped the tears from Hannah's eyes. "What's wrong, what's the matter?" Hannah said nothing, but rolled her face into the cushion, sobbing even louder. "What is it, Hannah?" pleaded Judah. Only a long silence followed. Then Judah watched her body shake as something terrible and painful played across her mind once more.

Finally, Hannah gained control of herself and faced him. Her eyes were red and swollen; mucous ran from her nose as she tried to wipe it with her hand. In a slow and deliberate voice, Hannah gave Judah the answer to his question.

"There is another thing you don't know about me."

"What?" replied Judah as he reached for the box of tissues on the coffee table.

"Do you believe me when I say I'm in love with you, Judah?"

"I want that to be so true."

"Well, when we were lying on this couch just a few minutes ago, what did you think was going to happen? Did you think I was going to have sex with you?"

Judah was stunned. He didn't know what to say and remained silent while Hannah continued.

"I wanted to, Judah. I wanted to give you that because I love you, but I've already had it taken from me." She had no more tears left, so she continued in an almost detached voice. "You see, Judah, Clark took from me what I had always wanted to give the man I loved. The last time he was here, he forced me to have sex with him. I'd never done anything like that before, and he took it away just like that. I was a virgin, Judah, and he robbed me of that. I didn't have a choice, it was like rape."

It was an unexpected blow for Judah, and Hannah could see it on his face. She wished that she hadn't told him. Judah remained still for several minutes, eyes closed, saying nothing. Finally, when he looked at Hannah again, her face was washed in fear.

"This has changed things, hasn't it?" she asked.

Judah didn't reply. Instead he lay next to Hannah, cradled her in his arms, and whispered, "Nothing has changed."

In this embrace they fell asleep, to awaken at five in the morning. After a good-bye kiss under an oak, Judah watched Hannah disappear into the general's quarters and the company of her sleeping sisters. Pulling the collar of his coat up around his neck, Judah picked his way over the dunes and onto the beach, where he would be alone with his thoughts and wait for the sun to appear over the slate-gray sea.

Desire

Desire is the very essence of man.
—Baruch Spinoza

SUNDAY MORNING dawned clear and cold, with a north wind bending back the sea oats and blasting sand across Judah's shoes as he trudged over the dunes back to his uncle's house. Cockspurs clung to his socks, and the wind off Tybee Sound stung his cheeks, as his eyes searched for activity in the general's quarters. It was after ten when he saw one of the girls carry an overnight bag out to her car. A few minutes later he was at the door.

"If you'd like, Hannah," he said in front of several other girls, "you can ride home with me. It'd keep somebody from going out of the way to get you back."

When they reached the crest of the Lazaretto Creek Bridge, Hannah and Judah could see for miles. The marsh grass was dry and brown, and they watched quietly as waves of wind swept through it like a giant comb. Hannah had been silent for too long; Judah was about to ask her why when she placed her hand on his. "Do you still feel the same way you did last night?"

Judah smiled and said, "I'm still trying to get used to the fact that you care so much for me. How about you?"

"I know it was a surprise for you, but the way I feel wasn't something that happened overnight. It's been building up inside of me for months. I meant everything I said last night, but we have to talk about what we're going to do."

Judah nodded.

"Until I've got things worked out," continued Hannah, "we

can't let anybody know how we feel about each other. I've got to handle this breakup properly or my mother will make me miserable for the rest of my life. Clark is coming back on Christmas Eve. You know that my parents are having a party that night."

"Yeah, I know, we've been invited."

Hannah moved uncomfortably in her seat. "Well, of course Clark will be there. Then on Christmas Day we've all been invited to dinner over at the Davenports'. I don't want to start something until after the holidays. I hope you understand."

"I do, but I hate the thought of him even being around you."

"I hate it too, Judah, more than you do."

"Listen, it's only Sunday, and he's not coming back until Friday. Will I get to be with you between now and then?"

"I don't see why not, but we've got to be real smart about it. You don't know what a scene my mother is going to make when I tell her I'm breaking up with Clark. I don't want her to know it's over you until a couple of weeks later. I hope this doesn't hurt you, Judah, but it's got to be this way."

Judah was silent for a few moments; then he glanced over at Hannah. "Does your mother know what he did to you?"

Hannah turned her face to the window and watched as the oleanders and palmettos flashed by. Then she let out a sigh. "No. Nobody knows but you."

When Judah pulled his father's burgundy Mercedes to a stop in front of Hannah's house, Mrs. Meldrim was waiting at the door. "Did y'all have a good time last night, sweetheart?" she asked as Judah carried Hannah's bag and dress up the steps. Hannah smiled and kissed her mother on the cheek.

"Yes, ma'am, everything was wonderful."

Mrs. Meldrim turned to Judah as he was laying Hannah's dress across a chair in the living room. "Judah, everybody was so impressed with you over these last few weeks. I can't tell you how happy we are that you were able to help Hannah out. With Clark away playing football at God knows where, you were a lifesaver for all of us. Even Mr. and Mrs. Davenport said you were the perfect stand-in for Clark."

Judah winced inside, but he replied without a hint of pain. "I was happy to be able to help, Mrs. Meldrim. Hannah's been a great friend, introduced me to so many nice people since we've been at Armstrong, that I couldn't turn her down when she asked. This whole thing has really been quite an experience for me. I'm just glad things worked out so that I could do it."

Hannah's mother picked up an elegantly wrapped gift from the mantle and handed it to Judah. "This is just a little something from Mr. Meldrim and me as a sign of appreciation for all that you've done for our daughter." Inside was a set of monogrammed cuff links and matching shirt studs. After Judah had unwrapped the gift, Mrs. Meldrim continued, "You've looked so smart in your tuxedo that Art and I decided you might need a set of these because you're gonna be a successful young man who goes lots of places where a tuxedo is required dress."

Judah thanked her profusely for his gift, and just as he was about to walk out the door, Hannah kissed him on the cheek. "You were wonderful," she said. "I think Pat and Julie and I are going over to the Triple X about four. Why don't you see if you can come by?"

The Triple X drive-in was located on the corner of Victory Drive and Ash, just across from Grayson Stadium. It was a popular hangout for teenagers and the place where the previous evening's adventures were hashed and rehashed. Inside was a large oak barrel with various soda pumps attached. There was also curb service, usually provided by an unfortunate-looking woman in her late thirties who hailed from the west side. By five o'clock on a Sunday afternoon, it was hard to find a parking place.

Judah still had his father's Mercedes when he pulled in next to Hannah and her friends. She was in the passenger seat of Patricia Roberts' car, and Julie McCloud was in the back. Almost in chorus, all three said, "Hey, Judah," as he climbed into the backseat next to Julie. Cigarettes were considered chic, so both Patricia and Julie had them dangling from their fingers. They, too, had made their debuts the night before and had also been at the Fort Screven party, so the conversation revolved around that. Cars slowly moved through the Triple X as passengers scanned the crowd for friends.

"There's Allison Deitz," said Patricia excitedly, "she's driving that new Riviera her father bought her!" Allison was another deb. She stopped when she reached Patricia's car.

"Y'all have just got to take a ride with me and see my new car," she called through the window. Hannah had other ideas.

"I'll stay here with Judah," she said innocently, "and keep him company."

Judah and Hannah watched as Allison steered her daddy's money onto Victory Drive. Then they smiled. Judah felt like kissing her, but he knew too many eyes were watching.

"When can we be together again? I mean just the two of us alone?"

Hannah thought for a moment. "You know, I like to go to Bonaventure Cemetery and sketch the monuments. I've done that a lot. My mother knows all about it. Maybe tomorrow around lunchtime, can you meet me there?"

For the rest of the afternoon and evening, all Judah thought about was Hannah. When he pulled through the gates of the cemetery the next day, he was afraid she wouldn't be there; but when he arrived at the Lawton family plot on the bluff of the Wilmington River, there she was, sketching a life-size statue of Jesus standing in a white marble archway beckoning the faithful to enter into paradise. She had gotten there early and had almost finished her drawing. After showing it to him, she closed her sketchbook, put her arms around Judah, and kissed him.

"Let's go back to Tybee," he whispered as he buried his nose in Hannah's hair and inhaled her scent. "Nobody's gonna be at my uncle's place."

"Seems like we were just here," giggled Hannah as she and Judah climbed the stairs to the second floor.

"There's quite a view of the ocean from up here," Judah said as he opened the door to the master bedroom. The room had twelve-foot ceilings, and on the far wall three floor-to-ceiling windows opened to sea and sky. There was an incoming tide, and a wind from the northeast whipped the waves high before they crashed against the seawall. It was cold and clear again. The beach was deserted, and for a long time they watched in silence as the gulls rode the winds. They seldom had to flap their wings. After watching for several minutes, Judah put his arm around Hannah and drew her close. He pressed his face against her hair, and once more enjoyed the glorious smell of Hannah Meldrim. Moments later they were lying on the bed.

The old house was cold, so Judah pulled up the quilt at the end of the bed. What would happen did not start quickly. It was a slow burn, tempered by what Hannah had told him the last time they were in this house. Nevertheless it burned.

Hannah had no intention of making love to Judah and he had no intention of asking, but as the situation slowly unfolded there would be a point of no return, of no longer refusing desire. It arrived with an intensity that neither had ever known or would ever forget. As the hours passed they would build themselves to this fulfillment again and again. Over the next few days, Judah and Hannah would find more and more ways to meet secretly—and with each encounter they would gladly surrender to overwhelming desire.

Winter Quarter

Look in my face; my name is Might-have-been;
I am also called No-more, Too-late, Farewell.
—Dante Gabriel Rossetti, *The House of Life*

AT THE MELDRIMS' party Judah was unprepared for the pain he felt as he watched Clark with his arm around Hannah. The calm and natural way she responded to her "boyfriend" in the presence of her family's guests gave him reason to fear that perhaps all they had said and done was only a sham, the dalliances of a troubled young woman. Having to shake Clark's hand and talk with him was even worse. It wasn't until the evening's end, when he and Hannah found themselves alone in the kitchen, that she was able to reassure her lover.

"I have to do this," she whispered urgently. "I love you, Judah, but for right now this must be our secret. It won't be for too much longer. When Clark leaves for the winter quarter, that's when I'll do it."

Judah had no recourse but to accept Hannah's reasoning—reluctantly. However, the thought of her being with Clark for the next ten days was agonizing. Visions of her being forced by Clark to have sex with him played again and again in his mind, and there was nothing he could do but wait. While Judah would be spending New Year's Eve alone, Hannah would be at another lavish affair, dancing in the arms of Clark Davenport.

The week between Christmas and New Year's dragged painfully by. Hannah would secretly call and confirm her feelings for him, but the sight of Clark's car in front of her house, and the image of them leaving together, drove the knife even deeper. Judah was certain that he could no longer bear the anguish—and then January the third arrived, and Clark Davenport departed.

The new campus of Armstrong College was located on the southern edge of Savannah at the end of Abercorn Street. For a city that size, the ride from Kensington Park to the college was considered a long one. Judah offered to drive Hannah that first day of class. She was glad to accept, because it would give them a chance to talk.

Hannah was not her usual bubbly self when she got into the front seat of Judah's car. She smiled and spoke, but Judah could tell something was amiss.

"Is anything wrong?" he asked as he pulled on to Waters Avenue and headed south.

"I don't know," said Hannah. "I guess I'm just tired."

"Did you tell him?"

"Yeah. I told him I didn't want to see him again."

"Does your mother know?"

"She knows."

"What did she say?"

Hannah managed to blurt out, "Oh, Judah, it was horrible," before bursting into tears.

For the rest of the ride she explained that she had been cool to Clark after Christmas and that he had pressed her for her reasons. "I finally told him on New Year's Day that I just didn't care anymore, that things had changed. He got real mad, Judah. He said he didn't care either and that he had plenty of girls in Atlanta who would love to go out with him." Then she started to cry again. This puzzled Judah: He thought she should be happy that it was over.

"Why are you still crying? Was it that bad when you told your mother?"

"It was that bad." Hannah turned away from Judah and stared out the window, her eyes swollen and red. A silence settled over her. Judah waited a few minutes before inquiring:

"Where did you go for New Year's Eve?"

"A party at Allison's out at Vernonburg."

"You told Clark the next day?"

Hannah didn't speak. She only nodded her head.

"How was the party?"

Once more tears started streaming from her eyes. Judah watched as they darkened the gray wool skirt she was wearing. He felt he had to insist.

"Did something happen out there?"

"He got drunk, Judah, real drunk."

"And?"

There was no response; and suddenly the image that Judah had so dreaded, and had fought so hard to cleanse from his thoughts, flashed again before his eyes. In a soft voice filled with torment, he asked, "Did that bastard rape you again?"

Hannah squeezed her eyes shut, and Judah watched as new tears ran down her cheeks and over the beautiful lips he so adored. The horrible truth could not be evaded.

Over the next couple of weeks, what Judah had hoped for did not materialize. He saw Hannah on a regular basis at school, but always she seemed a little distant. When he asked her out, she pleaded repeatedly that the time wasn't right yet, that she needed to smooth things over with her mother. Finally, on the third Saturday in January, Hannah agreed to an actual date.

Mrs. Meldrim was polite when she answered the door, but a hint of coolness tinged her voice. She didn't ask Judah in, but then Hannah was ready and appeared at the door immediately. All this registered with Judah at some level, but not consciously enough to make much of an impression. All he cared about was how Hannah acted, and she seemed in a much better mood.

Judah had his father's Mercedes again, and on its Becker Mexico radio the Righteous Brothers sang "Ebb Tide" as he drove east on DeRenne Avenue.

"Where're we going?" asked Hannah.

"To a Sigma Kappa Chi party down on Wilmington."

"Sigma" was a fraternity at Armstrong which had somehow managed to land a lease on a large dock house on the Wilmington River at the southern end of the island. The house was the envy of all and the scene of much college revelry. Billy Aprillia was a member, and he had invited Judah to a "Purple Jesus" party. Billy, the man in charge, had arranged the purchase of two quarts of 150 proof grain alcohol and had mixed it himself with two gallons of grape juice in a large punch bowl.

On the ride out Hannah had sounded normal, but she didn't seem to be as physically responsive as she once had been. Judah had leaned over and kissed her twice, but she had responded listlessly.

After their arrival it wasn't long before Hannah was in a tight knot with her friends, answering painful questions about her breakup with Clark. Judah basked in the fraternity's admiration of his having a date with Miss Savannah—but it took only one cup of Billy's special brew for him to tire of his newfound fame and seek Hannah's attention.

She had slipped away from the crowd, and when Judah found her she was outside, standing alone at the dock's railing, her eyes fixed on a blinking green marker near the far side of the river. He put his arm around her and inquired softly, "Is everything okay? You've seemed so different lately." Hannah said nothing for a few moments, but finally she turned to face him. "We Can Work It Out," by the Beatles, was blaring from the jukebox inside. Hannah almost had to shout.

"Can we please go now, Judah? I need to talk with you."

Neither said a word until they reached the Tybee Road. Judah turned right, heading east on Highway 80.

"Where are you taking me?" asked Hannah.

"To the beach."

"You mean to your uncle's place?"

"Sure, why not? That's a perfect place to talk."

"I don't think that's such a good idea."

The alcohol had worked its wicked magic, and Judah's frustration quickly turned to anger.

"That's funny, Hannah. You thought it was the greatest idea in the world only a few weeks ago." Judah had never spoken to her in such a harsh manner. At first it surprised her; but after that it made perfect sense. She knew how she had been acting, and she understood how Judah must have felt. She wanted to cry, but she was so emotionally exhausted that there simply were no tears left.

The night was cold, still, and clear. An immense crowd of stars had hurled themselves in a giant shawl over the marsh, and silver specks rose from horizon to horizon. A yellow moon hung over the top of the Tybee Lighthouse. Pearl-gray creeks heavy with the tide wound through the marsh on either side of the road as Judah and Hannah sped through the darkness in silence. Nothing was said until they were sitting on the same couch, looking at the same ocean, as they had done on their first night in Uncle David's beach house. Hannah was the first to speak.

"Judah, before I tell you what's happened, I want you to know that everything I've said to you has been nothing but the truth. You are the most wonderful boy I've ever known. I love you now and I'll probably love you for the rest of my life, but this just can't go on."

"It's because I'm a Jew, isn't it?"

"No, Judah!"

"Well, if you love me so much and you want to end it, then what else could it be? It's your mother, isn't it? She doesn't want Miss Savannah dating a slimy Jew, does she?" It was what Judah felt, but he wouldn't have said it like that if it hadn't have been for the Purple Jesus.

"No, it's not that!"

"Then what is it, damn it?"

Hannah put her face in her hands and rested them on her lap for a few seconds, then drew herself straight up. She turned to Judah, looked him directly in the eyes, and without blinking announced, "I'm pregnant."

Judah's mouth dropped open as he groped for words. Then his shoulders dropped as he exhaled a deep sigh. Hannah continued robotically.

"It's Clark's, and we're going to be married next weekend. I'll be moving to Atlanta and live there until he finishes school. Please don't make this any harder on me. I'll always have a special place in my heart for you, but we can never see each other again."

It took Judah months to get over the initial shock of Hannah's revelation. The simple act of leaving home each day forced him to look across the street at her house, which opened his wounds yet again. As he sat at his desk and tried to study, it seemed his eyes were always drawn to his bedroom window and its view across Althea Parkway. He found it hard to concentrate, and his grades began to fall. At the end of the winter quarter he barely scraped by with an overall 2.0 average, the minimum required to keep his draft deferment.

Judah's parents noticed the change with concern, but they never found out about Hannah. Nobody found out about Hannah, not even Billy. Of course everybody in Savannah knew she had been quickly married and immediately suspected what would shortly become obvious. But as far as Judah knew, no one ever became aware of his secret love affair with Hannah Meldrim. As spring quarter passed into the last week of April, he absorbed one final blow from his shattering affair.

It was a Friday afternoon and Judah was in his driveway washing his car when Clark and Hannah pulled up in front of her house. As they walked to the door, it was obvious that Hannah was heavy with child. Clark noticed him, waved, and said hello. Hannah gave a cheery greeting too, but the look on her face betrayed her. She was weary and resigned to her fate; she didn't even appear to be the same person he loved so much. It was painful for him to see her that way, but the shock of it made him realize that she was truly gone from his life. It was then that his scars began to heal.

Spring in Savannah defines the beauty of the city as no other season does. Around Valentine's Day tiny buds begin to appear on limbs and branches all over town. By St. Patrick's Day those buds have swollen to the bursting point. Patches of lavender, red, white, and pink dot the azaleas, while in the trees bright green leaves reach for the sun. By April Fool's Day Savannah is aflame with color, which seems to affect everything it touches. As the days grew warmer, Judah's outlook showed improvement and he began to think of Hannah less. His grades were also on the upswing; and although his old girlfriend Diane had dumped him because he had escorted Hannah to her debut, he had discovered another attractive Jewish girl at Armstrong. Life was getting better. Then the bottom dropped out.

It was three o'clock in the afternoon on Saturday, May 14th. Judah was sitting at his desk reading the *Iliad* for Dr. Strozier's English lit class when he noticed a dark blue 1965 Chevy Bel Air stop in front of his house. On the front door, in yellow letters, were the words United States Air Force. Below that was the Air Force seal. Two men were in the car, and he immediately recognized the one in the passenger's seat. It was Rabbi Ruben from Congregation Mickve Israel. Judah had been with him at services that morning. The other man was an Air Force officer; and as the two made their way up the sidewalk toward the Benjamin house, Judah knew that something serious had happened to Jacob.

"Colonel and Mrs. Benjamin," said Major Carpenter, "it is with the deepest regret that I must inform you that your son, First Lieutenant Jacob Benjamin, has been killed in the line of duty over the skies of the Republic of Vietnam."

It took two weeks for Jacob's remains to be found and shipped to Savannah. Hundreds of people were on hand when his plain wooden coffin was lowered into the ground in the old walled Jewish cemetery on the west side of town, which dated back to 1773. Judah's mother's ancestors were buried there. Even Hannah, now eight months pregnant, was present with her parents. She had returned to Savannah to have her baby. Judah was so devastated that seeing her again had no effect on him. The only thing that seemed to take his mind off his grief was working with Billy and Elijah on the *St. Patrick*.

II

THE EMPEROR OF THUNDERBOLT

The Legend Begins

When crew and captain understand each other to the core,
It takes a gale and more than a gale to put their ship ashore.
—Rudyard Kipling, "Together"

IN 1905, AT THE AGE of twenty, Charlie Aprillia's grandfather arrived in Savannah. Back in Italy Augustine Aprillia's family had all been fishermen, so it was the only thing he knew.

By luck there was a family of Italian descent in Savannah who owned a shrimp boat, spoke a little Italian, and agreed to take Augustine on. Five years later he would be married to one of that family's daughters, and thirteen years after that he would own the boat plus three more and have the largest wholesale seafood business from Jacksonville to Charleston. When Augustine died his son Charlie took the helm and guided Aprillia's Wholesale Seafood Company to continued success. When World War II began, Charlie was granted a draft deferment because he was engaged in an essential industry.

Because Italy and Germany were partners in their fight against the Allies, Americans of recent German and Italian descent were sometimes scrutinized by the F.B.I. for possible enemy sympathies and collaboration. At the start of the war, coastal towns were rife with rumors that shrimp boats were selling food and fuel on the high seas to the U-boats that prowled the Atlantic Seaboard. Savannah was no exception, and when word got out that the Feds had been asking questions in Thunderbolt, everybody immediately suspected Charlie Aprillia was the object of their investigation.When the rumor finally made it to Charlie's ears, he was so incensed that he went to the next town council meeting in Thunderbolt. There he proclaimed his innocence and then announced that he had joined the United States Navy to fight for his country, just in case there were any lingering doubts about his patriotism. As it turned out Charlie was able to lay those doubts to rest the very next day.

In the early months of the war a few U-boats had indeed surfaced, taken what supplies they wanted from the fishing vessels they had surprised, and then sunk them with their deck guns. Incidents like these seemed distant to the Thunderbolt fleet until the trawler *Norge* disappeared without a trace. Small ships like the *Norge* had no radios to sound the alarm, no Geneva Convention to offer even a modicum of protection from mistreatment, and, worst of all, no way to fight back. An action by the War Department remedied that situation.

In April of 1942 the Secretary of War declared that shrimp boats and other U.S. flagged fishing vessels were members of the Coast Guard Auxiliary and considered warships. This action gave crew members Geneva Convention protection. The government went even further when it provided the shrimp boats with radios, fifty-caliber machine guns for the bows, two roll-off depth charges for the stern, and a Coast Guard Auxiliary flag to fly from the mast.

It was sweet the next morning when Charlie prepared to set course in the *Miss Katie* for the Atlantic. His boat was topped off with enough fuel to venture out fifty miles, drag the nets all day, and return to safe harbor in Wassaw Sound, only to head out again the following day and repeat the operation. He was searching for the large prawn twice the size of his index finger.

Miss Katie was forty feet long, had a single Chrysler marine engine, and was named after Charlie's wife. As Charlie and his crew were preparing to shove off, a young F.B.I. agent showed up dockside and started asking questions. When the questioning seemed to intimate that special agent Carlson suspected Charlie of selling fuel to a U-boat, he was ready.

"Let me take you down to my boat," said Charlie, when asked about his activities beyond the horizon. "Then you'll understand why it would be impossible for me to sell fuel to those Nazi bastards." Charlie removed the filler cap from one of the tanks, then told the agent, "Stick your nose in there and tell me what you smell."

The agent complied. "I smell gasoline, captain. What else would I smell?"

"You're a smart boy, Mr. Carlson, but not that smart," said Charlie angrily as he replaced the filler cap. Agent Carlson was offended by that reply, so he decided to put a little pressure on his target.

"The government doesn't appreciate your disrespect for its agents."

Charlie folded his arms over his chest and smiled. "Do you know what kind of engines those Nazi subs have, Mr. Government Agent?"

"I, uh, I'm not sure. What do you mean?"

"What I mean is, do you know what kind of fuel those subs burn?"

"That's ridiculous," said Carlson. "The same stuff as this."

"Well, because you're just a young fella who doesn't know much, I'm gonna go easy on you, Mr. Carlson, and simply tell you that you don't know your ass from a hole in the ground."

The F.B.I. man's mouth tightened. His hand almost went to the shoulder holster under his double-breasted suit, but something gave him pause. Charlie laughed.

"Aw, hell, they have diesels on those subs, and they can only burn diesel fuel. You know, fuel oil, Number 2 Bunker, the same stuff your Momma up in New York burns in her furnace. The gasoline in these tanks would destroy their engines in a few seconds if they tried to use it. There ain't no way in hell I'm sellin' fuel to those U-boats. So if you have no further questions, I have work to do."

By the time *Miss Katie* had passed the General Oglethorpe Hotel on her way to the ocean, all of Thunderbolt was buzzing about the way Captain Charlie had put that smart-ass Yankee government man in his place.

Miss Katie sailed forty miles out into the Atlantic to set her nets.

The ocean was like glass when she lowered them and started dragging for prawns. As the hours passed the hold began to fill with prawns as Charlie's two strikers, Elijah and Clegg Roberts (whom everybody called Skeeter), dumped the nets' goody bag over and over again. The deck came alive with the twitching and jumping of the big shrimp, but around three in the afternoon, Charlie decided that they had worked long enough. He told his first mate, Elijah, to secure the nets and set a course for home.

Charlie was at the wheel and had just pointed *Miss Katie*'s bow into the setting sun when his eyes caught movement in the water about a hundred yards to his starboard side. Simultaneously he heard Elijah holler, "Some'in in da water over here, Cap'n Charlie!"

At first Charlie thought it might have been the dorsal fin of a right whale breaking the surface on its yearly migration to the North Atlantic. Moments later, however, a closer look with his binoculars clearly revealed a periscope. Charlie immediately grabbed the microphone on his government-supplied radio and told the Coast Guard station at Tybee what was going on. Then he yelled for Elijah to take the wheel as he bolted out the wheelhouse door and headed for the fifty-caliber Browning machine gun on the bow.

"Get the depth charges ready, Skeeter," he yelled as he loaded the machine gun with a belt of ammo, chambered a round, and swung the barrel toward the sub. By this time the sub had started to surface, and the conning tower had broken the water. Charlie took aim at the center of the conning tower and depressed the gun's trigger.

The Coast Guard had trained the shrimpers how to use the weapon, and Charlie had done pretty well with it; but when the first round came out the barrel, he still found the massive explosion startling. Charlie's knees went weak and he almost collapsed, but he regained control of himself and began firing bursts at the sub.

Every fifth round in the ammo belt was a tracer, and Elijah watched from the wheelhouse as the burning orange flash streaked over the water and hit the side of the sub's superstructure. *Miss Katie* and the sub were running a parallel course, and

Charlie was chopping up the water all around the U-boat as some of his fire plowed into the ocean. Just as quickly as the sub had appeared, it began a rapid dive below the surface. In moments it was gone, so Charlie ran to the stern and yelled to Elijah. "Steer the boat to where you think that sub is. I'm gonna roll off these depth charges. Let me know when you think we're over the bastards!" Elijah estimated the speed and course of the sub, jammed the throttle all the way forward, and made for where he thought the U-boat would be.

On the surface a U-boat could make almost twenty knots, but when submerged it was actually slower than a shrimp boat. *Miss Katie* had a good chance of catching it. While Charlie and Skeeter armed the depth charges, Elijah guided the boat to a particular spot in the ocean.

"You ready, Cap'n Charlie?"

"Yeah. Just say when."

They were in about seventy-five feet of water. Charlie had set the depth charges to go off at fifty feet, so he was concerned that the explosion might damage his hull. But his blood was up, and he decided to take the risk for a chance to sink a Nazi sub with his beloved *Miss Katie.*

"Now!" screamed Elijah from the bow. In an instant Charlie and Skeeter put their backs into the barrel-shaped weapon and rolled it off the stern. Then they scrambled to the other side to roll out the second depth charge.

No one said a word as *Miss Katie* scuttled away at eight knots, the fastest speed she could make. After about ten seconds, Charlie could feel the initial shock wave of an explosion. He thought the worst had passed until *Miss Katie* was rocked from bow to stern as the surface of the ocean erupted like a geyser. Then the second depth charge went off. The three men braced themselves.

Somehow *Miss Katie* survived. Charlie later swore it was because she was made from oaks harvested on St. Catherine's Island, the same as were in Old Ironsides.

"Cap'n Charlie," yelled Elijah from the wheelhouse, "Coast Guard done called and said they got a couple planes on the way to help us out." Everything grew quiet as all eyes scanned the water for signs of the U-boat. Ten minutes later they heard planes approaching.

On the way back in, Charlie, Elijah, and Skeeter huddled in the wheelhouse and debated whether or not they had sunk the sub. "Shit," said Charlie, "I can't believe what's happened. I'm wound up tighter than a two-dollar watch. I need a drink."

"Me, too," echoed Elijah.

"How 'bout you, Skeeter?"

Poor Skeeter's eyes were wide open and his hands were shaking. He had never been so scared in his life, but he had done his job and was proud of himself.

"Yes, sir, Cap'n Charlie, ol' Skeeter sure could use a drink right about now."

Charlie gave the wheel to Elijah and went back to the small cabin. In seconds he returned with a bottle of Jim Beam.

"Hope y'all like this stuff, it's all I got."

Two days later in the Savannah paper there was a photo of Charlie, Elijah, and Skeeter standing next to the machine gun on the bow of *Miss Katie*. "Shrimpers Take On U-Boat," read the headline. After that no one questioned the patriotism and loyalty of Charlie Aprillia. He was true to his word, however, and left for the Navy six weeks later. Katie would run the business, and Elijah would run the boats.

The Empire

Sweet childish days, that were as long
As twenty days are now.
—William Wordsworth, "To a Butterfly"

WHEN CHARLIE looked back on his war years, his attack on the U-boat seemed minor in comparison to the other battles he would have with the enemy. From the beginning of his Navy service, Charlie had been trained as the coxswain on a Higgins boat, the principal landing craft for beach invasions. His first taste of combat was in the Pacific at the battle of Tarawa Atol in November of 1943. Because the invasion planner had miscalculated the tides, his boat got caught on a reef as it headed to Betio Beach on Tarawa. He barely escaped with his life and collected his first Purple Heart.

Because of his bravery and experience, Charlie was transferred to the Atlantic, where he wound up in England practicing for the invasion of Europe. On D-Day he was again at the helm of a Higgins boat on the first wave to go in at Omaha Beach. He was injured by shrapnel from a German 88 that destroyed the Higgins boat next to him, killing everyone on board. Somehow he managed to make it to the beach and came back four more times to deposit soldiers from the 29th Infantry Divison below the cliffs of Normandy. He earned the Navy Cross for gallantry that day as well as his second Purple Heart.

After Japan surrendered in August of '45, Charlie had enough points to be mustered out of the Navy the next month. Shrimping season wasn't over until the end of December, and by the beginning of October he was heading *Miss Katie* out for Wassaw Sound. He still had the St. Christopher medal around his neck that he had worn throughout the war. Katie had given it to him the day he left Savannah, and Charlie was sure that her prayers and St. Christopher had brought him through.

Even though the war had introduced such things as fuel rationing and wage-and-price controls, Elijah had done an admirable job for Aprillia Wholesale Seafood and had helped to place the business on a firm footing. It didn't take Charlie long to realize that he was doing well enough to afford another boat. When he got it in May of 1946, he made Elijah the captain.

For the shrimping industry the postwar years were robust, and Charlie was selling every pound of shrimp he could catch from his wholesale operation in Thunderbolt. It didn't take him long to realize that he could make even more money by opening a retail store in Savannah. By 1949 Aprillia's Seafood was in operation on Jefferson, right across the street from the old City Market.

Soon Charlie had enough money to begin looking around for investments. He didn't know anything about the stock market and didn't trust brokers, bankers, or lawyers; but he did know that God wasn't making any more dirt, so he started buying up land. His first purchase was the lot next to Aprillia's Wholesale Seafood on River Drive in Thunderbolt. It was two hundred feet wide and ran from the street all the way to the Wilmington River. A few months later he bought the lot on the other side of his business; and now Charlie owned six hundred commercial feet on the Wilmington River. It was only 1951.

When a man has as much invested as Charlie did in Thunderbolt, it is only prudent for him to become involved in the governmental and civic affairs of the municipality that has jurisdiction over his holdings. In 1952, therefore, Charlie ran for city council. He was elected handily, because he was a natural politician. People used to say he could talk a hungry dog off a meat wagon, and he put that talent to good use at the council meetings. He was friendly, funny, the consummate hail-fellow; yet if the situation called for it, he could also be a hard-nosed bastard.

At thirty-two Charlie was the happiest man in the world. He

had a thriving business, a pretty wife he had loved from the first time he saw her, two daughters who looked like their mother, and a young son who looked like him.

During the colonial period the town of Thunderbolt was known as Wassaw; the Wilmington River was called St. Augustine Creek. The legend is that Thunderbolt got its new name during a violent thunderstorm when a bolt of lighting struck the ground and a spring burst forth that furnished enough fresh water for everyone.

Almost from the beginning Thunderbolt's economy was built around two things: shrimping and recreation. It was an easy trip to Savannah, so the shrimp boats could unload their catches onto waiting wagons and take the shrimp directly to the city for sale. In addition the prevailing winds along this part of Georgia coast are from the south, and the high bluffs along the Wilmington River where Thunderbolt sits have a generally south-to-southeastern exposure. Because of this the town was blessed with cooling breezes during the sweltering days of summer. This attracted large crowds in search of relief from the overwhelming heat in the days before electricity. In 1867 the first streetcar tracks were laid in Savannah; a line to Thunderbolt was included. Soon the town became a prime destination for city-dwellers seeking comfort on a hot day. Around the turn of the century, the Casino and Resort Hotel was built on the bluffs of the Wilmington River there. Bannon's Lodge, Butler's Wassaw Family Resort, the Savannah Yacht Club, and one of the area's fastest half-mile racetracks were also located in Thunderbolt.

The sometimes dangerous and always hard life of the shrimpers and the people who liked to gamble at the casino or bet on the ponies at Mike Doyle's racetrack combined to give Thunderbolt its personality and charm. As it evolved the town became very distinct from its big sister, Savannah, and more like its naughty little sister, Tybee Island. It was also very proud and protective of its independence, and tended to ignore the various attempts by outsiders to change the way Thunderbolt ran its business. It was an open secret that money placed in the proper hands could get zoning laws ignored or changed and make a speeding ticket disappear.

Such was the town where Charlie Aprillia had been raised and had his business. Now it was the town he helped to govern.

Charlie and Katie were typical examples of the Catholic subculture in Savannah. They had met in the first grade at Sacred Heart School; and when it came time for high school, Charlie went to Benedictine Military School. Katie attended St. Vincent's Academy. Neither had ever dated anyone who wasn't Catholic, and both felt somewhat isolated from and suspicious of the Protestant world around them. For twelve years they had been so methodically instructed in the fundamentals of their faith that something like skipping Mass or failing to make a weekly visit to the confessional never even crossed their minds.

When Billy Aprillia was born at the old St. Joseph's Hospital on Taylor and Habersham streets, Katie received the VIP treatment. Her oldest sister was a nun and the hospital's administrator, so there was no way that Sister Victorine Flannery was going to allow anything but the best for Katie and her baby.

From the very first moments of his life, Billy Aprillia was surrounded by people who were devoutly Catholic, from the obstetrician who delivered him to the nursing nuns working in the OB room to the pediatrician who would care for him. His parents' relatives were all Catholics, too, as were most of their friends. Some of Billy's earliest memories were of kneeling with his family in the living room while saying nightly rosaries led by his father. At the Aprillia house a crucifix hung in every room and a holy water dispenser stood at the front door, so all could properly make the sign of the cross when leaving. A statue of the Blessed Mother adorned the mantel over the fireplace. Another of St. Michael, the patron saint of fishermen, resided on the dresser in Billy's room.

The Aprillias attended Mass together every Sunday at The Nativity of Our Lord in Thunderbolt, on the corner of Victory Drive and Mechanics Avenue. Katie was president of the Altar Society and secretary of the Catholic Women's Club. Billy's father had served several terms as Grand Knight of the Knights of Columbus, and Billy had become an altar boy at the age of eight when the Mass was still said in Latin. Fond of making weekly novenas, Katie would often take Billy with her to the evening services. Religion was such a large part of Billy's life that by the fourth grade he had decided he was going to be a priest.

Charlie's political star was shining brightly in Thunderbolt. Only two years after winning his seat on the town council, he was approached by several of his fellow council members and asked to run for mayor.

In 1954 Thunderbolt had only about five hundred registered voters. The town was also small geographically, with only about a hundred homes. This meant that a candidate, if willing, could walk the streets and visit each household in about three days. All this gave Thunderbolt a very up-close and personal brand of politics—the kind that perfectly suited Charlie. When the votes were counted on the second Tuesday in September, he beat the incumbent in a landslide.

Charlie had a victory party that night at his house on River Drive, just across the street from his business. There were more than two hundred people present, and Billy was at his father's side when Charlie gave his acceptance speech. Years later he would look back on that night and remember how proud he was of his father. After his victory Charlie's friends hung a nickname on him: "The Emperor." If Charlie had evolved into the Emperor of Thunderbolt, then Billy had become its Crown Prince.

Charlie reveled in taking his son with him just about everywhere he went. At town council meetings Billy was always in the front row, watching how his father was able to persuade and cajole. For his age he absorbed a remarkable amount of information and understanding from these meetings; and much to his father's delight, he often quoted council members verbatim at the dinner table.

By the time Billy was ten, he was working in the family business. He had become an expert at filleting fish and could head and peel a shrimp as fast as any of the other workers at the processing plant. Then, in the summer between the eighth grade and high school, Charlie took Billy with him on his new boat, the *St. Anthony*.

Billy had been out with his father before, but never for more than a day. That summer of 1961 he would start spending a week at a time with Charlie—not just to be entertained, but to learn how to handle a shrimp boat and catch shrimp. Charlie was grooming his son to take over the empire he had built in Thunderbolt.

Charlie was reelected in 1956, 1958, and then again in 1960 and 1962. His business continued to prosper as he watched both it and his son grow. As far as Billy was concerned, things couldn't have been better. He was happy and secure, and he had a successful future in store for him.

As he entered his teens and then high school at Benedictine, his ideas about the priesthood faded as his interest in girls took off like a bottle rocket. He even began to have doubts about the existence of God and life after death, but it was more than his fascination with girls that was responsible for his diminishing interest in religion in general and the Catholic Church in particular. Billy was beginning to think for himself and rebel against authority of all kinds. By the end of his junior year at Benedictine, he was lying to his parents about attending Mass. When he entered Armstrong he dropped all pretenses and told his parents he was no longer going to church.

Billy's mother was so horrified that she made it her sacred mission to shepherd her wayward son back into the Catholic fold through prayers, novenas, holy cards, and candle-lightings at church. So fervent was she in her mission that it even got on Charlie's nerves. As for Charlie, he simply told his wife that Billy would get over it, that it was natural to question one's religion. He summed up his feelings about his son's attitude very neatly one night after dinner. "Relax, Katie. Billy's got a big C for Catholic branded on his brow. He's marked for life. He'll never be able to escape from it. It may take time, but he'll come back to the Church. Just don't push him further away with too much of that mumbo-jumbo you're so good at."

There was a great deal of tension for a number of months afterward. Billy even considered moving out, but he knew he couldn't afford it. He simply kept his mouth shut, bowed his head at the dinner table when his father said the blessing, and even made the sign of the cross when necessary—but it meant nothing to him. In a way he was sad to have lost something that had meant so much to him, but in another way he was angry to have been taken in by what he considered to be so much "bullshit."

Billy eventually decided that his discarding of religion was actually a liberating thing for him. He no longer felt constrained by the rigorous morality of the Catholic Church, especially regarding sex; and he was determined to have as much of it with as many girls as he possibly could. Soon the Sigma Kappa Chi fraternity house on the Wilmington River was his regular hangout.

Billy had been dating Evelyn Morgan since their junior year, and their relationship had taken pretty much the same track as his parents. They were both Catholics, who had gone to Benedictine and St. Vincent's respectively; and although they had done some heavy petting, nothing else had happened. Evelyn was sure she was in love with Billy and envisioned a life with him after college. Billy used to feel that way too, but after he disavowed his religion, he began to grow somewhat cynical, and even cold. When they were alone together, Billy became more aggressive with Evelyn, but for a while she was able to fend off his advances. It was a cold Wednesday night in February of 1966 when she finally surrendered.

"If you love me as much as you say you do, Evelyn, you'll do it," said Billy as he angrily pulled away from her and went to the cooler for another beer. The only light in the fraternity house was a Pabst Blue Ribbon sign hanging over the bar.

Evelyn knew how Billy felt about the Church and had sensed a change in him ever since he had told her, but she hadn't put the two together. Now she felt even more distance between them; she feared that she was losing him. When he returned and sat next to her sulking and sipping his beer, Evelyn's concern heightened. Finally she reached out and rubbed his back.

"You know I want to, Billy, but I'm afraid. I want to wait until we get married."

"Why?"

"Because it's the right thing."

"Oh, you mean because it's a sin to have sex before marriage? A sin. That is such bullshit."

Evelyn rose and put her arms around Billy and started to kiss him. Soon they were locked in an embrace as Billy sought to tear her clothes off. Years later Evelyn would sadly recall how quickly it all had happened. She had envisioned romantic tenderness and patience from her lover that first time, but it was not to be.

When it was over she sobbed softly as she dressed. Billy went back to the cooler for another beer. They would continue dating for several more months, but Billy eventually lost interest.

Over the next several years, he would continue going to Armstrong during the off-season and working for his father when the shrimp were running. Billy fulfilled his military obligation by joining the Georgia Air National Guard, and completed his basic training in 1967 at Lackland Air Force Base in Texas.

Smuggler's Paradise

"I think that counting all inlet waterways, we have in Georgia, we consider, about 2,500 miles of coastline that are almost a smuggler's paradise."

—D. C. Ghormley,
inspector for the Georgia Bureau of Investigation,
as quoted in the *Savannah Morning News*,
March 22, 1978.

WHEN BILLY and Judah entered Armstrong College in the fall of 1965, beer and hard liquor were the only intoxicants they had ever tried or even heard about. The word "marijuana" was only vaguely familiar to them. If questioned about it, they would have responded that they thought marijuana was something jazz musicians and ghetto blacks used up in New York City to get high.

At the beginning of the twentieth century, illegal use of drugs was something generally associated with the lower class and the fringes of American society. By the 1950s heroin was becoming more visible and was even seen as a major cause of crime, especially in the larger urban areas; but use of illegal substances was still far from a mainstream affliction. This would all change, however, when the late sixties arrived and the Baby Boom generation began to come of age.

Although drugs such as cocaine and LSD came into fashion for some, marijuana became the recreational drug of choice for the "hip" generation. In the beginning, hardly any cannabis was grown within the borders of the United States, so what was consumed had to be imported. As its popularity grew, ever-increasing amounts of marijuana were needed to satisfy demand. Some came across the Mexican border, but most was smuggled in along the South Atlantic Coast.

In the mid 1960s Colombia was the main supplier of marijuana and cocaine to the U.S.; and because of its proximity to that country, south Florida was the primary entry point for Colombian pot and coke. It took a while for law enforcement to recognize the extent of the smuggling, and even longer for it to figure out how it was being done and the ways to stop it. Eventually, though, enough heat was put on south Florida that the smugglers were forced to find another locale for their operations.

Aprillia Seafood had done well for so long that Charlie couldn't believe it when things started going downhill in the seventies. It seemed as if the shrimp had just disappeared. Some said it was pollution; some thought it came from over-fishing; and others decided that the unusually cold winters in those years had been responsible for the meager harvest. Whatever the reason, the shrimping business had been hit hard all along the Georgia coast, and shrimpers were desperate. Then came the oil embargo of 1974. Like gasoline, diesel fuel went through the roof. The bottom fell out for a lot of shrimpers. In 1965 there had been more than a hundred boats in the Thunderbolt fleet; by 1975 the number was down to thirty. From St. Mary's to Savannah, shrimpers were broke and looking for ways to feed their families. Then the smugglers in Florida moved north.

By most law enforcement estimates, only about ten percent of the drugs smuggled into the United States are actually confiscated. In August of 1972 188 pounds of marijuana were found floating in the Savannah River. At the time it was the largest haul ever found in the area. Then in April of the next year, five hundred pounds of pot were seized at the port of Savannah—discovered quite by accident on a freighter from Colombia. Four months after that the shrimp boat *Hazel B* was captured by U.S. Customs Patrol officers at Shellman Bluff as it was unloading thirty-six thousand pounds of marijuana onto a truck. It had long been rumored in Savannah that shrimpers were involved in drug-smuggling. The Shellman Bluff incident gave creditability to those rumors.

In the following months major marijuana seizures took place at Coffee Bluff and St. Marys. Then packages of ninety percent pure cocaine started washing ashore on Ossabaw Island. Suspicious eyes were cast at all shrimpers along Georgia's coast.

The 1976 season had been the hardest in memory for Thunderbolt shrimpers. It was so cold that winter that the marshes froze, killing most of the roe white shrimp. The state closed all of the sounds to shrimping and delayed the opening of shrimping season until July, forcing a new wave of bankruptcies and foreclosures along River Drive. The Emperor of Thunderbolt had never been so worried.

Charlie Aprillia would have starved to death before becoming a part of the drug trade. Billy was a little different. Although he wouldn't have been actively involved in smuggling drugs, he was not averse to turning a blind eye to those who were. Aprillia Seafood Company was tilting toward bankruptcy in the fall of 1976 when a stranger approached Billy at the Aprillia docks. He had a dark complexion, a Yankee accent, and wore an expensive suit. The man was polite and friendly, and to Billy he looked like a lawyer.

"Are you Mr. Aprillia?" he asked as he extended his hand.

"I'm one of 'em," replied Billy as he shook the stranger's hand and eyed him head to toe.

"Nice to meet you, Mr. Aprillia. My name is Barry Spence. I represent a seafood consortium that's interested in renting a couple of your boats."

"For what? The shrimp aren't running worth a shit around here."

"Oh, yes sir, we know that. My partners aren't thinking of shrimping in these waters. They want to go to the Dry Tortugas and Rebecca Shoals off the Florida Keys."

"Well, why don't you rent a boat down there?"

"Because there aren't any available, Mr. Aprillia. You see, the Golden Brazilians are running like crazy down there and all the local boats are in the hunt. Everybody knows you guys aren't doing a thing right now, so my partners and I thought you'd jump at a chance to make some money off an idle boat."

Billy knew all about the Golden Brazilians; the shrimpers in

Thunderbolt used to call them "pink gold." Back in '72 he'd taken the *St. Patrick* down to the Keys and kicked ass, taking in fifty boxes of shrimp in three days. Each box was equal to a hundred bushels or five thousand pounds of shrimp, but he hadn't heard anything about a "pink gold" run down that way recently.

Billy was immediately suspicious, but he needed the money. He was so broke he couldn't have raised enough cash to pay for the fuel to get to the Keys, much less provision his boat.

"Well, Mr. Spence, what's the deal?"

"We want the boats for two weeks, and we'll pay you $40,000 in cash when we leave the dock." Mr. Spence knew that was a lot of money for a shrimper in trouble.

"You gotta put up a bond for my boats, just in case they don't come back," said Billy, "and your captains have gotta have their papers, too. I don't want any half-ass at the wheel of my boat."

"Not a problem," said Mr. Spence with a smile as he extended his hand.

"When do you want to shove off?"

"I can have my people here the day after tomorrow. Is that okay with you?"

Billy was uneasy about the whole deal and suspected the boats would be used to smuggle drugs, but he was in a real jam and willing to take a chance. Besides, nothing had been mentioned about drugs, and boats were leased out all the time to independent contractors. If something happened he could honestly claim no knowledge of drug-running. The next two days were tense, and Billy didn't mention a word about the deal to his father. Charlie had been in declining health for the past few years and seldom involved himself in the day-to-day business of Aprillia Seafood.

Billy was waiting on the dock beside the *St. Patrick* and the *St. Anthony*, half hoping Mr. Spence wouldn't show, when he spotted him and four others getting out of a black Mercedes on the bluff. They started making their way down the dock.

"So good to see you again, Mr. Aprillia," said Mr. Spence in a cheery voice. He handed Billy a briefcase with one hand, and extended an envelope with his other. "Here is your fee. And here is the bond and papers you required." After Billy had finished checking the papers, Mr. Spence introduced the two captains. Both spoke with Latin accents, and to Billy they looked like Cubans or Puerto Ricans. He also thought they looked like really bad dudes.

Billy had a knot in his gut as he watched his boats ease away from the dock and start down the Wilmington River for Wassaw Sound. Then he and Mr. Spence made small talk as they walked to the Mercedes, where Mr. Spence extended his hand. "Perhaps we'll be able to do business again some time." Aprillia Seafood was safe again, at least for the next few months.

Two weeks later the boats returned to Thunderbolt as promised. When Billy checked their holds, he found no signs that shrimp had been in them, but he did find scattered bits of marijuana. Immediately he swept both boats clean. When he had finished Billy had collected enough pot to fill a grocery bag. He had it tucked under his arm while he climbed the ramp to Aprillia Seafood. When he got to the top, he was greeted by Brad Grady, Thunderbolt's chief of police.

"Whatcha been up to, Bubba?" asked Brad.

"Aw, I had to clean some trash out of a couple of my boats. I leased the *St. Patrick* and the *St. Anthony* to a consortium for a couple of weeks. Nothing but fuckin' spicks, and they left the boats a mess." Billy strolled over to a Dumpster next to his building and tossed in the bag of pot.

"How 'bout you, Brad? You been out keeping Thunderbolt safe from the crime wave that's hittin' Savannah?" asked Billy as he dusted off his hands, trying to remain nonchalant.

"I been writin' a few speeding tickets on the other side of the bridge. I always get a kick outta people who think I don't have jurisdiction just cause it's not in the town limits." Brad chuckled as he rested his right hand on his pistol.

"You off now?" asked Billy.

"Yeah, I guess so. I was heading to the barn when I saw you down on the dock and just stopped to see how things were goin'." The chief tilted his cap back. He had a full head of dark, curly hair.

"I got a bottle of Jack Daniels in the office. How 'bout a drink?"

"Shit," said Brad, "sounds like a winner to me."

The leather on Brad's pistol belt creaked as he sat in the chair in front of Billy's desk. His pistol thumped against the chair's arm when he shifted his bulk in an attempt to get comfortable.

"You still like it over the rocks, chief?" asked Billy as he opened the drawer to a filing cabinet on his side of the desk and produced a new quart bottle of Jack Daniels Black Label. Two drinks and a lot of small talk later, Chief Grady got to the real point of his visit.

"How did your deal with that Yankee Barry Spence turn out?"

Billy was surprised and afraid because he hadn't told anyone about the mysterious Mr. Spence. He fought to maintain an innocent demeanor.

"How do you know about that, Brad?"

Brad let out a snort. "Goddamn, Billy, I'm the fuckin' chief of police around here. I know everything! Besides, I'm the guy who put him on to you."

"You what?"

"That's right. Barry came to me first. He was lookin' for somebody who'd lease him a couple of boats, and I sent him to you."

"Son of a bitch," said Billy as he leaned back in his chair. He was staring at Brad in bewilderment.

"Did he treat you right?"

Billy wasn't about to tell the chief how much he had been paid, so he answered noncommittally, "Yeah, just fine."

"Did they catch anything down in the Keys?"

"Said they did, but I don't give a shit one way or the other. All I wanted was to be paid and get my boats back safe and sound."

There was silence in the room as Billy studied Brad's face. The chief knew an awful lot about his dealings with Barry Spence, and it bothered him. Finally he rested his elbows on the desk, looked squarely at Brad, and asked, "Why did you send this guy to me? Why didn't you send him to one of the other guys? Like your buddy on the other side of the bridge?"

"You hurtin' my feelin's, Bubba. It was your daddy who gave me this job, remember? I'm just watchin' out for the ones who were watchin' out for me. I know times have been hard for everybody around here, but shit, man, you're almost like family to me."

Billy had known Brad long enough not to be fooled by this line, but he bottled his scorn as he tried to assess the situation. His eyes kept drifting to the old safe sitting next to the closet door. His grandfather had purchased it years before, back when things were booming. He had locked the forty grand from Barry Spence inside, and now he wondered if Brad knew how much Spence had given him. After a few seconds he cupped his hands behind his head and leaned back in the worn-out leather swivel chair that had been his father's.

"Brad," said Billy with as much sincerity as he could muster, "I had no idea you were behind this Spence guy. You could have sent him to anybody, but you sent him over here and I really appreciate it. I think you deserve a finder's fee or something, know what I mean?"

The chief put his hands up in a "you don't own me a thing" gesture, but Billy knew he wanted a piece of the action and was there to collect.

"Naw, none of that, chief," said Billy as he leaned forward and rested his arms on the desk again. "You deserve something for your trouble."

Billy figured that Brad had a good idea how much he had taken in, but he wasn't about to open the safe and let him know for sure, so he decided to stall a little.

"I want you to give me a number you think is fair while I fix us another drink," said Billy as he stood and went onto the packing-room floor for some more ice.

"Shit," said Brad as Billy poured a slug of clear brown over the ice in his glass, "I don't know what's fair. Tell you what, I'll leave that up to you."

"You somethin' else," replied Billy with a smile as he pushed the cork back into his liquor bottle. "Tell you what, where're you gonna be around nine tonight?"

"Right next door," said Brad before he took a long pull from his glass.

The Thunderbolt city hall, police station, and jail were all located in a small, white-columned building next to the Aprillia property. As Billy parked his car next to the chief's cruiser, the knot in his stomach got tighter. It had been there ever since Barry Spence had laid the forty grand on him, and now he found himself wishing he had never gotten involved with Spence. "If I get in trouble for this," he said to himself, "it'll kill my parents."

After Billy closed his car door, his hand reflexively went to his right back pocket to check on the nickel-plated .357 Magnum he had been carrying for the last two weeks. When he walked by the chief's car, he leaned in the open window on the driver's side and stuffed a brown paper bag loaded with four thousand dollars under the seat. This was not the life he had dreamed about back when he and Judah were working the nets on the *St. Patrick*.

With the exception of an incurious radio dispatcher who was looking at a tattered issue of *Playboy* from 1973, the only other person in the station was Chief Grady. It hurt when Billy walked down the hall on his way to Brad's office and passed the portrait of his father hanging with the rest of Thunderbolt's past mayors. Brad's feet and gunbelt were both resting on the top of his desk when Billy stuck his head in the open door.

"What's up, Bubba?" said Brad with a mischievous smile.

"Oh, nothin'," replied Billy as he leaned on the doorjamb. "I just came by to say hello."

"Well, hello, then." Brad was in a jolly mood. "Let's go out and get some fresh air."

Billy and Brad rested against the trunk of Billy's car as they pretended to watch the traffic pass along River Drive.

"It's under the driver's seat in your cruiser," said Billy in a low tone.

"Thanks, Bubba, I appreciate it," answered Brad as he watched some people exit a seafood restaurant a block down the street. "If I run into our friend, I'll send you some more business."

Billy's arms were folded over his chest. He was quiet for several seconds before he said, "I don't think I can do this again, Brad."

"Why not? I thought you were hard up."

"I am hard up, Brad, but not that hard up, if you know what I mean."

"Hey, no problem, Bubba, I get your drift." Brad planted his hands on the car trunk and eased himself forward. "There're plenty of other folks who'd be glad to have the business, but like I said,

I thought of you first." He walked casually over to his car. Just before opening the door he gave Billy a wink. "I think I need to check on some of those characters down the street. They might've had too much to drink."

Brad backed his cruiser into the street and stopped next to Billy. "Be careful with that snake in your back pocket," he said sarcastically. "It might accidentally bite you on the ass."

Over the next few weeks Billy kept telling himself that not a word had been said about drugs with Barry Spence or Chief Grady, so he could reasonably assert he knew nothing about drug-smuggling. He kept repeating this over and over until he finally believed it.

Billy never saw Barry Spence again and Brad acted as if Spence had never existed. Nevertheless Billy couldn't help wondering who had been tapped for the Key West shrimp runs. In January of 1977 he got his answer in the form of a new red Corvette parked in front of Randy Sikes's dock.

From the beginning most of Thunderbolt's shrimping fleet had been Italian. Family names like Aliotta, Cafiero, Cannarella, Cesaroni, Ricupero, and Maggioni shared the ocean's bounty along with the Aprillias. There were some exceptions, and Randy Sikes was one of them. He was the mainspring in a group of Thunderbolt shrimpers known as the "Cracker Fleet."

Before Atlanta had the Braves, the city hosted a Triple A ball club known as the Crackers. All people from Georgia were tagged with the same nickname. In Savannah the term was honed to a finer point; a Cracker was white Protestant with blue-collar origins. Among shrimpers Crackers thrived in abundance along the Georgia coast south of Savannah, but in Thunderbolt they were somewhat of an anomaly.

Billy didn't have any problems with the Crackers, but he believed that living large during hard times attracted a dangerous brand of attention. His judgment would prove correct when Randy was arrested and his boat, loaded with fourteen million dollars' worth of marijuana, was seized at a dock in Richmond Hill. Word on the street was that Randy's high living had brought the law down on him.

River Storms

What deep wounds ever clos'd without a scar?
—Lord Byron

CHARLIE APRILLIA went down hard. He struggled against death as mightily as he had fought the ocean for its shrimp, but in the end no amount of willpower or dutiful perseverance could wrench the cancer from his body, which began in his lungs and then spread to his liver. Billy watched in frustration as his father, once the strongest man he had ever known, wilted. Finally he was swept away like a dry leaf in a November storm.

After the funeral several of Charlie's old political allies approached Billy and asked if he was interested in running for his father's old job as Thunderbolt's mayor. Business had been off for years, and Billy thought that being mayor couldn't hurt his situation, so he accepted and was easily elected. It turned out to be a beneficial business move that gave him a great deal of influence over property-zoning matters at a time when real-estate prices were increasing and available land, especially waterfront property, was becoming scarce.

Over the next few years, he traded favors with members of the city council for favorable changes in zoning codes; and with an eye on the future he was able to have the zoning ordinance on the land he owned on River Drive changed to allow him to build multistory residential units. That change made the land on which his seafood business sat significantly more valuable. Although Billy still had every intention of staying in the seafood business, he knew that one day he would want to stop. By that time sale of the property would be more than enough to retire on comfortably.

Even though he had never seen the mysterious Mr. Spence again, Billy continued to regard Chief Grady with a degree of fear and suspicion. Rumors about local shrimpers continuing to smuggle drugs into the coast persisted; and every month or so another article about a big drug-bust would appear in the Savannah paper. Billy couldn't sleep for a week after two federal narcotics agents came to his dock asking questions about a guy who sounded a lot like Mr. Spence. He went right to Chief Grady after they left.

"Shit, Brad," said Billy as he leaned on the chief's desk, "those two asked me if I'd ever been approached by somebody wanting to rent my boats."

"Well, what did you tell 'em?" Chief Grady rose from his chair, straightened his gunbelt, and peered out his office window as if he expected to see the Feds nosing around his town.

In a low voice Billy replied, "I had to tell 'em the truth, 'cause I sure had the feeling they already knew the answer."

Suddenly the chief's face grew darker. "What'd they say after that, Bubba?"

"Not much. Just shook their heads, gave me this card, and told me to call them if I ever saw Mr. Spence again. They scared the shit outta me, Brad." Billy thrust his hands into his pockets and stared at the floor.

"Lemme see that card." The gruffness of Brad's voice startled Billy.

After Brad read the name on the agent's card, he snorted. "This guy John E. Peters, I know him. He's a lightweight. He couldn't find his own ass with both hands in broad daylight. Quit worrying." Over time Chief Grady's advice proved to be correct, but one crisis replaced another as Billy's marriage began to fall apart.

When Billy married his Carol in 1975, it was the first time he had been in a Catholic church in twelve years. They had dated in high school and had fallen in and out of love with each other a couple of times before; but finally they decided they were made for each other and took the long walk down the center aisle of the Cathedral of St. John the Baptist—Carol's church—where they pledged their love forever. Forever lasted until December of 1979.

After that, Carol got the house on the Isle of Armstrong just across the Wilmington River from Thunderbolt, and Billy got a court judgment for child support and alimony for the next ten years.

After their daughter was born, a year after they were married, Billy thought she had lost interest in him sexually. She decided that he wasn't willing to spend enough time at home with her. Both of them were partially correct.

Following the birth of Claire, Carol never lost the weight she had put on during her pregnancy. She decided that she had become unattractive and was ashamed for her husband to see her unclothed. Billy had always been a sociable type who enjoyed making the rounds at the various establishments that sold alcohol in Thunderbolt. Sometimes he would come home tight, but most of the time he had only a couple of drinks spaced between a lot of schmoozing and backslapping. He considered it part of his job as mayor, and indeed it was: A lot more got decided in the lounge at Bill Hilliard's Restaurant before the town council meetings than during them. Carol didn't see it that way, and she had no inhibitions about making her feelings known—loudly and frequently.

As the situation began to deteriorate, Billy's eye began to roam. It wasn't long before he started appreciating the finer attributes of other women. He never had an actual affair, but the high he got from flirting with a pretty girl convinced him he needed out. His little girl Claire was all that kept him coming home, but Carol ended that when she had him served with papers as he stepped off the *St. Patrick* after five days of shrimping.

Billy was surprised at how depressed he became after the divorce. He always thought his life would follow the example set by his parents: He would grow old with Carol as they stood side-by-side, enduring the good and bad that comes with life. When that didn't happen he was riddled with guilt. Billy sought solace by throwing himself into his business. It helped; but there would be more storms to weather.

The seeds of what would become known as the Mariel Boat Lift were planted in Havana, Cuba, on March 28th, 1980. On that day six Cuban dissidents engaged Castro's police in a running gun battle through the streets of the city that ended when these desperate men crashed the bus they were driving through the gates of the Peruvian embassy and sought political asylum. The police surrounded the embassy, and a standoff ensued that lasted until April 4th. Then the police suddenly withdrew, and the government of Cuba announced that all those seeking asylum in the embassy would be allowed to leave. That was a Friday. By the next Monday more than ten thousand Cubans had overrun the embassy, frantically seeking asylum and a way out of the country. After that things started moving fast: Castro announced on April 20th that he would let anyone go who wanted to leave, and designated the port of Mariel as the exit point. He also took this opportunity to empty his prisons of common criminals and the insane asylums of their patients and to dump them on the shores of the United States.

News of Castro's actions spread quickly through the Cuban communities in South Florida. The next day what came to be known as the Freedom Flotilla began. Cubans in Florida with their own boats left for Mariel. Those without boats contacted shrimpers in Key West and other ports, offering them as much as $1,000 a head to sail to Cuba and rescue their loved ones. Word spread quickly up the coast of Florida and into Georgia.

Shrimping had been poor that year; and to make matters worse, the prices for what the shrimpers were able to catch had been low, the cost of diesel fuel high. Many shrimpers at Thunderbolt were teetering on the edge of bankruptcy, so when they heard how much could be made off a boatload of refugees, almost thirty boats set sail for Key West in early May with dreams of pulling a bad season out of the fire. Billy's three boats were part of that flotilla. Billy himself was at the wheel of the *St. Patrick.*

At first President Jimmy Carter supported the boat lift, but when it became evident how many people would be overrunning South Florida, and how many of these were actually criminals and the insane, he began to get cold feet. Quietly he started looking for a way out of the mess that Castro had maneuvered him into. Other things had happened, too—things the Thunderbolt shrimpers wouldn't find out about until they arrived in Mariel Bay.

It was true that, at first, the Cubans in Florida were offering

$1,000 a head for relatives; and fifty people could comfortably fit on a shrimp boat for an easy ninety-mile trip to Key West, which would yield hard-up shrimpers a $50,000 payday. Unfortunately the prices rapidly dropped to $10,000 a boatload, and they continued to drop as the Cubans started running out of relatives and money. By the time the Thunderbolt crowd arrived, competition was stiff and customers were few. What happened after that was a nightmare for Billy and his boats.

At Key West he was lucky enough to cut a deal with several Cuban families to bring out as many of their relatives as could fit on his boats for a flat fee of $6,000 per boat, half up front and half upon delivery of the refugees. He also figured that once he got to Cuba he would pick up some more money from some of the refugees who didn't have anybody in the U.S. but did have a few bucks of their own. Then, on May 12th, the *St. Patrick*, *St. Anthony*, and *St. Joseph* set a course for the city of Mariel, just across the Straits of Florida, and only fifty miles west of Havana—but as the *St. Patrick* sailed past the breakwater of the Mariel Harbor, what Billy saw stunned him. The entire harbor was filled with hundreds of fishing and pleasure craft of all descriptions. There was hardly a place to drop anchor, and armed Cuban gunboats prowled menacingly about. One of the gunboats peeled off from its patrol and approached the *St. Patrick*. In broken English the captain of the boat ordered Billy to follow him to an anchorage, where the Cubans took all the necessary information. Then he ordered Billy and his boats to wait until they heard from the government. Billy gave the Cuban captain a paper with a list of names on it, saying, "These are the people I'm here to pick up. Would you please see that this gets into the right hands so I can load up and get out of your way?"

The Cuban gave a "Yeah, right" kind of look, cracked a sarcastic smile, and said, "Sí, Captain, right away." Then he flipped off a sloppy salute, climbed over the side of the *St. Patrick*, and left. Two hours later the gunboat returned with twenty weary-looking souls standing on the deck holding all their worldly possessions, some with only the clothes on their backs. Billy wouldn't let any of the people aboard until he had correctly identified them. He quickly discovered that only one person was on his list. Much to the disgust of the Cuban captain, that person was the only passenger Billy took on his boat.

The passenger was a lean man in his thirties named Augusto Camacho, who spoke perfect English. He told Billy he had learned to speak the language by working as a busboy in one of the gambling casinos owned by the American Mafia before the revolution in 1959. He said his father ran the gambling tables at the casino owned by Meyer Lanksy and that, from time to time, he would be sent to the States on errands for Mr. Lansky. He said his father would occasionally take him with him on those trips.

"When I saw *Thunderbolt* painted on the stern of your boat, captain, I thought that sounded familiar. Once my father went to the city of Savannah to visit some men at a hotel called the General Oglethorpe. I remember passing through a town called Thunderbolt on the way to the hotel. I am correct, captain?"

"You sure are," said Billy with a smile. "When was that?"

"I believe it was 1957. I had just turned thirteen, and getting to go on the trip was a birthday present. I remember swimming in a pool in front of the hotel and jumping off the high diving board. I could have anything I wanted to eat. When I look back on that trip, I think it was probably the happiest time of my life. After the revolution, everything changed. My father was arrested by Castro and placed on trial, as hundreds of others had been. It was shown live on TV. He was accused of treason because Castro said he had cooperated with the Mafia and they had corrupted the government and abused the people. He was found guilty. Two weeks later Castro hanged my father."

Billy looked at the hundreds of boats jamming Mariel Bay, then turned back to his new passenger and asked, "Why didn't you get out after that?"

"I tried, believe me, but my family was on the police watch list so I couldn't. Finally I have this chance, and I have taken it."

Augusto also said the situation at the docks was in turmoil and that it was only by luck that he had wound up on the *St. Patrick.* He explained that no one sought him out by any list, but that he was herded into a group of strangers and shoved onto the gunboat that brought him. "Captain, Castro intends to fill every one of these boats with as many of the people he calls '*guasamos*' or 'worms' as he can and get them off the island. Only the ones at the very beginning went with the boats that came searching for them in particular. Right now, if the boats refuse to accept anyone, the military won't force them on board—but that won't last long, you just wait and see. Pretty soon, when that boat returns, you will accept whoever they say. It will be at gunpoint, and they will shoot you if you don't obey them. I feel bad for those still left behind, captain, but if I were you, I wouldn't stay much longer in Cuban waters."

Billy looked back at the entrance to Mariel Harbor. Two heavily armed Cuban Navy boats were lurking in the vicinity. He turned back to Augusto. "I think I'll take a chance and stay a little longer. What I've collected so far won't even cover my fuel. I can't afford to go in the hole for this, but I do appreciate your advice, Mr. Camacho."

"Just call me Gusto. All my friends do." Gusto offered his hand to Billy; and as Billy shook it, he said, "Thank you for coming, captain. You and my friends in America have saved my life."

That night Billy met with the captains and crew of his other two boats and gave them the bad news. Then he went to his cabin, poured several stiff vodkas, and tried to sleep. Mariel was a hell of a lot hotter and more humid than Savannah had ever been. The air was heavy and still, and Billy couldn't sleep. Around three in the morning he knocked back two more shots and finally fell asleep, only to be awakened at six by the rising sun and a pounding hangover.

His three boats rested in Mariel Harbor for three more days; then he received more bad news over the radio. President Carter had done a one-eighty on the boat lift that he had at first supported. On May 14th, the White House announced that from then on, any boats returning to the U.S. with refugees aboard would be seized and impounded.

"Son of a bitch!" hissed Billy when he heard what his government was doing. Then he whirled around to face the captains of the *St. Joseph* and *St. Anthony* and growled, "Up anchor, boys, we're getting the fuck out of this place."

St. Patrick was in the lead as the three boats picked their way through the crowded anchorage and moved toward the harbor's exit. About a quarter of a mile from the exit, Billy watched as two Cuban boats positioned themselves to block his passage. Then his radio came alive with a Cuban-accented voice. "This is the Cuban Navy. The three vessels attempting to leave Mariel Harbor are ordered to turn about and return to your anchorage immediately. No one is allowed to leave this harbor until further notice by order of the President, Fidel Castro."

Gusto was standing by Billy's side when the order crackled over the radio. When he saw that Billy wasn't stopping, he put his hand on Billy's shoulder and cautioned him. "You better do as they say, my friend. If you don't they will sink us, I promise you that."

Billy's head dropped. Then he looked over at Gusto, let out a long and throaty "Shee-it," grabbed the microphone, and said, "Okay, boys, we gotta turn back."

The *St. Patrick* and her sister ships were trapped in Mariel Harbor. Billy had no idea how long they'd be there. After a week all boats were running out of everything but sweat and grime. There were supplies for sale, offered by locals who went from boat to boat plying their goods. The only problem was the high prices. Beer was going for $35 a case, a fifth of rum for $40, and water was selling for a dollar a gallon. Every boat in the harbor was being picked clean by Castro. Then, two weeks into their ordeal, things began to happen.

On the morning of May 28th, the same battered gunboat that first guided Billy to his anchorage pulled alongside the *St. Patrick*. The fifty-caliber machine gun mounted on the bow was manned by a scraggly looking youth of no more than twenty who trained the weapon on.the *St. Patrick* with an obvious desire to use it. On the deck stood three sailors brandishing AK-47s. The captain of the vessel got on his loudspeaker and ordered Billy and his other boats to raise their anchors and follow him.

The gunboat led Billy to a warehouse wharf where armed Cuban soldiers waited on the dock and ordered him to tie off. Moments later the large doors to the warehouse opened and a mass of refugees was marched to Billy's boats at gunpoint. The soldiers kept packing people onto the three shrimp boats until there was standing room only. Billy guessed he had at least eighty people on his deck, in the hold, and even sitting on top of the wheelhouse. When the Cubans decided they'd loaded about all the people the boats could manage, they loosed the lines, pointed their guns at Billy and the other captains, and shouted, "*Vamoose, Yankee, vamoose pronto*!"

The trip to Key West was a twelve-hour ordeal punctuated by the wail of crying babies; the sound of the pitifully seasick as they hung themselves over the gunnels and retched their guts out; and the nauseating smell of feces that flowed out of the ship's overtaxed head and onto the decks. There was one other thing of a sinister nature that gave Billy great cause for concern.

During the loading at the dock, Gusto stood by Billy's side and looked carefully as each person was placed on the boat. Later, after they had left Mariel Bay, he walked among the passengers, spoke with many of them, and then went to the wheelhouse.

"Captain," said Gusto in a low voice, "it appears we have a few very bad types on this boat."

"What'cha mean, Gusto?" asked Billy.

"I heard rumors that Castro was emptying the prisons and sending them to Mariel to be shipped to the U.S. It looks like we've at least three of them mixed in with the rest."

"How do you know that?"

"I know my own people, Captain Billy, but in addition, I spoke with the ones who are legitimate, and they feel the same way."

"You got'em spotted, Gusto? I mean, you know who they are?"

"Yes."

"Well, what do we do?"

"If there's no problem from them, I suggest we wait until we reach Key West, then we inform the authorities. These people are scum, deserving of nothing from your country."

"What if they make trouble?"

"Captain Billy, do you have a gun on board?"

The blood drained from Billy's face as he looked over at Gusto. He hesitated before replying, then said, "Yeah, I got one," but didn't say where. Gusto had been a great help and Billy liked him, but he wasn't going to tell where he stored his weapons. He wasn't going to turn over ultimate power to a man he had only known for a few days. Not yet, at least.

Gusto's face was very dark as he asked, "Have you ever killed a man, Captain Billy?"

Billy kept his eyes on the horizon. After a second he shook his head, let out a sigh, and said, "No."

"Then don't worry, my captain, I have, and if anything happens, I can take care of it. Hopefully not with a gun, but I ask you now, if I tell you I need your gun, please believe me and don't hesitate."

"Shit," said Billy, his hands tightly gripping the ship's wheel, "I sure as hell didn't bargain for this when we left Thunderbolt. Yeah, I'll get it for you, but look me in the eye, Gusto."

Gusto's eyes locked with Billy's for several seconds before Billy finally said, "Remember what you said back at Mariel about how my friends and I had saved your life?"

"I do, and I meant it."

"I hope you do, Gusto, 'cause I'm trusting you. Now, how 'bout gettin' out on deck and keepin' an eye on things?"

As Gusto stepped through the cabin door, he turned and looked at Billy. His eyes were soft and moist as he said, "I will never betray your trust, captain."

The Cubans on board the *St. Patrick* were mostly women, children, and old men. Almost the only young men were the three Gusto had pegged as convicts. When he looked around the boat the first time, one of the bad guys was near the bow, one was sitting at the stern, and the third was huddled in the hold, where the old women and the young ones with infants had sought refuge from the blistering sun. On his second reconnoiter Gusto discovered that all three men had taken up residence together in the hold.

When he peered into the darkness below, Gusto noticed that his suspects were sitting around a girl of about sixteen. She was boxed in. They were talking wildly and making what appeared to be lewd gestures; the girl had a horrified look on her face. The other women shrank away in fear, and the one old man present helplessly dropped his head, refusing to see. In a few moments one of the men produced a knife he had made in jail and held it to the girl's throat while the other two started to fondle her breasts. Gusto shouted at the men to move away from the girl, and in the Spanish equivalent of "fuck you" the men invited him to climb down into the hold and stop them if he were man enough. Gusto was certain he was man enough, but when he started down the ladder, two other blades appeared. Gusto quickly retreated.

"Three pieces of *merda* with knives have a girl pinned down in the hold," said Gusto as he entered the wheelhouse. "I think they intend to rape her. I can't take on three men with knives. Where is your gun, Captain Billy?"

Billy looked at Gusto for a second, then opened one of the drawers under the instrument cluster, removed a stainless steel Colt .45 automatic, and handed it over.

"You know how to use this thing?" he asked.

"Oh, yes, quite well." Gusto took the weapon and pulled back the slide to see if a round was in the chamber. When he saw the chamber was empty, he racked the slide all the way back, then released it and watched as the bolt shot forward, peeling off a big-nosed copper-jacketed round from the top of the pistol's magazine and shoving it into the firing chamber.

Gusto hadn't been out of the wheelhouse three seconds before Billy turned to Tran, one of the strikers who'd come with him from Thunderbolt, and said, "This is some bad bullshit! Here, take the wheel, I'm gonna help him." Then Billy went to his cabin, got the same .357 magnum he had carried after the Barry Spence episode, and headed for the hold.

Just as he stepped out of his cabin door, Billy saw the three convicts emerge from the hold with their hands over their heads. Gusto was bringing up the rear. When the people on deck saw what was happening, some cried out in fear, and all of them quickly got away as fast as they could. Billy was frozen in his tracks as he watched Gusto, pistol trained on the men, take his last step up the ladder and plant a foot on the deck. What happened next was a rush of movement and flashes of light that came so fast that he didn't have time to react.

Gusto took his eyes away from his charges for only a moment to check his footing, but that was all these streetwise prison toughs needed. Instantly they made their move. When Gusto looked back up, they were coming at him. The pistol was still trained on the three, but he had only enough time to point and pull the trigger quickly. He hit the one on his left squarely in the gut, which caused the man to bend, crumple, and fall. In a fluid motion he then panned the pistol to the center and hit the second fellow in the chest. He slammed backwards, then collapsed into a sitting position against the gunnels. Gusto wasn't so lucky with number three, who was already on him with his arms wrapped around his middle as the two fell backward and down into the hold. When that happened Billy ran toward the action, but before he could even get to the hold he heard a shot, then another. Arriving at the open hatch, he held the .357 at the ready and snatched a quick look into the hold, all the time believing he would have to use his weapon. Bad guy number three was big and burly, and when Billy looked into the hold he was atop Gusto. Both were struggling furiously.

Then there was another, muffled gunshot. All movement ceased. Billy had his pistol pointed at the convict's back. He was ready to shoot, but he feared that the round would carry through the man and hit Gusto. All the women and the one old man were in a hard knot, pressed against the boat's hull, shivering with fear.

"Gusto," shouted Billy. No response. "Gusto, goddamn it, answer me, man!" Still nothing.

Without taking his pistol off the convict's back, Billy carefully climbed down the ladder and into the hold. When he got to the bottom, he screamed his friend's name as hard as he could and inched his way toward the two men. When he was about a foot away, he saw the man on top of Gusto begin to move. Billy almost fired, but he stopped short as he watched the body roll away and turn face-up. Gusto was covered in blood—but it wasn't his.

"I got him in the leg with my first shot, I think," said Gusto as he struggled to stand. "That was while we were falling. When we hit bottom he was on top. I had the breath knocked out of me, but I was able to press the pistol to his side and shoot again. I think that was a good hit, but he was still fighting, so I shot him again. And that was it."

Billy helped Gusto to his feet, then looked him over head to toe. "I just can't believe this is happening." He was about to say something more when cries from above got his attention.

"What's goin' on, Gusto, what're they saying?"

One of the women on deck shouted into the hold. Gusto listened, then shook his head in acknowledgment.

"They're saying one of the men is still alive and they're scared of him."

When Billy got to the top of the hatch and poked his head up, he saw Gusto's first target clutching his stomach and rolling around the deck in pain. The other man was long gone. Gusto's bullet had passed though his heart and out his back.

"This guy is hurt bad," said Billy as he and Gusto squatted next to him. "We need to call the Coast Guard and get a chopper out here and take him to a hospital or he hasn't got a chance."

Gusto looked at Billy and calmly said, "I'll take care of him, Captain Billy. Go to the wheelhouse, guide your boat, but don't call your Coast Guard. Do you understand?"

Billy's mouth dropped. He didn't know what to say. Then he stood and almost robotically started walking toward the bow.

"Captain," called Gusto, "you forgot your pistol."

In a daze Billy looked down at the gun in his hand. He didn't understand. Then Gusto said, "Not that one, this one," as he held out the .45 he had used to shoot the three Cubans. Billy said nothing as he returned, to take the pistol. He looked Gusto in the eyes for a long time, then did an about-face and left.

"You and you," said Gusto in Spanish, "go below and get the one down there." Then he pointed to two more people and gestured to the dead man. "You and you, throw this one over the side." The wounded convict was moaning loudly now, and blood was spreading over the deck. Gusto stood over him and pointed to one more person and said, "I need your help with this one."

"What are we going to do with him?" asked the man of about sixty.

"He's going over the side, too."

"But he's still alive."

"Not for long."

"Our Holy Savior," cried the man, "I cannot do this. It is murder!"

"Suit yourself," answered Gusto as he pulled the wounded man into a sitting position, tossed him over his back, and staggered to the rail, where he unceremoniously dumped the convict over the side. Gusto then turned to face his fellow passengers.

"All of you come in close and listen to me."

The women in the hold climbed up to the deck. Those on the bow and stern gathered with the others.

"Speak nothing of what you have seen here today," said Gusto. "Forget what you have seen, if you can, but never speak of it. It can only bring harm to you. I did what I did to protect you. Now go."

"I've spoken with your passengers," said Gusto as he stepped into the wheelhouse, "and they won't whisper a word about what has happened. Not that you or I are at fault, but we just don't want unnecessary and time-consuming inquiries." Billy didn't answer; he just stared over the bow and nodded his head. A long silence settled over the *St. Patrick*'s wheelhouse as Billy piloted his boat to the north-northeast. The quiet was finally broken when he announced, "We're about three hours from Key West now." After that the silence descended again, only to be broken once more by the roar of a low-flying Coast Guard plane as it buzzed the *St. Patrick* several times before heading in the direction of Mariel Bay and the long stream of boats leaving the harbor. About twenty miles from Key West, Billy and his three boats were stopped by a Coast Guard cutter. Armed sailors boarded each boat. They gave instructions not to go to Key West, but rather the port of Miami.

At the dock in Miami, as the boat was being unloaded under the watchful eyes of a dozen immigration officials and armed Marines, Billy saw Gusto approach two of the officials and engage them in conversation. In a few moments he returned to the boat and thanked Billy for taking him to freedom. "If I ever get to Thunderbolt again, I'll look you up and take you to dinner. I'm going to be a success in America." Then he shook Billy's hand, thanked him once more, and returned to the two waiting officials. Billy watched with curiosity as they escorted him not to the holding area, where the other refugees were, but to a U.S. government car.

The agents used the car's radio. A few minutes later Gusto and the agents got into the car and drove off.

Billy hadn't even begun to digest what he had just witnessed when a Coast Guard lieutenant and a U.S. marshal boarded the *St. Patrick*. "Are you the ship's captain?" asked the lieutenant.

"Yes, sir," replied Billy, "what's wrong?"

"We need to see your papers, captain."

Billy reached into the same drawer where he had kept the .45, produced all the necessary documentation, and handed it over to the lieutenant. For several minutes the man studied the papers, then sternly handed them back. "Captain Aprillia, your boat is now seized and will be impounded until further notice. The charges against you are twofold. First, you are operating well out of the geographic area granted by your license. Second, you are licensed to carry no more than six passengers. My men counted eighty-one people on this vessel when she tied up."

Without a word the marshal took a warrant from his vest pocket and placed it in Billy's hand. "Captain Aprillia, you have now been served. You are remanded to your own custody, but you are ordered not to leave the country."

When Billy heard those words, he went into overload and let loose with a stream of invective and obscenity of such volume and quantity that it even got the attention of the Marines on the dock. The lieutenant and the marshal stood patiently throughout and let him vent his rage. They'd been through this same scenario a dozen times over the past few days; and when Billy was finally spent, both men told him they understood and sympathized with his plight, but the law was the law and they were only doing their jobs. Their parting shot, however, was the most devastating. Billy was informed that he was facing a fine of $1,000 for each illegal immigrant he had on his boat, and would also be charged for dockage.

Billy stood silently as he watched the men leave his boat, then went to find a pay phone to call his lawyer in Savannah. He figured he had lost about $20,000, and since he couldn't work his boats he had no way of making any of it back. The meter would be running at the dock.

What happened next was the most intense and emotionally charged politicking Billy had ever been involved with. Countless times over the next three weeks he would be thankful for the contacts he had made in Washington while serving as mayor of Thunderbolt. It would all pay off on June 28th, when he got word from his lawyer that he and all the rest of the Thunderbolt shrimpers could bring their boats home. By the middle of July, the government had decided to drop all charges and fines against them and bring an end to their ordeal.

A short time later a story ran in the *Savannah Morning News*, in which Billy stated that "It's like a thousand-pound weight has been taken off my shoulders. I feel a hell of a lot better looking out my front door (near the Thunderbolt docks) and seeing those boats."

At its conclusion what came to be known by some as the Freedom Flotilla and by others as the Mariel Boat Lift would be responsible for placing 125,262 Cubans and 10,211 Haitians on United States soil. Five months after the charges were dropped against Billy and the others, President Jimmy Carter would lose his job to Ronald Regan in a landslide.

A warm, late-September breeze swept through the *St. Patrick*'s wheelhouse as Billy steered her on a southerly course, paralleling Ossabaw Island. It was almost seven o'clock and the sun was hanging low in the sky behind a mass of deep purple clouds miles away on the horizon. Rays of orange and gold pierced through holes in the clouds and fanned out on a sky of robin's-egg blue. His catch had been good the last few weeks and his nets were straining under the weight of another bountiful haul. Billy's face was tanned and warmed by the sun, and days like this made him glad to be a shrimper. On a gently rolling sea, he throttled back to idle speed and told Tran, his striker, to bring the nets in: They were heading for home. Then he dug his hand deep under the ice in the cooler he kept in the wheelhouse. He ignored the Diet Cokes and orange juice and continued digging until he found what he had been looking for: a bottle of Moosehead beer. Billy didn't drink beer on the way out or during the workday, but he always brought a few for the trip back, the time when he could afford to relax and enjoy the ride. With a smile he cracked the bottle open, took a long pull, put it back into the ice, and went to the stern to help Tran haul in the nets.

Tran had first seen Savannah in the summer of 1966, when he was being trained at Hunter Army Air Force Base to be a Huey helicopter pilot in the Vietnamese Army. He was nineteen then, and some of the area reminded him of his home near Saigon, particularly the marshes and rivers. When South Vietnam finally collapsed in 1975, Tran had been a pilot of some distinction, ultimately reaching the rank of major. He was one of the lucky few who were able to commandeer a helicopter, collect his family, and head for one of the U.S. aircraft carriers lingering off the coast. In a feat of daring and skill, he crash-landed the craft on a carrier deck and secured asylum for himself and his family. He was ultimately offered the chance to live in America; without hesitation Tran requested Savannah for his home. By what he considered unbelievable luck, he was granted his request and settled in a small rental house on the outskirts of Thunderbolt. The government had already arranged a job for him with Aprillia Seafood, and in 1978 he started as a striker on the *St. Patrick*. It seemed to Billy that Tran worked harder than anyone else, including himself; and he had grown to respect and admire him.

It took about an hour to pull in the nets, sort the catch, then ice it down in the hold. When Tran had thrown the last shovelful of ice over the twitching shrimp, Billy grinned. “Know what time it is, Tran?” Tran smiled broadly, exposing teeth badly in need of dental care, and replied in an accent no longer as thick as it used to be, “Yeah, boss. Time for cold beer, right?”

“Right.” Billy pulled the beer he had been working on from the cooler, fished around until he had found one for Tran, then set course for Thunderbolt.

It was after nine when the *St. Patrick* passed into Wassaw Sound and started her journey up the Wilmington River. The tide was high, and in front of the boat the river reflected an orange glow from the lights in the sky over Savannah. Behind it the Atlantic sky was inky, spotted with the first stars of the night, and punctuated by a rising crescent moon. "It's beautiful, isn't, Tran?" Billy eased the ship's wheel a little to starboard as he passed the bend at Priest Landing.

"Beautiful, boss," replied Tran.

Things had been going so well since the Mariel fiasco that Billy was beginning to think he just might make it after all. He even had a new girlfriend he had been seeing for the past two weeks; it seemed as if that might be going somewhere, too. Billy had a natural smile on his face for the first time in a long while. He was lost in his pleasant reflections when he was interrupted by Tran.

"Boss, you mind I ask you question?" The look on Tran's face bordered on sadness.

"No, go ahead, feel free."

Tran hesitated for a moment, then continued. "Boss, why you no go Mass anymore? I see your parents at Mass every Sunday, but never you. Why that, Boss?"

Billy was surprised but not angered. He leaned back in the captain's chair, cocked his head to the side for a moment, then replied, "I'm not really sure, Tran. I used to go to Mass every day. I was an altar boy and even wanted to be a priest, but something just clicked inside me and it all began to turn me off. I don't know what I believe. I guess I kind of think that if God doesn't bother me, I won't bother Him."

Tran's expression remained grave."Not good. You need go Mass, boss. It help you like it help me. I know, I almost die in Vietnam, but pray and go to Mass. I never stop going and now, look, here I am in paradise!" As Tran spoke those last words, his face was transformed by a serene smile.

"Maybe one day, Tran. Maybe I'll go back one day."

The river god continued to favor Billy until February of 1981, when his dealings with Barry Spence came back to haunt him. It all started with a knock on his office door by DEA agent Johnny Peters, the man Chief Grady said couldn't fine his own backside with both hands. Agent Peters informed Billy that he had busted the chief, along with six other Thunderbolt men, at a deserted farmhouse up in Effingham County, over a truck containing eleven tons of marijuana. He further informed him that the chief had implicated him in a drug deal several years prior in which Billy had leased one of his boats for the known purpose of smuggling marijuana into the state. Then he placed Billy under arrest and applied the cuffs. While his employees watched, a stunned Billy was marched to a waiting police cruiser.

The front-page headlines the following morning announced Chief Grady's arrest and the details of the smuggling operation. Billy had made bail by the time the afternoon paper carried the news of his arrest and those of other locals implicated by Brad Grady. Word on the street was that the chief had cut a deal and was making more noise than a 747 as he fingered everybody he could think of in order to save his own skin.

In the end his attorney convinced him to plead guilty to a lesser offense. In a plea bargain Billy wasn't given any jail time, but he did have to serve five years of probation and pay a fine of $10,000. Two days later he was forced to resign his job as Thunderbolt's mayor. To make matters worse he had to sell a portion of his precious River Drive property to pay the fine and cover his lawyer fees. After that his banker buddies who held the notes on the *St. Joseph* and the *St. Anthony* weren't as friendly as they used to be.

Billy was able to keep Aprillia Seafood running, but only on the thinnest of margins. Behind his back wild and inaccurate stories circulated about him; and when he would walk into one of the restaurants in Thunderbolt, he could tell by the looks on their faces that people believed what they had heard.

Billy's fall from grace was steep and swift and weighed very heavily. The little boy who had once been the Emperor of Thunderbolt's son and heir to his empire was now a thirty-seven-year-old felon living on the edge.

III

LIVING ON THE BIGHT

Low Tide

> Ye marshes, how candid and simple and nothing-
> withholding and free
> Ye publish yourselves to the sky and offer yourselves to
> the sea!
>
> —Sidney Lanier, *The Marshes of Glynn*

Present Day

ONLY A SLIVER of morning sun was visible over the marsh on the other side of the Wilmington River when Judah rolled out of bed and planted his feet on the floor of Billy's guest room. He hadn't bothered to close the curtains the night before and watched transfixed as the sun seemed to pulsate with a golden light while it edged its way ever higher over the bright green grass of spring. He had seen many a sunrise, but they had mostly been behind the backdrop of Washington's skyline. He had wished for this moment so often .

Making the decision to leave Washington had been hard at first, but as things progressed the move seemed inevitable; and when the moment of truth finally arrived, it came with such ease that Judah was surprised. Now it was decompression time, time to soul search, to think about the rest of *his* life: not the wants and needs of the powerful, but those of Judah Benjamin. There was something deep within him that whispered, "Surely there is more to life than this."

Judah opened the window and breathed deeply, searching the cool morning air for the scent of the river. Over and over he filled his lungs with a saltwater breeze tinted by the smell of the marsh and the shrimp boats moored down river. For him it was the elixir of youth, and his mind was instantly filled with sweet memories. He stood at the window and even allowed himself to remember Hannah. Tears filled his eyes. Then he shook his head and muttered, "I can't let that stuff get me down." Judah looked over at Moshe Dayan, who was still curled at the foot of his bed, lost in deep sleep.

"Moshe," called Judah as he headed for the bathroom, "let's go for a run." In an instant the big dog was awake and standing at the bedroom door with his leash in his mouth. The house was still as Judah and Moshe went down the stairs and slipped out the front door. Billy wouldn't rise for another hour or so; up at first light wasn't his style.

Judah and Billy had pounded back almost a fifth of vodka between them the night before. Now he was suffering from a slight headache, but his never-fail cure would take care of that. Somehow vigorous exercise always seemed to purge him of the poisons he had been pouring into his system—which had become all too frequent of late.

Bonaventure Cemetery had always been one of his favorite places in Savannah, so he decided that a jog through a forest of tombstones and statuary would be a good place to clear his head and mend his body. He was fond of visiting cemeteries and believed that death had a way of bringing the important things of life back into focus. As Judah guided his Jag through the gates of Bonaventure, he could feel the beginnings of an attitude adjustment.

After parking his car near the gate, Judah let Moshe out and stood for several moments as he surveyed this city of the dead. Stands of marble and granite spread themselves out on the high bluffs overlooking the Wilmington River. Here and there he could make out the top of an obelisk piercing through the oak canopy, needling the sky, making him wonder about those below.

The Christian section of Bonaventure, his favorite, provided a real contrast in cultures with the Jewish side of the cemetery. There were no magnificent statues of angels and saints, no crucifixes of stone, no ostentatious display of family wealth and importance in

Jewish Bonaventure. It was stark there and almost uniform in appearance; visits by loved ones were marked not by a potted plant or a bouquet of flowers, but rather by a single stone left on the grave. Judah understood and embraced the reasoning behind this, but the Christian part of the cemetery attracted him because it was filled with works of art that, for him, were aesthetically pleasing and spiritually evocative.

Moshe anxiously circled around while waiting for his master to begin. Judah looked down the long, oak-lined drive that led to the river, took a deep breath, and started his run. The azaleas were at their peak; heaps of lavender and red lined either side of the road. With Moshe close by his side, Judah had broken a sweat by the time he had reached the bluff. He turned right and ran with the river as he looked for the Lawton family plot, where he knew a marble Jesus beckoned beside the door to eternity. Then he began to think.

"What Billy wants," he thought, "is going to be a hard sell." Judah wasn't quite sure where to start, but he would figure it out. He would try for his old friend, but he was damned uncomfortable with the thought. "I came home to get away from the Washington crowd, and now Billy wants me to jump right back in." He didn't think Billy realized how tricky the situation really was now. Nine-eleven had changed everything. Approaching the Department of Defense and telling them that a buddy of yours knows where he can find one of their H-bombs was tricky enough; demanding money for this knowledge could be an invitation to some very serious consequences. "Shit," thought Judah, "we're talking about involvement not just with Defense, but with Homeland Security, the Department of Energy, the F.B.I., probably some C.I.A. types too, and that's not counting what the White House will think once they hear about this. Naw, I gotta tell him this is out of my league."

Judah was maintaining a steady pace as he passed the grave and imposing bust of Civil War General Robert Anderson. There he ran deeper into the confines of nineteenth-century Bonaventure, where the graves became even more ornate; and it was at the grave of Gracie Watson that Judah's thoughts turned elsewhere. Gracie had died in childhood, and her grieving father had had a life-size statue of her placed there. It was a poignant and haunting sculpture, the most famous in all of Bonaventure—and the sweetness of the dead child's face reminded him of Hannah.

"What was it about her," Judah asked himself as he jogged past Gracie's lot and caught the stone smile on her face, "that's affected me for so many years?"

The best explanation Judah had ever received for his long-term heartache had come, surprisingly enough, from an old girlfriend about ten years before. The night she broke up with him, she gently told him she believed each person had a soulmate, made uniquely by God. She said she had come to realize that she was not this person, and that when he had found her, he would know. Nothing else would seem right after that. Judah had decided that "when" had already come and gone with Hannah Meldrim.

All the windows were down on his car as he maneuvered along the curving Bonaventure Road heading back to Thunderbolt. The woods were filled with blooming pink-and-white dogwoods, and the sweet soft smell of honeysuckle and marsh grass filled the car. It was still early morning, but the day was already making bright promises. Judah's run had been helpful for both body and mind, and he assured himself once more that quitting Washington had been the proper thing to do. It was a wonderful feeling to know that he had no meetings with the campaign staff, no power lunches, no polls to analyze—and nobody he had to force himself to be nice to. He used to have a knot in his stomach from the time he got up until he had his first drink sometime around six in the evening. His gut was easy now.

After he crossed Victory Drive, the rows of condos along the Wilmington River came into view. Judah flinched. They completely obscured any view of the river, destroying what used to be Thunderbolt's most charming asset. Judah understood that money didn't talk: It screamed. "How in the world," he wondered, "could the town do this to itself?"

Billy was fixing breakfast when Judah and Moshe hit the front door. The house was filled with the scent of bacon cooking and the sound of the Beach Boys singing, "I wish they all could be California girls."

"You want grits, don'cha, Bubba?" asked Billy without looking up from the frying pan.

"A pile of 'em," replied Judah as he headed for the shower. "They make a stab at 'em up in Washington, but they're always too watery and they never add salt when they cook 'em." When he got to the bathroom door, he turned and yelled down the hall, "Yankees don't know shit about cookin' grits." Then as an afterthought he added, "God, it's good to be home!"

Over breakfast Billy talked about how he and Hannah had gotten together. Judah forced himself to listen. Billy went on about how nice Hannah was, and said that he thought their relationship was turning into something that might be permanent. From somewhere inside, Judah wanted to ask if he and Hannah had been sleeping together. In some silly way he hoped they weren't, but he knew at this stage in their lives there would be only one answer. Judah chided himself for even thinking about it.

After breakfast they took their coffee to the balcony overlooking the river. It was getting warmer, but springtime temperatures would go no higher than the low 80s and both men noted how good the morning sun made them feel. There was a long pause in the conversation until Billy broke the silence.

"You think you can help me with this bomb thing, Judah?"

Judah shifted in his chair and hesitated for a moment. "I've been thinking about that all morning, Billy. What you've got to understand is that you've stuck your nose into a real stink pile, man. I'm even thinking that you could get into a shitload of trouble just for pulling those stabilizer fins up and not telling the Feds about it. They're off the fuckin' wall right now. They aren't takin' any chances on anything, if you know what I mean."

Billy shrugged and nodded his head. "I understand all that, but what the hell, at least I can try, can't I? I mean, do you know what those motherfuckers put me through with all that Mariel shit?"

Judah looked down at his hands, and then swung his eyes up again at Billy. "I know all about it. I was up in Washington then, working for Will McQueen, remember? Will was the man who pulled your shit outta the fire. Of course I know how bad you got screwed."

"I know you do, Bubba," said Billy plaintively, "but hell's bells, after they broke me, after that dumb-ass Jimmy Carter made like he wanted us to go down to Cuba and get those people out, then sicked the law on us, I figure if I can get something out of the damn government for finding that bomb, then I deserve every dime."

"I do, too, but that's not the point. The point, you hardheaded wop, is that what you're talking about is a hydrogen bomb in a post nine-eleven world. You're not just playing with fire, Billy, you're playing with a fuckin' thermonuclear bomb. Our government looks upon that in a most serious way."

"I understand all that, I really do, but there should be something in it for me, shouldn't there? I mean, they've been looking for that bomb for almost fifty years, and it's got to be worth a lot of money. I heard the plutonium in it's worth a couple or three million just by itself. All I want you to do is just ask around. You know, find out if they're interested."

"Oh, I can guarantee you they're interested, on that you may rest assured. What I don't know is if they'll cough up any cash for the location or if they'll just come and haul your ass off to some place like Gitmo and hold you there till you decide to tell 'em where the bomb is. That's my concern."

"Well, will you at least give it a try?"

Judah let out a sigh. "I'll make some inquiries, but don't push me on it, okay?"

"You got it."

"Also, keep your big fat mouth shut about this. I mean completely shut. Do you read me loud and clear, Bubba?"

"I understand, Judah. I haven't said a word to anybody about this, not even to Hannah."

"Who else knows about that thing in your garage?"

"I had two strikers with me when I pulled it up, Tran and this black guy I just hired about a month ago named Abdul. I never said a word to either one about what I thought it was. When we hauled it in, I told them I was going to take it back in and drop it off at the dump so nobody would snag their nets on it again. We've pulled all sorts of crap in and this was just another piece of junk metal as far as those two know."

"Tran's been with you a long time, hasn't he?"

"Yeah, and he's loyal. Even if he knew exactly what was going on, he'd keep his mouth shut. He's the kind of guy who doesn't forget the people who helped him when he first got here."

"What about this Abdul character?" asked Judah with a hint of concern in his voice.

"He's a relative of Elijah's. He grew up here, didn't have much of a father to lean on, and got in trouble when he was younger. Mostly petty crime stuff, purse-snatching, selling weed, things like that. He did two years at Reidsville, and when he came back he announced that he was a Muslim. He's into the skullcaps and dashikis, all that kind of Black Muslim bullshit. I wouldn't have taken him on if Elijah hadn't asked me to. He shows up on time, works hard, and keeps to himself. I can't ask for more. I don't think he knows his ass from a hole in the ground, so I'm not worried about him."

Judah looked out over the marsh, then turned to Billy. "I can't promise you anything except that I'll look into it. You know I came home to get away from stuff like this, so don't pressure me, okay? With the election coming up, it's a bad time to be approaching anybody about something as sensitive as this. Just keep your big-ass mouth shut."

Billy faked a hurt look, then broke into a smile as he said, "I appreciate anything you can do, Judah. Now, let's talk about tonight 'cause I've got a real sweet little gal I want you to meet."

For the next week Judah was Billy's guest as he waited for his new home to arrive. Judah had always wanted to live on the bluff at Isle of Hope in a house with a dock. But, when he made his decision to move and checked with real estate agents, he soon found that none of the homes along Bluff Drive were available. Not to be deterred in his dream to live there, he arranged for the purchase of a seventy-foot trawler, which he would have moored at the Isle of Hope marina and live on until something along the bluff came up for sale.

The seventy-foot *Aleutian* is the largest boat in the Grand Banks lines. Judah had found one in Maine, and while he waited at Billy's, the boat was making its way down the Intracoastal Waterway to Savannah. It would fulfill his dream of living on the water at Isle of Hope as well as providing him with access to the entire coastline. He named it *Solitude*, and on his trip from Washington to Savannah he had passed the driving time by planning trips to the anchorages where he and Billy had spent so many nights on the *St. Patrick*'s deck watching the stars fill the night sky.

Judah realized that it may be impossible to capture the past, that people and things change, even in Savannah, but he had a yearning for something he knew he could find only at home. He wasn't sure what that something was, but he was determined to try to find out, and in searching, maybe, just maybe, discover someone with whom he could share the rest of his life, that soul mate his old girl friend Carla had talked about.

Looking for Miss Savannah

> If thou hast heard a word, let it die with thee; and be bold, it will not burst thee.
>
> —Ecclesiasticus 19:10

JUDAH HADN'T been on the *Solitude* for ten seconds before his cell phone started ringing. He had just returned from his morning run and was dripping with sweat when he put the phone to his ear.

"Judah," asked Billy excitedly, "have you seen the paper this morning?"

"Not yet. I just got back from my run. After I take a shower, I'm gonna get some coffee, go topside, and read up there. Why?"

"Right on the front page there's a story about my bomb. There's some retired Air Force colonel who claims he knows where the bomb is. They even got a map of Wassaw Sound showing the area where this character says the bomb is located. It's up on the northern end of the sound. He can't be right; I found that stabilizer at the southern end of the sound, that's where the bomb is. This colonel wants the government to come up with a bunch of money so he can find it for them. Have you called your people yet and told them about what I showed you? This son of a bitch is trying to steal my thunder!"

Judah's lips tensed up; he put his free hand to his forehead and nervously rubbed it. He was on the stern deck; and before he replied to Billy he took a seat on one of the deck chairs. His voice was very angry.

"Billy, you listen to me and you listen real good. You don't talk about things like this on the phone, ever. You have no idea of who might be listening, got me?"

There was silence for a moment. Then Billy replied, "Yeah, you're exactly right. I'm sorry, it won't happen again."

"Good. Be sure it doesn't. Let me get cleaned up and read the paper. Why don't you come on over here in about an hour and we can talk then? Maybe even take the boat out for a while."

Judah's voice had lightened, and Billy warmed to the idea. "You got enough beer for a cruise? It's suppose'ta warm up today. Let's take her out to Wassaw Sound, and I can show you how much it's changed since the last time you were there."

"Yeah, that sounds like a winner. I don't have much more than a six-pack, so you better pick up enough for a couple of old Benedictine cadets and a day on the water."

The sky was cloudless when Judah stretched out on the top deck, took a sip of coffee, and opened the morning paper. Just below the fold the headlines read, "GROUP CLAIMS TO KNOW LOCATION OF TYBEE BOMB." The text of the story stated that retired Air Force Lt. Col. Derrick Earl from Statesboro, a well-known figure in the hunt for the missing H-bomb, had formed a consortium to search for the bomb. The story went on to say that Earl claimed to be in possession of extremely sensitive radiation- and metal-detection equipment that had discovered a plume of radiation and the presence of a large metal object at the northern end of Wassaw Sound, a little east of tiny Williamson Island. Just as Billy had said, there was a map of the area with an "X" marking the spot where Colonel Earl claimed the bomb was resting. The article went on to say that Earl had been in contact with Congressman Will McQueen's office and that McQueen has asked the Defense Department to meet with him and discuss his findings. The last sentence read: "Colonel Earl estimates the cost of finding and recovering the bomb to be in the neighborhood of $2,000,000 and that his company is prepared to begin searching for the bomb immediately."

When Judah read that line, he let out a snort and chuckled. "I'll bet he's ready. Two mill ain't a bad payday for a Cracker boy from Bulloch County." Then he snapped the cell phone off his belt, hit the speed-dial key, and waited for the assistant to the chief of staff at the White House to answer.

"Walker? Judah Benjamin here. Is the boss around?"

"Yes, sir."

"Great. Tell him I need to speak with him"

"How are you doing, Judah?"

"I'm doing fine, a lot better, thanks for asking."

"Judah?" said another voice.

"Carl. It's good to hear you again."

"Judah, we thought you'd gone into seclusion or something."

"I just need a rest, that's all. You remember just before I escaped from that town you work in, to pray that The Haunted Tree got the nomination?"

"Yep," Carl replied. "And it looks like our prayers are gonna come true. The next best thing is that he's got a real kook for a wife. Rich, but a goofy-looking kook."

Judah laughed into the phone. "I ran the numbers the other day, and I'm thinking 52-48 our boy, but that's not why I called. Why don't you call me back on a secure line? I've got some interesting things to talk about."

He hung up and went two decks below to his stateroom, which was paneled in mahogany and accented with antique furniture he had bought up North. Even though a king-size bed was the room's focal point, there was still plenty of space left for an old but very fine rolltop desk he had found at an estate sale in Philadelphia. It had come with documentation linking it to the first president of the Pennsylvania Railroad. He seated himself in a leather swivel chair that had, at one time, belonged to the office of General George C. Marshall when he was chief of staff during World War II. The dark burgundy leather was worn in the seat and the headrest, but he didn't care. Just sitting in it made his hair stand on end. He liked to imagine General Marshall's fanny placed exactly where his was now as the general planned Operation Neptune, the code name for the invasion of Normandy. For a few seconds he was sixty years away, but he was called back to reality by a ringing in the top right hand drawer. A small key unlocked the drawer, and Judah answered the phone.

"Okay, Judah, what's the deal? Are you coming back to work after all? You know you've still got a job up here."

"No, Carl, I'm not coming back, please don't start on that shit again, okay? You can tell Mac I'm still here for y'all, but I needed to step away."

"He might be pissed at you, Judah, but he still thinks you're the best there is in your field."

"I know he does, and I appreciate his sentiments, but that's not why I've got you on the dark phone. Listen, have you heard anything about an H-bomb that was lost down here near Tybee Island in the fifties?"

"Yeah, your congressman, Will McQueen, is pushing for Defense to conduct another search down there to find the thing."

"Yeah, it said in the *Savannah Morning News* today that McQueen had gotten involved. Listen, I have information indicating that Colonel Earl doesn't know his ass from a hole in the ground. That the bomb isn't anywhere near where he says it is."

"How do you know that?"

" I just know. Trust me."

"Okay, Judah, what do you want me to do about it?"

"I want you to put me in touch with the right guy on this over at Defense."

"Not a problem."

Judah took the secure phone and placed it on the nightstand next to his bed, where he sprawled out and waited for a call from the Defense Department. About five minutes later the phone was ringing again.

"Judah Benjamin here."

"Judah, this is Gary Webb. I've been told you have some info on the Tybee bomb and want to talk about it."

"Yeah, colonel, I sure do. But what I need right now is some background on the accident and for you to check out this Colonel Earl for me, find out what his MOS was when he was on active duty. I don't want a pile of technical crap on the bomb, I want it boiled down. Seems that Colonel Earl claims the bomb has its plutonium trigger in place. From what I'm reading in the local paper, you guys are saying the trigger was never placed in the bomb, that it was a practice mission and y'all didn't do that back then."

"That's our position, Judah."

"One other thing, Gary. What do you think the chances are that DOD or whatever agency is involved with this thing is going to pay Earl to find the bomb?"

"We're not at that stage. Why do you ask?"

Judah closed his eyes for a moment and rubbed his brow. "Because there's someone else who claims to know where the bomb is, and it appears that this individual has some real solid evidence indicating he's right. What are the chances you boys would pay a reward for this information, providing the information is correct?"

"That depends. I think reward money for information leading to the recovery of a thermonuclear device is quite reasonable, but I'll have to discuss that with folks who have a higher pay grade than I do. They'd be the ones making the decision."

Judah had always wanted to follow in his father's footsteps and become an Air Force pilot. Even though he had a draft deferment as a sole surviving son, he applied to and was accepted by the Air Force's Officer Candidate School after graduation from Armstrong—much to his mother's dismay. Unfortunately poor eyesight dashed his hopes of becoming a pilot. Instead, after his commissioning, he was assigned to military intelligence in Vietnam, where he did bomb-damage assessment. From there he was attached to the unit responsible for the storage and deployment of nuclear weapons in the Southeast Asian theater. Judah did his job quite well and wound up at the Pentagon, where he completed his obligation to the Air Force. He was encouraged by his superiors to make a career of the service, but his stay in Washington infected him with a political virus that led first to a life as a professional pollster and ultimately to working for the Republican Party. The top-secret clearance he acquired while working with nuclear weapons and the scores of friendships he had made while in the Air Force enabled him to move with ease through the military-industrial complex and the political mazes of the capital. When Judah left Washington to return to Savannah, he was president of a large political consulting firm in Washington and a direct adviser to the president's reelection campaign. Over the years he had made millions of dollars and hundreds of friends. These were the connections that gave him access not only to the White House but to the Pentagon as well.

Judah was about to nod off when he heard Billy coming aboard. He got up, slipped on his Georgia Bulldogs T-shirt, and went topside to greet his friend—who had a case of Pabst Blue Ribbon under one arm and a bag of ice under the other. He made his way to the cooler on the fly bridge.

"Man," said Judah, "I'll bet I haven't had a can of Pabst since I was in college. I thought they'd stopped making the stuff."

"Me, too," said Billy, "but it's making a comeback. I spotted it at the BP station in Sandfly and decided to bring some along for old times' sake."

Judah was always happy to have Billy along whenever he took the *Solitude* out. He held a master's license, and handling the *Solitude* was easier than driving a shrimp boat; but Billy was always happy to teach Judah everything he knew about the waters and how to handle so big a boat . . . and Judah was always happy to learn.

When the *Solitude*'s twin 1,140 horsepower diesels had warmed up, Judah handled the dock lines as Billy expertly eased the boat away from her berth at Isle of Hope and headed up the Skidaway River toward the Wilmington. Billy made piloting the big boat look easy, and Judah commented on his skill as they passed the old Roebling plantation on Skidaway Island, which was now Georgia's marine research center. Once they'd left the no-wake zones and were in the middle of the Wilmington, Billy opened the throttles. Even he was impressed at how effortlessly the *Solitude* rose to a plane and was soon doing twenty-five knots as they made the turn at Priest Landing and headed for Wassaw Sound.

"Every time I take the wheel of this boat, I find something else that impresses me." With a grin Billy surveyed the glittering instruments arrayed before him. "The electronics you've got are much better than I have on *St. Patrick*, and she's a working boat that uses them all the time."

"You seem to do pretty well with what you've got."

"I know, but this is the latest stuff. Your sonar and radar are out of this world. You can paint the bottom with this sonar like nothing I've ever seen before, at least commercially." Billy stared as detailed graphics of the river bottom passed by under the *Solitude*'s hull. "Look at that, I'll bet that's an old crab trap, and the detail on the fish-finder is really fine. This GPS plotter is sweet, too."

Off in the distance they watched as the northern end of Wassaw Island came into view. Judah held his hand a foot away from his face and pinched Wassaw's tree line between his thumb and forefinger. The island was less than a sixteenth of an inch high.

"How far are we from the Wassaw's north beach?" asked Judah as he placed a pair of binoculars to his eyes.

"Right at four miles when we passed Priest Landing."

Judah had his glasses trained on a wood stork rookery near the inlet to Joe's Cut and counted over twenty-five of the large white birds perched in the branches of a dead oak, their broad wings folded neatly over their backs. He lowered the binoculars, pulled air in through his nostrils, then exhaled slowly.

"In my entire life," he said, "I've never grown tired of this place. It's always a thrill to come around that curve back there and see the limits of the sound laid out before me and to know that only a few miles away there's nothing but open ocean between the sound and the coast of North Africa."

Judah leaned down and opened the beer cooler, snagging a couple of cold Blue Ribbons. Without saying a word he opened them both, and silently passed one to Billy. Both men remained quiet as they put the bottles to their lips and pulled the beer into their mouths, savoring its taste before swallowing.

"This stuff tastes pretty good," said Judah. "I don't know why I ever stopped drinking it."

"You got your ass up in Yankee land and started drinking all that imported shit," answered Billy before he took another long pull off his bottle.

"You know," Judah said as his eyes followed Wassaw's tree line to the south until it dropped below the curve of the earth, "I think the marsh is something that's viewed in the horizontal plane."

"What the hell are you talking about?"

"Well, I mean when there aren't any clouds in the sky, like today, it's not a vertical world. What we see is just a strip of olive water, then a thread of marsh mud, and then a line of marsh grass itself. Like over on Beach Hammock."

Billy looked in the direction Judah pointed as he continued.

"Look, nothing has any height out here. There aren't any mountains or hills, nothing like that. Everything's flat, and what we do see in the distance are only horizontal lines."

Billy smiled at his friend. Even when they were teenagers, Judah had had a knack of pointing out the obvious and then putting it into perspective. "You're a smart sum'bitch, Judah," said Billy with grin, "I'll betcha that's why you're so damn rich!"

Judah laughed. "I wish it were that easy. There's blood, sweat, and tears in it too."

"I thought we'd take her by the beach on Wassaw. You know, check out who's there, then I'll take you to the spot where I found the bomb. I bet your sonar can spot that thing."

Judah said nothing for several seconds, then turned to Billy slowly. "This morning when you were talking about the bomb over the phone and I jumped your shit about it . . ."

"Yeah, what about it? You were right, I shoulda known better."

"Maybe. But I was a little rough on you and I'm sorry, okay?"

The wind was plastering back Billy's hair, and Judah couldn't see his eyes because of the sunglasses; but he did notice a smile on Billy's lips as he reached over and gave Judah a pat on the back. "I never even thought about it, Bubba, but I am impressed by your apology. You must really be in touch with your sensitive feminine side today!"

"Aw, man, fuck you. But I do want to emphasize how careful we've got to be whenever we talk about this thing. Okay?"

"Yeah, I can dig it, Judah."

"Good. So, what I think we should do whenever it's necessary to talk about the bomb over the phone or around other people is to use a code name for it."

"Good idea."

"Since you're dating Hannah," continued Judah, "and she used to be Miss Savannah, I think that we should call the bomb Miss

Savannah. That way, if anything was ever said about who Miss Savannah was, we could always say we were talking about her."

Billy shrugged, but then he nodded his approval and said, "You really are into this cloak-and-dagger stuff."

"Like I said earlier, Billy, it's a whole new world after nine-eleven. We may not always be right, but this government is dead serious now, and if they get wind that you know where that bomb is—well, I've already expressed my fears about what could happen, so let's just play it safe."

When they reached the Wassaw beach, Billy throttled back, held the *Solitude* about a hundred yards off the gently sloping sand, and motored forward at idle speed. It was early, and only a few boats were anchored in the surf.

"Check out the one in the yellow bikini," said Judah as he took the wheel while handing Billy the binoculars. "I think she's got potential."

Billy worked the focus back and forth a couple of times, then asked, "How do you score her?"

"I'm givin' her a seven, maybe even an eight."

"I don't know about making judgment calls from this distance," said Billy as he kept his eyes to the binoculars. "But I can see how somebody who's been out of training for as long as you could make a mistake. Look at that, she just turned sideways, and boy does she have a gut with a big ass to match! Here, Judah, take the glasses and see for yourself."

Solitude sailed past the old concrete gun emplacement on the beach that had begun to sink under the sand prompting Judah to remark, "Holy shit, I can't believe how much that thing has sunk into the sand since I was out here last. That must be ten years ago and it hadn't shifted anything like it is now. I'll bet it's resting close to a thirty-degree angle."

The Fort Morgan gun emplacement was named after Lt. Harry Sims Morgan, a young West Point graduate who lost his life in 1897 while trying to pull some Italian sailors out of Tybee Sound during a storm. It was made of steel-reinforced concrete and erected during the Endicott period of fortress-building just after the Spanish-American War, at the same time the much larger Fort

Screven was built on Tybee Island's north end. It had been placed more than three hundred feet inland, situated among a stand of windswept oaks. A hundred years later the fort was almost covered by the tide, irrefutable evidence of the first law of barrier islands.

Along the coast the islands that abut the ocean are washed away at their northern ends and built up on the southern ends. From the beginning of time, the Georgia coastal islands have been making a slow but steady migration southward, carrying their entire ecosystems with them, including the sounds. In another hundred years Wassaw's northern end will have retreated three hundred feet from the old fort, which will have disappeared under the sand forever.

As Billy watched the familiar landmark pass by, he said, "The forces that cause that old fort to be under at high tide are the same ones responsible for me finding Miss Savannah."

"How is that?" asked Judah as he watched the *Solitude*'s wake break against the walls of the fort.

"Well," said Billy as he fished in his pocket and pulled out a piece of folded notepaper, "it's like this. The channel we're in right now has been moving to the south for thousands of years. You can look at the fort and see that. I snagged our girlfriend just at the southern boundary of the channel. I went back and checked the 1960 chart for this channel, then plotted these GPS coordinates"—Billy held up the paper—"and back then this plot had a mean low depth of only two feet. It was well out of the channel. Today the mean low depth where I found the bomb is eight feet and inside the channel—only by a little bit, but still the channel has moved over the place where that damn thing buried itself."

Billy handed the coordinates to Judah. "Plug these into your GPS. This ought'ta put us right on top of it. We'll be able to make it out on your sonar, too. Last time I was here, I could see an image on my sonar that sure looked like a something big stuck straight up in the sand with a washed-out depression surrounding it, just like a piling on the beach would look like at low tide."

Billy paused for a moment and let what he said sink in. Then he continued. "That's the bomb, buried nose down and straight up almost fifty years ago. Back then, when it hit, I figure it went down about twenty-five feet. Now, fifty years later, the channel's moved south. It's eroded away the sand that covered the bomb, exposed the stabilizer section—that was probably weakened as the bomb traveled through the sand. That's what I snagged, and after I put the juice to the winches, it broke off from the body of the bomb. Like I said when I first showed you what I've got in my garage, I hit the GPS. We're headed to that spot right now."

Judah pointed to the video screen on his GPS, which displayed an electronic map of the sound. The *Solitude*'s position was indicated by a small arrow that traveled across the screen as the boat moved. "Show me where we're going."

Billy put his finger on the chart. "See this spot, this is where the military said the bomb went down. I went on the Net after I brought up the stabilizer and did a lot of research. The government puts the bomb approximately at the intersection of Bull River and Lazaretto Creek. That's the area I'm pointing to. It's right at six miles north of where we are now, right on this curve in Lazaretto Creek. The government searched this whole area for six weeks and never found a thing."

Billy moved his finger down the chart to the number eleven green buoy that marked the southern limits of Wassaw Sound's channel. "Close to here is where I snagged the bomb. It's the same east-west coordinates the government had, but as you can see, the north-south coordinates were off by over six miles." Billy tapped his finger on the chart for emphasis. "This is where we're headed."

Judah was fascinated. He looked up at Billy in admiration. "Damn, Billy, you've really done your homework. I'm impressed. I can't help noticing that area was out of the channel then. Only small boats would go into water that shallow. I guess that was all underwater back in '58, wasn't it? Is that why the search team missed it?"

"Yeah," answered Billy, "it sure was."

"I imagine that didn't help in the hunt for the bomb, either," said Judah. "I mean those guys had to be looking for a crater."

"Right again, my man. The first thing they did was to put divers down on those coordinates up in Lazaretto Creek and have them feel along the mud for a depression. When they didn't find anything up that way, they moved the search further south and into the sound itself. Only problem was that the tide and wave action is really strong out here, and by the time those divers were on the bottom, probably days after the bomb was dropped, the movement of the water had completely erased any sign of a depression. Then all they had to go on was a magnatometer. Back then I guess they weren't all that great."

Judah nodded as he looked at the GPS screen, then over the bow of his boat. "Very interesting." His eyes once more fell on the GPS monitor. "How did the Air Force come up with the coordinates they used when they looked for the bomb?"

"Good question. At first I thought they came from the navigator of the plane. Then when I dug a little deeper I found out they were from Hunter's radar. They were tracking the plane as it approached and they were able to pick up the bomb when it was released. Looks like they got the east-west part of the plot okay, but the readout on the north-south wasn't quite up to snuff and they plotted the impact area a lot farther to the north than it really was. That Colonel Earl guy thinks he's found the bomb along the same east-west line and he puts it a lot more to the south too, just off Williamson Island. He needs to be about two more miles south."

"Again, captain, I'm impressed. I'll approach the president and recommend a medal for such brilliant work."

"Fuck a medal," responded Billy. "I want cash."

"I'm working on it, Billy. Just be patient and discreet."

Thirty thousand feet above Wassaw Sound, the contrails of six jets marked the light blue sky like so many lines of chalk. One of the planes was following the Georgia coast as it made its way toward Jacksonville, its contrail curving in the same direction as the coastline below. Billy pointed up.

"Look at all those Yankees up there hurrying from New York to Miami."

"That jet's contrail is shaped just like the coastline, isn't it?"

"Exactly. That curve in the coastline from St. Mary's up to around Charleston is known as the Great Atlantic Bight. Not many people realize it, but Savannah is the westernmost point on the Atlantic Coast. The way the coast curves in here and the position of the Gulf Stream is why we don't get all the hurricanes that Florida and North Carolina do."

"The Great Atlantic Bight," repeated Judah. "That's interesting. I've never heard that term before. So we're living on the Great Atlantic Bight. Can't wait to use that bit of trivia on my know-it-all colleagues in D.C."

"We're here," said Billy as he slowed the *Solitude* and pointed to the GPS coordinates. "We should be within twenty-five feet of the bomb. At least that's what this system is supposed to be capable of. I'm going to make several passes over this area and try to spot it. Keep a sharp eye on the sonar."

The *Solitude* crept over the area as Billy and Judah watched the sonar paint the pattern of the ocean floor in shades of tan and gray. It took several runs before an image appeared on the screen, prompting Billy to shout, "That's it, damn it, that's the bomb!"

Athough the sonar Judah had on his boat was sophisticated, it was not a side-scanning sonar, the type used to map river bottoms and investigate shipwrecks and capable of rendering almost three-dimensional images. *Solitude*'s sonar worked by bouncing sound waves off the bottom. It then interpreted those waves and displayed what it saw, not as if the user were looking down on the ocean floor, but rather as if he were looking at a side section of the floor. What Judah and Billy saw was the flat ocean bottom with a funnel-like depression that measured about ten feet across. In the center of the depression was an object in the vertical position. Judah's sonar was capable of measuring the height of the object and also of distinguishing metallic from nonmetallic objects. Whatever was sticking up in the center of that depression was metallic.

"See, I told ya," said Billy excitedly.

"Yeah," answered Judah in a serious tone. "I see what you mean now."

The Cadet Corps

> Foresake not an old friend; for the new is not comparable to him: a new friend is new wine; when it is old, thou shalt drink it with pleasure.
>
> —Ecclesiasticus 9:10

THE INTENSE HEAT of summer had arrived early. June felt like July, but Judah didn't care. The morning air was still cool enough for him to jog comfortably through Isle of Hope, then make his loop at Dutch Island for the return run back to the *Solitude.* As he climbed aboard his boat and headed for the shower, he was thinking about the fresh cantaloupe and grapes he would have for breakfast up on the fly bridge. Ten minutes later he was headed topside, breakfast and newspaper in hand. Judah's head had just cleared the top of the hatch when he caught sight of a woman's legs. As he climbed higher, more of his mystery guest came into view.

"Hi, Judah. Surprised to see me?" asked an attractive, forty-something, expensively dressed brunette.

Judah shook his head and smiled. "Yeah, Page, I'm surprised. You bet." Then he just stood for a moment, holding his plate of fruit, trying to grasp the situation. Finally he asked, "Oh, uh, would you like to share breakfast with me? Your favorites, if I recall correctly."

Page's white shorts highlighted a pair of nicely shaped legs, which she uncrossed while looking seductively at Judah. "I'm touched that you remembered. Yes, I'd love to share with you."

Judah sat next to Page and laid the plate between them. The

diamond tennis bracelet she wore sparkled when it caught the morning sun as she reached for some grapes. For a while there was silence as Judah watched Page pop a grape into her mouth. Her red lips were very full. She never shifted her eyes from his as she took another grape, held it up for his inspection, and placed it into his mouth.

She was wearing a sleeveless blouse that matched her lipstick and opened past the second button to reveal a tantalizing glimpse of cleavage, which Judah knew very well. Page giggled when she saw Judah's eyes drift downward; and she held another grape in her expertly manicured fingers before placing it in his mouth.

After Judah swallowed the grape, Page offered him another, but he put his hand up. "Okay, what's this all about, Page? What are you doing in Savannah?"

She faked a hurt look and said, "Judah, I thought you might be glad to see me. After all, it's been over three months since we were together. Haven't you thought about me just a little?"

"Sometimes I think about you a lot, Page, but you still haven't answered my question. What's going on?"

"Maybe I came down just to see if . . . "

"Maybe you did, that might be a part of it, but I doubt you'd be taking off from your job right now to see if there was anything left for us, especially after what happened the last time I spoke with you. I thought I'd made myself pretty clear."

Page's mouth tightened a little as she looked away for a moment. "God, I don't see how you stand the humidity in this place."

"Sorta like D.C. in August, isn't it?"

Page let out a sigh, then looked back at Judah. "Carl sent me. I've got some papers for you. I guess they could have been mailed, but he asked me if I wanted to see you again. Hell, he knew I did, so he told me to deliver these to you in person." She reached into the briefcase sitting next to her on the deck and pulled out a manila envelope. "This is the material you requested a few weeks ago." Her voice held a note of sadness.

Judah opened the envelope and examined the papers while Page finished the grapes and began eating one of the cantaloupe halves.

Judah glanced up, said, "Save some for me," then buried his face in the papers again. Five minutes later he stacked the papers on his knees and put them back into the envelope.

"I need to go over these more closely, but that can be done later." Judah leaned back and studied Page for a moment. She had dropped her head and was fidgeting with her bracelet when he asked, "How did you get here?"

"I flew down yesterday and rented a car."

"Where are you staying?"

"At a B-and-B called 17Hundred90. It's really quite nice. You know I work for the White House now, and your buddy Carl told me about it."

"Yeah, I know it well. A classmate of mine from Benedictine owns it." Judah thought for a very long moment. "Listen, how long had you planned on being here?"

"Well," Page said hesitantly, "I, uh, guess I'm going back tomorrow."

Judah smiled. "Why don't you stay here tonight? If you want, maybe even stay a day or so longer. Think the campaign could function without you for a few days?"

It was after three when the two of them returned to the boat with her luggage. The drive back had been pleasant, and Judah had enjoyed showing Page some of the sights around town. She hadn't said anything to him about their relationship, and Judah was relieved. He just wasn't in the mood for "relationship talk" and had questioned himself on the idea of inviting her to spend the night on the *Solitude*; but she had tugged on his heart a little and he actually did like her, except when she got into one of her moods. That, unfortunately, had been all too often, the real reason he had broken it off with her; but "What the hell," he said to himself, "she's acting like maybe she gets it now. What have I got to lose?"

"Looks like it's going to rain," Judah said as he carried Page's bags to the stateroom across from his and then placed them on the bed.

"I love the rain," Page said while looking out the window at the river.

"Yeah, me too. I especially like thunderstorms. Come on, let's go topside and watch the front move in. The rain will cool things off before everybody gets here."

After Page had decided to stay, Judah had made some quick calls and invited a few friends over for cocktails. Page had heard about his buddies, but had never met them.

"It was nice of you to invite your friends over to meet me," she said as she climbed the ladder to the fly bridge. Judah was below her and couldn't help admiring her calf muscles as they flexed sinuously with each step. His eyes followed them with interest all the way up.

Page took pride in her looks. She never missed an exercise class and, her personality notwithstanding, Judah had to admit that he found her next to irresistible, or had for a long time. His feelings for her, however, had run in sync with his feelings for Washington, and one day enough had been enough no matter how pretty she was.

The wind had shifted: It was coming out of the east as the low-pressure system moving in from the west pulled the air to it. Thunder that had been distant only thirty minutes before was now loud and persistent. Judah and Page sat side by side and watched as the first drops of rain splashed across the river and a towering thunderhead blotted out the sun. The big oaks along Bluff Drive swayed in the wind like marsh grass, and the temperature dropped off ten, thirteen, fifteen degrees as the storm approached. Soon the rain was heavy with fat drops that flattened the river into a fuzzy stream. The wind picked up as flashes of lightning popped out of angry, bruised clouds rolling in over Isle of Hope. A gust of wind-blown rain splashed across Page and plastered her blouse to her breasts as she shouted above the thunder, "God, I love storms, Judah!" Then, with a blinding flash and a deafening clap of thunder, a lightning bolt struck Burnt Pot Island just across the river. Judah stood quickly and announced, "It's not safe up here anymore. Let's get below."

As she stepped into her cabin, Page said, "I guess I need to get into some dry clothes."

"Me too," responded Judah.

Judah hadn't been in his cabin more than two minutes before Page appeared at his door with nothing on. She was, indeed, a sight to behold; and two hours later Judah was asking himself if he hadn't been a little too harsh in his judgment.

John-Morgan and Ann Marie Hartman, the first guests, arrived just before sunset. They had walked from Driscoll House, their home on Bluff Drive, the ancestral manse of John-Morgan's mother's family. He and Judah had been classmates at Benedictine, where John-Morgan had been cadet colonel, only to be reduced in rank following an incident involving a stolen tree—the centerpiece of Benedictine's Christmas dance back in their senior year. John-Morgan had recently retired after thirty years of practice in internal medicine; and now he spent his days researching Savannah's Civil War history.

Judah had been a major on John-Morgan's staff and, like the entire student body, had greatly admired his refusal to rat on his classmates over what, in Benedictine folklore, became known as The Great Christmas Tree Caper. He had been severely wounded in Vietnam and still walked with a slight limp, but Judah could tell the years had been kind to John-Morgan. He was a little gray now, just like Judah; he had a bald spot on the back of his head and couldn't read without his glasses; but there was still that little mischievous smile when they talked of old times; and Judah was thrilled to see him.

A few minutes later the Right Reverend Monsignor Lloyd Bryan arrived. Now it was Page's turn to be surprised. Judah hadn't said anything about Lloyd apart from the fact that he had also gone to Benedictine and was a Catholic priest. What greeted Page was a six-foot-four, very muscular black man with silver-gray hair and a beard to match. Afterward all she could say was that Lloyd looked like a black Moses, "maybe the most impressive man I've ever seen."

In 1963 Lloyd had been handpicked by the Bishop of Savannah to integrate Benedictine Military School, and during his first year he had been the only member of his race in the Corps of Cadets. He had been an outcast at first, but his athletic abilities propelled the school into the state football playoffs, and any lingering animosity toward him in the Corps soon dissolved. As it happened Judah was one of the first boys to offer Lloyd his hand in friendship, a friendship that would blossom when Lloyd came to Washington to play for the Redskins back in the seventies.

The sun had just slipped behind the oaks along the bluff when Will and Charlotte McQueen stepped aboard. Will wasn't a B.C. boy—he had graduated from Savannah High School—but everyone present was well acquainted with him. After high school Will had entered the Military College of South Carolina, also known as The Citadel, and had done a tour in Vietnam with the Navy. As the result of combat action, he had lost both legs below the knee.

Will McQueen was a member of one of Savannah's most socially prominent and politically connected families, and after he had learned to walk again, he entered politics. He was elected to the United States Congress, and represented the First District. Will's campaign was the first really big one that Judah managed; its success was the springboard for the rest of Judah's career. Will and Judah saw a great deal of each other up in D.C., and it was Will who had counseled Judah to take an extended leave of absence when he saw the toll that a stressful life was taking on his friend.

When Billy and Hannah arrived, everyone was topside enjoying the cool air ushered in by that afternoon's storm. In the twilight the sky had a lavender tint as a butter-colored moon rose from behind the trees on Skidaway Island.

Although Page had never met Hannah, she had heard a great deal about her from Judah—perhaps too much. Once, when he was drunk, he had started talking about the loss of his brother and how badly it had hurt him. It wasn't long before he was recounting other painful episodes of his life—and his romance with Hannah became front and center. When Judah informed Page that Hannah and Billy were dating and that she would be at the party with him, she asked if it bothered him that she would be there. "Naw," he replied, "that's all been a long time ago. You know what they say about time, don't you? It heals all wounds."

"No matter how deep the wound?"

"No matter how deep."

As the party progressed the women soon gathered in a knot of conversation at one end of the boat, while the men did the same at the other. For a while Judah and Will entertained their friends with Washington tales. Then, out of nowhere, Will casually inquired, "Have y'all been following that story about the lost H-bomb in Wassaw Sound?"

Judah couldn't help cutting a startled look at Billy; and, afraid that Will had noticed, he quickly chimed in, "Yeah, I've been reading about it in the paper. Seems like some retired Air Force Colonel thinks he knows where the damn thing is. As a matter of fact, Will, the story said your office was involved. What gives?"

Will took another sip of his second Glenfiddich on the rocks, then shook his head wryly. "The colonel's a pretty intense fella. He says he's certain he knows where the bomb is and that he'll get it for us for the reasonable sum of two million dollars."

"Yeah," said Judah, "I read that in the paper too. Is he gonna get the money?"

"Well, what wasn't in the paper was that he was informed by DOD that if he found the bomb and tried to raise it, they would put his ass under the jail. Their position is pretty much let a sleeping dog lie, and that trying to recover the thing could cause the casing to crack and lead to a radiation leak."

"What did Colonel Earl have to say about that?" asked Billy.

"He was none too happy, and he told me he was going to the press with the story that it was dangerous not to be able to account for a hydrogen bomb and that our terrorist buddies surely knew of the bomb's existence and that they would certainly try to get their hands on it."

"Do you think terrorists could locate and then retrieve that thing from the sound?" asked Lloyd.

"Good question, Monsignor. The DOD really doesn't see that as a viable threat. I kind of have to agree with them, too."

"Why?" Billy wanted to know.

"Well, if the government can't find the bomb with all of the resources at its disposal, what makes you think some bunch of ragheads could find it? But, let's suppose they do find where the bomb is resting. Then they have to get the thing up and out. It weighs 7,500 pounds. It would take a barge with a crane and God only knows what other additional equipment to do the job. I've seen the stuff Colonel Earl claims to have at his disposal. It's big and it's a lot. An operation that size would take days and would attract lots of attention. Defense just doesn't believe terrorists can snatch the bomb up from Wassaw Sound right under our noses—and I have to tell ya'll, I tend to agree with them on this."

"From what I've read in the papers," said Lloyd, "the big concern seems to be whether or not the plutonium capsule is present in the bomb."

"That's correct, Colonel Earl insists the plutonium is there. The government says it isn't. The reason the plutonium is so important is that, if the bomb's casing is somehow ruptured, it's quite possible that the plutonium could leak out and poison the entire Atlantic Seaboard. It would certainly render this area uninhabitable for the next couple of hundred thousand years. The uranium isn't the problem. Nobody believes there's gonna be a nuclear detonation, either. It's the plutonium that's the rub."

Lloyd thought for a moment, then asked, "With something as dangerous and important as an H-bomb, how could there be any dispute about the plutonium? I mean, the government must keep pretty tight controls and records over something like that, right?"

"One would hope so, but Earl has come up with a document from the 1960s that seems to dispute the government's claim. There was a hearing back then about the bomb, and an Air Force officer who was supposed to know about that kind of stuff stated on the record that the bomb had its plutonium trigger in place."

"Well, then, why does the government keep insisting that it doesn't?'

Will smiled, took a sip from his drink, and said, "The plot thickens. You see, this colonel who testified to that committee saying the plutonium was in the bomb later retracted his statement saying he had been mistaken. He claims the Air Force doesn't lose track of its plutonium bomb parts and that the particular amount of plutonium in question had been accounted for and couldn't possibly be in the bomb."

"Whatcha think's gonna finally happen, Will?" asked Billy.

"Nine-eleven put the pressure on the government. I think they'll go along with a search of some kind, but I don't think they'll find anything. What we've done so far just hasn't turned up any evidence of the radioactivity Colonel Earl claims to have found, so I guess we'll just have to wait and see."

"Let's turn our attention from bombs to broads," said Billy jokingly. "Tell us about Page, Judah. How come she just popped up? I thought that whole thing was over with."

Judah cut a look in Page's direction and said in a low voice, "I thought it was too. She just showed up here today with some papers from my old boss in Washington. I mean, I like the girl, but I don't think I could live with her."

"Well," injected John-Morgan, "she ain't bad lookin' at all."

"Agreed," said Judah, "but pretty is as pretty does. Isn't that right, Lloyd?"

Lloyd smiled, put his hands up in a defensive manner, and said, "One of the great advantages of being a priest is that I'm not confronted with such vexing personal issues. So I'll just confine my comments to saying that it may be time for an old fart like you to think about settling down with some nice girl, whoever she may be, and leave it at that."

Everybody laughed as Judah nodded in agreement. Then the conversation turned to politics. After that topic was exhausted, the men began reminiscing about their high school days. By eleven everyone but Hannah and Billy were gone.

"Have you heard anything?" asked the latter as he and Judah rested their arms on the railing and looked at the stars.

"Page brought down some papers today about the bomb, and I looked 'em over. I also talked to one of my buddies about having a friend who claims to know where it is and I kinda got the cold shoulder. Like you heard tonight, the government's real touchy about stuff like that. We've got to go real slow and careful now, okay?"

Billy looked down at the river. "I understand. I just think it's kinda funny this Colonel Earl is leading the Feds on a wild goose chase up at the northern end of the sound while I got the damn thing nailed down two miles to the south."

Judah was quiet for a moment. "Look, Billy, we're not certain that what you've found really is the bomb, okay? I mean, we're gonna need absolute proof. Somebody who knows what the hell they're talkin' about is gonna have to put an eyeball on that thing. Either on the bottom of the sound or when it's been hauled up. This is some really tricky shit you've got me involved with."

"I know it is, and I don't want to get you in hot water. Sometimes I think I should just go to the government and tell'em about it, but when I think about what those bastards did to me back with that Mariel bullshit, that's when I say, hell no, I want something for my trouble."

"I know," said Judah, "just be cool. Let me see what I can do."

After Billy and Hannah had gone, Judah and Page went topside once more to look at the stars. The night was particularly clear, and from their vantage point Judah was able to point out the constellations and stars he had learned from Elijah back when he and Billy had worked on the *St. Patrick*.

Pointing directly overhead, Judah said, "There's the Big Dipper. Look at the two stars that make up the end of its cup. Those are called the pointers because if you run a straight line off of them to the north, they're pointing directly at Polaris, the North Star. See, Page, Polaris is the end star on the handle of the Little Dipper."

"I wish I'd taken a course on astronomy in college," Page said as she followed Judah's hand across the sky.

Judah pointed to the east. "There's the Summer Triangle. Its three points are the first magnitude stars Vega, Altair, and Deneb. Can you see the Milky Way cutting right through it?"

"Oh, God, I can," said Page excitedly, "I never get a chance to see anything like this up in D.C. This is just overwhelming! What's that big star over there?" She was pointing to the south.

"That's not a star, that's the planet Jupiter, and just by it are the stars of the constellation Leo. That's your sign, isn't it?"

There was silence for a moment, until Page turned away from the stars to look at Judah. "I want to be back with you."

"Over in the northwest sky we could see Mars and Saturn if the trees weren't in the way." Judah did not take his eyes from the heavens.

"Judah . . . "

"I heard you, Page."

"Well?"

Judah dropped his gaze from the sky, turned to Page, and said, "Maybe too much has happened to start over again. Know what I mean?"

"We can try, can't we?"

"Page, I'm not leaving this place again and I'm not going back to Washington to live, ever. You made it pretty clear that you didn't want anything to do with the South, remember? You said the South was full of ignorant rednecks, right?"

"Maybe I can change my mind." Suddenly Page seemed desperate.

"Maybe you can," replied Judah. "But I doubt it."

Page put her arms around his neck, kissed him, and said, "Come on, let's go to bed. We can talk about this in the morning."

The next morning after breakfast, Page took Moshe on a jog through Wormsloe Plantation while Judah settled onto the sofa in the ship's salon to read the material she had brought from Washington. The cover letter was written by an old friend he had served with during his tour at the Pentagon.

Dear Judah,

I trust this letter finds you in good health. It was nice talking to you last week, and attached, you will find the material you requested. None of it is classified. I'm well acquainted with the so-called "Tybee Bomb" and will offer a summary of the attachments for your convenience.

The ordinance in question is a Mark 15, Model 0, 3 megaton thermonuclear device, serial number 47782. It was lost on February 5, 1958 in Wassaw Sound, Georgia. After an extensive, but fruitless search, the weapon was declared irretrievably lost on April 16, 1958.

It is the government's position that the plutonium trigger was not on board the aircraft and that the bomb is, in all likelihood, buried under many feet of sand and, if not disturbed, presents no danger at all. While I fully realize that retired Lt. Col. Derrick Earl has come forward with evidence that the bomb does have its plutonium capsule in place, the Air Force has the original temporary custody receipt signed by the plane's commander, Captain Howard Richardson, stating that not only was no capsule present, but that Richardson was not to "allow any active capsule to be inserted at any time." The declassified top secret history of the Strategic Air Command clearly indicates that at the time this bomb was lost SAC did not "have the authority to launch alert aircraft with the nuclear capsules aboard."

Let me now address the evidence that Lt. Col. Earl puts forth in his assertion that the plutonium trigger capsule was indeed inserted into this bomb. Lt. Col. Earl has a letter from William Jack Howard, the Assistant to the Secretary of Defense in 1966, listing four U.S. nuclear weapons that were lost and never recovered. Two of the bombs were described by Mr. Howard as "complete," meaning they had their plutonium capsules in them. One of these bombs is the Tybee Bomb. This information was obtained by Lt. Col. Earl in 1996 after it was declassified. Since that time, Mr. Howard has recanted that statement, claiming he made a mistake. Lt. Col. Earl has not come forward with any other evidence supporting his assertion that the capsule was present.

The Air Force has decided to conduct a survey of the area where Lt. Col. Earl claims the bomb rests. This should be in the next few months, and I will be happy to keep you posted. Until then, Debbie sends her love and looks forward to seeing you again in the near future.

Sincerely yours,

Gary D. Webb, Colonel, U.S.A.F., Assistant to the Secretary of the Air Force

Judah placed the letter aside and went through the rest of the papers. Some of them were technical; most were copies of letters and transcripts of testimony about the missing bomb. None of them, however, added anything to the content of Colonel Webb's summary. As he placed the papers back into their envelope, Judah sighed and whispered, "Looks like Billy knows as much as they do, maybe more. Maybe a whole lot more."

After putting the papers away, Judah went to the stern, seated himself in one of the wicker chairs, and waited for Page to return. He hadn't had sufficient time to sort through how he felt about her visit; but his only real question was, What would he do if she said she'd come and live in Savannah? Did he care enough about her that he wanted to start over again? He didn't know, but he had enjoyed the lovemaking. She was beautiful and fifteen years his junior, and all that did make him feel good most of the time. But she was so damned pushy, such a social climber, and so critical of people, that he sometimes wondered what she said about him behind his back. Whenever they'd argue, and it became all too often, she could cut to the bone—and Judah was surprised that he hadn't heard a negative word since she had stepped on board the *Solitude*. He was shaken from his thoughts when he noticed Page walking down the dock towards the boat. Judah couldn't help admiring her.

Anne Page Adams was a Connecticut native, a graduate of Dartmouth, a WASP who looked like one, and had once been married to a Wall Street lawyer. She was childless by choice, intelligent to a fault, aggressive by nature; and she had been smitten by Judah when they'd worked together on the presidential campaign of 1996. For three years Page had lived with Judah at his townhouse and had seen him slowly crumple under the weight of his work—and she couldn't understand it. She thrived on competition and loved the high-stakes politics inside the beltway. Page in no way considered herself a bad person, but she had no intention of backing away from the hot fire of a Washington insider's life. She did love Judah, however. At least that's what she sincerely believed at the moment.

"How was the run?" asked Judah.

"Great," she answered as she gulped greedily from the bottle of Evian Water Judah handed her. Page flopped into the chair across from his and grew silent.

"How did you like the party last night," Judah asked as he gazed down the river, which he followed with his eyes as it passed John-Morgan's white-columned home.

"Fine."

"What did you think of Lloyd Bryan?"

"He has a lot of charisma and presence. He'd make a great politician."

"I guess he already is in a way. I hear he's in line to become the Bishop of Savannah. It takes a good politician to handle that job."

Page said nothing for a few moments, then twisted in her chair a little. "Well, did you enjoy yourself last night?"

"Yeah, I had a good time. I always enjoy being around my B.C. buddies."

"I noticed you sure had a lot to say to Hannah." Her tight voice held more than a hint of sarcasm.

"We talked. So what?"

"You couldn't keep your hands off each other. Every time I looked around, you'd be touching her to make a point, or she'd be touching you."

"We're Southerners, Page, people down South do that kind of thing. It doesn't go any further than that."

"Really?" Her sarcasm had now turned to irritation. "When we were talking with John-Morgan and his wife and Hannah was on the other side of the cabin with the others, I noticed how you kept looking at her."

"Like I said, Page. So what?"

"So, are you still in love with her?"

"Look, we've been down this road before, and I told you how I felt about her. So let's just let it drop, okay?"

"For the life of me, I can't understand what she sees in that shrimper. She has so much more class than he does."

Judah had wondered when she would start; so now he settled back in his chair and waited for the individual appraisals he knew were in the offing.

"And John-Morgan's wife, what a typical example of Southern womanhood! Demure, soft-spoken, doesn't give a shit about anything but her house and her children. That accent of hers made me want to scream."

Then Page leveled her sights on Hannah. "Your old girlfriend must be some kind of a religious zealot. The first damn question she asked me was where I went to church. Then she launched into this spiel about how impressive a speaker Lloyd Bryan is and what an influence he had had on her life and Billy's. Ann Marie Hartman was standing there lapping it all up like it was cold beer on a hot day. I'll never understand these people."

Judah thought for a moment, then stood, stretched his back, and asked in a flat tone, "When does your plane leave tomorrow?"

Things Unknown

Work on,
My medicine, work! Thus credulous fools are caught.
—William Shakespeare, *Othello*, 4. 1. 52–54

JUDAH DIDN'T KNOW he was being watched as he carried Page's luggage to his car. He also didn't know that somebody had been keeping tabs on him for almost a week; and he had paid little attention when a forty-foot Sea Ray tied off at a berth four days before, just a couple slots down from his. He had noted its name, *Eventful*, and that Miami was its home port. He had even spoken to the man he assumed was its owner on the dock; but other than that Judah hadn't given the matter much thought.

The captain of the *Eventful* was an operative for the Defense Intelligence Agency, the intelligence-gathering arm of the Department of Defense. He had been sent to Savannah after Judah called Washington with the word that he had information concerning the Tybee Bomb. DOD had been alerted. They also knew about the papers Page had brought; and these only served to heighten their interest. The fact was that DOD didn't put much faith in Lt. Col. Earl's claims; so when a person as high up on the D.C. food chain as Judah Benjamin offered to lead them to the bomb for a fee, and even stated he had proof for his assertions, it was raw meat to them. The man who had been watching Judah had been in the employ of the U.S. intelligence community in some fashion for many years. His name was Augusto Camacho.

Gusto had been a C.I.A. agent back when Billy picked him up at Mariel Bay. He had made his connections the same way he had learned his English: through his association with organized crime and their hazy, symbiotic collaboration with the C.I.A., especially the agency's efforts to depose Castro by any means, including assassination.

Gusto didn't actually work for the D.I.A. His cover was completely different, but he was presently taking orders from them. After nine-eleven Gusto had been actively involved in hunting down suspected terrorists outside of the U.S. and had been responsible for the capture of several really dangerous actors, one of whom Gusto was forced to terminate with extreme prejudice. He was in the twilight of his career, and men his age usually didn't spend much time in the field; but Gusto had special talents when it came to patiently putting the pieces together, and he jumped at the chance to take his boat from Miami and spend some time keeping an eye on a burned-out big shot who might know too much for his own good.

The way Gusto had it figured, the likeliest person to stumble across the bomb was a shrimper. "Who else drags huge nets across the ocean bottom out where the bomb was lost?" he asked himself. When he saw Billy Aprillia show up for Judah's party, he recognized him at once and realized that Billy could well be Judah's connection with the bomb. This prompted him to recommend eavesdropping on both Judah and Billy's cell phones. He also sought permission to search Judah's boat and Billy's condo. The cell phone recommendation was followed, but permission for the searches was denied. Judah still had friends looking out for him, even if he didn't know it.

For the next few days, he watched from the secrecy of his boat as a variety of people visited Judah. He watched with interest as Billy showed up each afternoon and sat on the sun deck as the two men drank beer and talked. He noted the remarkable black man with the silver hair and clerical collar who joined them one afternoon, along with the white man who arrived by boat from his home just past the bend in the river. He had seen them all at Judah's boat party. When Congressman McQueen's green Silverado eased into the marina parking lot, Gusto watched Will through binoculars as he walked down the ramp to the *Solitude*. While Judah and his friends talked and laughed, Gusto removed his Nikon F-3 with a 200mm telephoto lens and began snapping pictures of the crowd on the boat. Two days later they would be on a desk at the Pentagon.

Other than Billy Aprillia, Gusto discounted the possibility that anyone else he had seen Judah associate with knew where the Tybee Bomb was. He made a call to the Pentagon with his summary.

"If, indeed, Mr. Benjamin has knowledge of the bomb's whereabouts," Gusto said to the ears in Washington, "I believe it can only be through the shrimper, Billy Aprillia."

"Makes sense," replied his handler.

"What did you get from the wiretaps?"

"Pretty bland stuff. A lot of cutting up and talking about old girlfriends, but nothing that ties them to the bomb. We listened to a lot of stuff about the campaign from Benjamin, but that was between him and Republican National Committee boys. As far as conversation between Aprillia and Benjamin goes, it looks pretty clean unless they're talking in some kind of code, but I doubt it. Several times there were conversations about a Miss Savannah. I'd love to know who this gal is, but that's about it."

"I already found out," said Gusto. "I did some asking around about Aprillia and found out that his girlfriend was Miss Savannah about forty years ago. If you'd seen her you'd know why. She still looks pretty good. That's who they're talking about."

"Okay," said his contact in the Pentagon, "hang around for a few more days. If nothing else comes up, pack it in."

Abdul Aleem had been born at Savannah's Memorial Hospital on the hottest day of the year in 1970. His mother, Cassandra, hadn't seen his father, Willie, better known by his street name Pork Chop, since she had first informed him that she was expecting his child. The name on Abdul's birth certificate was Tyrone Connor; he would answer to that until his stint at the state prison in Reidsville. Tyrone had a rough time growing up in Hitch Village, a low-income housing project on Savannah's east side. He had lived with his mother until he was six, when a succession of her abusive boy friends finally prompted his grandmother to take him into her home on West 37th Street.

Mae Bell Connor was a widow who lived on her husband's Social Security check and a small retirement fund she had managed to build up while working at a local doctor's office. Cassandra had been her only child and had shown great promise in the beginning, but after her father died on her twelfth birthday, Mae Bell was forced to find a job; Cassandra was left to her own devices until her mother returned home in the late afternoon. Things went well until Cassandra started high school and began running with the wrong crowd. She was pregnant for the first time at sixteen. That pregnancy ended in a miscarriage, but by her senior year she would be carrying Tyrone. It was then that the relationship between Cassandra and her mother really took a nosedive.

Mae Bell was a devoutly religious woman who took the admonitions in the Bible against fornication very seriously. She was a deaconess at the Church of the Most Holy God in Christ and was willing to forgive Cassandra's first transgression; but when her daughter continued in her obviouly wicked ways, she was told that after the baby was born, she was on her own. Mae Bell was at the hospital for Tyrone's delivery, however, and after she had held her only grandchild in her arms, she softened her stance. Her daughter could continue to live with her; but Cassandra, unbeknownst to Mae Bell, had been to the welfare office and had made arrangements to have her own place.

By the time Mae Bell finally intervened to rescue Tyrone from his mother's tawdry life, the damage had been done. She was now in her sixties and suffering from heart disease; and although she tried as hard as she could, Tyrone was soon in trouble both in and out of school. Because he was a good liar, Mae Bell didn't know that anything was seriously wrong until the police arrived at her front door and arrested Tyrone for burglary. He was thirteen at the time and spent two years in juvenile detention. There he learned to become an even better criminal; but it was the two years he spent at Reidsville for armed robbery that truly changed his life.

Tyrone's cellmate was a thirty-eight-year-old doing long time for attempted murder. Hakeem Shabazz, formally Germaine Driggers, had converted to Islam shortly after his arrival at Reidsville; he was the driving force in bringing Tyrone into the Nation of Islam. The tenets of self-reliance, hard work, clean-living, and devotion to prayer fostered by the Nation of Islam—all had such a positive effect on Tyrone that he, while in prison, cast aside what he considered a slave name forced upon him and his ancestors by their white oppressors and assumed the Muslim-African name of Abdul Aleem, which meant "servant of the omniscient." Unfortunately the positive ideas accepted by Abdul were tainted by the overt racism espoused by the Nation of Islam, which declared whites to be devils and collectively responsible for every calamity suffered by blacks from slavery to AIDS to drug addiction. By the end of his stay at Reidsville, Abdul was sure he knew the reason he had been incarcerated. He was certain that it had nothing to do with his own behavior.

Abdul's great-uncle was Elijah Deveraux, so when Abdul was released from the penitentiary, Elijah arranged a job for him as a striker on the *St. Patrick*. On board Abdul kept his political opinions to himself and worked hard. When not on the boat, he stayed out of trouble and attended the Massid Jihad Mosque with regularity. There be began to gravitate toward a couple of politically charged mosque members whose ideas were in sync with those of radical Islam. When nine-eleven happened Abdul and his friends all expressed admiration for the terrorists; and in the coming months he began to accept more and more of their radical beliefs. When the Savannah Islamic Center was firebombed and burned to the ground in August of 2003, Abdul's feelings hardened even more.

While he may have been politically naive and easily led, Abdul was shrewd, streetwise, and by that time suspicious of everyone who was not a Muslim. So, even though Billy thought that Abdul had accepted his explanation about what they'd pulled up in Wassaw Sound, he hadn't been fooled. He had read the articles in the paper about the Tybee bomb and recognized the stabilizer fins for what they were the minute they hit the deck. Unknown to Billy, Abdul had also slipped into the wheelhouse and copied the coordinates on the GPS. At the time he didn't know how he would use this knowledge, but he vowed to think of a way to employ it against the infidels who were trying to destroy Islam.

The handling of *Solitude* was not a one-man operation; whenever Judah took her out, at least two extra hands were needed to work the lines when docking and shoving off. At Billy's suggestion Judah employed Abdul and Tran for these tasks as well as the general maintenance and cleaning of his boat. Both were experienced and willing hands who could also pilot the boat when Judah had friends aboard, freeing him to mingle with his guests; so Abdul and Tran had also been spotted by Gusto.

It took only a single trip to the Thunderbolt chief of police to find out the scoop on both of them. All Gusto had to do was flash his I.D. and badge, and the chief was more than happy to tell him all he knew. When Chief Steve Smith told Gusto that Abdul was an ex-con and a Muslim to boot, his ears perked up. That information was at the Pentagon two hours later.

The next day the F.B.I. was in touch with Gusto to tell him they had already infiltrated Abdul's mosque and knew all about his political leanings. They considered him essentially harmless, but still a person they'd keep an eye on. Gusto chose not to share his suspicions about Billy, so after a few more days of snooping proved fruitless, he pointed his boat south and headed home.

Judah had just finished watching the Hannity & Colmes show and was pleased with the way the Republican guest had fielded the questions. He was about to call the senator and congratulate him when his phone rang.

"Judah," said the deep baritone voice, "whatcha up to?"

"Oh, Lloyd, hey, I was just watching one of my clients on the tube."

"How'd he do?"

"Fine, 'cause he did just like I told him. What's up with you?"

"Well," said Lloyd, "I got a new boat today and I was wondering if you might like to take a little ride on it in the morning."

"Yeah, I'd love to. What time?"

"I'll come by for you at nine, is that too early?'

"No, that's fine. I'm usually up before seven. Can I bring anything?"

"Not a thing, I gotcha covered. See ya at nine."

"Yeah, but what kind of boat did you get?"

"You'll see when I get there," was Lloyd's reply.

There were times when Lloyd Bryan questioned the wisdom of entering the priesthood. He had given up so much when he had deprived himself of a woman's love and affection, forgone the happiness of children, and taken to his heart the spiritual and physical sufferings of his flock. Sometimes what he saw and heard was overwhelming, and his spirit would buckle under the burden; but over the years he had learned that, with prayer and patience, those feelings were transient, especially when he forced himself to focus on the good things he had accomplished with his vocation. Nevertheless he needed to step back from time to time and find diversions that would allow his mind to cool and rest.

Although Lloyd had taken a vow of celibacy and obedience upon his ordination, he had not taken one of poverty. During his years with the Washington Redskins, he'd blown a lot of cash riding in the fast lane before he had had his personal moment of truth—a close encounter with what he considered to be God—but he had also made some wise investments. They had paid off handsomely. He was generous to a fault with his money and rarely spent any on himself.

Lloyd and Judah had fallen in love with the water when they worked together as strikers on the *St. Patrick*. That love had not died in either of them. Lloyd had yielded to that passion several times over the years in a succession of modest boats that a parishioner allowed him to keep at this dock on Richardson Creek. Boats were precious to Lloyd because they afforded a feeling of freedom and detachment from the pressures of his work; so when time and weather permitted, he was on the river heading to his favorite spots. Two days before Lloyd called Judah, the same parishioner had come across a boat that was only a year old and much larger than the one Lloyd presently owned. The man drove a hard bargain with the seller on Lloyd's behalf purchasing the boat for a good price.

Summer mornings on the rivers around Savannah can be as sweet as a vase of freshly cut flowers; and as Lloyd guided his boat out of Turner's Creek and pointed the bow towards the Skidaway River, he savored the scent of the marsh and watched a great blue heron take to its wings. Twenty yards off his port bow, four dolphins frolicked as they broke the surface, their steel-gray backs glistening in the sun. Lloyd listened as they exhaled, took deep breaths, and disappeared into the river, only to surface again farther on and repeat their breathing cycle.

The sun felt good on his skin as he checked his gauges before pushing the throttle forward to bring his boat on to a plane. His engine was a four-cycle Mercury, quieter and more responsive than the two-cycle he had had on his old boat. The new one was a twenty-foot Trophy with a walk-around cuddy cabin and a hard top. The name "Eleventh Commandment" was painted on the hull in Old English script.

"Whoa," said Judah as he climbed aboard, "I like this!"

"Well, it's no seventy-foot yacht, but I'm happy with it. Wait 'till I open it up. With this one-seventy-five, it'll do fifty!"

"I bet it will." Judah looked admiringly around the cabin and examined the fittings. "Where'd you get the name from?" he asked as he watched Lloyd maneuver the boat into the middle of the river. "Is that like Reagan's eleventh commandment? You know, thou shalt not speak ill of another Republican?"

Lloyd laughed, then put his sunglasses on to shield his eyes from the sun's glare. "Naw, man, it's the eleventh commandment according to Monsignor Bryan." The smile across his face widened.

"Okay, you got me," said Judah. "Just what is that?"

"Grab me a beer and I'll tell you." Lloyd pointed to the cooler. "Get one for yourself, too."

"Well," said Judah as he opened the cooler and pulled out two Mooseheads, "it's five o'clock somewhere. So, what's your eleventh commandment?"

Lloyd took a slug off of his beer, turned to Judah, and said, "After thou hath kept the first Ten Commandments, then thou shalt have as much fun as thou possibly can."

Judah shook his head and laughed. "Damn, I love it! I hope you're the next Pope. It'll be one rockin' church!"

There were several places Lloyd liked to go where he would drop anchor and simply sit and talk if he had company, or think if he were by himself. His destination this day was the slough behind the beach at the northern end of Wassaw Island. There was always a nice breeze from the ocean, and soon he and Judah were stretched out in their chairs. The boat swung lazily from its anchor line.

Behind them the tree line on Wassaw was filled with cabbage palms, longleaf pines, cedars, and live oaks; its dark green contrasted with a light blue cap of sky interrupted by an occasional cauliflower cloud drifting over the Atlantic. The marsh has several different hues that time of year, ranging from forest green at the base of the spartina grass to lime near its top, where a dusting of dead grass the color of goldenrod rested, waiting for the next spring tide to carry it out to sea. In front was the beach, littered with the shells of channeled whelks, sand dollars, angel wings, and an occasional horseshoe crab. Up in the dunes amid the sea oats and morning glories, there might be a diamondback rattler waiting for a marsh rabbit to pass, or a terrapin in search of snails. Down at the water's edge, Judah and Lloyd watched as a laughing gull stole a fish from the beak of a brown pelican, while an osprey soared overhead, scanning the water below for its breakfast.

"You glad to be home?" asked Lloyd, knowing full well what Judah's answer would be.

"Yeah. It all got to be too much. I just couldn't hack it anymore, know what I mean?"

"Uh-huh, I know. Why do you think I got this boat?"

There was silence for a while as both men listened to the waves as they rushed up onto the beach and the sound of the wind as it blew through the sea oats. Then Lloyd asked, "What happened to that nice young lady you had at your party a few weeks ago? Didn't you say you had something going on with her before you came back home?"

"That's over, man. She turned out to be a real pain in the ass, and I'm too damn old for that shit."

Lloyd said nothing for several seconds. Then he twisted in his chair to face his friend. "You act like you've got something on your mind, Judah. You know, we've been friends since B.C. If there's anything I can help you with, just ask me."

For perhaps five minutes not another word was said. Then suddenly Judah blurted out, "I'm fucked up, Lloyd. I feel empty inside, like I've got nothing to hold on to. I mean, hell, I've got plenty of money and all kinds of 'things,' but I don't have anything to really live for, no wife, no children, none of that. I don't have anybody I want to grow old with. I don't think I believe in God anymore, either. It's really awful not to have that inner peace I hear so many people talk about. That's why I'm home again, I'm looking for something and I don't know what. I'm drinking way too much, but, shit Lloyd, I really don't give a fuck. I just want to blot a whole lot of bullshit out of my mind."

"I can't tell you how many times I've heard those exact same words and feelings, Judah," said Lloyd as he looked out over the horizon. "The first thing you've got to get through your head is that you're not different from anybody else. You're lucky, Judah. You know there's a problem and you've taken that most important first step."

"What's that?"

"You got the hell out of the situation you knew was eating you up inside. A lot of people don't have the resources to just up and haul ass from their jobs like you did. You also realize a need for something spiritual in your life, to believe in something that's bigger than you are. You're gonna be fine. It'll take some time, but you've got that hunger for something better."

"Well, what else do I do from here, Lloyd?'

"First things first, Judah."

"What's that?"

Lloyd smiled. "Hand me the boiled peanuts and another beer. Then spill your guts out if you feel like it—and remember, even though you're not a Catholic, I consider everything you say to be under the seal of the confessional. It will go no further than this boat. Understand?"

Judah had tears in his eyes when he began to speak. He had to stop a couple of times to gain his composure. "I think it all started when my first marriage ended. The whole marriage was really a disaster, but still, knowing I'd failed hit me hard."

"No, Judah," Lloyd interrupted, "I think it all started with you know who."

Judah let out a sigh, then nodded. "Yeah, you're probably right, but let's get to that later. Right now you need to hear about all the sorry-ass, shitty little things I've done or had done to me. They've brought me to where I am now. Then we can talk about her."

For the next couple of hours, Judah bled his heart out as he had never done before, not even to the expensive, social-climbing psychiatrist in Georgetown he had seen weekly for almost two years. Dr. Kesselman had put him on Prozac, then Zoloft, sometimes Halcion for sleep, and finally Sinaquan before Judah fired him after deciding he would rather tough it out on Absolut and tonic. When he had finished talking, he felt as if he had been wrung out, but at least he felt better. It was getting close to noon when he changed the subject. "Lloyd, there's something else I need to tell you about."

"Fire away, Judah."

"This has also got to be under the seal, okay?"

"You have my word."

"You see the old gun emplacement down there?" Judah pointed to the old fort sinking into the sand.

"Yeah. It sure has been slipping away over the years. What about it?"

"You're not gonna believe this, but just about a mile east of that thing, Billy Aprillia found what he thinks is the missing H-bomb lost back in fifty-eight. Do you remember that incident?"

"Yeah. There's been a lot about it in the paper lately."

"Well," continued Judah, "I think Billy's probably right. I think he did find it. Only problem is, I've been put between kind of a rock and a hard place by him. He wants me to help him get some reward money for the thing, and it's got me in a bind with my buddies in the White House. I don't know how to get out of it without hurting Billy, know what I mean?"

"Yeah, not hard to imagine. What do you think will happen?"

"I'm getting the impression from my friends that they don't want to play ball," said Judah as he rose from his chair and looked out over the sound. "It's going to get a little tricky with this thing. I think the proof Billy has is pretty solid, but I don't think the feds are gonna want to come up with the cash. I'm afraid that if Billy is able to prove he knows where the bomb is, then the government is going to say, 'Tell us all about it for free. If you don't we're going to make your life miserable'—and believe me, Uncle Sam has the resources to do just that. I doubt there's a lot of sympathy up in Washington for a guy who knows where that H-bomb is sitting and won't tell the government. I also doubt there's very much sympathy in the minds of the general public, either. I gotta be real careful, Lloyd. The last thing I need is for this situation to blow up in my face."

"I wish I could help, but this is way out of my league."

Judah returned to his seat. "I know that. I guess I just wanted you to know what else was eating at me."

"Can I change the subject a little?" asked Lloyd.

"Sure."

"I want to thank you again for your help in getting that money for my youth program. It seems to be working, and the money let me hire two more instructors who have really made a difference."

"I was glad to do it. When the president's man for faith-based initiatives saw the proposal, he really loved it. Your proposal kind of sold itself."

"Well, anyway, I just wanted to thank you again."

Judah reached over, flipped the cooler's lid up, and pulled out two more beers. "Has all that sex-abuse scandal stuff had any affect on you?"

Lloyd shook his head from side to side. "Aw, Judah, that really broke my heart. You just don't know. Before that, whenever I went anywhere with my collar on, it was like a key to people's hearts. You could just feel the warmth and respect. Now I see people looking at me funny, some with disgust—I haven't done a damn thing!"

"Good lord, Lloyd, I never thought you did!"

"I know you don't, Judah, but that whole thing really hurt the

Church and the entire priesthood. I've got to be on my guard all the time now. I don't even let myself be alone with a kid anymore—and that's really sad, because so much can be accomplished one-on-one, especially the youngsters I deal with. Most of them don't have a daddy around the house, you know, no positive male role model, and I've tried to be as much of one as I can, but all that crap really put me on my guard. I hate to have to think that way."

"This diocese didn't have any problems, did it?"

"No, not really. We had this one priest from Maryland, that's where he was in the seminary, and he turned out to be a problem. The bishop canned him before anything serious happened. That was before the whole sex-abuse thing broke. About six months after it all hit the fan, a complaint was filed against him by some guy in Maryland and he was arrested, tried, and found guilty. He's doing time now." Lloyd let out a long sigh. "We had a close call, but that's about it." Then he glanced at his watch and said, "Looks like it's time to head back in, Judah."

Hurricane Season

June—too soon;
July—stand by;
August—look out you must;
September—remember;
October—all over.
—Admiral Nares,
Hurricanes in the West

JUDAH WAS WATCHING a story about hurricanes on the Weather Channel when he heard someone knocking on his stern door. He was surprised to find it was the owner of the boat *Eventful.* He was even more surprised when the man produced identification stating he was special agent Augusto Camacho of the Department of Homeland Security.

"Mr. Benjamin, may I have a few words with you?"

"Yes, please come in. May I fix you something to drink."

"Yes, it's quite warm today."

"What would you like?"

"A Diet Coke would be fine, if you have it."

"Not a problem, Mr. Camacho. Please have a seat. I'll be right back."

Gusto removed his coat and placed it over the back of a soft brown leather chair, into which he then sank. For a while he studied the paintings and photos that adorned the paneled walls of the *Solitude*'s main salon. There were a dozen or so pictures of Judah and various politicians whom Gusto easily recognized, but the centerpiece was a photograph of Judah and the president in front of his desk in the Oval Office. Inscribed by the president himself were the words, "To Judah, a faithful friend and fearsome warrior." Below that was the president's signature. Gusto nodded and said to himself, "Pretty impressive, amigo. Pretty impressive." On the opposite wall was a large Ray Ellis canvas depicting a thunderstorm over marshland. Gusto recognized Ellis' work: indeed he owned a couple of his own; and he admired the way the artist had captured the grandeur of a storm moving across the open marsh. When Judah returned with the Diet Coke, Gusto was standing in front of the painting.

"Nice piece, Mr. Benjamin. Very nice. I imagine you can look out your window across the river any summer afternoon and have a pretty good chance of seeing exactly what Mr. Ellis has portrayed."

"Yeah," said Judah as he handed Gusto his drink. "We had a boomer yesterday that took down a couple of trees on the island. The rain was coming in sideways, and those sailboats anchored out there were bouncing around like toys—but, to tell you the truth, I loved every minute of it."

"So would I, Mr. Benjamin. I think it's the power of the storm that impresses me the most."

"Me too. I've liked them since I was a little boy. Once my father had to pull me from my tree house when there was a storm coming. I had planned to ride it out up there just to see what it was like."

Gusto laughed. "I don't want to take up any more of your time than I have to. May I explain the reason for my visit?"

"Sure," said Judah. "Have a seat, let's talk."

"Mr. Benjamin, as I told you, I work for Homeland Security, but right now I'm attached to the Defense Intelligence Agency. I know you're familiar with the D.I.A."

"Quite," said Judah. "Deputy Director Russell Fredrich and I are old friends."

"Yes, sir, I know. As a matter of fact, Director Fredrich is the one who sent me down here to talk with you. It's about the Tybee Bomb."

"I've been expecting someone to contact me about that. What do you want to know?"

"Mr. Benjamin, DOD is quite interested in what you know about the bomb, but they're having a hard time accepting the validity of your friend's claims, especially since Colonel Earl seems so certain he knows where the bomb is. Is it possible that both your friend and the colonel are talking about the same location?"

"From what I know, we're talking about sites that are miles apart."

"And what about the evidence you have, may I see it?"

"Let me ask you something, Mr. Camacho. Is the government willing to compensate my friend if the bomb is found?"

"They are."

"Gee, that's different from the vibes I've been getting. How much are they talking about?"

"Two hundred thousand. But it comes with strings attached."

"Why am I not surprised?" asked Judah sarcastically.

"Well, the main string is complete secrecy. No newspaper stories, no bragging rights, nothing. The money will be deposited in an offshore account when the government is satisfied that the information provided is accurate. Other than that it's standard boilerplate government lingo I'm sure you're familiar with."

"Are you going to be in town for a few more days, Agent Camacho?"

Gusto handed Judah one of his cards. "I'm here as long as I'm needed. You may contact me anytime at this number."

"It may be a day or two before I can get back to you, but rest assured you'll be hearing from me."

Judah didn't call Billy until nine that night. It was Hannah who answered.

"Hey, Hannah, it's Judah."

"I'd know your voice anywhere, Judah. How have you been?"

"Okay, I guess."

"Oh, Judah, I was just thinking about you. Tell me, is Page coming back anytime soon? I thought she was such an attractive girl."

"Don't think so. Tell me, is Billy around?"

"Sure, he's downstairs. I'll get him." There was a slight wait, and then:

"What's up, Bubba," asked Billy.

"I was just thinking about Miss Savannah, and thought I'd call and see how she was."

"She was your girlfriend before she was mine, remember?"

"Yeah, I sure do. Listen, I was wondering if you'd like to take the *Solitude* out with me tomorrow and spend the night down at Bradley Point."

Hurricane Debbie was conceived between the equator and the tropic of Cancer about a hundred miles from the west coast of Africa. The seminal event was a cluster of thunderstorms set off in the tropics by some type of surface convergence. Once this organized area of convergence formed, massive quantities of heat were released, causing a drop in atmospheric pressure. This forced more air to converge; and as it came together, the air mass was compelled to rise. This rising motion spawned even more thunderstorms, which released ever-increasing amounts of heat, reducing the pressure even more as the system moved westward.

The earth's rotation causes a weather phenomenon known as the Coriolis force; this force makes the weather spin along the equator when air is put into motion. As more air rises in a storm, additional air is forced toward its center, causing the circulation to become even brisker.

In the upper elevations of Debbie, during its embryonic stages, a high-pressure system formed, ensuring a steadily falling pressure through the net removal of air. This acted as a kind of high-level exhaust fan. Midway across the Atlantic, because of the Coriolis force, little Debbie had achieved well-defined circulation and sustained wind speeds high enough to earn her the status of a tropical depression. By the time she was approaching the Caribbean, her sustained winds were fifty-five miles an hour. Now she was a tropical storm. It was then that people along the southeastern Atlantic coast began to pay attention.

Judah was stretched out on his bed channel-surfing when a pretty young lady standing in front of a weather map got his interest. "We're keeping our eyes on this system about five hundred miles south of Hispaniola," she said, pointing to the map and turning sideways to show off her figure, "and we expect this system, now called Tropical Storm Debbie, to increase in strength over the next seventy-two hours and perhaps begin to threaten the Dominican Republic and Haiti sometime toward the end of the week. Stay tuned to the Weather Channel for further updates."

For some reason Judah had a funny feeling about that storm. He had been watching hurricanes move up the Atlantic seaboard all of his life, and the only other time he had had the same feeling was when he started tracking Hurricane Hugo back in 1989. He had been in Washington at the time, but he followed the storm's path closely because it was predicted to hit Savannah with 145 m.p.h. winds. Judah had been watching an update about the storm on CNN when Flip Spiceland, the weatherman, said, "Don't ask me why, but the National Weather Service predicts that Hugo will collide with a low-pressure system right about here, and if it does, that will throw its path off about one degree causing it to hit Charleston rather than Savannah." Savannah was spared while Hugo tore Charleston apart.

The last really devastating hurricane to hit Savannah was on August 27 and 28 of 1898, when a storm with winds estimated to be in excess of 130 m.p.h. made landfall just south of Tybee Island. It put Tybee and most of the other barrier islands underwater and took more than 2,500 lives along the Georgia and South Carolina coasts. The hurricane made landfall during a full moon and at high tide; and the storm surge was so great newspaper accounts reported that people standing on the bluff at Thunderbolt could see nothing but water where Wilmington and Whitemarsh islands are located.

In 1911, 1940, and 1947 Savannah took direct hits from weak Category 2 hurricanes, sustaining moderate damage and loss of life. On Labor Day of 1979 Hurricane David, another weak Category 2 storm, was the last to pass over the city. It caused no loss of life and only minor damage.

As opposed to Florida and the upper Carolinas, the Georgia coast leads a relatively charmed life when it comes to hurricanes. This has nothing to do with luck, however, but rather with geography and the Gulf Stream. Positioned as it is on the Great

Atlantic Bight, Georgia's coastline is about a hundred miles west of the historic hurricane tracks. These tracks are heavily influenced by the flow of warm water in the Gulf Stream. Although Savannah has many times felt the effects of hurricanes that hit along the Gulf Coast and then moved across the state from the south, those storms were mostly spent by the time they reached the city, carrying only drenching rains and little wind. For the most part a hurricane is a rare event along the Georgia portion of the Great Atlantic Bight.

"Did you hear about that storm down by Haiti?" asked Billy as he sat with Judah on the *Solitude*'s flying bridge and watched him pilot his boat through the Skidaway Narrows.

"Yeah, I sure did. I've got a bad feeling about that storm," said Judah just before he radioed the bridge tender at the narrows to say that he was coming through and needed the span raised. Billy nodded.

"They said it's already a hurricane, and it's expected to brush by Haiti this afternoon and gather strength. It's real far out, but the projected path brings it right up the Atlantic coast of Florida. We're in the strike zone," Billy grinned sourly as a line of cars started to form on the bridge after its center spans parted.

"Well," said Judah, "Debbie is still at least ten days away from here, so we don't have anything to worry about for a while."

"Yeah, but it's the beginning of July. Having a storm this early is kind of unusual."

Judah guided the *Solitude* past the Moon River, then Burnside Island, Vernon View, and into the Vernon River. They headed for their anchorage at Bradley Point on the northern end of Ossabaw Island. It was ten in the morning but the sun had already heated the marsh, causing the odor of spartina grass and the blue-black mud in which it grew to rise and float with the south wind in their direction. When they'd reached Green Island they turned south and began their passage through Hell Gate, where the smell of marsh and ocean were even stronger. Overhead Billy counted a dozen jet contrails making their marks across the sky before he inquired, "Whatcha thinkin' about, Bubba?"

"About you and me on the *St. Patrick* and all the times we spent up in Bradley Creek or over in the Odingsell River. They sure were good times, Billy."

"That's a long time ago, Judah. I remember what a hurry I was in to grow up and be on my own. I didn't know how good I had it." Billy sniffed the air. "Damn," he said, "I always thought the marsh smelled a lot like roasted marshmallows, but I've never smelled it so sweet. All of a sudden it smells like Juicy Fruit gum or something." Then Billy put his hand to his head. He was a little dizzy but didn't say anything to Judah. After a few moments the dizziness and the sweet smell passed.

That night after dinner Judah and Billy sat topside and watched the first meteor shower of the summer cut orange streaks across the indigo sky. The Constellation Aquarius rode low over the Atlantic.

"I've been contacted by a government agent about Miss Savannah," said Judah as he worked on his third Grey Goose over the rocks.

"I figured you had when you called. What did he have to say."

"They've offered two hundred K if it really is the bomb, but they want to see your evidence first."

"What did you tell the guy?"

"That I'd get back to him in a few days. What do you think?"

"I was hoping for a whole lot more, you know, in the millions."

"Do you want to at least show this guy the tail fins and see what he says?"

"I don't know," said Billy. "I'll think about it. Right now I'd like another drink."

Abdul Aleem's apartment on West 32nd Street was the top floor of a sprawling Victorian-era mansion that had seen better days. It sat close to the corner of 32nd and Montgomery streets in a high-crime area where the sound of gunfire sometimes punctuated the night. The apartment's furnishings looked as battered and weary as the old house, and the only decorations Abdul had were a few pieces of African art he had purchased from a store on Broughton Street that specialized in such items. Most of the clothes he wore when he wasn't working came from the same store, and that wardrobe consisted primarily of North African–style garments like dashikis. He also had a penchant for the galabia, which resembles a priest's cassock, and Moroccan Zaytuna cloaks, like the ones he had seen Libya's Mu'ammar Qaddafi wearing on TV. Along with his ever-present skull cap, he often wore these clothes to prayer services at the Massid Jihad Mosque. Abdul's ardor for his new religion paralleled that of most religious converts, and as a result he spent a lot of free time reading publications from the Nation of Islam. His best friends were two other black men he had met at his mosque.

Hussam Udeen, whose name meant "The Sword of Faith," was a thirty-six-year-old from Harlem. His former name was Robert "High Five" Greene until he had been converted to Islam by an apostle of Louis Farrakhan. Hussam had been a cab driver in New York who'd moved to Savannah when summoned by his childless great aunt Lucile, who'd promised a healthy sum of money if he would look after her in her old age. She died just two years after Hussam had come to Savannah, and he had inherited her home along with the tidy nest egg she had planned to live on. Although Hussam had never been married, he did have two children back in Harlem, with whom he had very little contact. Just as in New York Hussam drove a cab in Savannah. Through his work he had come to know the city and its people well.

Abdul's other friend was thirty-eight-year-old Alphonso Simmons from the Cabbagetown district of Atlanta, a rough area of poverty close to the Braves baseball stadium. Alphonso had attended Morehouse College on a football scholarship and had shown great potential until he was accused of assaulting one of the cheerleaders. The charge was false and he was ultimately acquitted, but the damage had been done. As a result he became embittered with the justice system in particular and America in general, which made him ripe pickings for the style of radical Islam that painted all blacks as victims of white oppression. Alphonso joined the Nation of Islam and eventually started rubbing shoulders with Islamic radicals of Middle Eastern descent who had contact with other radicals in their countries of origin. One of these individuals attended his mosque.

After the debacle at Morehouse, Alphonso drifted through a couple of different jobs until he landed a position at one of the Hyatt Hotels in Atlanta. He fared well there, and was ultimately promoted and transferred to the Bay Street Hyatt in Savannah. He had been married once, had fathered a child that he supported, and was dating a girl who was also a radical; but unlike Abdul and Hussam, Alphonso eschewed the gaudier trappings of Islam. His style of dress was more mainstream, but he was every bit the radical: He could hold his own with anyone when it came to religious and, especially, political discussions. Alphonso paid close attention to current events and spent his off-hours on the Internet, reading and researching all he could find on Islamic fundamentalism and its war on Western civilization.

One Friday after evening services Abdul and his friends met at his apartment for an impromptu dinner. When Abdul clicked his TV on, Bill O'Reilly filled the screen blasting a Muslim cleric from a mosque in Washington that he believed supported terrorist activities.

"That cracker," said Abdul as he watched O'Reilly drill Mullah Omar Akmed, one of Louis Farrakhan's lieutenants, "I'd like to shoot him for treating our brother that way."

"Me, too," chimed in Hussam, who looked like Mike Tyson with a beard, "but shooting would be too good for him. I'd like to castrate him and stuff his nuts down his throat first."

"How 'bout cuttin' his head off on camera like our brothers do in Iraq?" said Alphonso. "That would really send a message to every cracker in this stinking country, wouldn't it?"

"Yeah," responded Hussam.

Abdul nodded and said "Uh-huh, it sure would."

Over a dinner of frozen chicken pot pies, the three continued their discussion of politics and how unjust life in America really was. Their collective anger and resentment grew. When they returned to the living room there was a story on the TV about a white police officer in Los Angles who had shot and killed a black teenager he thought was armed, but wasn't.

"I wish I could do something to this country as payback for all they've done to us," Alphonso spat out through gritted teeth.

Abdul turned the sound down, and looked squarely at Alphonso. "You really mean that, brother?"

"I'm as serious as a heart attack, Abdul—but what can I do? About all I could do is ride around and shoot a few crackers like those two brothers did up in D.C. before they finally killed me. I want to hit 'em hard, like on nine-eleven."

Abdul said nothing for several seconds. Then he looked at Alphonso and Hussam in turn and said firmly, "I know how to do that."

Both men stared at each other; then Hussam snickered. "How you gonna do that, with an atomic bomb or something?"

A smile crept across Abdul's face. "That's exactly how I can do it. You remember hearing about that H-bomb that's lost out in Wassaw Sound?"

Both men nodded. Hussam said, "Yeah, I remember. There was something on the news about it a few weeks ago."

"Well, my brothers, Allah be praised, because I know where it is." Abdul swore his friends to secrecy and explained, to their astonishment, what he had witnessed on the decks of the *St. Patrick*. He finished his account with the statement that he had the GPS coordinates hidden away, waiting for someone to help him use them against America, The Great Satan.

Hannah and Billy were having dinner with Judah at a tucked-away restaurant in Sandfly called the Driftaway Café when Billy had his second episode of dizziness accompanied by a sweet aroma.

"Damn, there it is again," said Billy.

"There what is?" asked Hannah as she dipped her fried shrimp into the cocktail sauce.

"I'm dizzy again like I was on Judah's boat." Then he added, "What smells so sweet all of sudden? Did somebody come through here with a can of air freshener?"

Hannah and Judah both sniffed the air. "All I smell is food being cooked," said Judah.

"Me, too," added Hannah. "I don't smell anything sweet."

"Well, I sure do." Billy leaned back in his chair. "This is weird."

"John-Morgan and Ann Marie are meeting us here in a little while," said Judah. "Why don't you ask him about it."

With a perplexed look on his face Billy replied, "The smell's gone now, but that's a good idea."

After dinner Billy managed to get John-Morgan aside in the cocktail lounge. "Listen, I've been having dizzy spells, and at the same time I start smelling something real sweet. What's going on, John-Morgan, is it anything to be concerned about?"

Dr. Hartman felt a stab in his stomach when he heard Billy's question. He looked directly at his friend and asked, "How long has this been going on?"

"The first time was a few days ago out on Judah's boat. Then I just had another episode while we were eating dinner before y'all got here."

John-Morgan thought for a moment, then asked, "Have you had any headaches or nosebleeds, anything like that?"

"No, I just get dizzy and smell something sweet. It only lasts a short time."

John-Morgan looked down at the floor and toyed with his drink for a few seconds before he looked up at Billy and asked, "You want the straight no bullshit scoop?"

"Hell, yeah, I want the straight scoop. What the fuck's going on with me?"

"Billy," said John-Morgan slowly, "what you're having is referred to as an olfactory aura."

Billy blinked and said, "You mean the smells?"

"Exactly. The dizziness could be caused by a number of things, but to my knowledge an olfactory aura can be caused by only one thing."

"Yeah, what's that?"

"An expanding mass in your brain," responded John-Morgan, who tried as hard as he could not to sound too grave.

Billy felt as if he had been punched in the gut. He swallowed hard and asked, "You mean a brain tumor?"

"Yes, Billy, that's exactly what I mean."

Billy dropped his head. His eyes wandered across the barroom floor while he tried to digest what he had just been told.

"Billy," said John-Morgan as he put his hand on his friend's shoulder, "I could be wrong. God knows I've been wrong about things before, but you need to have an M.R.I. pronto. I'll call somebody in the morning and get you set up for that, okay?"

Billy, though dazed, managed to nod. In a whisper he said, "Yeah, whatever you say. How bad is it, man?"

"Let's wait and see. We won't know anything until we get that M.R.I., so until then I'm going to assume that whatever's causing your problem is benign. I want you to do the same thing, okay?"

"Will I have to have brain surgery?"

"Look, let's cross that bridge when we get to it. I've been honest with you, and I'm being honest again when I tell you that I want you to be concerned but not panicked, all right? Can you do that for me and for yourself?"

"Is it okay to have a drink? I mean, I need one."

"Hey, man, not a problem at all. As a matter fact, I'm buying."

Two days later Billy had his M.R.I. The results were not good. He did indeed have an expanding mass in his brain that had been exerting pressure on the olfactory nerve, causing his hallucinations. John-Morgan referred him to a neurosurgeon, who scheduled him for a craniotomy and tumor debulking that would allow for a pathological examination. In a room at St. Joseph's Hospital, Judah and Hannah watched WTOC's weatherman Pat Prokop while they waited for Billy to return from surgery.

"The National Weather Service has just issued its noon update on Hurricane Debbie," said Pat as he stood before a satellite image of the storm, "and those coordinates put her eye about two hundred miles due east of Barbados. Debbie is moving on a northwesterly path at about three miles an hour with sustained winds in excess of 125 miles an hour. That makes her a strong Category 3 storm on the Saffir-Simpson scale. Debbie is expected to strengthen and increase in speed over the next twenty-four hours. She has winds extending out for over five hundred miles, and right now the eye-wall is projected to pass somewhere very near to the islands of Antigua and Barbuda within forty-eight to seventy-two hours, depending upon what happens along the way. Several computer models show this hurricane making landfall in a wide area from central Florida up to about the South Carolina–North Carolina border; as you can see Savannah sits at the center of this cone. There's no need for concern right now, but you need to stay tuned to WTOC for all your weather updates as this monster makes it way through these warm Atlantic waters."

Judah turned the sound down on the TV as he looked over at Hannah, who was sitting by Billy's empty bed. "Something else to worry about," he said. Hannah smiled.

"When it rains, it pours."

"Yep." Judah let out a sigh. "How much longer do you think Billy'll be in surgery?"

"From what Dr. Baker said, probably a couple more hours." Hannah reached out and put her hand over Judah's. "I'm glad you're here with me. It's bad enough as it is, but without somebody, especially you, I don't think I could make it through."

Judah patted her hand. "And I'm glad you're here, too, because I feel so damned helpless right now."

This was the first time they had been alone together for any great length of time, and at first their conversation was dominated by Billy's plight. After a while, however, the enormity of the circumstance exhausted them; their conversations began to wander. Finally it was Hannah who brought up the topic of their long-ago love affair.

"Did you ever hate me for what happened, Judah?"

"I hated what happened, but I never hated you. I was too much in love with you to hate you. The pain I felt numbed me from a lot of emotions for a long time, but I could never be angry with you. I understood that you had to marry Clark because you were pregnant, but it was just losing you that hurt so much. It was like I lost an arm or a leg or something. Everything was fine one minute, and then the next minute it was over." Judah looked plaintively and even miserably at Hannah, who smiled. Tears came to her eyes.

"There's a lot you don't know about, Judah. Maybe one day I'll feel like telling you."

"What do you mean?"

"I mean the reason I did what I did, Judah. It's not exactly what you think it is."

"You broke up with me and got married to Clark because you were pregnant, didn't you?"

Hannah grew silent. She dropped her head for a moment and then looked at Judah again. "This isn't the right time, Judah. There's just too much for both of us to deal with right now. Let's wait until things calm down a little. Then we can talk, okay."

Judah started to say something when the room door opened and two attendants pushed a gurney in with Billy on it. He was groggy, but he managed to give Hannah a thumbs-up as he was transferred to his bed. For the next couple of hours he would drift in and out of sleep; but by the time Dr. John West was making his afternoon rounds, Billy was sitting up in bed sipping apple juice.

"They told me you did just fine in the O.R." said Dr. West in a soft Alabama accent as he placed his stethoscope to Billy's chest and listened. Billy didn't wait for the doctor to finish his exam.

"What did they find?" he asked.

Dr. West removed the stethoscope from his ears and let it hang around his neck. He pushed back the sides of his open lab coat, sank his hands deeply into his pockets, and took a deep breath. "Billy, how long have we known each other?"

"From the time I catered your first oyster roast back in 1979."

"That's a long time to know somebody, isn't it?"

"Yeah," said Billy slowly. He was now anticipating bad news.

"I guess I kinda read you as the type of person who wants the truth fast and hard, so I'm not gonna beat around the bush with you." Nevertheless the doctor paused for a moment. "The results of your frozen section biopsy indicate that your tumor is something called a glioblastoma multiforme. This is the worst kind of brain cancer there is. I emphasize these are the preliminary results. We'll know something more definitive when the tissue has been further processed, but right now it's not good. I'm gonna want to see you in my office in a few days. By that time we'll have all the information, and we'll be in a position to talk about treatment options and anything else you want to know about." He placed his hand on Billy's shoulder, then continued. "It's hard to tell people these kinds of things, Billy. I'm sorry it's not better news."

"I know you are, Dr. West, and I don't envy your position, but I'm not surprised. I had a hunch I was in serious trouble."

Two days later Billy and Hannah were sitting in Dr. West's private office. Billy's head was still bandaged, and sometimes he felt a little woozy; but all in all he was doing a lot better than he had expected. He had done a lot of soul-searching since the surgery and had had long conversations with Hannah, Judah, and Monsignor Bryan as he fought to come to grips with what had befallen him. He had even entertained thoughts that the preliminary results were wrong. Those thoughts were fleeting as he prepared himself to hear the worst.

Bowties were a trademark of Dr. West. Today he was wearing a yellow one with blue polkadots when he entered his office and greeted Billy and Hannah. The white shirt he had on was neatly pressed, and his kind eyes looked sympathetically at Billy from behind a pair of round, owlish glasses.

"So, how are you feeling, Billy?"

"Better than expected."

"Well, I have all the results." Dr. West casually took his seat behind his desk. "And they're just what I feared. Your tumor was a glioblastoma multiforme."

Billy nodded slightly. "I've been preparing myself for that. Can I be cured?"

Dr. West glanced down at a stack of papers on his desk, then looked back at Billy. "I'm going to tell you what my personal experience has been with this tumor, and what all the literature says about it." The doctor drew a breath and continued. "Billy, this tumor is going to kill you. How long it takes depends on what you choose to do, and it is entirely your choice; but even if we hit this thing with all we've got, it's been my experience that you probably won't live longer than two years at the most."

Hannah was sitting next to Billy. Her grip on his hand tightened when she heard the insidious words, "two years." She had been hoping for so much more.

"What kind of treatment are you talking about, Dr. West?"

"Dr. Baker took out all of the tumor he could find, but it'll grow back quickly. You could have it removed once more, only to have it recur again. That will give you some more time. You can also have radiation treatment, but it's not really that effective against this type of tumor. You can also take chemotherapy, which will give you better results, or you could take a combination of chemo, radiation, and even surgical resection if you wanted to. Most people opt for the chemo and radiation, which seems to work best."

"I heard the chemo will make me sick as a dog."

"Unfortunately, you're correct. There are a number of side effects with these drugs, and they're all unpleasant. The dilemma facing you is a quality-of-life issue versus a longevity issue. You have to ask yourself if living a couple more years and not feeling very good is worth it as opposed to doing nothing at all and having a few good months before this disease begins to really take you over and eventually kill you. It's not an easy choice you have, but it's one you'll have to make."

Billy leaned back in his chair and sighed heavily. "Whew. I never dreamed I'd be hearing something like this, at least not at my age." Then he thought for a moment and asked, "What if I decide to do nothing? How long do you think I'll have before things get bad?"

"Well, your tumor was detected before it was very large, and this is in your favor. What I'm going to tell you is a guess, but it's an educated guess."

"I understand, Dr. West."

"My experience with a patient like you has been about three to four months where you feel fairly well, where you feel like doing things—you know, enjoying the time you have left before this disease begins to incapacitate you. After that, you could last another couple of months."

"What happens to me then?"

This was the question Dr. West dreaded the most.

"Generally you'll start getting headaches at first. You'll have nausea and vomiting. We can control most of those symptoms with medications. Then as the tumor begins to really increase in size, you'll start having seizures, which can also be controlled somewhat. Toward the end you could have some paralysis, sensory loss, visual loss, personality changes, and of course loss of bowel and bladder control. It's not going to be pretty, but I'm confident I can keep you comfortable and out of pain."

"When can you start me on the chemo and radiation?"

"Immediately."

Billy was quiet for a few seconds. "I want to go home and think about it, Dr. West. I'm not so sure two years of feeling rotten is any better than three months of feeling good and then two dying. What do you think?"

Dr. West smiled. "I know what I'd choose, but I'm not going to tell you because this is a decision you have to make on your own, and I don't want to influence you in any way. It's your life, Billy, not mine."

"Give me a few days, Doc, and I'll let you know what I want to do."

Three days later Billy called his doctor.

"I'm opting for a few good months, Dr. West. I have some living to do."

Softly, Dr. West replied, "That would be my choice too, Billy."

Whenever Abdul and his two friends were together, their conversations always centered on how they could utilize the Tybee bomb as a weapon against the United States. No matter how hard they tried, however, they hadn't been able to come up with a feasible plan.

"We could try to pull it up with the shrimp boat I work on," said Abdul as the three of them sat around his rickety kitchen table one afternoon, "but I don't know how we'd do that. Maybe just drag over it and hope it got snagged."

"Them winches strong enough to pull the bomb up?" Hassam asked.

"My Uncle Elijah say they can lift eight thousand pounds," answered Abdul. "One of them articles in the paper said the bomb weighed seventy-five hundred pounds, so I guess the boat could lift the bomb. But it'd be close."

"Okay," interjected Alphonso, "let's say we somehow manage

to get your boss's shrimp boat all to ourselves; and let's say we manage to snag that bomb in the nets; and let's even say we even manage to haul the thing up and drop it into the hold. Then whatda we do?"

A silence fell over the room as the three plotters struggled to come up with a sensible answer. After a moment Abdul said, "We could sail to Cuba and give it to Castro."

"What good would that do?" asked Hassam. "He isn't about to use it against America, man."

"Well, if we do get the thing into that boat," said Alphonso, "couldn't we contact somebody in Al-Qaeda and turn it over to them?"

"You know anybody in Al-Qaeda?" Hassam asked.

Alphonso dropped his head and quietly said, "No." In actuality he did know someone who had an Al-Qaeda contact, but he had decided to keep this information to himself.

"Well, neither do I, and if we go nosing 'round askin' questions 'bout who you know in Al-Qaeda and stuff like that, then the Feds will be comin' by for a visit," replied Hassam forcefully.

The three grew quiet again until Abdul shifted in his chair. "You know, I remember readin' in the paper that there's no way the bomb's gonna go off. What they're really afraid of is a radiation leak. They're even afraid that if the bomb does get pulled up it might crack open and leak radiation into the environment. Then it could poison all the water up and down the coastline and make it unlivable for thousands of years."

Hassam was the shrewdest and most cunning of the trio. What Abdul said started him thinking.

"You're on to something, brother," said Hassam as he stroked his beard and thought about the bomb. "You know, if we was able to crack that bomb open, then we wouldn't have to worry about hauling it up or nothin'. Think about what a blow it would be against all these white devils in their fancy houses to have radiation running right up on their lily white beaches!"

All three smiled as they thought about millions of people being evacuated from the shoreline and the closing of harbors from Savannah to who knew where as a plume of highly radioactive

Plutonium 239 worked its way to the Gulf Stream and crept northward toward New York City. It would be a disaster of unimaginable proportions.

"How do you propose cracking that thing open?" asked Alphonso, who liked the idea immensely. "Use a jackhammer or something?"

Hassam shook his head. "No, brother, a jackhammer wouldn't work. What we need are some explosives. All we need to do is blow that bomb up to crack it open. And we don't need that much, either."

"What are you talkin' about?" asked Abdul.

"Remember when you said you read in that newspaper article that there were four-hundred pounds of TNT in the bomb that was used to get the atomic reaction going?"

"Yeah—and I remember the article said they were worried that the TNT might go off if the bomb was ever moved, too. I remember that part, Hassam."

Hassam nodded in approval and continued. "What I'm saying is that if we can plant some stuff around the bomb, that when we set it off, the TNT inside the bomb will probably go off too, so we need just enough to rock it real good."

"Yeah, I understand," said Alphonso. "But where do we find explosives for that kind of thing?"

With a sinister smile on his face, Hassam sat back in his chair. He was silent for a few moments before he said, "We live just about thirty miles from Fort Stewart. It's the largest military reservation east of the Mississippi. You know why it's so big, Alphonso?"

"No."

"'Cause even the biggest guns the Army has can't shoot a round outta the boundaries of that fort, that's why."

Alphonso blinked and said, "Okay, so what?"

"Not all of them shells they shoot go off, Alphonso, and they been shooting some big shells ever since World War II. That means there's probably thousands of unexploded ammunition of all kinds sittin' in the woods at Fort Stewart."

Alphonso thought for a moment, then said dubiously, "So what you want us to, go down there and hunt some up?"

"That's not necessary, my brother. I know some people who've already done that."

Billy was on the fly bridge at the helm of the *Solitude* as he slowed the boat to a stop off Beach Hammock Island at the north end of Wassaw Sound. "Is this good enough, Judah?" he asked.

Judah looked around, then checked the depth finder. "It's low tide, and we've still got eighteen feet under us. Go ahead and drop the anchor, Billy."

John-Morgan and Lloyd were also on the fly bridge. They watched Billy closely as he depressed the remote switch for the windlass and listened as *Solitude*'s anchor chain played out. All they could think about was how their friend was going to handle the catastrophic news he had been given only a week before. So far he seemed to be doing well, but both physician and priest knew by experience that outward appearances often disguised turmoil and anguish. Instinctively both men glanced at each other. They exchanged looks that betrayed their concern.

"This trip was a good idea, Judah," said Lloyd as he twisted the cap off a bottle of Budweiser, causing the muscles of his well-developed forearm to flex and expand. "I really needed some time off, and the only way I could get away for two nights was during the week. The weather's fine and this spot's perfect." Then Lloyd held his beer up. "To my buddies and a good time."

The news of Billy's cancer had darkly affected all of his friends, but Judah was hit the hardest. At first he tried to talk Billy out of his decision to take no treatment; he said that money was no object and he would fly Billy anywhere in the world and pay for all treatment if only he would try to fight the disease. All of his pleadings, unfortunately, were in vain; finally he had to relent. "Okay, then, I'll shut up only if you'll promise to tell me if there's anything special you want. I mean like a trip to Europe or something. Whatever you want, I want to get it for you."

"All I want is to be around my friends and live like I always have," said Billy. Then he thought for a moment and added, "Actually there is one thing I'd like for you to do."

"Anything."

"Let's take your boat out to the sound for a few days. You know, just you, me, John-Morgan, and Lloyd. We can fish, swim, grill out, get drunk, and just have a good time."

Judah jerked his head up, and with a smile on his face said, "Just tell me when." That was the seed of the trip Judah was hosting, and it gave him immeasurable satisfaction to be able to do something for his friend. Now he settled into one of the chairs in the main salon and flicked on a forty-eight-inch HDTV.

"In an hour or so we'll take the tender and cast for some shrimp. If we're any good at all, we'll have some fried shrimp just like Elijah used to make when we worked on the *St. Patrick*. Remember, Billy?"

"We didn't know how lucky we were," said Billy as he put his head back and relaxed.

The TV was tuned to the Weather Channel, and the forecaster from the National Hurricane Center in Miami was giving an update on Hurricane Debbi.

"As everyone knows by now, Debbie slammed into San Juan, Puerto Rico, with sustained winds of 140 miles an hour, causing heavy damage and killing at least fifty people. At the present time we're showing the eye of the storm to be located at approximately 67.5 degrees west and 22.3 degrees north. This puts the center of Debbie near the tropic of Cancer."

All the men fell quiet as they watched the satellite image of the hurricane swirling in the Atlantic.

"Debbie is moving in a generally northwesterly direction at a little over five miles an hour. If our predictions are correct we expect her to land a glancing blow on the Turks and Caicos islands in about twenty-four hours and to continue along this general path, which will take her just east of the Bahamas sometime this weekend. Folks along the Atlantic seaboard need to be keeping a sharp eye on Debbie, as we predict she'll make landfall somewhere between Jacksonville and Charleston in about nine days."

"What are you gonna do with the boat if it looks like that thing is coming here?" asked John-Morgan.

Judah shrugged. "I think this boat's too big to anchor in the river if we're having winds over a hundred miles an hour. I don't think there's an anchor made that can hold a boat this size in place, not in that kind of wind. I'm sure as hell not leaving her at the dock. It'd be a wreck in short order. When the storm's path is more clearly defined, I guess I'll get Tran and Abdul and we'll run like hell in the opposite direction. Probably south if it looks like Debbie will hit Savannah or above. I guess north if it's below Brunswick somewhere. This is a fast boat, and I can go comfortably on the outside even if the seas are up. We're here for three days. I'll start worrying about Debbie when our party is over."

Judah and John-Morgan took the tender up House Creek to cast for shrimp while Billy and Lloyd stayed behind and sat on the stern, where they drank beer, ate boiled peanuts, and watched a half dozen shrimp boats dragging just outside the sound. The two hadn't been alone together since Billy had his surgery; and Lloyd was happy that Billy had opted out of shrimping and had stayed behind to keep him company.

"You feelin' okay, man?" he asked. Sunlight filled the deck; and Billy was wearing a Benedictine Cadets baseball cap to cover the area of his head that had been shaved and bore the scar from his surgery. After a moment he pushed his Ray-Bans back on his nose and fished around in the cooler for another beer.

"I don't feel bad, not physically at least, but I just don't know how I feel right yet. I mean I'm just numb right now. Kind'a tryin' to sort out how I feel, you know?"

"Yep, I know where you're comin' from. Unfortunately I've known too many people who've been in your shoes. It comes with my line of work. I just want you to know that I'm always here for you, twenty-four-seven, any hour of the day or night. You call, I'm there for you."

"I know, Lloyd. You've already done a lot for me. I mean helping me get back into the church and all. I don't think I'd be able to handle this in the right way if I hadn't come back to my roots."

"It's a hell of a thing you're going through, Billy—I think you've made the right decision. I just want you to realize that you're in a unique position."

"How's that?"

"Have you ever heard the question about what a man would do if he knew he had only a few weeks or months to live?"

"Oh, yeah," answered Billy as his eyes followed a pelican that crash-dived into the water just yards away and emerged with a fish in its beak. "I'm that kind of guy."

"Yes, you sure are, and it's an opportunity that nobody envies. But everybody wishes they had the moral gumption to live like they knew tomorrow was their last day. This has really put things in focus for you, hasn't it?"

Seconds after Lloyd's question Billy suddenly buried his face in his hands and began to weep uncontrollably. His shoulders heaved, and soon his tears splattered upon the deck. Lloyd reached over and placed his hand on Billy's back. He patted it gently.

Through his sobs Billy managed to say, "I'm sorry. I'm sorry for this, Lloyd."

"No, my sweet friend, there's nothing to be sorry for. You've got to let your pain out, it's a good thing. Is this the first real cry you've had?"

Billy pulled his T-shirt up and wiped his face with it. Then he nodded. "Yeah. I knew this was coming, I just didn't want to break down in front of anybody. Especially Hannah."

"There'll be more tears, Billy, and there's nothing wrong with that. After a while they'll get less and less as you begin accepting what's happening and you start seeing and feeling God's love for you. You have your faith to carry you through this, and I promise it will be like a soothing balm. I know, I've seen similar situations many times, and it seems that these people grow to be almost joyous in their plight because they're drawn closer and closer to God. I wish I could feel that kind of joy. The saddest people of all, and the ones who seem to suffer the most, are the ones who have no faith. It's an agonizing thing to watch."

Billy's eyes were red and swollen. Mucous ran from his nose, and he used his shirt tail to wipe it off.

"I'm just scared and pissed off, Lloyd. I'm not so much scared of dying—hell, everybody has to die. I'm just scared about what's going to happen to me before I die, and I'm pissed because I had so much to live for. I mean I was happy with Hannah, happier than

I'd ever been before with anybody, and she was happy with me. Now that's all gonna end and it pisses me off!"

Billy and Lloyd talked for another hour or so; and by the time Judah and John-Morgan had returned with a cooler full of shrimp, Billy was feeling and looking much better. That evening the shrimp were headed and peeled, dipped in Elijah's special batter, deep fried to a golden brown, and washed down with more cold beer than any of them had consumed in a long time. All of the old stories they'd told about themselves and their friends were dusted off and told once again to howls of laughter. As the stars filled the sky and the heat of the day was shooed away by an east wind, the world seemed in balance for the crew of the *Solitude*, and Billy felt at peace.

Hurricane Debbie

> When it is evening, ye say, It will be fair weather: for the sky is red.
>
> And in the morning, It will be foul weather to day: for the sky is red and lowring. O ye hypocrites, ye can discern the face of the sky; but can ye not discern the signs of the times?
>
> —Matthew 16: 2–3

JUDAH WAS AWAKENED the next morning by his cell phone. With his eyes still closed and his head throbbing from too much alcohol the night before, he felt for the phone on the night stand next to his bed, grabbed it, and pressed it against his ear.

"Hello."

"Mr. Benjamin?"

Judah managed to prop himself up on his right elbow while he shifted the phone to his left ear and squinted at the sunlight that poured through the port-side window.

"Mr. Benjamin," asked the voice again.

"Yeah," said Judah.

"This is Agent Gusto Camacho. I haven't heard back from you in a couple of weeks and I was wondering if anything had changed regarding the subject we most recently discussed."

"Oh, Agent Camacho, please forgive me for not getting back to you sooner. Yes, something has come up, something quite serious, and to be completely frank, what has happened really just put everything else on the back burner."

Gusto's voice had an air of concern as he asked, "Has something happened to the object we discussed, Mr. Benjamin?"

"No, it's not that at all. As far as I know nothing has changed with that, but my friend who provided me with the information we discussed has become seriously ill since we last talked. It was sudden and unexpected, and it's very serious. Quite frankly he has a fatal disease, a brain tumor, which was diagnosed only days after our meeting, and it's thrown both him and me for a loop. He's not expected to live more than a few months."

"I'm very sorry to hear that, Mr. Benjamin."

Judah was now sitting on the side of his bed, trying to remember if he had any aspirin on board. He numbly replied, "Look, just call me Judah and I'll call you Gusto, okay? All this formal bullshit gets on my nerves."

"That's fine with me, Judah. After speaking with Director Fredrich, I feel like I know you well enough to be on a first-name basis anyway."

Judah stood, walked over to the dresser, and looked at himself in the mirror. Rough, he thought.

"Well, next time you see Russ, give him my best, will you?"

"You bet—but does your friend still have an interest in making a deal? I mean is he even capable of talking, know what I mean?"

"Yeah, oh yeah. As a matter of fact he's with me right now. He and a couple of our old friends are spending a few days on my boat. We're anchored out in Wassaw Sound, just kinda decompressing you might say."

"Is he or anyone else within earshot, Judah?"

"No, not at all. We partied down pretty hard last night and it's my guess everybody else is still sleeping it off."

"Good. I'm sure I don't have to remind you about the gravity of this situation."

Judah, irritated by that comment, shot back angrily. "Come on, Gusto. Russ Fredrich must have made it abundantly clear to you that I didn't just fall off some fuckin' turnip truck!"

"I'm sorry, Judah, but being careful is part of my job."

Judah rubbed his head and sighed, "Hey, I'm sorry too. I've got a bad hangover right now and I didn't mean to pop off at you like that. It's been a really rough couple of weeks for me and my buddy. Let me talk things over with him again, you know, about the proof you wanted, and I'll get back to you sometime after, say, one or two this afternoon. Okay?"

Judah dumped three or four St. Joseph's aspirins into his hand—he wasn't sure how many—then made his way to the galley, where he pulled a long-necked Bud from the fridge and used it to wash them down. He braced himself against the sink for a few seconds, fully expecting to puke them back up. When the wave of nausea finally passed, he put the bottle to his mouth and sucked down half of it. He was about to finish off the rest of the bottle when he was startled by a voice from the salon.

"Hair of the dog?" asked Lloyd, who'd been up since sunrise. Judah was a little embarrassed, but not enough to lie about it.

"Yeah, Monsignor, I guess you might say that." Judah flopped onto the sofa, put his head back, and waited for the aspirin to do its work. "You aren't hurting?" he added, keeping his eyes closed while he pressed the cold bottle against his temple.

"A little bit, but I didn't put the pedal to the metal quite as much you boys did. Plus, I took the tender to the beach for a run. Kinda got the poisons outta my blood stream, if you know what I mean. I even watched the sun come up over the ocean as I ran. Really an impressive sight."

"I bailed out early last night, at least early for me," said Judah. "How did Billy do?"

"John-Morgan and I put him to bed a little after one. I imagine he'll be one hurtin' buckaroo when he finally opens his eyes this morning."

"Poor bastard," answered Judah, "I don't know what I'd do if I were in his shoes. I'd probably stay fucked up all day long." Judah turned the TV on, and as he waited for it to warm up, he finished the rest of his beer. "Let's see what's happening with Hurricane Debbie," he said as he walked to the galley and grabbed another one.

When Judah returned the Weather Channel's Jim Cantori was giving a live report from Nassau in the Bahamas. He was standing on a beach; behind him a row of tall palms swayed in the wind in front of a group of deserted condos outlined by a slate-gray sky.

"Right now," said Cantori, "it looks like Debbie is going to miss the Bahamas. As a matter of fact, the computer models at the National Hurricane Center are predicting that Debbie, within the next twelve hours or so, will make a turn to the northeast, taking her out into the open waters of the Atlantic and away from our coast. That's the good news. The bad news is that these same projections show Bermuda as Debbie's next likely landfall, perhaps over the weekend. Of course we'll be here with all the information about this dangerous storm, but for right now, let's turn our attention to the west coast of Africa."

Judah and Lloyd watched as a satellite photo appeared on the screen, showing a band of thunderstorms forming off Sierra Leone and moving westward. "Here's something else we'll be keeping our eye on over the next week or so," continued Cantori. "This system seems to have all the elements needed for the formation of another hurricane as it moves across these warm waters and picks up steam. But for now it looks like residents along the Florida, Georgia, and Carolina coasts can relax. From Nassau in the Bahamas, I'm Jim Cantori for the Weather Channel."

Billy had walked into the salon as the announcer was summing up. He remarked slyly to Judah, "Well, Bubba, looks like the hunch you had about that hurricane was wrong."

Judah smiled. "Thank God." He slid to one side of the sofa and gestured. "Here, take a load off, and tell us how you're feelin'."

"Not bad," responded Billy. "Not bad at all."

Judah snorted. "I find that hard to believe, 'cause I feel like shit and I know you knocked back more than I did."

"Well—I've got a little secret hangover weapon in my arsenal."

Judah grinned. "Really? I bet I know what it is. You took a shower, didn't you?" He glanced at Lloyd, winked, and continued. "I had the Monsignor bless my freshwater tanks before we left, so that was holy water you were showering with. The holy water did it, because only a miracle could account for the way you feel this morning."

Lloyd laughed. "That was just a temporary blessing, though. It's got to be renewed every twelve hours or the magic wears off."

Billy reached into the right pocket of his shorts and produced a medicine bottle. "I owe it all to this Percocet Dr. West prescribed for me. He said if I had any pain, to take a couple of these, and believe me, when I woke up this morning, I was a hurtin' puppy!"

Judah and Lloyd chuckled, then Lloyd jokingly said, "Hand'em here, I'll bless'em for you. Then they'll work twice as good."

Judah and Billy laughed out loud, then Judah added, "Holy water, holy pills, all the same to this Jew-boy."

There was silence for a few moments as the gravity of Billy's illness quietly forced its way back into the thoughts of all three men. Judah glanced over at Billy and noticed his eyes were downcast and moist. Deep inside Judah knew the agony his friend was forced to bear. He searched for something, anything, to break this spell, and blurted out, "I'd like to take the Whaler over to Williamson Island and jog along the beach before it gets too hot. Do you feel like a little exercise? I mean are there any restrictions on what you can do, Billy?"

Judah stood at the wheel of the fourteen-foot tender, steering it through the narrow mouth of the slough that separated Williamson Island from Beach Hammock. A quiet, four-cycle, seventy-five-horse Mercury hung on the stern, and Judah had to tilt the motor up as the boat passed over the shallow bar that blocked entrance to the slough at low tide. After this obstacle the slough widened considerably into a river that wandered through marsh and sand dunes. Billy was standing next to Judah, and as his eyes passed over the dark green marsh, then up to the tree line on Beach Hammock, he asked, "You remember when we were kids and came out here all the time in your father's fifteen-foot Cobia?"

"I used to think about that a lot when I lived up in D.C. We had some wonderful times back then, didn't we?"

Billy smiled and nodded. "This slough used to go all the way to the other side. We could get back into the ocean this way, but now it's blocked off. And Williamson Island, I remember when it was underwater at high tide. Now it's got dunes and sea oats growing on it. The whole area is building up, while the north end of Wassaw is being washed away. That's the reason I found that bomb."

Judah nudged the boat's bow up onto the beach. Billy set its anchor in the sand, and then they began the climb across the dunes to the island's ocean side, where they'd run on the hard-packed sand.

"I got a call this morning from the Feds about the bomb," said Judah as he and Billy trotted side by side just yards away from the breaking surf.

"Funny, I was thinking about that while we were coming over here. I've really thought about it a lot, but with this damn brain tumor I have, I really didn't feel like talking about it. What'd they say?"

"The agent who called is the same one I've been dealing with all along. He wanted to know why I didn't get back to him like I said I would. You know, only two days after I spoke with him, you got sick. I don't think either one of us gave much of a shit about the bomb after that."

As he jogged Billy watched a couple of shrimp boats dragging a mile off the beach. One looked like the *St. Patrick*.

"Yeah," said Billy, "a fatal brain tumor can kinda fuck up your whole day, can't it? The bomb just isn't a priority item right now, but I'd still like to know if I'm right about it. And if I am I'd like to get something for my trouble. The money's not for me, though. How the hell could I spend it in the time I've got left? Any money I get out of this, I want it to go to Hannah. Everything I have will go to my child when I die, as it ought to. But I'd still like to leave her something. She's doing all right, but I'd like to see her be able to quit selling real estate and have some time and money enough to enjoy life."

"You're a good man, Billy. I'd like to see that happen for her too. If you still feel like going through with this bomb thing, we need to show the feds what's in your garage, and then take them to where the bomb is."

"Okay, fine, Judah. Tell'em I'd like to meet just as soon as we get back." Billy pointed to one of the shrimp boats and said, "I'm pretty sure that's the *St. Patrick* out there."

"Who've you got running the show now?"

"Tran at the wheel, Abdul on the nets. Elijah's just too old to go out anymore. I think they're doing pretty well. The only thing that's kicking their ass is all that farm-grown shrimp imported from Asia. Think the president can push through those import duties on that stuff? It sure would help the shrimpers."

"If he wins I think it's a done deal. Believe me, he's catching heat about those imports from every coastal congressman from Texas to Maine."

"Let's stop for a minute."

Billy bent over and rested his hands on his knees. Sweat poured from his forehead. "I think I've had enough. I'm a little nauseated, maybe from all that booze last night, could be from the Percocet. I read the package insert, and it said the drug could make me puke. I sure hope the way I feel right now isn't caused by my sweet little brain tumor."

"Hell," said Judah, "I've had enough too. Let's walk back to the Whaler. When we get back on the *Solitude*, I'm going to buy you the coldest beer in Savannah."

Billy stood up straight, put his hands on his hips, and watched the two shrimp boats as they pulled their nets across the sandy ocean bottom. Judah watched, too. He remembered the good times he and Billy had enjoyed as they worked the *St. Patrick* in that same spot of ocean forty years earlier. Billy finally interrupted the silence.

"There's something else I want out of the government, something maybe more important than money. Especially now."

"What's that, Billy?"

"I want a presidential pardon for that marijuana bullshit they put me through. I want my record wiped clean. After I'm dead and gone I don't want my grandchildren or anybody else to ever know that I've got a criminal record."

Gusto watched as Judah parked his Jaguar next to the rented Ford Taurus he was driving outside the Driftaway Café in Sandfly. He wasn't surprised when Billy Aprillia got out of the passenger's side and followed him into the restaurant. When Judah approached Dottie, the hostess, and spoke to her, Gusto saw her point toward his booth; he stood to greet the pair while he waited for them to make their way through the crowded bar. He noted with amusement Billy's expression when he caught sight of him, and he could see that Billy was trying to recall his face. Even after Judah had introduced Billy and seated himself across the table, Gusto could tell Billy still hadn't recognized him. It wasn't until Gusto said, "Captain Billy, it's been a long time since we last met," that Billy remembered.

"Holy shit," he blurted incredulously. "You're that guy who was on my boat back during the Mariel boat lift, aren't you!"

"That's right, Captain Billy, I was right there with you. That was quite a ride back to the States, wasn't it?"

Billy sat back and shook his head. "This is just unreal. I haven't thought about it in a long time, but I remember after it was all over that something just didn't jibe with who you said you were. I mean, with your story and the way you acted. Damn, I remember watching you get into that government car and thinking, this guy must be some sort of C.I.A. dude or something."

Judah was even more surprised than Billy. "You two know each other?"

"This is the guy I told you about. You, know, the one who killed those dirtbags on my boat when we were coming back from Mariel Bay and dumped them over the side."

"Yeah," responded Judah, "I remember the story well. So, Gusto, you were working for the government even back then?"

Gusto caught Dottie's eye and motioned for her to come to their table, then replied, "Yeah, I've been working for Uncle Sam in one capacity or another for a long time."

"You want your regular, Judah?" asked Dottie.

"That'll be fine, sweetheart."

Dottie turned her attention to Billy. "What would you like, honey?"

"Jack and ginger, plenty of ice, please."

After Dottie left to place their order, Gusto got right to the point. "Judah has told me that you think you've found the Tybee Bomb and can prove it."

"That's correct. I've got the GPS coordinates and some solid evidence hidden away on dry land that should nail it down."

"When can I see this evidence?"

"How 'bout we finish our drinks, then I'll take you right to it?"

Gusto nodded in approval, then smiled, "So, Captain Billy, tell me what you've been up to since we last met."

When Billy snatched back the canvas that hid the stabilizing fins of the bomb, he did it with the same style and flourish as when he had shown them to Judah. Gusto seemed just as impressed as Judah had been. He inspected everything carefully, noting that the fins didn't appear to have been in the water for almost fifty years.

"That's 'cause I used a pressure washer to knock off the barnacles and all the other crap that covered it. The way I read the situation, this section of the bomb hadn't been exposed to direct saltwater for more than a few years. It had been buried in sand just like the rest of the bomb until the littoral currents washed away the sand that was over it and exposed the fins."

"Excuse my ignorance about such things," said Gusto, "but just exactly what are littoral currents?"

"Those are the currents that run parallel to the shoreline," replied Billy. "Along this coast, the littorals run from north to south. Just the opposite of the way the Gulf Stream flows, but on the Georgia coast the Gulf Stream is about 125 miles out."

"So, these currents wash away the northern end of the barrier islands and carry the sand to the southern ends of the islands, correct?"

"Exactly right."

"And it is this current that has exposed the tail of the bomb and allowed you to snag it with your nets?"

"Yep."

"So, correct me if I'm wrong, but eventually this current will expose the entire bomb?"

"Right again."

Gusto nodded, then took out a high-end digital camera and proceeded to take an extensive series of photos.

"I'll get this off to the Pentagon today by courier plane from Hunter air base. Someone from D.C. should be reviewing this by no later than noon tomorrow." Gusto neatly placed the camera back into its carrying case.

"Okay," said Billy quietly. "Where do we go from here?"

"After I get the go-ahead from my boss, I guess the next move is to go out into the sound and take a look."

"We can use my boat," said Judah. "We've been there before with it, and the sonar picture is pretty fine. The unit has the capability to run a paper copy of what it sees. You can send that up to Washington, too."

"So," asked Billy, "when do you think we'll be going back out to the sound?'

"Probably within the next three days or so," said Gusto.

The following day Abdul and his two buddies were sitting on the open porch at Tubby's Tankhouse, a combination restaurant and bar located on River Drive in Thunderbolt, directly across the street from Billy's condo. It was an unlikely place for three non-drinking Muslims to meet, but the *St. Patrick* was docked just down the bluff from Tubby's, and it was a convenient location for Abdul to gather with his friends. It was early on a weekday and the lunch crowd hadn't started filtering in yet, so the three men had the entire porch to themselves.

"You find anything yet, Hassam?" asked Alphonso.

Hassam cautiously looked around before quietly answering, "Yeah. I got two M-3 hand grenades."

"Where'd you get that from, man?" asked Abdul just before he cut his eyes toward the windows of Billy's condo.

Hassam snickered. "From this crazy cracker who lives over close to Montgomery Street. I think he's some kinda Nazi or something. Anyway, I met him about three months ago when I had him in my cab. I picked him up from this redneck joint out on Highway 17. He was a little drunk and said he and this girl he was with had a fight and she had taken off with his car. Just left him high and dry, that's why he needed a cab. Anyway, we start talkin' on the way to his place and he starts braggin' 'bout how he used to be in Special Forces back in Nam, know what I mean?"

Abdul nodded. Alphonso stoked his goatee and murmured, "Probably thinks he's some kinda badass or somethin'."

"Well," continued Hassam, " he pulls out some reefer and starts smokin' it in the back of my cab. Gets really high, understand?"

"Yeah," said Abdul. Alphonso just nodded and continued fingering his goatee.

"Anyway, he starts talking shit about all them slopeheads he popped the cap on over in Nam. Next thing I know he's tellin' me about all the stuff he has, you know, automatic weapons, explosives, and shit like that. Claims he bought a lot of it from some G.I.'s when he was workin' over at Fort Stewart. I don't know, but we kinda get to be friends 'cause he wants me to find him some more reefer. I do, and over the next few weeks, next thing I know he's saying if I ever want to buy some bad stuff, he can get it for me. So the other day I stop by his place, tell him what I need, and then go over yesterday and pick it up. Cost me three hundred dollars, but I think it'll get the job done."

"You think those grenades are powerful enough?" asked Abdul. He seemed impressed.

Hassam had been in the Army during the first Gulf War and had served in an infantry platoon, so he was well versed on different munitions and ready with an answer.

"They're M-3 anti-personnel grenades, man. The manufacture date on 'em is 1978. They're kinda old, but I'm sure they're still live."

"Where are they?" asked Alphonso.

"Hid away real good."

"How you know you can trust this honky?" was Alphonso's next question.

"Yeah," chimed in Abdul, "how you know this cracker isn't settin' you up, brother?"

"Just 'cause'a the way it all came down. I mean, dude didn't know me from nothin', right? I never asked him for anything. He was just runnin' his cracker mouth. I score him some weed the next day an' he's all like, hey man that's cool, ever need anything let me know. It's just a feelin' I got, know what I'm saying?"

Abdul sat back and thought for a moment while Alphonso stroked his goatee with greater intensity, then said, "You don't tell us where that shit is, got it? We don't need to know anything till the time comes when we're ready to use it. We got the explosives we need, so now we gotta come up with the way we do it."

Hassam and Abdul both nodded in agreement. They were oblivious to what was on the TV inside the bar. WTOC's weatherman, Pat Prokop, stood in front of an animated satellite image of the Atlantic: "The latest on Hurricane Debbie is that her movement to the northeast has stalled, and if you'll notice on this latest satellite photo, she appears to be taking a more westerly track. Right now we're not sure what Debbie will do, but some projections show her taking a track that could put her somewhere over the Georgia-Carolina coasts within seventy-two hours. As you can see, there are rain bands that extend out five hundred miles from the eye of the storm, so this is a real monster with barometric pressure of only 28.01 inches and recorded sustained winds of 125 miles an hour, making Debbie a strong Category 3 on the Saffir-Simpson scale. The National Hurricane Center will be issuing an update on Debbie at noon, so stay tuned to WTOC for all your weather information."

When Judah called, it was Hannah who answered Billy's phone.

"As far as I can tell, I think he's doing all right. He said he really had a good time on the boat, Judah. It's all he's talked about since he got back."

"I think the trip was therapeutic for everybody, not just Billy. It gave us all a chance to honestly face what's going to happen to him."

For a second Judah regretted what he had said when he heard Hannah sigh deeply and grow silent, but then he decided that refusing to confront reality wasn't going to do anybody any good. "Is he there? I need to tell him something." A few seconds later Billy came to the phone. "I spoke with our friend a little while ago, Billy, and he said to tell you how impressed everyone was with those pictures of Miss Savannah."

"Oh really? I guess he wants to meet her in person now."

"Yeah, that's what he said, but we've got a problem. Have you seen the weather?"

"Can you believe that storm?" asked Billy in astonishment. "I guess your hunch about Debbie might turn out to be right after all. We don't have time to introduce Gusto to our lady, 'cause if that storm keeps headin' this way, I gotta get Tran and Abdul set up to anchor the *St. Patrick* in the Wilmington. Have you thought about what you're gonna to do with your boat?"

"I'm in kind of a jam with it, 'cause it looks like the storm is gonna sweep up the Florida coast starting a little below Daytona, then follow the coastline up past here and probably come ashore somewhere north of Charleston. I sure as hell ain't runnin' south, not right into the teeth of that damn thing, and I'm afraid to take her north too, 'cause who the hell knows what's really gonna happen? Plus, even if I did decide to make a run for it, Tran and Abdul are tied up with your stuff, and I sure as shit can't handle this thing by myself. Looks like I'll take my boat out into the river and do the same thing you're planning to do."

"What were the winds last time you heard?"

"I was listening to the Weather Channel just before I called, and they're saying it's dropping off a little, but its forward speed is picking up. That really limits our choices, doesn't it?"

"Listen," said Billy, "don't worry about Tran and Abdul; I'll help you with your boat. If the winds stay below a hundred, I'll ride that bastard out aboard the *Solitude*. We set two good anchors, play out plenty of line, keep the engines running and in gear, point her bow into the wind, and enjoy the ride."

"You're nuts," replied Judah, "you could get killed that way. She's fully insured, so I'll just leave her and stay at your place during the storm."

"You think I'm worried about dying?"

"Come on, Billy, you know what I mean."

"Lemme tell you something, Bubba. You remember Hurricane David?"

"Yeah, back in the early eighties. I was living in New York back then, married to my second wife, who was just about as crazy as you're actin' right now."

"To be exact," said Billy, "David hit over Labor Day weekend, in September of 1979. It was the last hurricane to hit here. It had sustained winds of around eighty miles an hour. I spent the entire storm at the wheel of the *St. Patrick*, anchored out in the Skidaway River in front of Modena Island. My father was in the *St. Anthony* just down the river from me, and Elijah was in the *St. Joseph* a little further on down. It was no big deal, I'm tellin' ya. The only problem I had was that I gave out of Jack Daniels before the storm was over and I couldn't hear that funky eight-track player I had in the wheelhouse over the howl of the wind."

Judah laughed. "You crazy bastard! Okay, but if I agree, I'm stayin' with you. If the winds are above a hundred, we anchor it and leave. If they're below a hundred, we stay and ride it out."

The eye of Hurricane Debbie passed over Isle of Hope three days later at two in the afternoon. Sustained winds barely reached hurricane strength, and Savannah's shrimping fleet, along with other vessels too large to be removed from the water, were anchored up and down the Intracoastal Waterway, where they successfully rode out Savannah's first hurricane in more than twenty-five years. Although Debbie's winds weren't very destructive, she did hit at high tide.

With the exception of Eastport, Maine, which has an average tidal fluctuation of 19.4 feet; Portland, Maine, with one of 9.11 feet; and Boston, with 10.4 feet; Savannah's 8.3-foot tidal variance is the greatest along the U.S. Atlantic coast, because of its position on the Great Atlantic Bight. During hurricane season this can be a good or a bad thing, depending on when the storm hits. Before its eye passed over the city, Debbie had dumped almost twelve inches of rain on Savannah before she actually hit the city. The incoming tide greatly impeded water runoff which led to widespread flooding and shut the city down for several days.

There is a phenomenon that occurs twice in each lunar month when the sun, moon, and earth are directly aligned. This allows the sun and moon to exert their gravitational forces in a mutual or additive fashion, producing the highest highs, also known as spring tides, of that lunar month. This happened when Debbie hit Savannah with a predicted high tide of 9.1 feet. Flooding was the major problem in the city, but the barrier islands fared far worse: Debbie's winds, though not severe, were completely unimpeded by the waters of the open Atlantic. Parts of Tybee, Wassaw, and Ossabaw islands were underwater for most of Debbie's visit along the Georgia coast. The dramatic tide, combined with Debbie's winds and the storm surge they produced, shifted hundreds of thousands of cubic yards of sand all along the coast, particularly in Wassaw Sound, where it rearranged long stretches of beach, sand bars, the sound's channel—and the bomb.

"This is a magnificent boat, Judah," Gusto remarked as he let his eyes wander around the appointments on the interior of the *Solitude*. "I can't get over how much teak there is in this thing. This boat really puts that Sea Ray I have to shame."

"Thanks. Teak is kind of a Grand Banks signature item. They all have a lot of it."

Billy was on the flying bridge preparing to start the engines when Gusto and Judah joined him. Gusto took the seat next to him. "I guess handling something this large is no big deal after a lifetime of being at the wheel of a shrimp boat."

"This boat's a pleasure," said Billy as he turned the key to the port side engine, sounding the start-up warning bell. He engaged the ignition and the engine rumbled to life. As soon as the big diesel smoothed out, he did the same with the starboard engine. Judah watched with confidence and satisfaction as Billy carried out a litany of other start-up procedures, then turned to Gusto and said, "It's nice to have a buddy who knows what's going on with a boat this size. That means I can just sit back and enjoy the ride."

With the engines running at idle, Billy leaned back in his chair and took off his B.C. baseball cap. Once more the shaved area on the right side of his head became painfully prominent. "See how much my hair has grown back?" he said. "I wonder if it'll be back to normal length before this tumor finally gets me."

Gusto was unprepared and stunned by Billy's bluntness, but Judah wasn't. "By that time you'll be wearing a ponytail," he said before turning to Gusto. "When did you say those two divers were supposed to show up?"

Gusto looked at his watch, then up at the bluff. "Right about now. As a matter of fact, they just parked next to your car."

Two Navy divers had been flown in the day before to inspect whatever it was that Billy had found. As they walked down the dock toward the *Solitude*, Gusto told Billy, "These guys are the best. It shouldn't take them long to identify what's out there."

"If they say it's the bomb, how long before I get paid?" Billy wondered. "And how long before that pardon is issued?"

"I'm not exactly sure, but I'd say we're talking about days for the money transfer and maybe a week or so with the pardon."

"I gotta pay taxes on that money?"

Gusto laughed. "No, Captain Billy, it's all tax-free. But remember, you've gotta keep your mouth shut about the money and this whole damn thing, okay. You too, Judah. Either one of you gets loose lips and some serious shit will start happening very fast."

Billy looked Gusto in the eye and asked, "You mean more serious than dying from a brain tumor, amigo?"

Gusto glanced away, thought for a moment, then said, "No, my friend."

Judah could not help being a little exasperated. "I know what you're going through, Billy, but can you cut the shit for just a little while? You know, ease up on yourself and everybody around you?"

Billy put his cap back on and quietly said, "I'm sorry. It won't happen again."

Gusto reached out and put his arm around Billy. "You can say anything you feel like around me. You were the one who took me to freedom, remember?"

It had been only three days since Debbie had blown through Savannah, so Billy had to maneuver around a number of vessels that remained at anchor in the river. When the *Solitude* had passed the marina at Priest Landing and the river was clear of traffic, he advanced the throttles; in no time the big boat was cutting through the water at thirty miles an hour, headed for the north end of Wassaw Island.

Checking the GPS coordinates, Judah pointed to a spot on the chart laid out before Gusto. "We're getting close. This is where the bomb is resting."

By design Billy had brought Gusto to the bomb site on an outgoing tide. He reasoned he would need enough water beneath *Solitude* to allow for maneuvering while the ship's sonar searched the bottom; then, after they had located the bomb, he would drop anchor and wait for low tide. When the tide is running, the current is quite swift, at times close to ten miles an hour, so going into the water at dead low meant the divers didn't have to deal with the current.

"We should be seeing something over there in just a few minutes," said Billy, pointing to a spot about half a mile due west of green channel marker number nine. He approached the area at idle speed while keeping his eye on the GPS and watching as the numbers on its display grew closer and closer to those he now knew by heart. Judah and Gusto also watched the sonar display as Billy edged the boat forward, finally saying, "We should see something any second now, right Judah?"

"Yep," replied Judah. "This is the spot." His eyes kept shifting back and forth from the GPS to the sonar, fully expecting the sonar screen to momentarily reveal the familiar shape he had seen only a month before; yet for a very long time the only sound on the bridge was the distant throbbing of the engines and the whisper of the wind as it blew across the open cockpit area. Finally Billy cut the ship's wheel hard to starboard. "Let's make another pass. We may have been off just a little. I think this GPS is only accurate to within thirty feet. The storm may have moved the bomb a little bit, too."

For the next two hours Billy scoured the bottom in a widening circle that centered on the original GPS coordinates, but found nothing. Finally he threw his hands up and said to Gusto, "The storm surge has either rolled the bomb away from here or buried it again. But we had something the last time we were out here, didn't we, Judah?"

"We sure did," answered Judah. "As a matter of fact, I stored what we saw in the sonar's memory. I'll play it back right now."

Gusto watched as Judah scrolled through the sonar's memory to reveal the image they'd come looking for, but which had now disappeared. Disgusted and dejected, Billy watched as the two Navy divers began to pack their gear. Then he said, "Take the wheel, Judah, I don't feel worth a damn."

The Other Side of Town

"For, once a select quarter, Savannah's Old Fort district has crept westward and encroached, bringing with it the noisy vitality of shanty Irish and Negroes; and a bastard architecture."

—Harry Hervey, *The Damned Don't Cry*

TECHNICALLY THE HOUSE Lloyd Bryan had grown up in wasn't in the Old Fort district of Savannah, but it was close enough for him to get the full range of its texture. Most of the Old Fort's residents were working-class Irish who attended the Cathedral of St. John the Baptist on the corner of Abercorn and Harris streets. Though Lloyd's home on Harris and East Broad streets was in the shadow of the cathedral's spires, he had come up during the era of segregation. As a result he had attended Mass at all-black St. Benedict the Moor Catholic Church only a few blocks from the cathedral and was educated at St. Pius X, a Catholic school for black children. He was a student at St. Pius until he was selected by the bishop of Savannah to be the first black cadet at Benedictine Military School.

Lloyd's mother, a fervent Catholic, had been the bishop's housekeeper. She had taken the position out of necessity caused by the absence of Lloyd's less than admirable father. Because of her unyielding influence, Lloyd was a dedicated and devoutly religious student who eventually caught the bishop's eye. The bishop's faith in his character and abilities was richly rewarded by his success first at Benedictine, then later at the University of Notre Dame. For a while, however, during his career with the Washington Redskins,

Lloyd allowed himself to be distracted from what his mother believed to be his spiritual destiny.

In his third and most successful year in professional football, Lloyd was living the dream of many young men from all social, financial, and racial backgrounds. He was blessed with both fame and fortune, the sum of which allowed him to attract a panoply of the most beautiful and willing women any man could desire. His lifestyle, however, had stripped him of the Divine underpinnings that had permitted him to accomplish so much with so little. While he was adrift in a secular world filled with instant gratification, his spiritual needs were ignored—until the wee hours of the morning following a particularly important victory in his team's march to the Super Bowl. Lloyd had been a key player in the Redskins' triumph, and he sought to celebrate this accomplishment with some fellow players at a party dusted with cocaine and hosted by several Redskins groupies.

On the way back to his apartment at the Watergate, Lloyd saw an innocent child gunned down in a drug deal gone awry. He would later describe what he saw as being not unlike St. Paul's encounter with Jesus on the road to Damascus and the event that changed his life. A few months later Lloyd quit professional sports and entered the seminary. Six years after that he would be ordained by the same bishop who had selected him to desegregate Savannah's parochial schools.

In Savannah the percentage of the black population who were Catholics was dwarfed by those of the Protestant denominations; Lloyd was the first homegrown black priest the city ever had. His initial assignment was as assistant pastor of St. Benedict the Moor, his home parish, just around the corner from his mother's house.

Although the rules of social order in Savannah were changing, the process was slow. For many years Father Bryan's appointments alternated between the more stately St. Benedict's on East Broad and the smaller and humbler St. Mary's parish, a rough location in the center of Abdul's old neighborhood, and the only other black church in the diocese.

In the early nineties Lloyd was appointed assistant pastor of the Cathedral of St. John the Baptist. A few years later, in another precedent-setting move likened to the appointment of an African-American as archbishop of Atlanta, he became rector of the cathedral. Even though Father Bryan's duties at the cathedral consumed most of his time and energy, his heart was really in working with children in the neighborhood around St. Benedict's.

The twenty-third chapter of the Gospel according to Luke recounts how Jesus was crucified between two thieves. The thief on His left taunted Jesus, calling on Him to save Himself, while the one on His right chided the other thief for mocking Jesus and asked to be with Him in Paradise—a request that Jesus granted. According to legend the thief on the right, also known as the "good thief," was named Dismas.

Lloyd had always been touched by this story, so when the youth center he had worked so hard to create finally came to fruition, he called it The St. Dismas Center. Judah had been influential in acquiring the government grants that allowed him to hire full-time staff and stood next to him while Congressman McQueen presided over the opening-day ceremonies. The center was open to all young people, but Lloyd's primary focus was on teenage boys from fatherless homes, those he considered to be the most at risk.

St. Dismas Center offered a wide array of programs and activities along with a well-furnished gym and health club. Since the amount of time Lloyd could devote to the center was limited, he chose to spend it in the weight room, where he could interact with the boys while working out at the same time. A sports legend already, Lloyd easily drew a healthy crowd of teenagers eager not just to lift weights with him, but also to share their thoughts and problems. The center quickly grew into the ministry Lloyd had always dreamed of; and in recognition of his hard work, the Church bestowed the title of Monsignor upon Lloyd in 2003.

Most but not all of the young men Lloyd came in contact with at St. Dismas went on to productive lives. Some were harder to help than others, and there were those few who were so full of anger that not even Lloyd could get through to them. This seemed to be the case with fifteen-year-old Damian Small, who went by the street name "Skeebo."

Monsignor Bryan detested the use of street names, believing them to be demeaning and the product of the "Hip Hop" culture he despised, and which he blamed for many of the ills that afflicted black society. Although Lloyd viewed his job as pastor to his (mostly white) congregation as his most important, very close behind was his quiet devotion to elevating both the material and spiritual well-being of his own race. In doing so he refused to accept excuses for failing to try at self-improvement. This attitude produced results, but gained him a reputation as a harsh taskmaster.

Lloyd first noticed Damian one afternoon while doing bench-presses: big for his age, hair done in dreadlocks, cut off from his surroundings by headphones. (He was listening to the music of a local rapper known as "Camouflage," while bouncing his head to the rhythm of the beat.) Standing in front of a full-length mirror, Damian was working with a set of twenty-five-pound dumbbells trying to build up his biceps. He knew who Lloyd was but had chosen to ignore him. Between sets Lloyd sat on the bench and watched as the boy struggled with the weights. After a few moments Lloyd wiped the sweat from his face, got up, and approached him.

"I think you'd do better with a lighter weight for now," said Lloyd as Damian, using poor form, struggled to lift the dumbbells by arching his back and swinging them up.

"I'm doing okay," replied Damian, who tried even harder to control the weights.

"Naw, man," answered Lloyd, "it's not just about lifting the weight, it's about form, too. You'll be able to work with these weights after a month or two, but right now you need to be using about fifteen pounds. Lemme show ya."

Lloyd took a pair of fifteen-pound dumbbells from the weight rack and handed them to Damian. "Now, go through the movement slow and easy." Damian did as instructed and watched his biceps in the mirror as they contracted into a tight knot just below his shoulders. "That's the way," said Lloyd with a smile. "Good form. Hey, after you finish this set, think you could spot me for a couple of minutes?"

Lloyd didn't really need any help with his bench-presses, and there were other boys standing around who'd jump at the chance to help him with his workout. But he had seen something in Damian's face and wanted the opportunity to know him a little better. As they walked over to the bench-press area, Lloyd extended his hand. "I'm Monsignor Bryan. What's your name?"

Reluctantly Damian shook the proffered hand and mumbled, "Skeebo."

"Naw, man, I'm not talkin' 'bout what they call you on the street, I mean your name, man, you know, what your Momma calls you."

"She calls me Damian."

Lloyd sat on the bench, then laid back and looked up at the barbell over his head. "What's your last name, Damian?"

"Small."

"Where do you live?"

"On Price, about a block from Gwinnett."

Damian was standing behind Lloyd and watched as he tightened his grip on the bar. "Okay, here we go, help me off with this."

Damian helped Lloyd lift the barbell and watched as he did twelve well-executed repetitions before assisting Lloyd as he rested the barbell into its rack.

"How much you got on here?" he asked as he examined the plates on either end of the bar.

"Three-fifty."

"Um-um, that's a lot. How long you been doin' this?"

"Ever since I was your age." Lloyd slipped from under the bar and sat upright on the end of the bench. "This your first time here?"

"Yeah. I mean yes, sir."

"Well, I tell ya what, Damian, I'm here about this same time every Monday, Wednesday, and Friday. If you want you can work out with me. As big as you are it won't be long before you'll be benching this much, too."

Over the next several weeks Damian became a regular at St. Dismas. The process was slow, but he opened up as Lloyd had hoped. In the beginning Lloyd surmised that many things in Damian's life would be similar to those he had experienced at the same age. He quickly discovered this speculation was substantially incorrect. They were worse.

Damian had two younger sisters living in the same house along with his mother and Ronnie, her live-in boyfriend and father of his youngest sister. Damian's biological father was none other than Abdul Aleem, who'd enjoyed an intense if brief affair with his mother, Sharee, before being imprisoned. Abdul knew of his son's existence, contributing nothing toward his financial welfare, and was only a sporadic presence in Damian's life. Lloyd also learned that Damian's relationship with Ronnie was mercurial at best; it sometimes erupted into physical matches that occasionally, when Ronnie was drunk, culminated in Damian's administering a sound thrashing. This usually resulted in another confrontation the following day.

As with many inner-city youths, Damian's grandparents were the strongest positive influence in his life. Unfortunately Howard and Yvonne Small were rapidly approaching their seventies. Both were frail and easily deceived, but they provided a stable and loving atmosphere to which Damian retreated with regularity. Their high morality and strong work ethic was the overwhelming norm in Savannah's black community.

The Small home was just east of the railroad tracks on Gwinnett Street, not very far from the St. Dismas Center. As Lloyd's relationship with Damian grew, it was the grandparents whom Lloyd decided to visit one Sunday afternoon after celebrating eleven-thirty Mass at the cathedral. Mr. and Mrs. Small had heard much about Monsignor Bryan over the years, most recently from Damian, who seemed to have finally found a positive male role model in his life. When the Monsignor appeared at their door, he was greeted warmly.

Howard Small was a retired postal worker and Yvonne a former teacher at Beach High School. They were financially comfortable and would have been able to enjoy retirement had it not been for the actions of their daughter Sharee. She had broken their hearts early on with a cocaine habit that spiraled out of control. After repeated and unsuccessful attempts to help her, the Smalls resigned themselves to her fate. Instead they focused their energies on salvaging the lives of their grandchildren.

"Preacher," said Mr. Small, "when Damian told us that he was going to St. Dismas three days a week and exercising with you, we both said 'Thank you, Jesus,' 'cause we knew our prayers had been answered."

"He's a good boy," chimed in Mrs. Small, "but only the power of God can keep him away from all that bad stuff out there on the street. God knows we pray for him every day and night, 'cause he ain't gettin' no direction at home, none at all."

Lloyd played with the brim of the white Panama hat that protected the bald spot on the back of his head during the summer and said, "Yes, ma'am, I think he's a good boy, too. But, like you said, there're lots of temptations on the street."

As Lloyd stood to leave he handed Mr. Small his card. "If you ever need me for anything, you can get me at this number."

A Trip to the Sound

> Man that is born of a woman is of few days, and full of trouble.
>
> —Job 14:1

"BILLY GOT A LITTLE dizzy today, Judah," said Hannah as she sat across the kitchen table from him in Billy's condo.

"How's he feeling now?" Judah was sipping a can of Diet Coke as he studied the expression on Hannah's face.

"I think he's okay, he's been napping for about the last hour or so. He took one of his pain pills, and they seem to make him sleepy."

"Was he having pain, too?"

"I don't know, but I don't think so." Hannah looked exhausted. "I went on-line and read about that drug. One of the side effects is euphoria. I think right now he takes it because it makes kind of not give a damn. Know what I mean?"

Judah looked down at the Coke can. "Yeah, I know exactly what you mean. I don't blame him one bit for wanting to feel better."

"I don't either. I'm just scared that when the pain really starts, the medicine won't work anymore. That article I read said it was easy to build up a tolerance to the drug, and that would lessen its effectiveness."

"I spoke with John-Morgan about that kind of stuff, and he told me that if that happens, there're plenty of other drugs much stronger. He said Billy won't be in physical agony." Judah was quiet for a moment before he added, "It's the mental torture I worry about . . . his . . . and mine."

"Me, too."

There was silence for several minutes. Judah thought he could hear snoring from Billy's room.

"Has Billy mentioned anything he'd like to do or anywhere he'd like to go?" he finally asked.

Tears formed in Hannah eyes; she wiped them dry with the back of her hand before taking a breath and answering.

"He said he wants to die on the water. He wants to die on his boat, not in this condo and certainly not in some room at Hospice. The time he spent on your boat was really special to him, Judah. I believe it really got him thinking."

Judah, his eyes fixed on the top of his Coke can, rubbed his finger around its rim as he thought for a moment. "I can understand why he'd want to take his last breath out on the water, but I don't think that old shrimp boat is going to be comfortable or big enough." Then he shifted his eyes to Hannah's. "But my boat is plenty big enough, and I know he'll be comfortable on it. In the meantime, while I look into what we'll need on it before he gets really sick, he can take the *Solitude* out anytime he wants. He's still in pretty good shape and I know he can handle that boat. I'll check and see if Tran can go out with y'all in case anything happens."

"What about you, Judah?" Hannah asked. "Why can't you just go."

Judah stood and walked over to the windows overlooking the river. With his back to Hannah he said, "The two of you should have as much time to yourselves as you possibly can. I'll stay here while you're gone. I think that would be best."

Abdul was sitting between his two friends in the back of their mosque, waiting for Friday evening services to begin, when he whispered quietly, "I got some really great news, my brothers."

Hassam and Alphonso glanced at each other, then leaned in close to hear what he had to say. Proudly, Abdul related his story.

"This morning Aprillia called me to his house. He told me he's dying with a brain tumor and probably won't live more than a few months. He said that little Jew friend of his was loanin' him that nice big boat he's stayin' on so's he and that bitch he's seeing could take it out and live on it for a while. He says he takin' that chink Tran with him to work the boat and I needed to get me some strikers of my own. Also until further notice I'm the captain of the *St. Patrick.*" Abdul waited for Hassam and Alphonso to absorb what he had told them, then continued. "This means we got that boat all to ourselves now."

Hassam smiled slightly and whispered, "You're saying we can take that boat out and find the bomb without nobody else on it?"

"That's just what I'm sayin'." Abdul leaned back with a supremely satisfied look on his face.

Hassam nodded in approval as Alphonso stroked his goatee, slightly rocking back and forth while digesting what he had just heard.

"When do we go bomb-huntin'?" asked Hassam with undisguised glee.

"Tomorrow's the Sabbath, so we can't go then, but both'a you brothers got Sunday off, don't ya?"

Hassam nodded in affirmation. Alphonso answered with a low and menacing, "Yeah."

"Good. Then we'll meet at the boat at six Sunday morning." He looked at Hassam and asked, "You got the stuff?"

"My what?"

"You know, man—the fireworks."

"Yeah, I got it."

"Then bring it with you on Sunday."

"Man, I'm not about to go get that shit till I'm sure we got the bomb for real."

Harshly Alphonso stated, "I said don't disrespect this place of worship with that kind of language."

Hassam looked at Alphonso and in a voice louder than a whisper said, "Fuck you," prompting a man of Middle Eastern descent seated two rows ahead to turn and glare at the trio. He was Hamza Muhammad, called "The Lion" by his friends in Al-Qaeda. The Lion had immigrated from Syria to the U.S. ten years earlier. He was also Alphonso's secret friend: Alphonso had told him everything he knew about the bomb. For almost a minute everyone was quiet until Abdul whispered, "Okay, Hassam, have it your way, but we're still meetin' at the boat on Sunday morning, right?"

"I'll be there," replied Hassam.

"Me, too," added Alphonso, whose eyes momentarily locked with The Lion's.

The cruise to Wassaw Sound took up a slow and easy Saturday morning in August. Billy wanted to anchor off Beach Hammock again so Hannah sat next to him as he guided the *Solitude* down the Wilmington, into the channel at the south end of the sound, and out into the ocean. As he did so his eyes kept drifting to the spot on the water where he had last detected what he thought was the Tybee Bomb; all the frustration and disappointment he had felt after Hurricane Debbie started seeping back in. He hadn't wanted to come this way, but with the *Solitude* at seventy feet, she was too large to pass through Tybee Cut, the quick way to Beach Hammock. At red marker ten, Billy turned the boat north and pointed her bow at the south end of Little Tybee.

"Judah and I shrimped these exact waters when we were kids," he told his girl as he eyed the instrument cluster, then the horizon. "We had lots of days just like this one. Not a cloud in the sky, ocean calm as it can be and not too hot." Billy looked at Hannah, smiled, then continued: "And a date with a pretty girl when we got back in." Hannah returned his smile and put her arm around his shoulder.

"How do you feel today? Any more dizzy spells?"

"Naw, not since day before yesterday." As they entered the channel in front of Williamson Island, Billy called for his assistant. "Let's make ready to drop anchor, Tran."

"Right, boss." Tran had made himself scarce down below in his own cabin. He wanted to allow Billy and Hannah as much privacy as possible.

Solitude was easily the largest boat in the sound and an imposing sight as it rested at anchor off Beach Hammock. Its fly bridge stood more than twenty feet above the water, affording an unimpeded view of the ocean over the tops of the wind-brushed oaks that grow just past the island's dunes. The incoming tide forced a line of gulls standing along the edge of a sandbar to retreat as the water claimed more and more of their space. Billy watched as pelicans crashed themselves headlong into the water, trying to snatch the fish they had spotted. On the stern the single-star Bonnie Blue flag snapped in the breeze. Billy listened to it while he thought.

Hannah had one of Billy's white dress shirts on over her one-piece black bathing suit. As she stood to slip it off, Billy couldn't help admiring her figure.

"You still look pretty damn hot, baby," he said.

"And you're still trying to make an old broad feel good."

"No, I mean it, you can still turn heads on guys half your age. No joke."

Hannah smiled, gave him a peck on the cheek, and said, "I'll bet you'd like a cold beer, wouldn't you?"

Billy was stretched out on a lounge chair, enjoying the sun while he worked on his second beer and listened to the album *Endless Summer* by the Beach Boys. He was wearing a pair of khaki shorts with no shirt; his gold crucifix rested in the center of his chest. Hannah had given it to him, and after she had placed it around his neck, he had never removed it—for anything. Even now he was tan and handsome; and his broad shoulders and muscular arms not only held Hannah but actually seemed to give her shelter. As she looked at him she fought to banish thoughts of how he would appear when his disease really took hold. Billy took a long pull from his beer, then said, "It doesn't get much better than this, does it, Hannah?"

"No, sweetheart. This is beautiful."

"You know, Judah said we could have the boat as long as we want it."

"I know, Billy, he told me the same thing."

"Damn guy, he won't even let me pay for fuel or anything. He's even picking up the tab for Tran."

"Judah loves you very much, Billy."

His eyes were hidden by sunglasses. Hannah watched as he nodded his head, but Billy said nothing. After a few moments she noticed tears starting to streak down Billy's cheeks.

"You think I've done the right thing by not taking any treatment?"

"Yes, sweetheart, I do. If you hadn't, then we wouldn't have had this day, would we?"

That evening, Tran fixed dinner as Billy and Hannah sat on the stern under a canopy of stars. Later, while she lay next to him in bed, Billy's head started spinning, but he said nothing, allowing her instead to slip away into a peaceful sleep.

Around four the next morning a thick fog rolled in from the ocean. Visibility in Wassaw Sound was reduced to less than a hundred feet.

"Man, I can't see a thing," protested Hassam as he and Alphonso stood next to Abdul in the *St. Patrick*'s wheelhouse. "Turn this motherfucka 'round before we hit something and sink. We can try another day."

"Take it easy," responded Abdul. "See this little arrow up here on the screen?"

"Yeah."

"That's us. And this here is the marsh, and this right up here is Wassaw Island, and this dot here is another boat. You might not be able to see anything, but our radar sure as hell can."

Hassam grunted a couple of times, then settled down as the boat moved along at five knots, probing her way through the fog with electronic eyes.

First light that morning was a little before six. The sun had already started to burn away the fog when Abdul neared the coordinates he had copied only months before from the same GPS to which his eyes were now glued. He had taken the *St. Patrick* about a mile out from the mouth of the sound, and was three miles away from the *Solitude*. When Abdul started his search at seven-thirty, visibility had increased to fifteen hundred yards, but the *Solitude* was still cloaked by the fog. Abdul assumed the large blip just off Beach Hammock was just another shrimper.

Hannah was up before Billy. She helped Tran in the galley as he prepared bacon, eggs, grits, and biscuits.

"Where did you learn to cook biscuits and grits, Tran? Y'all didn't have food like this in Vietnam, did you?" Hannah was tasting the grits and testing them for consistency.

"Remember, Miss Hannah, I come from South Vietnam," replied Tran with a grin on his face.

Hannah laughed. "Well, you've got the grits just right, and that's something a lot of people from around here have trouble with."

Tran wiped his hands on a towel tucked into his pants, then turned to face Hannah.

"Miss Hannah?"

"Uh huh."

"Captain Billy gonna make it?"

Hannah looked at Tran, dropped her head for a moment, then replied softly, "No, Tran, I'm afraid he's not going to make it."

"How long he have?"

"Maybe a couple of months, maybe three, we're really not sure."

There were big tears in Tran's eyes when he said, "Captain Billy a good man, a real good man. He take me in when I come from Vietnam. He need me for anything, anything, I there for him, Miss Hannah."

"You sure you got those numbers right?" asked Alphonso after two hours of fruitless searching.

"Yeah, I'm sure," said Abdul as he steered the *St. Patrick* over his target area for the sixth time. "We gotta be patient. This a big ocean."

Hassam left his perch on the bow, came into the wheelhouse, and stood next to Abdul. For the next half hour he was silent as he watched Abdul troll for the bomb. Around nine Hassam decided he had had enough.

"This is a waste of time, Abdul," said Hassam with an angry look on his face.

"Yeah," repeated Alphonso. "A waste of time."

Three miles to the north, in front of Beach Hammock, Hannah was in the shower, and Tran was clearing away the breakfast dishes while he kept his eye on a shrimp boat he had been watching ever since the fog lifted.

"Boss, you see that trawler over there?" he asked as he pointed to a boat about a mile off the north end of Wassaw Island. Billy twisted in his chair and looked across the sound.

"Yeah, I see it."

"I not sure, but I think that your boat."

Billy lifted his sunglasses and squinted.

"It could be, after all Abdul was supposed to find a replacement for you and go out this weekend."

"Yeah, boss, I know, but something not right."

"What do you mean?"

"Boat just going in circles, boss."

Billy went over to the locker under the ship's wheel and got a pair of Swarovski 10x42 binoculars. Judah had shopped around for the glasses, and even though he got a good deal over the internet, he still wound up paying $1,600 for them. As he said, however, they were the world's finest. Billy could tell the difference when he brought them to bear on the boat Tran had pointed out.

"You might be right, Tran, that does look like the *St. Patrick.*"

"He been there all morning, just sailing 'round and 'round same spot, boss. And he no have his nets out 'cause outriggers still up."

Billy adjusted the focus a little, and without taking the glasses away from his eyes, he said, "Yeah, I see what you mean. That is kinda strange, especially when he's supposed to be out catching shrimp. He's in a good spot for it, but he's not doing anything."

Billy passed the binoculars to Tran. "Take a look," as he went to the chart rack and picked NOAA chart number 11512 for Wassaw Sound. He unrolled the chart and spread it across the table.

"I no see anybody on deck, either, boss," said Tran as he watched the boat slowly turn until its stern was presented. "That boat *St. Patrick*, Captain Billy, no other boat have paint job like that. Here, look."

The boat was much too far away to read any lettering, but Billy could tell by the color scheme that he was looking at his boat. He thought for a moment, then studied the chart as he sought to fix *St. Patrick*'s location on it.

"Tran," said Billy without looking up.

"Yeah, boss."

"Light up the radar."

Judah had gone all out with his Sperry Marine naval radar, as he had done with his binoculars and everything else. Soon the entire sound and everything that was on it was displayed in full color. For ten minutes, Billy and Tran watched as the *St. Patrick* passed back and forth over an area about the size of two football fields.

"Boss?"

"Uh-huh."

"You remember when we get snagged and pull up that piece of metal?"

"Yep."

"I think your boat in same spot."

"So do I, Tran," said Billy as he looked away from the radar screen and picked up Judah's fancy binoculars again.

"What you think Abdul doing, boss?"

Billy had the binoculars fixed intently on his boat. "I don't know, Tran, but I'd sure as hell like to find out." For the next few minutes Billy alternated between watching the *St. Patrick* through the binoculars and following its movements on the radar plot.

"Do you know who Abdul's got out there with him, Tran?"

"I think he has friend of his."

"What friend?"

"You met him, boss. He come to boat one day to pick up Abdul. It early on a Friday afternoon. I think they same religion and go same church."

"Oh, you mean that black dude who wears a little skull cap just like Abdul?"

"Yeah, boss, that one. I think he named Hassam. I no like."

"I no like either, Tran."

Billy looked again at the radar screen, then turned to Tran. "We're going back in tomorrow. When we get back I want you to find out who's been out there with Abdul. But whatever you do, don't tell anybody about this. And for God's sake, don't let on to Abdul that we saw him, understand?"

Billy and Tran watched the *St. Patrick*'s unusual behavior for another ten minutes before they saw the outriggers come down and the nets drop over the side. The boat started dragging about a mile off the beaches at Wassaw, and Billy kept an eye on her until she disappeared heading for the southern end of the island. The crew aboard the *St. Patrick* had been so intense in their search for the bomb that they never even noticed the *Solitude.*

"Abdul knows about the bomb," said Billy as he stood in his garage, pulled the canvas off the stabilizers, and ran his hand over the fins. "I'm sure of it."

"Well," asked Judah, "suppose he does know? What difference does it make now? It's not there anymore. If we can't find it, how can he?"

"It's somewhere close," replied Billy, looking at his piece of the bomb. "That thing weighs seventy-five hundred pounds; the tides can't push it that far away. He can just troll around the area like we did and maybe get lucky."

"Okay, say he stumbles across the bomb. Then what?"

"Abdul is a fuckin' Muslim, Judah! So are those two bastards he had on his boat with him. They're radicals; they're Black Muslims, man. Can you imagine what they'd try to do with that bomb if they did find it?"

Judah was quiet for several seconds then said, "Maybe they'd just want to sell the information like you did?"

Billy pulled the cover back over the stabilizers and said angrily, "What the fuck is wrong with you, Judah? All I wanted was some cash and a pardon in exchange for the location of the most dangerous weapon ever invented. These characters want to hurt us. Just ask Tran, he'll fill you in on Abdul and his buddies."

"All right. So what do you want to do now?"

"Get hold of Gusto," replied Billy. Then he gestured to the object under the canvas and said, "Tell him he can come and pick this thing up if he wants it. And tell him about Abdul and Hassam and whoever that other jerk was out on my boat. Tell him I want to talk to him."

Billy and Judah were alone in the condo as they climbed back up the stairs from the garage. Billy, feeling dizzy and weak, had to hold the railing to steady himself. When he got upstairs he flopped into a chair, saying, "My head hurts." Thirty seconds later he was in a full-blown seizure: limbs rigid, jaws clenched shut, eyes rolled back as foam bubbled at the corners of his mouth. Two hours later he was lying in his bed, exhausted and depressed.

"I'm glad I came back early," he whispered as Judah watched from the foot of the bed. "I would'a scared the shit outta Hannah if I'd pulled this trick out on your boat."

"Don't underestimate her, Billy. She'd have done just what I did and given you a shot of Dilantin, like we'd been taught to do if you had a seizure."

Billy rubbed his forehead. "I've still got a terrific headache."

"You want me to get you anything?"

"Yeah, get me three of those Percocets, and I'll wash'em down with a nice cold Blue Ribbon."

Judah hesitated. He started to say something about taking it easy on the drugs and alcohol, and Billy frowned at his reluctance.

"Afraid I'm going to overdose?"

"Naw," answered Judah as he picked the bottle of Percocet off Billy's dresser and shook out three ten-milligram tablets. "But tomorrow you've got to see Dr. West. He said he'd have to put you on some cortisone after you started seizing. It helps to control the swelling in your brain and suppress the seizures. You'll probably be taking Dilantin by mouth along with the cortisone."

"Yeah, I know. He told me that stuff would make me fat. I guess I've done pretty well, though. I've gone a whole month since I was diagnosed, and this is the first real problem I've had."

Judah had a beer in each hand when he returned to the bedroom. Billy offered a toast to their friendship before swallowing his pain meds.

"Promise me you'll watch out for Hannah after I'm gone."

"I've already done that, but I'll promise you once more."

"She told you I wanted to die on the water, didn't she?"

"Yep."

"Guess that can't happen now, I'd be too much trouble."

"I've made arrangements with the hospice people, Billy. You're going to live on my boat and have around-the-clock care, right to the end. We'll take the *Solitude* anywhere you want. John-Morgan and Lloyd have agreed to make daily trips in their boats and bring out anybody who wants to visit."

The Street

And his hunger burns
So he starts to roam the streets at night
And he learns how to steal
And he learns how to fight
In the ghetto
—Elvis Presley, "In the Ghetto"

AS LLOYD CHANGED into his workout clothes in the locker room at St. Dismas Center he was thinking about how well Damian seemed to be doing. He glanced at his watch and noted that Damian was a little late, but he didn't think much about it. When an hour had passed, however, he was concerned enough to call his grandparents.

"Oh, Lord, preacher," said a distraught Mrs. Small as she held the phone to her ear while looking out the window for her husband, "he had a real bad fight with Ronnie yesterday; and to make matters worse that no-account father of his showed up just after and carried him away with him. I think he's stayin' over at his place."

Standing in front of the door to Abdul's apartment, Monsignor Bryan could hear loud talking inside and listened for a moment before knocking. He was able to pick out Damian's young voice, but the two older ones weren't familiar. Lloyd guessed one was Abdul's. Dressed in black and wearing his Roman collar, Lloyd delivered three sharp raps on the door.

"Who is it?" demanded Abdul gruffly.

"I'm Monsignor Lloyd Bryan and I'm here to speak with Damian. Open up."

Abdul turned to look at Hassam. "Ain't this somethin'. Some priest I don't know from nobody comes to my door and starts givin' me orders!" He unlatched a series of three different dead bolts protecting his apartment, and yanked the door open.

Abdul was wearing a tan-colored Moroccan robe with an embroidered skullcap planted firmly on the back of his head. He gave Lloyd a head-to-toe once-over before finally saying, "You not speakin' with my son, now get."

Lloyd could see Hassam, dressed in the same sort of garb, standing by the old coal-burning fireplace with a picture of Louis Farrakhan hanging over the mantle. In the center of the floor was a richly woven Persian prayer rug. Lloyd cut his eyes to the right and noticed Damian on a tattered sofa, framed by a pair of tall windows that looked out over the street. He had his head down and did not acknowledge Lloyd's presence. Making no attempt to enter, Lloyd called out, "You all right, Damian?"

Damian didn't speak, but he did nod.

"You sure?"

"I'm sure," replied Damian meekly.

"Didn't I tell you to get your black ass outta here?" said Abdul forcefully while Hassam approached, arms folded across his chest, a menacing look on his face.

Lloyd didn't move a muscle as he returned Abdul's glowering stare with one of his own. He knew the rules of the street; and rule number one was never show fear, even in the face of overwhelming odds. It was a matter of honor. After a few moments he looked into Hassam's eyes and saw the same rage and evil as in Abdul's. Without looking away he said, "Damian, you want to leave with me? They can't keep you here against your will."

Lloyd watched stoically as Hassam moved close to the baseball bat Abdul kept next to the door.

"Damian," Lloyd repeated in a louder voice, "do you want to leave?"

"No."

"Look at me, Damian."

Slowly Damian raised his head revealing a swollen right eye.

"Who did that to you?" Lloyd demanded as he returned his eyes to Abdul and gave him a stare-down look.

"Ronnie did it," replied Damian, lowering his head and fixing his eyes on the floor.

With a sarcastic emphasis on Lloyd's clerical title, Abdul sneered, "Satisfied, Reverend Father?"

Lloyd didn't reply, but he returned Abdul's cold stare as Hassam picked up the baseball bat and slapped it in the palm of his left hand.

"Time for you to get your nigga ass back in the street," said Hassam as he tightened his grip around the bat's handle.

Lloyd didn't budge as he looked over at Damian. "You need me, you call me, understand?"

"Yes, sir."

Abdul and Hassam broke into sarcastic laughter, then Abdul even mimicked Damian's response. "'Yes, sir!' Ain't them fine manners? This cornbread-eatin', handkerchief-head, inside-the-house colored boy has trained my son how to be a well-behaved Negro, ain't he?"

Lloyd plastered Abdul and Hassam with one last steely glare; then turned again to Damian. "You know where to find me," he said tonelessly; and without another word he left Abdul and Hassam snickering in the doorway.

What followed was a continuation of Damian's indoctrination into radical Islam by Abdul and Hassam.

"I'd be back in prison," said Abdul, "if it wasn't for the teachings of The Prophet and all the brothers that delivered them to me when I was locked up. The Honorable Elijah Mohammad gave the black man a blueprint on how to live in a society that keeps its heel on the necks of all people of color."

"That's right, Damian," said Hassam. "My life turned around when I threw off the yoke of the slave-master's religion and put on the armor of Islam. What's happened to you and all our brothers and sisters isn't anything but the product of this racist country we live in and the bunch of crackers that runs it."

Abdul sat next to Damian and softly said, "I know I haven't

been much of a daddy to you, but that was in the time when I was lost and under the influence of white devils who made a livin' offa givin' me drugs they knew was gonna keep me in my place. But things is different now, son. The light of The Prophet, all praise be to Him, has shined into my soul, and I'm a different man now. No more drugs, no more booze, no more trashy livin' and talking and whoring around. They all things that our slave-masters were happy to provide 'cause they knew it kept the black man weak. I'm your daddy and I'm ready to accept my responsibilities now and try to raise you up in the way of The Prophet, all praise be to him; and if that Ronnie ever put his hands on you again, he ain't gonna have no more hands."

That night Damian accompanied his father and Hassam to evening services at their mosque. The next day he was enrolled in the Islamic equivalent of Sunday school and quit going to St. Dismas.

"It's hot out here," said Billy as he and Hannah closed the door to the *Solitude*'s main salon, "but the inside of this boat is like the cooler at my store."

Judah smiled and said, "Remember how hot it used to get when we were kids?" He removed his feet from the coffee table to stand and kiss Hannah on the cheek. When he glanced at Billy he could see the swelling in his face caused by the water-retaining effects of cortisone. "I can cut the air back if you'd like." Judah walked to the galley and opened the refrigerator.

"Naw, man, this feels good. All that crap I'm taking makes me feel hot all the time."

"You want anything, Hannah?" Judah asked as he pulled two beers from the fridge. He knew he didn't have to ask Billy.

"Well, it's after six, and I'm not working tomorrow. I think I'll have a mixed drink, maybe a Cosmopolitan. Think you can make one as well as Tony does at the Yacht Club?"

Judah could only smile. "I'll give it one hell of a try."

The TV remote in one hand and a beer in the other, Billy settled back with a sigh into one of the salon's large chairs. He was tired—awfully tired now; and although he had noticed his strength slipping away on an almost daily basis, he had tried to hide it as much as he could from Hannah and his friends. The weakness in his arms and legs seemed to be getting worse; he staggered a little when he walked and struggled when he attempted to stand. These things he couldn't hide. In spite of the medication he had had several more seizures. His speech was sometimes slurred, but Billy refused to surrender to the bed. Recently there'd been long visits with Lloyd Bryan, which consisted mostly of repeated confessions of sins long ago forgiven. When Billy left his condo to get on board the *Solitude* that afternoon, he knew he would not return.

"Tran's on board and we've got everything here we need," said Judah. "You'll be sleeping in my cabin, and when you've decided where you want to take the boat, we'll set sail."

"Who's gonna wipe my butt when I get too weak to do it?" asked Billy. "I don't want Hannah doing stuff like that."

"I'll wipe your butt," said Judah. "But I'm not kissing it."

Billy laughed, raised his bottle, and said, "Touché" Then he turned the sound up on the TV.

"Savannah-Metro police sealed off a neighborhood around Montgomery Street yesterday," said Sonny Dixon, WTOC's news anchor, "in response to a blast from a suspected bomb."

Judah and Billy watched the video of police inspecting a green Dumpster as they listened to the reporter's voice-over.

"There was a loud explosion about nine yesterday morning in this trash container located outside this Montgomery Street business. Police say the explosion was caused by the detonation of a rocket-propelled grenade, also known as an RPG, very similar to those used by the insurgents in Iraq. No one was hurt, but as you can see the surrounding homes were evacuated and the area searched. Around noon today, responding to a tip from the Crimestoppers' Hotline, Metro police executed a search warrant on the house you see behind me. Inside police found what they are describing as a cache of weapons, some of which included hand grenades, fully automatic rifles, thousands of rounds of ammunition, and two RPG's just like the one that exploded in the Dumpster. Two men have been taken into custody and are expected to be arraigned tomorrow on weapons charges. For WTOC's Action News, I'm Kim Angelastro."

"Thanks, Kim," said Sonny. "Now let's have a look at the weather from Ron Wallace."

The weatherman was standing in front of a satellite image of Africa's west coast. "Well, Sonny, as you know, it's a busy time for this area of the Atlantic, and we're starting to enter the peak of the hurricane season. So it should come as no surprise to find a tropical disturbance of this magnitude moving across the Atlantic. The hurricane center in Miami has designated this as a tropical depression twelve and thinks it could easily intensify to hurricane strength over the next few days. We'll have more on this and our local weather forecast after these important messages."

"How the hell do you get hold of an RPG?" asked Billy as he struggled to get up and use the head.

"Maybe Gusto can tell you. He's coming tonight, too."

"Oh, great." Billy placed his hand on the bulkhead to steady himself while he made his way to his cabin.

Nobody knew exactly how long he had left, but it was evident to everyone, especially Billy, that he was fading fast. The number of quality days was eroding at an even quicker pace. With this in mind Billy wanted to gather his closest friends around him while he was still able to enjoy their company. He had asked Judah to host a party the night before he left on what he was convinced would be his final voyage.

Standing on the stern with Judah and Hannah by his side, Billy greeted John-Morgan and Ann Marie, who arrived carrying two bottles of wine; then Lloyd, who was wearing his favorite Hawaiian shirt. A few minutes later Will and Charlotte McQueen stepped aboard. Congressman McQueen had postponed his return to Washington in order to be present; in his pocket he carried a special gift for Billy. Just after the McQueens, Special Agent Camacho appeared. He embraced Billy emotionally. "I can never forget how you rescued me from that godforsaken island, Captain Billy. You saved my life!" Finally Hannah's son, Matt, and his wife, Pam, stepped aboard.

Billy had grown close to Matt over the past several months, and he had especially appreciated Matt's help in getting his legal and financial affairs in order. Judah had also grown fond of Matt, seeing him frequently at Billy's condo, and Matt had developed similar feelings for Judah.

Several miles to the west a line of thunderstorms rolled across I-95, their towering, anvil-shaped cloud formations blanking out the sun while the storm's low pressure gradient sucked cooler air off the ocean. The temperature had dropped almost fifteen degrees; the breeze that swept across the Skidaway River allowed Billy's guests to enjoy themselves on the *Solitude*'s spacious stern. Tran and his wife, Min, circulated among the guests with platters of boiled shrimp pulled that morning from the Atlantic. Billy had his arm around Hannah while he expatiated on the finer points of a boat like the *Solitude* for Matt.

Around seven, distant flashes of lightning appeared in the western sky, and the rumble of thunder shook across Isle of Hope with the first drops of rain. Billy leaned against the railing and watched as the wind blew through Hannah's hair. "God," he said to no one in particular, "I don't want to leave this place." For a few moments, his burden was lessened.

After supper everyone gathered in the main salon, where Congressman McQueen tapped on his glass and said he had an announcement to make. Billy was seated on the sofa with Hannah on one side and Judah on the other when Will raised his glass and offered a toast in Billy's honor.

"We've all known Billy for many years, and our lives are richer for the experience. There's no one here who wouldn't make any personal sacrifice if they thought it would mean a cure for our friend; and we all share the same feelings of frustration for being so completely unable to help him. At a time like this I doubt there's anything Billy wants more than for his friends to gather around him as we are this evening. There is no greater gift than the love of friends and family." Will had worn a blazer to the party, which he had removed early on. As he spoke he lifted the jacket from the back of his chair and removed an envelope from the inside pocket.

"Billy, I always thought you got a rotten deal from our country back during the Mariel Boatlift fiasco, and I also thought you got an equally rotten deal when Brad Grady put the finger on you and plea-bargained his way out of that drug bust. He slung a lot of dirt on a lot of folks, including innocent people, in an attempt to save his own hide."

Will paused for a moment, then smiled. "You didn't know it, but for the past few weeks Judah and Agent Camacho have been raising a ruckus in Washington on your behalf. I'll bet I've spoken with Judah at least twice a day for the last week. He and Gusto are mostly responsible for what's in this envelope by pointing me in the right direction."

Hannah was holding Billy's hand. She could feel his grip tighten as Will spoke. He held up the envelope.

"I was at the White House last week, and the President personally placed this in my hand. What this is," said Will as he opened the envelope, removed its single-page letter, and passed it to Billy, "is a full and complete pardon from the president of the United States exonerating you for any wrongdoing in connection with the Grady case. Billy, your record has been wiped clean."

"Did you know about this, Hannah?" asked Billy as he unfolded the president's letter and read it.

"I knew Judah was trying to get the pardon for you, but I didn't know it had come through. I'm so happy for you."

"Thanks, Will," he said, fighting back tears as handed the letter to Hannah. "You too, Gusto. Judah, you've been a wonderful friend. Thanks."

As those gathered talked and finished their after-dinner drinks, Gusto approached Billy. "Judah says there're some things you wanted to talk about."

"Yeah. But I think Judah and Will should be in on this, too. I'll tell Will to hang around until everybody else has left."

A little after ten-thirty Will, Judah, and Gusto were gathered with Billy in his cabin, while Hannah and Charlotte remained topside. Billy quickly described the activities of the *St. Patrick* the day he and Tran had watched the boat move in circles over the area where he thought he had found the bomb. He also said he believed Abdul knew what had been hauled up from the ocean floor and dropped on the *St. Patrick*'s deck; and he suspected that Abdul and his friends Hassam and Alphonso were up to no good.

"This Hassam character," asked Gusto, "do you know his last name?"

"Uh huh, it's Udeen."

Gusto looked at Will for a second. "That's interesting, because just today I got a call from Washington telling me the Savannah police had arrested a father and son on weapons charges. Apparently they were in possession of some hand grenades, RPG's, and fully automatic rifles. When the locals found that stuff, they notified A.T.F., who then put the info out to Homeland Security. The way things work now, anything of that nature comes under close scrutiny for possible terrorist connections."

"Yeah," injected Will, "that was on the TV today. Didn't one of the RPG's blow up in a Dumpster?"

"Right, Congressman. But what you didn't hear was that the two who were arrested have started talking in an attempt to cut a deal with the F.B.I." Gusto looked at Billy and grinned, "You're gonna love this."

"Love what?"

"It just so happens that the father in this team has told the FBI he sold a couple of hand grenades to a black dude who drove a cab and went by the name of Hassam. They checked out the story, and this cab driver turns out to be a well-known Muslim militant who calls himself Hassam Udeen."

"Is he the same guy who's working on my boat with Abdul?"

Gusto reached into his shirt pocket and produced a photo of a black man dressed in army fatigues. "This is a photo of Hassam Udeen when he was in the Army during Operation Desert Storm. Does he look familiar?"

Billy held the picture in his hand and studied it for a moment, uncertainly. "It could be, but the Hassam I'm talking about has a beard. Could we ask Tran to take a look?"

"That's him, boss," said Tran as he tapped the picture of Hassam with his finger. "I know him anywhere. I can tell by eyes. He have cold, hard eyes. I no like, boss."

"Thanks, Tran," said Gusto as he placed the photo back in his pocket. “This is probably nothing at all, but we still want you to keep quiet about this. Not a word to anyone. Not your wife, your kids, and especially not to Hassam. Just act normal around him, understand?”

Tran stiffened his back, looked squarely at Gusto, and replied, “You got my word. I no say a thing.” Then he motioned towards Billy and continued, “I love America, you just ask Captain Billy, he tell you how much Tran love America. I kill many enemy in Vietnam. Hassam try hurt this country, I kill him, too. One more make no difference now.”

“I don’t think that’ll be necessary,” said Gusto, “but I do want you to keep your eyes and ears open, okay?”

Tran gave a quick nod of his head, then looked at Billy again. “Okay I go now?”

Billy smiled. “Sure, that’s fine, Tran. And thanks.”

After Tran closed the door Will looked steadily at Gusto. “Tell me more about Hassam Udeen.

“He’s a bad actor, Congressman,” answered Gusto, who was sitting at Judah’s desk in General Marshall’s chair. “I don’t know if Abdul Aleem is in the same league with him, but I tend to doubt it. After the first Gulf War Hassam got a general discharge from the Army because he was stirring up trouble in his barracks. Seems he believes any black who isn’t a Muslim is betraying his race and is a tool of American imperialism, and he wasn’t shy about expressing his opinions. You remember that G.I. who tossed the hand grenades into the officers’ tent just before we invaded Iraq?”

“Yeah,” responded Will, “he was a black guy who was also a Muslim, wasn’t he?”

“Yes, sir.” Gusto leaned forward and rested his elbows on his knees. “His name was Hasan Akbar, and he was a sergeant in the Hundred and First Airborne. Sergeant Akbar was a recent convert to Islam—and guess who one of his best friends was?”

“You talkin’ about Hassam?” asked Billy.

“That’s exactly who I’m talking about. Hassam was also in the Hundred and First, that’s how they met. Hassam used to be a member of the Nation of Islam, you know, Louis Farrakhan’s bunch, but he was also an apostle of a guy by the name of Khallid

Muhammad. Khallid was one of Farrakhan's lieutenants. He was a vicious anti-Semite along with a list of other twisted beliefs."

"I remember him," said Judah. "He was one of the worst."

"That's right," said Gusto, "and it may seem hard to believe, but one day he went too far in his remarks about Jews, even for Farrakhan, and Farrakhan slapped a muzzle on him. It seems Khallid was none to happy with what Farrakhan did, so he bolted from the Nation of Islam. After that he dug up the old Black Panther Party, dusted it off, and called it the New Black Panther Party." Gusto was smiling when he looked at Billy and said, "Guess who one of his first members was."

"Our guy, Hassam?"

"Right again. Hassam joined up just after the Army discharged him. He was quite active, but not a very big cog in the wheel until after the death of Khallid Muhammad in February of 2001. It just so happens that one of his best buddies was a character who went by the name of Malik Zulu Shabazz."

"Wait a minute," interrupted Judah, "wasn't Malik Shabazz really Malcom X? How could Hassam be friends with Malcom X? He's been dead since 1966."

Gusto leaned back in his chair, dumped a Cuban cigar into his hand from the cigar case he carried in his shirt pocket, stuck it between his teeth, and started chewing on the end.

"You're right and wrong at the same time, Judah. Malik Shabazz was, in fact, the Muslim name Malcolm X adopted when he converted to Islam. But I'm talking about Malik Zulu Shabazz, who's a lawyer from Chicago and the same age as Hassam. Malik Zulu Shabazz took that name in honor of his hero, Malcolm X, but inserted the Zulu so as not to be confused with Malcolm."

"Okay, I see. I'm sorry for interrupting."

"No problem, because these names can be very confusing. In fact I'm impressed that you'd know something like that."

"When you're a Jew," said Judah, "it pays to have a keen ear for those who'd like to kill you. But please, continue what you were saying about Malik Zulu."

Gusto took the cigar from his mouth and held it between his fingers while he spoke.

"Malik Zulu was tight with Khallid Muhammad, and when Khallid died, Malik was positioned to take over the number one spot in the New Black Panther Party, which he did. This meant that his buddy Hassam moved up a peg or two in the business."

Congressman McQueen, listening intently, was troubled by what he had heard. "Okay, Gusto, sounds like there's no question that Hassam is a pretty bad guy, right?"

Gusto nodded. "I concur with that assessment, Congressman."

"And you have pretty reliable information that he has at least two hand grenades?"

"Yes, sir."

"And given what Billy and Tran have told us, Hassam probably has a pretty good idea of where the Tybee Bomb may be?"

Gusto stuck his cigar back between his teeth, and from the corner of his mouth replied, "Yep."

Will walked over and sat next to Billy on the bed, then looked at Gusto indignantly. "Then why in the hell hasn't he been picked up? I mean we could bury this dirt bag on the weapons charges alone."

"I understand your concern, Congressman, but right now he hasn't done anything. Hassam might be a bad guy, but he's not stupid. I seriously doubt he's hiding those grenades in his house. We execute a warrant to search his home and don't find anything, then he's on the alert. Look, we've known about Hassam for quite some time, and he's shrewd. He has street smarts, and the guy is tough. He knows he's been watched. I think he moved down here, not to take care of his aunt, but so he could cool down and have some of the heat taken off him. We just want to keep an eye on him and see what he's up to. He might lead us to an even bigger fish. We can bust him anytime we want."

"Reverend Bryan," whispered a voice on the other end of the line.

"Yes, ma'am."

"This here is Yvonne Small."

"Yes, Mrs. Small?"

"He doesn't know I'm callin', but Damian's over here at our house. I think he's high on something. Anyway he's here wanting money from me and his granddaddy and when we told him no, he went and got real mad, even pushed my husband and started going through the drawers in our bedroom."

"Is he still there?"

"Yes sir, that's why I'm callin'. We scared of him. I don't want to call no police, but neither one of us can handle that boy."

"Sit tight, Mrs. Small, I'll be right over."

When Lloyd opened the front door to the Smalls' house, he could see Damian standing in the kitchen helping himself to whatever he found in the refrigerator. Damian heard the noise of his entry, looked over his shoulder, smirked, then returned his attention to the half-gallon container of milk he had been drinking from.

Lloyd stood at the kitchen door for a few seconds, then said, "I'd been wondering what would happen to you after you stopped coming to the center. Are you still staying with your old man?"

"Yeah," replied Damian, without looking at Lloyd.

"I heard you haven't been going to school regularly. Is that right?"

"I'm helpin' my father on the shrimp boat, sometimes I ain't got time for no school."

"What kinda shit you been doing today?" Lloyd looked over his shoulder at Damian's grandparents and motioned for them to stay in the living room.

"What the fuck's it to you, man?" Damian kicked the refrigerator door shut and took another swig of milk.

"I thought you might make something out of yourself, Damian, and I still do, but you can't if you're laying outta school and smoking weed or taking something."

"Who put you in charge, man?"

"Your granddaddy and grandmomma love you, Damian. They want the best for you. It hurts them to see you this way."

"Fuck them."

"You put your hands on your granddaddy, Damian?"

"Man, fuck you. All I wanted was a little piece of money. They got plenty."

Lloyd looked again at Mr. and Mrs. Small, who were huddled together in the corner of their living room, then asked, "Whatcha need money for, more dope?"

"Man, fuck you. You ain't nothing but a colored boy all dressed up in that preacher's suit and prancing around like a trained monkey to the tune of your white masters. Who the fuck do you think you are, stickin' your nose in other people's business?"

The sound of Yvonne's sobbing could be heard as Damian casually opened one of the kitchen cabinets, pulled out a box of Ritz crackers, tore it open, and stuffed two into his mouth.

"Where you keep the booze around here now?" he shouted to his grandparents. "You use ta keep it back here. You hidin' the shit now?"

"Oh Lord Jesus," cried Mrs. Small, "I can't stand no more of this."

"Okay, Damian," said Lloyd, "you're leaving this house right now. Let's go."

"Fuck you, I ain't going no damn place. That bitch called you over here, didn't she?"

When Lloyd was a teenager and working on the shrimp boat with his Uncle Elijah, he had once seen him take on a drunken dock worker with a move so fast, furious, and effective that he had never forgotten it. A white boy of about twenty, who worked on another boat, had decided, for no other reason than to feel superior to Lloyd and his uncle because they were black, to taunt Lloyd as he washed down the *St. Patrick*'s deck following a long day of hard shrimping.

"Be sure to put that hose on yourself," called out the boy, who stood on the dock wearing white shrimper's boots and no shirt. He had a quart bottle of Old Milwaukee in his hand. "Hey, nigger, you hear me?" he shouted. "I said to turn that hose on your nigger ass so it don't stink so much."

Two other white men of the same ilk who were also standing on the dock thought it great fun to watch as Lloyd tried to ignore the insults. From the corner of his eye, Lloyd watched as Elijah emerged from the wheelhouse, climbed off the boat, and approached the troublemaker.

"I'm sorry, mister," said Elijah softly, "but I didn't catch what you were sayin' to my nephew." All the three men broke out in derisive laughter. Then, in one seamless movement, Elijah grabbed the big talker by his testicles with one hand while pinning him against a piling with the other. When this happened the other two men started to move against him. Elijah calmly shouted, "You two crackers come any closer and I'll squeeze his balls off." This stopped the crackers in their tracks. Elijah then continued to the white boy, whose face was only inches from his. "I ever hear you talk like that again, I swear to God, you'll be singin' a high 'C' for the rest of your life, 'cause I'll cut your nuts off."

Lloyd's tormentor retreated rapidly, and when Elijah had climbed back aboard the *St. Patrick*, all he said was, "Moses McQueen taught me that move years ago. Works every time, 'specially with cowards." Lloyd, internally, was almost smiling at the recollection.

"I said that bitch call you over here?" repeated Damian.

Lloyd gave no reply while he watched Damian rifle through another cabinet in search of his grandfather's Early Times.

"Shit," said Damian, "she called you, I just know it." Then he shouted, "Where you keepin' your damn liquor?"

"That's enough, Damian," said Lloyd. "You're leaving right now."

"What part of 'fuck you' don't you understand?"

Damian had turned to face Lloyd.

Damian hadn't gotten the words out of his mouth before he found himself pinned against the cabinets he had been picking through only a moment before. As Lloyd squeezed his testicles he lifted him a foot off the floor, pressed his face against Damian's ear, and calmly said, "I don't understand that part of 'fuck you' that says you want to keep your balls, 'cause if you don't leave this house right now, you're gonna lose 'em."

Damian's eyes and mouth were stretched to the breaking point, and the pain he felt was so great that he couldn't even cry out. Lloyd tightened his grip on Damian's crotch and dug his forearm into his throat as he whispered, "I ever hear about you mistreating these wonderful people again and I will gladly go to hell for the pleasure of killing you, but not before I rip these worthless nuts off." Lloyd waited for a moment as Damian lamely struggled to free himself before sarcastically adding, "What part of 'rip your nuts off' don't you understand?"

When Lloyd finally loosened his hold on Damian, the boy crumpled to the floor, sobbing and holding his crotch. Lloyd reached down, pulled him to a standing position, grabbed him by his shirt collar, and hustled him out the front door.

"I'll deal with you later," he said as he watched the boy stagger down the steps. "In the meantime, if you come back around this house giving your grandparents trouble, you better give your heart to God, 'cause your ass is gonna be mine!"

The sun had just started peeping over the oaks on Beach Hammock as Judah and Billy sat in lawn chairs at the water's edge and watched the *Solitude* gently rise and fall with the swells caused by passing boats. They dug their feet into the sand and let the waves lap over their ankles and the breeze from the sound carry away the horseflies. Billy's face was even puffier from the cortisone, and his appetite had fallen off dramatically. The beer he had been nursing for the past twenty minutes was now warm; and he had only eaten a couple of the boiled peanuts Hannah had prepared that morning. She had waded across the slough that separated Beach Hammock from Williamson Island, where she walked with Judah's dog Moshe and watched as he chased seagulls across the sand. Billy's health seemed to be deteriorating rapidly, and she wondered if he would last through the end of September.

Hannah climbed to the top of the dunes, where the panorama of Wassaw Sound unfolded. The water sparkled with sunlight, and she watched as a dozen trawlers dragged their nets across the ocean floor. The surf's white noise was very pleasant. She turned her head back to Beach Hammock, where she could see Billy and Judah, sitting side by side, and thought how ironic it was that these two friends, both men she loved, would be with her in such a beautiful place. She wondered what would happen with Judah after Billy was gone.

At noon the temperature was close to ninety-five. The sun beat down on Beach Hammock like a sledgehammer and drove everyone to the confines of the *Solitude*'s air-conditioned salon. Billy was looking through Judah's DVD collection while he listened to the local news on WTOC. Suddenly his head snapped up, and he hollered plaintively for Judah.

"Savannah-Metro police took Monsignor Lloyd Bryan into custody this morning following a charge by Abdul Aleem of Savannah, who says the Catholic priest sexually molested his son two days ago."

Billy, Judah, and Hannah stared at the TV in disbelief as they watched videotape of their friend in handcuffs being led up the steps of the police barracks on Oglethorpe Avenue.

"The police haven't released any details about Mr. Aleem's accusations, nor have they revealed the name of the alleged victim. Monsignor Bryan has not yet been formally charged, and WTOC has learned that he is expected to be released sometime today on his own recognizance. A full investigation is pending, and police spokesman Bucky Burnsed says that after the investigation is completed, formal charges may be brought against the fifty-eight-year-old priest. The Catholic Diocese of Savannah has declined to comment on the Monsignor's arrest."

Lloyd had already planned to visit Billy that afternoon, and the trip to Wassaw Sound proved to be a welcome respite from the sudden storm that now swirled around him.

"I don't believe a word of it," said Billy as he embraced Lloyd.

"Neither do I," echoed Hannah when Lloyd turned to her. She put her arms around him.

Tears were in Lloyd's eyes as he said, "Come on, let's go inside. I'll tell you the whole story."

Judah was seated in the salon with a cell phone pressed against his ear when Lloyd entered. He put is hand up, signaling that he would be off the phone momentarily, and continued his conversation with the person on the other line.

"That's what I thought." Judah listened for a few more seconds, then said, "Get back to me when you know more." He also stood and embraced Lloyd. "I was just talking with a buddy of mine at the D.A.'s office. They think this is all bullshit, but with the way things are now, they have to do a full-court press with their investigation."

Lloyd wiped the tears from his eyes while he said, "Sit down, and I'll tell you all what happened."

The Thousandth Man

One man in a thousand, Solomon says,
Will stick more close than a brother.
And it's worth while seeking him half your days
If you find him before the other.
—Rudyard Kipling, "The Thousandth Man"

AS THE SHADOWS of Billy's life lengthened, he became ever more focused on the disposition of the immortal soul he now believed he possessed. Indeed, when he was alone, many of his waking moments were spent in reflection as he pondered the sins of his past life, rebuking himself for each one, and regretting the lost moments spent on frivolous distractions. More frequently his thoughts returned to his early days when his life was defined by the religiosity of his parents and the devotion of the priests and nuns who taught him. He sought for some tangible way to recapture a small part of what had been a happy and serene childhood. As it turned out, Lloyd Bryan would be that way.

"I've been temporarily relieved of my priestly duties until this investigation is completed," said Lloyd after he had finished explaining what had happened during his confrontation with Damian. "But the Bishop has given me permission to administer the sacraments to Billy out here on the boat. I also have permission to say Mass on the boat and brought everything I'll need with me."

"You mean we can have Mass right here?" asked Billy, his words slightly slurred.

"If Judah has no objection, I'm prepared to say Mass tonight."

"It would be an honor," said Judah.

"One more thing," added Lloyd with a sly smile—his first since the accusation had been made. "I also got permission from the bishop to say the Mass in Latin."

Billy's eyes opened wide; and in them, a long-absent brightness appeared. "I haven't been to a Latin Mass in probably forty years. I remember how much I loved it, and I was just thinking today that maybe . . . I don't know . . . maybe when it was dropped . . . maybe that was part of why I quit going. That would be wonderful, Lloyd."

The day was unusually cool and the humidity low as Lloyd sat with Billy on the stern and watched clouds shaped like elephants, lady-faces, and giants with clubs float overhead. The ocean breeze pushed the burnt-marshmallow smell of the salt marsh fronting Beach Hammock across the *Solitude.* Billy closed his eyes and remembered the days when he would stand on the seawall at Tybee as a sunburned child and hold his mother's hand while eating cotton candy. The sound of an approaching boat brought him back.

"That's Gusto's boat," he said with surprise as the *Endeavor* positioned herself about a hundred feet from the *Solitude* and dropped anchor. In a few minutes Gusto and a dark-haired woman were in their boat's little Zodiac tender headed in their direction.

"This is my wife, Carmella," said Gusto as he introduced her. About thirty minutes later John-Morgan in the *Graf Spee* was also tying off to the *Solitude.* With him were Ann Marie, Hannah's son Matt, and his wife Pam. A little later Will and Charlotte McQueen arrived in a perfectly preserved 1947 all-mahogany Garwood sedan hardtop named the *Little Feats.*

"Something's going on here," said Billy to Hannah as he leaned against the railing and surveyed all the friends who had gathered on Judah's boat. She slipped her hand around his arm.

"It's a surprise for you."

The moon rose early that evening. It floated over the Atlantic like a giant scoop of vanilla ice cream. As the sky darkened the Milky Way appeared low on the eastern horizon and the Little and Big Dippers became visible overhead. Mass would be said on the flying bridge, and Judah had placed kerosene lanterns all about to provide a warm, almost golden light.

Lloyd set up a simple altar in front of the helm, which consisted of a twelve-inch brass crucifix, an altar cloth embedded with the relic of a saint, a pair of beeswax candles in hurricane lamps, and two cruets, one containing water, the other wine. John-Morgan would serve as acolyte. Everyone gathered for the service just as the last speck of the sun's orb slipped behind the trees on Skidaway Island, leaving the sky to burn in orange and gold. What happened next startled Billy.

John-Morgan emerged from the stairwell, his hands together in prayer and dressed in an elaborate red cassock with a finely embroidered white linen surplice over it. He was followed by Monsignor Bryan, who wore pre-Vatican II vestments. It was the feast of St. John the Baptist, a martyr, and in his honor the chasuble he wore was blood-red. A white Crusader's Cross adorned the front and back of the vestment. It was a sight that had rarely been seen since 1963.

Lloyd intoned the prayers in Latin, and John-Morgan answered in kind. Then it was time for the homily.

"I'm going to make everybody happy," said Lloyd with a smile on his face, "because my sermon this evening will be brief." His almond-shaped eyes and coffee-colored skin were framed by silver hair and beard. His deep voice was very gentle; and when he spoke his words were like honey.

"We're gathered here tonight on this magnificent boat to be with our dear friend Billy Aprillia. We all know what lies ahead for Billy. It is no different from what lies ahead for all of us."

Without another word, Lloyd returned to the altar, genuflected before it and with the words, "Credo in unum Deum, Patrem omnipotentem factorem coeli et terrae, visibilium omnium et invisibilium," began to repeat the Nicene Creed as a profession of faith.

"I believe in one God, the Father Almighty, Maker of heaven and earth, and of all things visible and invisible."

From the back shadows of the fly bridge, Judah watched the ritual of the Mass. He had always been impressed by the formality, the pomp and circumstance, the vestments, and the artwork of the Catholic Church; and to him the strenuous dogma and rules of behavior required of its adherents were similar to the parades, pageantry, and order of the military culture in which he had been raised.

At Benedictine, Jews and other non-Catholics were not required to attend religious services, but Judah would often leave study hall and slip into the choir loft of the church, where he would watch the Mass. The power of its symbolism had not been lost on him; and although it had been almost forty years since he had last witnessed a celebration of the Mass, the aura of majesty and mystery still remained for him. It was the Last Supper, the Passover meal of his ancestors, complete with unleavened bread and wine. There may have been no bitter herbs, or the four Seder questions, but the similarity was unmistakable.

As he listened to Lloyd's repetitions of the ancient Latin prayers and supplications, Judah's eyes wandered to those present. Billy was closest to the altar, on his knees, with Hannah by his side. He would tell it to no one, but Judah envied Billy, even in his present state. He had Hannah. Then he looked at Tran and his wife Min, also kneeling, hands together. He envied them, too. They had each other. So it was with Will and Charlotte, and John-Morgan and Ann Marie.

Then he looked at Gusto, who was also kneeling with his wife. Carmella had been a novice in the convent of Mount Saint Agnes in Baltimore before she decided against a life with the Sisters of Mercy. Gusto met her at the F.B.I. headquarters in Washington, the first job she had after college. They were married a year later. Judah had learned a lot about Gusto, and he wondered if Carmella had any idea what her husband had done as a government agent. He wondered, too, if those things weighed upon him now—and if, as he knelt before the altar, Gusto felt the need to seek forgiveness. Nevertheless, he envied Gusto. He and Carmella had been married for more than twenty-five years. Judah was jolted from his melancholy state when John-Morgan rang a crystal bell as Lloyd elevated the consecrated host over his head, followed by a golden chalice of wine.

When Mass was over everyone retired to the main salon, where Tran and Min had laid out a smorgasbord of Vietnamese food: gha gio (fried spring rolls), banh tom (crispy shrimp pastries), bun (a type of rice vermicelli), hue (sour shrimp), called tom chua, and cau mong beef. For Judah, John-Morgan, and Will, all veterans of the Vietnam war, it was a walk back in time. Gusto had been in Vietnam too, but he couldn't talk about it.

As the evening progressed Judah began to notice a change come over Billy. He seemed genuinely happy, and when he laughed the old sparkle that had gone from his eyes returned. He mentioned this to Hannah, who told him she had also noted the change. It became infectious as the glow in Billy's eyes became apparent to all, and for the rest of the evening no one gave much thought to Billy's illness; not even Billy.

There were sleeping quarters for everyone on the assemblage of boats anchored that night at Beach Hammock; and as the evening drew to a close, Billy rose to his feet with little difficulty and announced, "Tonight I understand how Lou Gehrig felt when he stood on the diamond in Yankee Stadium and said, 'I consider myself the luckiest man on the face of this world.'"

After everyone else had gone, Lloyd administered the sacrament of Extreme Unction to Billy in his cabin. Only Hannah and Judah were present as an exhausted Billy lay on the bed while Lloyd prepared for the rite. The same crucifix and candles used earlier for the Mass were in place on the night stand, as were holy oils. The sacrament is intended to give both physical and spiritual strength to the sick and dying.

Judah listened while Lloyd repeated a series of prayers and watched as the Monsignor anointed Billy's eyes, ears, nose, lips, hands, and feet with oil, because they represented the means by which most sins are committed. Judah recognized that this rite, too, had its roots in Judaism.

After the rite was completed and Lloyd and Judah had gone to bed, Hannah held Billy in her arms while the effects of the Halcion he had taken allowed him the escape of sleep. After Billy had drifted away, Hannah put her head on the pillow next to him. She listened quietly to his breathing until she, too, was overtaken by Hypnos, the god of sleep.

At about two in the morning, Billy was awakened by a headache.

It was nothing new for him, but this one seemed a little worse than the others. As he slipped away from Hannah, sleeping soundly next to him, he grabbed his bottle of Percocet off the night stand and stuffed it into the pocket of his shorts. Quietly he climbed the stairs to the galley, where he picked up one of Judah's Harmony Club tumblers and filled it with ice. Then he found a fifth of Jack Daniels and crept through the salon, where Judah and Lloyd were stretched out on the sofas, lost in sleep. When he got to the cabin door, Billy turned and gazed upon his friends. Tears welled in his eyes. "Good men," he said softly. "Very good men." Then he headed for the bow of the *Solitude*.

The sky was incredibly clear and full of stars as Billy sat in the lounge chair in which Hannah had been sunning that day. He stretched his legs out, rested his back, and lifted his head toward the heavens. Then he pulled out his medicine bottle and dumped four Percocets into his lap. After that he poured some Jack Daniels over the ice and listened as it cracked in the glass when the liquor hit. Billy popped all four pills into his mouth and washed them down with a good swill of Tennessee sour mash.

The meteor showers of August—the most intense of all—were in full swing after 2:00 A.M. Billy pointed his chair toward the southeast horizon. Streaks of burning Perseid meteors immediately ripped across the blackness. They had traveled millions of light years from the constellation Perseus, and now they burned themselves out in a show that only the heavens could produce. Billy sipped from his glass as he watched and remembered how his mother had told him that shooting stars were really souls leaving Purgatory for Heaven. Billy smiled and whispered, "Must be millions leaving tonight."

The pain inside his head receded faster than he had expected, and soon he began to feel really good. "It's the Percocet," Billy said to himself as his eyes followed one burning dot of orange after another. He seemed to lose track of time as the stars rained down; and he remembered being on board the *St. Patrick* with Judah and Lloyd as they lay on their backs four decades earlier and watched this same spectacle unfold.

At some point an overwhelming sense of well-being washed over

Billy like a spring tide; his body felt light. Every fear of death was lifted from him. "This can't be the drugs," he thought as he rested his head while his eyes beheld the cosmos. "Thank you, Lord," said Billy just before his eyelids became too heavy and he surrendered to a deep sleep on the waters where he had lived his life.

Judah was first up the next morning, and after he had turned the coffee maker on and downed a couple of aspirin he climbed to the flying bridge to survey the sound. He smiled when he saw Billy asleep on the bow, a bottle of Jack Daniels on one side of the lounge chair and an empty glass on the other. He was tempted to go and wake him just so he could have somebody to talk with, but then he decided, "Let the poor bastard sleep. He deserves it."

Judah had been down below for almost thirty minutes before he climbed back topside with his coffee and his latest copy of *National Review*. He looked once again at Billy, who had not changed positions. As he sipped his coffee he watched Billy more carefully; and after a few minutes he put the cup down and headed for the bow. Judah approached Billy quietly. When he was only a few feet away, he stopped and watched carefully for the rise and fall of Billy's chest. There was none.

John-Morgan knelt by the lounge chair, and for perhaps fifteen seconds all he did was look at Billy. Then he placed his hand on his chest, just over his heart, for a few more seconds, and afterward lifted his eyelids. When he removed his hand Billy's eyes remained open. John-Morgan gently closed them again.

"I'm afraid you're right, Judah," he said quietly. "He's gone." Then John-Morgan stood, and without another word he walked to the railing and looked out across the sound. It was only seven. The air was still cool, and the sun had not fully risen from behind the ocean horizon. The tide was coming in, and the sound of the breakers on the other side of the dunes was carried by the wind to the *Solitude*.

Judah came and stood by John-Morgan's side. Both men were silent for several minutes before John-Morgan finally said, "I've seen a lot of people die in my life. The ones who've been sick for a while, the ones I knew weren't going to make it, they all seemed to rally at the end; and if I wasn't with them when it happened, their friends and relatives all told me how good they seemed just the night before or maybe even hours before they passed away. It's like on some level they knew their suffering would soon be ending and that something better than this world was waiting for them. I can't help thinking that's what we saw last night in Billy. I don't know if he was consciously aware that he would be dead in only a few hours, but I think his spirit knew, just like the spirits of all the other people I took care of over the years."

"We need to get Lloyd before we tell Hannah," said Judah as he fought back his tears.

"You stay here with Billy," answered John-Morgan. "I'll go get Lloyd."

As John-Morgan worked his way to the stern, Judah went to Billy and knelt beside him. Tears now streamed down his face, and in uncontrolled sorrow Judah put his head on Billy's chest and wept. When John-Morgan and Lloyd returned, they found him cradling Billy's lifeless body in his arms as he sobbed at the loss of his dearest friend. When Judah felt Lloyd's hand on his shoulder, he eased Billy back onto the lounge chair. Lloyd knelt next to him; and with an upraised right hand made the sign of the cross over Billy's body. He prayed for the disposition of his soul.

"We can't leave him out here," said John-Morgan, who began to unfold the blanket he had brought back with him. After Billy's body was covered the three men stood for several minutes in silence as they looked at the lifeless form under the blanket. Then Lloyd reached down, took Billy in his arms, and carried him to the main salon, where he placed him on one of the sofas. It was also he who knocked softly on the door to Billy's cabin; and when he heard Hannah's sleepy voice call out, "Who is it?" he gently answered, "It's Lloyd, Hannah. I have something to tell you."

Billy's funeral was held three days later at the Cathedral of St. John the Baptist. All three local TV stations were at the noon Requiem Mass to cover the passing of a local legend. In addition, cameras and reporters from Fox News and CNN were also present. Their interest wasn't in Billy but in Monsignor Bryan and the charges of child molestation, which had now gained national attention. From the back of the church they focused their lenses on Lloyd as he said the Mass and delivered Billy's eulogy. The television crews were even present in Bonaventure Cemetery as seven members of the Air Force's funeral team fired three volleys from their M-16's. That evening an attractive female reporter appeared on Fox's seven o'clock news.

With moss-draped oaks and sun-bleached tombstones in the background, the reporter related how Lloyd had been relieved of his priestly duties by the Bishop of Savannah, but had been given permission to preside over Billy's funeral because of their close friendship. She also identified Judah as one of the pallbearers and former adviser to the president's reelection campaign. She even attempted to interview Judah, but was cut short with a terse "I'll have no comment for the time being."

One person who did not shy away from the cameras was Abdul who, dressed in full Muslim garb, stated he was present to honor the memory of his former captain while at the same time taking numerous shots at Monsignor Bryan and vowing to have him sent to prison for what he had done to his son. That evening Judah hosted a gathering of Billy's friends and family on his boat and watched in sadness as Shep Smith of Fox News said, "And now live from Savannah, Georgia, our own Gayle Stanley with a story about another possible child-abuse scandal involving a monsignor in the Roman Catholic Church. Gayle, what have you got for us tonight?"

Lloyd and Judah sat next to each other as they listened as Ms. Stanley's recapitulation of every detail of Damian's allegations, followed by an interview with Abdul. Billy's flower-covered grave served as a background. Later in the evening Lloyd told Judah he was at the lowest point in his life.

Sowing the Wind

> For they have sown the wind, and they shall reap the whirlwind: it hath no stalk: the bud shall yield no meal: if so be it yield, the strangers shall swallow it up.
>
> —Hosea 8:7

THREE DAYS after Billy's funeral a tropical depression formed in the Atlantic off the coast of Florida. The storm quickly developed gale-force winds as it moved northward, skirting the coastline. When it reached the Georgia-Carolina border, it slowed to a stall, punishing the beaches from Charleston to Brunswick with furious northeast winds for more than twenty-four hours. Beach erosion was severe on both Tybee's northern end and Wassaw Island.

Billy had left almost everything to his daughter Claire, who had been approached by Abdul with an offer to lease the *St. Patrick* from her. She agreed; and two days after the storm had passed, Abdul took the boat down the Wilmington and into Wassaw Sound in search of shrimp. With him were Hassam and Damian.

At Wassaw's northern end lies a shoal that points its finger out into the ocean for more than a mile. It is covered by varying depths of water when the tide is in, but at low tide the shoal is completely visible.

Over the last 150 years, Wassaw Sound and the adjoining waters have been littered with all manner of man-made objects, from a sunken Confederate blockade runner to the contents of wrecked barges. Strong northeast winds, which stir these waters like a cook's ladle, often reposition this long-resting bottom debris.

In May of 1980, for example, a barge filled with scrap metal began listing and dumping its contents about a mile off Wassaw Island, very close to the shoal at the northern end. Most of what was lost consisted of old refrigerators, washing machines, and junk car bodies. Over the years some of them would be washed up onto the shoal. The sight of this and other flotsam resting on the shoal was nothing new to those familiar with the area, so when the *St. Patrick* passed no more than twenty yards away as she headed out, Abdul was not surprised to see the junk washed up by the recent northeaster.

The *St. Patrick* was coming up on green channel marker thirteen as Hassam stood in the wheelhouse with a pair of binoculars and studied the sandy shoal, while at the same time extolling the virtues of Islam to a bored and frustrated Damian. He noticed an odd shape ahead, which he quickly recognized as a tree stump. Then the rusted hulk of an old car half-buried in the sand caught his eye; and he kept the glasses fixed on it as the *St. Patrick* passed close by. Hassam was about to shift his attention further down the shoal when something unusual next to the car body caught his attention.

At first glance Hassam thought it was an old fifty-five-gallon drum lying on its side at an angle about half under the sand; but as he sharpened the focus, he could tell it was much too long for an ordinary oil drum. The boat was starting to move away from whatever was on the shoal as Hassam still had his glasses fixed on it. He was about ready to put the binoculars down when he suddenly shouted, "Abdul, stop the boat! I think that might be the bomb up there on the shoal."

"Lemme see what you're talkin' 'bout," replied Abdul as he throttled back. Hassam handed him the binoculars. Abdul kept the glasses to his eyes for maybe a minute, and Damian watched curiously as his father's fingers worked the focus back and forth.

"I don't know," said Abdul, "let's take a closer look." He handed the binoculars back to Hassam and spun the wheel to bring the boat around.

Shrimp boats don't draw much water, and the shoal drops off at a fairly steep angle, so Abdul was able to get the bow of the *St.*

Patrick to within about ten yards of what Hassam had seen. They all went forward and looked carefully at what lay in the sand.

"I don't know much about bombs," said Abdul, after a very long and expectant examination, "but I guess that kinda looks like it could be one."

"That's what I think, too," answered Hassam as he tried to use the binoculars at close range. Finally he said, "Get me in close as you can. I'm going over the side and have a look at that thing."

It was dead low tide, so there was no current, and Abdul had the bow of the *St. Patrick* planted in the sand. Hassam slipped over the side and breaststroked part of the way to the shoal, then waded in the last few yards.

The sand on the shoal was wet and soft; Hassam's feet sank in above his ankles as he trudged over to the mysterious object. What he found was a barnacle-encrusted blunt-nosed cylinder about four feet in diameter. It was resting at a fifteen-degree angle with six feet showing above the sand. Hassam had no way of knowing how much more was buried, but whatever he had found seemed to be large when compared with the conventional bombs he had seen in the military. After he circled the cylinder a couple of times, Hassam took the Buck knife he always carried and tapped it against the cylinder's side. Whatever he was looking at wasn't hollow. Then he took his knife and scraped away some of the barnacles; underneath was what Hassam thought might be olive drab paint. With a little more work he was able to scrape down to bare metal. Then he took the point of his knife and scratched. "Looks like aluminum to me," he said to himself. After a few more seconds, he stood and shouted back to the boat, "Get me one of the shovels, Damian."

For the next fifteen minutes Hassam sweated and grunted as he dug sand from around what he thought was the Tybee bomb. The sand was wet and heavy; seawater quickly seeped into the trench he had dug along the top of the cylinder in an effort to see how long it was. He finally had to quit, but he had uncovered an additional four feet of the object.

"Tide's turned now," shouted Abdul. "We gotta get goin'. This'll all be underwater in another hour."

When Hassam stepped into the wheelhouse, the first thing he said was, "You hit the save button on the G.P.S.?"

"Yeah," replied Abdul, pointing to the overhead instrument, "that's the coordinates right there."

Hassam quickly scanned the horizon. "I don't see nobody else around. That thing'll be covered by water pretty soon, so nobody else will see it either."

As Abdul backed his boat away from the shoal and turned toward the ocean, Hassam was caught in deep thought. Finally he turned to Abdul. "I think that's the bomb you and that cracker Billy found. Hurricane Debbie moved it some, and that northeaster we just had must'a rolled it up on that shoal. Now we know where it is."

Damian knew nothing about the lost hydrogen bomb, or Abdul's belief that it had been discovered while he was working on the *St. Patrick*; but he was absorbing everything that Hassam and his father said. When he had first started living with his father, he was numb to his surroundings: he was numb in every way. Very little registered with him; and when Abdul gave him an order, he obeyed almost robotically. As time progressed, however, he became less and less enamored of the lifestyle he was forced to lead under his father's "care." Abdul was rigid and demanding; and when he and Hassam were together—which was often—they treated Damian more as a servant than a child. On the boat Hassam was particularly offensive, making Damian perform almost all of his tasks while he stayed with Abdul in the wheelhouse, where they discussed the teachings of Minister Farrakhan for hours as the *St. Patrick* dragged the waters. When Abdul and Hassam were together, it was almost as though Damian were invisible to them—except when it came to work.

When he was alone with his father, Abdul was cold and harsh. He tolerated no behavior that deviated even slightly from what he believed to be the teachings of Islam; and if Damian stepped out of line, he never spared the rod. When the incident involving Monsignor Bryan occurred, Abdul was able to manipulate Damian's anger, and thus control his behavior. Under his father's roof Damian experienced few of the simple joys of life and youth; and he had begun to contrast this life with what he had been exposed to in his grandparents' home. It wasn't too long before he began to suspect that his father wanted him around only because he believed there was a big financial score in his pending case against Monsignor Bryan and the Diocese of Savannah.

When the nets were hauled in for the first time that day and the goody bag's knot pulled loose, it was mostly Damian who sorted out the trash fish under the pounding sun, and then shoveled the catch into the hold and iced it down. When he heard Hassam talk about how the white devils had enslaved and mistreated people of color for hundreds of years, his rants began to ring hollow.

On the way back to Thunderbolt two days later, Damian overheard snippets of conversation between his father and Hassam. He didn't know exactly what they were talking about, but he did hear things like "pollute the environment and use the grenades." Whenever he entered the wheelhouse the conversation would become hushed and secretive. Damian realized that something ominous was in the air.

Immediately after Monsignor Bryan was arrested on allegations of child molestation, Bishop Burke launched a full-scale investigation of the incident. The panel of three priests and three laymen he headed, along with the Church's attorneys, interviewed Mr. and Mrs. Small, Monsignor Bryan, and Damian. Also present was Matt Davenport, Lloyd's personal attorney.

Abdul was present when Damian was interviewed. So was Alan LeRoi, the attorney Abdul had hired in anticipation of a large cash settlement with the Diocese of Savannah. Every aspect of Lloyd's life was placed under a microscope, especially his activities at St. Dismas Center, and particularly his relationship with the young people there. The Church hired the best private investigator in town, who conducted a meticulous inquiry into Lloyd's private life, including his friends and the places he frequented.

Damian's testimony before the panel was well scripted; he had been coached by Abdul. He denied being under the influence of alcohol or drugs and painted a picture of Lloyd's actions as more sexual in nature than violent. Abdul appeared at the hearing in full

Muslim regalia; his hostility was apparent when he was questioned about Damian's behavior following the incident. The panel also took testimony from a score of character witnesses who appeared on Lloyd's behalf, the most prominent of whom was Otis Adams, Savannah's black mayor. Judah also appeared before the committee on Lloyd's behalf, as did ministers from various Protestant churches in Savannah.

At the conclusion of the hearing, Bishop Burke announced that the panel would take several weeks to study the testimony before it delivered its findings to the public. Privately he informed Lloyd that, although he did not approve of what he had done when confronting Damian, he did not consider it to be abusive, and certainly not sexually abusive. Lloyd was also informed that he would not be able to resume his priestly duties until after the panel had released its report.

Lloyd was relieved by the bishop's support, but still faced criminal charges, and undoubtedly a civil action as well. The grand jury was set to convene in little more than a week, and he assumed it would return a bill of indictment, forcing him to undergo a very public trial on charges of child molestation. There was a constant knot in his stomach, and he sought peace by taking his boat to Wassaw Sound almost daily, where he could think and pray in solitude.

As horrible as the situation was, one positive thing emerged for which Lloyd was most grateful: not a single one of his friends had deserted him. Judah in particular was supportive, and Lloyd found himself having dinner on the *Solitude* almost nightly. After a while Lloyd came to believe that Judah needed his support and counsel almost as much as he needed Judah's.

"How much you think you gonna get?" asked Hassam as he stood next to Abdul in the *St. Patrick*'s wheelhouse. He was watching an electronic map of the Wilmington River displayed on the G.P.S. and following the little arrow that represented the boat as it moved toward the sound.

"Goin' by what my lawyer says, answered Abdul, "could be three or four million. It'll all be Damian's, but I got his power of attorney and I'll control what happens to it."

"Three or four million," said Hassam in wonder. "Man, that's a lot!"

It was close to eight in the evening when the *St. Patrick* neared the shoal where the bomb rested. The tide was dead low. There was only another hour of daylight left when Abdul nudged the shrimp boat's bow into the sand. The old car body was still there. So was the bomb.

Because it was a weekday Alphonso couldn't be with his friends as they sought to crack the casing on the bomb, but he knew what was going to happen. And he had quietly informed The Lion about the scheme.

Abdul and Hassam had assumed that there would be very little chance that any recreational boaters would be around to see them. They figured it was about the same for commercial vessels. Abdul watched intently as Hassam took the two olive-drab, baseball-size hand grenades he had bought months ago and placed them into a gym bag, followed by two sixteen-ounce mason jars and a piece of PVC pipe four inches in diameter and six inches long. The pipe was capped on both ends and packed with black powder Hassam had legally purchased only days before at a local gun shop. Inserted into one end of the pipe bomb was a coil of water-proof fuse that would burn twenty minutes before it reached the black-powder bomb.

When Hassam was in the Army he had learned that, during the Korean War, the light planes used for artillery-spotting carried no armament. Out of frustration the pilots tried to come up with a way of dropping a type of small, improvised bomb on the enemy soldiers they frequently saw taking shots at them with rifles. Hand grenades would have been the perfect answer, but their three second fuses would have exploded well before they hit the ground. Then some resourceful pilot realized that a hand grenade fit perfectly into a sixteen-ounce Mason jar and that it would be possible to pull the safety pin on the grenade and slip it into the jar without the grenade exploding. Dropped from a plane, the grenade wouldn't detonate until it hit the ground, broke the jar, and released the firing pin. This trick was also extensively used in Vietnam, and Hassam always thought it was slick as hell. It also solved the problem of how he could set the grenades off next to the bomb and live to tell about it.

Once Hassam was on the shoal Abdul lowered the gym bag by a rope over the bow. Hassam scurried to the bomb and scooped a hole out under it as deep as he could. Then he pulled the pin on one of the grenades and carefully slipped it into the jar; repeated the process with the second grenade; and put both into the hole. His hands were shaking a little as he nudged the PVC pipe between the two Mason jars. That completed, Hassam stood and spooled the fuse out across the sand. When he got to the end he looked up at Abdul to make sure he was ready. Abdul gave him a thumbs-up. Hassam lit the fuse, then as fast as he could run through the soft sand he headed for the *St. Patrick.* The second Abdul knew Hassam was safely aboard, he backed his boat off the shoal, pointed the bow into Wassaw Sound, and gave his engines full throttle. As the *St. Patrick* moved away from the bomb at ten knots, Hassam stood on the stern, watching it anxiously through his binoculars.

Hassam had read everything he could find on the Tybee Bomb. He had spent hours on the internet at the Bull Street public library in research; and among other things he had discovered that the bomb in question held four hundred pounds of TNT used as an accelerant to initiate the nuclear chain reaction. He had even found pictures of the Mark-15 on the internet; and he was certain that what he had found out on the shoal looked just like those pictures. He had also read that, by this time, the TNT had probably become unstable, and that the government was afraid it might detonate if the bomb were discovered and then moved. Therefore he had every reason to believe that the shock of the two hand grenades going off under the bomb would ignite the TNT and expose the environment to the radioactive material inside.

The *St. Patrick* was just abeam of Battery Morgan when Hassam saw the white smoke from his black-powder bomb billow over the shoal. He counted to three, and just as planned he saw the black smoke from the hand grenades puff up, too. Four hundred pounds of TNT should make an impressive blast; but as hard as Hassam looked and hoped, no such explosion followed.

"Allah has willed it," he said as he went to the wheelhouse and told Abdul about the failure.

"Well, whad da we do now?" asked Abdul, who had been counting on a real knockout punch against the infidel America.

"Don't worry," replied Hassam. "I got another idea."

Across the Street

I will spend my whole life through
loving you, loving you.
Winter, summer, spring-time, too,
loving you, loving you.
Makes no difference where I go or what I do.
You know that I'll always be loving you.
—Elvis Presley, "Loving You"
Words and music by
Jerry Leiber and Mike Stoller

IT HAD JUST STOPPED raining as Judah passed Wormsloe Plantation and headed over the causeway toward Sandfly. The street was slick with the rain, and the reflected afternoon sun caused him to squint. When he reached Montgomery Crossroads he turned left; and in moments a Wal-Mart Supercenter rose on what had once been thousands of feet of woods filled with giant moss-draped oaks. He strained to see the screen of the old drive-in theater he had been to so often as a teenager, and finally he caught a glimpse of it behind some pines the bulldozers had managed to spare.

Judah was on his way to Hannah's house; and the thought of being there again after so long had him thinking about how so much of his beloved hometown had changed. It saddened him when he made his turn onto Waters Avenue and noticed that the big oaks that had stood next to the old Standard Oil station on the corner were gone, cut down to make the traffic flow better. Waters Avenue wasn't a sleepy two-lane blacktop through forest and farmland anymore, but a busy four-lane highway bounded by condos, office complexes, and cheesy fast food restaurants. It seemed the things he had built his memories on were gone now—like Billy. He almost had tears in his eyes when he turned left onto Althea Parkway and entered Kensington Park, his old neighborhood.

When Hannah's house came into view, he admonished himself for his melancholy, forced a smile, and checked in the rearview mirror to make sure his shirt collar was just right.

As he pulled into her driveway Judah decided the house looked pretty much the same as it had forty years before. Even his old house across the street hadn't changed much, and that was reassuring. The tall sweet gum in which he had built the biggest tree house in Kensington Park was still standing, and the azaleas his mother had planted along the front of the house were all neatly trimmed. He had held on to the house after his parents died, mostly because of its sentimental attachment, but had sold it a while back when he had decided to start downsizing. He never thought he might come home again. Now he wished he had kept it.

Judah stood next to his car for a moment and looked at the picture window in Hannah's living room. He remembered how some nights he had sat in his bedroom, hoping he would catch a glimpse of her, then shrugged and started for the front door. Just before knocking he looked over his shoulder at his old bedroom window.

"The old neighborhood bring back some memories?" asked Hannah as Judah stepped inside.

"Like you wouldn't believe," he replied as he embraced her and kissed her on the cheek.

"I hope they're all good." She was smiling the smile that had won his heart when they were at Armstrong together.

"You're not going to believe this," Judah said as he looked around the living room, "but I remember this furniture. This is the same stuff your mother had, isn't it?"

Hannah smiled again. "Most of it is. My mother had expensive taste, and my father indulged her." Her voice trailed away a little as she added, "Seemed to keep the peace."

For a moment their eyes connected. Each seemed to sense the sadness in the other until Hannah broke the spell by cheerily saying, "Anyway, I'm so glad you could come over. I've prepared a real Southern meal for you, something I'll bet you didn't get much of up in Washington. We're gonna have roast beef with rice and gravy, yellow squash, butter beans, corn bread, and iced tea. And for dessert I made a pecan pie. Now come on back to the den—you do remember my den, don't you?—and I'll fix us something to drink."

Judah smiled broadly; and, "This looks pretty much the same, too," he said as he followed Hannah into the pine-paneled room. "But that sofa is new. That's not the one we sat on while I helped you with your homework."

"No, that was a Simmons Hide-A-Bed. My grandmother would sleep on it when she came up from Lyons. I got rid of that thing years ago. I always thought it was awful."

Judah sat on the sofa and watched as Hannah put ice into a couple of tumblers bearing the seal of the St. Andrews Society. Her father had been a member for many years. She was wearing rose-colored slacks with a sleeveless silk flower-print blouse, and Judah would have sworn that she hadn't gained a pound over the years. He wondered how she could do it. When she sat next to him he could smell the slightest hint of a very pleasant perfume. The conversation was light, mostly centering on what old friends were doing, and that carried them through the meal. After dinner they returned to the den and sat next to each other again. Judah leaned his head back against the sofa and let out a sigh.

"That really was a wonderful meal. Thanks again for inviting me."

Hannah put her hand over his, looked at him steadily. "Judah, there's something I've got to tell you that's very important."

Judah sat up straight with a shock. "Oh God, don't tell me there's something wrong with you! You're not sick, are you?"

Hannah tightened her grip a little and quietly said, "No, my dear Judah, this is good news. At least I think it is."

"Okay," he replied pensively. "I could use a little good news, so fire away."

Hannah was quiet for a moment; her eyes were fixed on the coffee table. Then she drew a breath, turned to Judah, and said, "This is something I've had to hold inside me for many, many years. It was something I wanted to tell you so badly, but I just couldn't for a whole bunch of reasons; and when you find out what it was, then I think you'll understand."

Judah was gazing fearfully into Hannah's eyes. All he could manage was a slight nod. Then she took another deep breath and said, "Judah, you know my son Matt." Judah nodded again, "Well, Clark isn't his father. You are."

For several moments Judah's eyes remained locked with Hannah's as her revelation sank in. Then Hannah placed her hand on Judah's cheek and said softly, "It's true. Matt is your son. It was your baby I was carrying when I married Clark, and I knew it—but my mother wouldn't allow me to marry you. She wouldn't let me tell Clark, either, she was so set on me marrying him." Tears streaming down her face, Hannah continued. "I loved you, Judah, with all my heart. But I couldn't do anything about it."

"Because I was a Jew," said Judah angrily. "That was it, wasn't it?"

Hannah's eyes were closed tight as the tears flowed. She was unable to speak. Eventually she regained control and was able to look at him again. "I wanted to marry you; I wanted to be with you, Judah—but my parents wouldn't stand for it. Oh, God, you should have heard Mother screaming at me. She called me a slut and a whore and said nobody in her family would stand for me marrying a Jew. I felt like killing myself."

Judah was silent for several seconds. "Does Matt know about this?"

"No, I never told him."

"Does Clark know he's not Matt's father?"

"Yes. After Matt was born and started growing up, the Davenports started talking about how he didn't look a thing like Clark. By that time I already had another baby and was pregnant with my third; and Clark and I were fighting all the time. He was angry with me for messing up his football scholarship by getting pregnant, and when his family started planting seeds in his head, he started turning on Matt. It was just pitiful. I wanted to leave him, but I couldn't. I had three children to take care of."

"Does Clark know I'm Matt's father?"

"Yes. One night he was particularly hard on Matt and spanked him for practically nothing. Then he turned on me. He accused me of sleeping around on him and said that Matt looked just like you. At that point I gave up and just admitted the truth. It was a really nasty scene, Judah, but there was also something liberating about it. I think that's when I started to realize that sooner or later, I'd have to leave him."

Judah stood, went over to fix them both a drink, and said, "So, you stayed in a very unhappy marriage because of your children; and after they were out of the nest, you decided to divorce Clark?"

Hannah's mascara was running down her cheeks. She dabbed her eyes with a cocktail napkin as she nodded. "That's pretty much the story. I was married for twenty-two years to a man I never loved. He despised me and my son. When it was over I was happy. I never looked back. At least until tonight."

Judah could only shake his head over and over again as he sat down next to her. "I don't think I've ever been more taken aback by anything in my life." Then he let out a breath that puffed up his cheeks. "Yeah, I think this is good news. I'd kind of given up on ever having any children. I mean at first I didn't want any; and then as I got older and my own biological clock started ticking down, I decided I really wanted them. You don't know much about my life after I left Savannah for Washington, but my third wife, Marcia, she got pregnant. When she informed me I was elated. She was distraught. She was an up-and-coming reporter on the CBS affiliate in D.C. and informed me that a baby would mess up her career track. She had an abortion. Things started falling apart not too long after that. I remember how utterly callous I thought it was of her to do that. Money was no problem for us at all, so what she did caused me to see her in a whole new light. When I look back now, I think that's what started me on my way back home. There just had to be a better life."

Hannah placed her hand on Judah's as he turned to face her. He could see the signs of aging, the rough road she had traveled, but somehow her eyes had retained all of the enchantment he had seen in them forty years before.

"Judah, I want you to know that I have never stopped loving you. Not once in all these years. When I divorced Clark I wanted to call you, but I found out through Will McQueen that you were married. I put that love away inside my heart and tried to live my life. I dated some, went with some really nice guys, but never any that I wanted to spend the rest of my life with. I'd hear about you from time to time, mostly from Will, so I know a lot more about your time in Washington than you think I do. It seemed like every time I wasn't involved with somebody, you were married or engaged to be. Do you remember when Will first ran for Congress and you were his campaign manager?"

Judah smiled. "Of course I do. I used to see you and Clark at all those political functions. It ate my guts out to see you with him, but he was a heavy hitter for Will, so I had to be polite to him and act as if nothing ever existed between us."

Hannah looked down and nodded. "I remember seeing you, too. As a matter of fact I was the one who pushed Clark to help Will. I was the one who made him go to all of those functions. I did it just so I could see you. That's how much I loved you."

Judah sat in silence for several seconds before he said, "Do you remember seeing me at all those other social functions, like those fund-raisers for the Symphony and the Telfair Museum? Well, the main reason I went to those was that I knew you'd probably be there. I wanted to keep checking, to see if you really looked happy. I was wishing you weren't. I used to fantasize that you'd leave Clark and we'd get together again."

"I know the feeling well," said Hannah softly.

"All these years, and you felt the same way about me that I did about you. It wasn't any different from when you lived here and I lived across the street. When we first fell in love and had to keep it a secret." Judah thought for a very long moment, then slowly said, "Please don't misunderstand what I'm going to say, okay?"

"I won't."

"What about Billy? Didn't you love him, either?"

"Judah, Billy was a wonderful, warm, and caring man. He came into my life when I least expected it, and yes, I loved him. But not the way I've loved you."

Judah had dropped his head after asking his question, so Hannah placed her hand under his chin and gently lifted it. Then she looked into his eyes and continued, "It was like this, Judah. Every time I heard your name mentioned, or if some random thought about you popped into my head, I'd get a little twinge in the pit of my stomach. Every single time. That's the kind of love I've had for you. What I felt for Billy was different. Maybe that twinge I felt was a little bit of guilt for what happened, but it was mostly just how much I cared for you and the fact that it all seemed so impossible, that you'd been lost forever because I didn't have the courage to stand up to my parents. I was weak and scared and took the easy way out. Please forgive me."

Judah slipped to one knee, took her hands into his, and said, "To know that I have a son with you and to know that you've been in love with me all these years is the most wonderful thing that has ever happened to me. Those are the two things I guess I hoped for all of my life, like there was some little voice that's been whispering in my ear for all these years and I just couldn't quite understand what it was saying. Now I know. I'm not a religious man, Hannah, but from my perspective, I can only describe what you've just told me as nothing short of a miracle. It makes me believe that there really is a God and that He's merciful."

"Oh, there's a God, Judah, and yes, He is a God of Mercy. I realized that when He took Billy the way He did."

"Yeah," said Judah, "I don't think he suffered much." Then he grew silent. Judah dropped his head again as he searched for the right words. Finally he raised his head once more and looked into her eyes. "Hannah, do you think we could try again? Do you think we could be sweethearts once more?"

Hannah's eyes welled with tears as she pulled Judah toward her. Just before their lips met she whispered, "I hope so."

The Trial

If you can wait and not be tired by waiting,
Or being lied about, don't deal in lies,
Or being hated, don't give way to hating,
And yet don't look too good, nor talk too wise . . .
—Rudyard Kipling, "If"

THE ARCHITECTURE of the Chatham County Courthouse on Montgomery Street in downtown Savannah is starkly out of sync with the historic district in which it resides. Its predecessor on Wright Square had character; the new one is simply an ugly box with a façade of concrete and rectangular windows. As Lloyd and Matt walked to the courthouse entrance, Lloyd decided he would have felt more comfortable at the old building.

"Don't say anything," said Matt quietly as they approached the knot of TV cameras at the front door.

"Don't worry," answered Lloyd just before a microphone with a CNN logo was thrust into his face.

"Monsignor Bryan," shouted a young female reporter wearing a dark blue suit wet with perspiration, "do you have any comments you'd like to make?"

"I have no comment," said Lloyd as he tried to make his way through the crowd, while a photographer for *The National Enquirer* shot photo after photo of him. It was cool inside the lobby; and as Lloyd looked back at the clutch of cameras and reporters outside, Matt said that he hoped it reached a hundred degrees.

When Lloyd and Matt got off the elevator at the third floor and went to the waiting area outside the grand jury room, they found

Damian, his father, and Hassam already present; dressed in Muslim robes, skullcaps atop their heads. The two older men glared at Lloyd menacingly . . . but Damian only kept his head down. Mr. and Mrs. Small were also in the hallway, but they had chosen seats as far away from the trio as they could get. When Lloyd and his attorney entered, the Smalls stood. They smiled as Lloyd approached to speak with them.

"Monsignor Bryan," said Mrs. Small in a quiet voice, "we're so sorry all this has happened. If I hadn't called you that day, none of this would be going on."

"That's right," said Mr. Small, "you were only trying to help us with Damian, and now this stuff has done come up and we feel terrible about it. There's no way you were molesting that boy."

"I appreciate what you've said," answered Lloyd, "and please don't blame yourselves for all this. Remember, I was the one who gave you my card and told you to call if you had any trouble."

Just as Lloyd finished speaking the doors to the jury room opened and a deputy came out. "Damian Small," he said in a loud voice. Damian looked up and said, "Yeah." The deputy motioned. "Come with me."

In grand jury proceedings the accused aren't generally called to testify, but on occasion they are. This was one of those occasions. Matt saw it as a good sign; Lloyd didn't know what to think, never having been accused of any criminal activity before. Just after Damian disappeared behind the big oak door, Mrs. Small said, "We gonna tell 'em just what happened, just you wait and see, Monsignor."

Lloyd smiled. "I appreciate that, Mrs. Small, but all you have to tell is the truth." After that he took a seat on one of the benches in the hallway and waited.

"Would you state your name, please?" said Spencer Lawton, Chatham County's district attorney. Normally, one of the assistant D.A.'s would be handling a case like this, but this was a high-profile affair. Mr. Lawton wanted to see that it was carried out properly and had chosen to present the state's evidence himself.

"Damian Small," mumbled Damian as he stared at the floor in front of the D.A.

"I'm sorry, Mr. Small, but you're going to have to speak up so we can all hear you, okay."

"Yeah, okay."

"Will you please tell the jury what happened the day Monsignor Bryan visited your grandparents' house?"

Damian squirmed in his seat and scratched the back of his neck with his right hand.

"Um, you know, he . . . he grabbed me in my privates."

"Why would Monsignor Bryan grab your privates?"

"I don't know."

"Had he ever done anything like that before?"

"No."

"Were your grandparents in the house when this occurred?"

"Yeah. I mean yes, sir."

"Where were they?"

"The next room, the living room."

"And where did this all happen?"

"The kitchen."

"Could they see what was happening?"

"I don't know."

"Tell us what was going on just before Monsignor Bryan grabbed your privates."

"We was arguing 'bout something."

"You and the Monsignor were arguing?"

"Yes, sir."

"About what?"

"I don't remember."

"Were you at your grandparents' house often?"

"Yes, sir. I used to stay there a lot."

"You didn't live with your parents?'

"They divorced and I stayed with my momma sometimes, but mostly with my grandparents."

"And now you live with your father, is that right?"

"Yes, sir."

"How long did Monsignor Bryan hold on to your privates?"

"I'm not sure, maybe a minute."

"Was he holding them kinda soft or was he holding them hard?"

"Hard."

"So, I guess that kinda hurt, didn't it?"

"Real bad."

"Did Monsignor Bryan do anything else to you while he had hold of your privates?"

"He lifted me up and pinned me against the wall and shouted at me."

"What did he say?"

Damian paused, then dropped his head as he fought to control himself; but after a few seconds he lost the fight, and tears began to fall on the county's freshly buffed linoleum tile. Mr. Lawton rested an elbow on the witness box and waited for Damian to regain control, but soon Damian began to sob.

"Would you like to have some time to get control of yourself, Mr. Small, before we continue?"

Damian suddenly jerked his head up and blurted out, "I don't want no more time for nothin'. I don't want to do this no more. I want to go back with my grandmomma and granddaddy. I don't want to stay with my old man no longer. I just want to leave this place right now. Monsignor Bryan ain't been nothing but nice to me." Damian's face was contorted with pain; mucous ran from his nose as he looked at the startled jury members and continued. "I was high that day and he came over to take care of me, that's all. He didn't mean nothin' nasty when he grabbed me."

Damian looked at Mr. Lawton, who stood before him in a daze. "I want to go back with my grandmomma and stay there. I want to go back to St. Dismas Center too, 'cause I'm sorry for what happened."

It was quiet in the grand jury room for what seemed like an hour before the D.A. put his hand on Damian's shoulder and said, "I don't have any more questions for you, Damian. You can go now."

When Damian returned to the hall, he was still crying. Abdul surmised that he had given a tearful account of the depths of Monsignor Bryan's depravity, just as he had been instructed to do. Damian cut a look over at his grandparents, who had risen from their seats when they'd seen him in tears, and the pained looks on their faces caused him to weep even more. Triumphantly Abdul put his arm around his son and snarled at Lloyd. "You gonna pay for what you done to my son, you faggot. You just wait and see, you gonna pay."

Mr. and Mrs. Small were called to testify next. They, too, told a story that not only exonerated Lloyd, but praised him. When they were finished Lloyd took the stand and simply told the truth. The grand jury sequestered themselves for about fifteen minutes before they returned, refusing to indict Lloyd for any crime.

That evening, back at his house, Abdul was in a rage over what had happened; and after a great deal of threatening, and abuse,was able to extract Damian's testimony from him. Then he got a belt, beat Damian, and locked him in his room. Later that night Damian climbed out the window and walked all the way to his grandparents' house. The next morning Abdul found Damian's Muslim robes stuffed into the toilet, wet with urine.

Hurricane Hannah

> They call her Hard Hearted Hannah, the vamp of Savannah,
> The meanest gal in town;
> Leather is tough, but Hannah's heart is tougher,
> She's a gal who loves to see men suffer!
> To tease 'em and thrill 'em, to torture and kill 'em,
> Is her delight, they say,
> I saw her at the seashore with a great big can,
> There was Hannah pouring water on a drowning man!
> She's Hard Hearted Hannah, the vamp of Savannah, G–A!
>
> —Milton Ager, "Hard Hearted Hannah"

LLOYD CALLED Bishop Bourke from the courthouse to deliver the good news. The bishop told him that, although it would be another week before the findings of his committee of inquiry would be made public, they had also found him innocent of any wrongdoing.

"When can I say Mass again, Bishop?"

"I guess I could let you resume your priestly duties tomorrow, Monsignor, but I'm going to wait until after the committee makes its findings public," answered Bishop Bourke in a thick Irish accent."

"But why?"

"Because if I don't, then it would appear that I had undercut my own committee, which would take away from its importance and authority. Surely you can appreciate that."

"I do, Excellency." Nevertheless Lloyd was dejected.

"Now listen, my dear Monsignor," continued Bishop Bourke

in an accent honed in County Offlay, "I know just how you feel, but there's an upside to not going back to work right away. I'm of the mind that you're needin' a good rest after all you've been through. I know you're thinkin' you haven't worked in a while and that's vacation enough, but I'm talkin' about sleepin' the sleep of the innocent and saved. Get away somewhere, Lloyd, and let all your pain just drain out from you. When you come back, everything will be the same, I promise."

Lloyd had no choice but to accept the bishop's advice. When he called Judah to tell him the news, Lloyd happily accepted his invitation for a little victory celebration the following night on the *Solitude*.

Tran and Min were in the galley preparing the food when Lloyd arrived. Hannah was there, too. She greeted Lloyd with a big hug. "I told you so, didn't I?" Matt and Pam were also invited, as were John-Morgan and Ann Marie. When everyone was aboard Judah edged the *Solitude* away from its berth and pointed the bow north in the Skidaway River. There would be a sunset dinner in Wassaw Sound.

Judah had the helm; Lloyd was seated next to him on the flying bridge as the boat glided past Modena Island, made a right turn into the Wilmington River, and headed for the sound. There would be more than an eight-foot tide that evening; the creeks were rapidly filling as the floats on the crab traps were pushed sideways by the inrushing water. The marsh was still lush and full, with occasional lime-colored streaks running through a carpet of forest green. In the far west thunder clouds were building and the tops of some of them touched the sun. Rays of gold and magenta rushed across the sky. The day had been killer hot, so Lloyd savored the cooling eastern breeze that now came in off the ocean. He was thinking about what would happen to Damian when his cell phone rang.

"Monsignor Bryan, this is Yvonne Small."

"Oh, Mrs. Small, I'm so glad you called. We never had the opportunity to speak yesterday after the grand jury delivered its opinion. Thank you for you support."

"All we did was like you said, Monsignor, we just told the truth about what happened and we sure are glad things came out the way they did."

"So am I, Mrs. Small."

"Well, the real reason I'm callin' is to let you know that last night Damian ran away from that nasty father of his and showed up here at one in the morning. He had welts on him from where that no-good beat him with a belt."

Lloyd put his hand to his forehead. "How bad, Mrs. Small?"

"He didn't draw no blood, but he put a whippin' on Damian, that's for sure. Damian said he was mad 'cause he didn't say you had molested him like Abdul wanted him to do."

"I'm not in the position to come over right now, but I really think you should get a restraining order against his father to keep him away from your home. I'll try and come by tomorrow."

"Well, there's more," said Mrs. Small. "Damian told us that the last time he was out working with his father on his boat, he thinks they found some kind of a bomb out in Wassaw Sound. He thinks they want to blow it up or somethin'."

"He says they found a bomb in the sound?"

"Yes, sir."

"I'll get back to you tomorrow, Mrs. Small. Thank you very much for calling."

When Judah heard Lloyd say, "They found a bomb in the sound," he sat straight up. He was looking intently at Lloyd when he got off the phone.

"Did I hear you say somebody found a bomb in the sound?"

Lloyd let out a heavy sigh. "Yep, you heard right."

"Do you know who found this bomb?"

"It was Damian's father Abdul and his buddy Hassam, some really bad actors, Judah. What do I do now?"

"Lloyd, there's something I need to tell you about." Judah filled him in on everything he knew about the Tybee Bomb, Billy, Gusto, and his own suspicions.

"Take the wheel," he said when he was finished. "I'm going below and get Gusto's number. He needs to know about this. It could be serious."

After dinner everyone gathered in the salon, where the TV was tuned to the Weather Station. Nobody was paying much attention until the tropical update came on.

"This is the latest satellite image of the Caribbean," said the reporter, "and if you'll notice this tropical depression about a hundred miles northeast of Puerto Rico, well, the National Weather Service is predicting that it will strengthen over the next twenty-four to thirty-six hours and reach hurricane strength. If that happens it will be the eighth named storm of the season and will be called Hurricane Hannah. We're projecting a track that could take it somewhere near the tip of south Florida in about a week." Several of her friends kidded Hannah about the hurricane named in her honor. She could only laugh.

When the *Solitude* returned to Isle of Hope later that evening, Hannah told Matt she had some business to discuss with him and asked him to stay after everyone else had gone. Tran and Min were the last to leave the boat; after she saw them get into their car she sat in a chair opposite Matt and his wife and smiled. Judah was sitting at the bar, hoping he would be able to control himself.

Just before Hannah started to speak, Pam placed her hand on Matt's; she had been told the news earlier in the evening. Then Hannah made eye-contact with Judah, looked back at Matt, took a deep breath, and started.

"Matt, what I'm going to tell you will come as a surprise, a very pleasant one I hope. I've wanted to tell you this for so many years, but it just never seemed right until now." She drew herself up straight in the chair and looked directly at her son. "I've been thinking about how to tell you this all evening. I even talked it over with Pam and Judah, and we all think the best way is to be direct and not beat around the bush."

Pam closed her hand tighter around Matt's, and when he looked at her she smiled sweetly saying, "Everything's fine, baby."

"Matt, you remember me telling you about when I made my debut and how Judah was my escort to many of the functions because your father was off playing football for Tech and couldn't be there to take me to the parties?"

Matt nodded and quietly said, "Yes, ma'am."

"Well, there was a whole lot more between Judah and me than

just friendship. We were in love with each other, desperately in love. I loved Judah more than any man in my whole life, but it was a doomed love because my family—it was mostly my mother—would never approve of my marrying a Jew, do you understand?"

Again Matt nodded, and glanced at Judah, but said nothing.

"Honey," said Hannah with tears in her eyes, "Clark Davenport is not your father, Judah Benjamin is."

Matt settled back on the sofa. His mouth dropped open. First he looked at his mother, then at Judah again.

"I know how you feel, Matt," said Judah. "I only found out about a week ago. It takes time to sink in."

"Well, does my father know?" asked Matt. "I mean, I guess he's my stepfather actually, isn't he? Does he know?"

"Yes, son, he's known since you were a little boy. That's the reason he treated you so harshly, that's the reason we got divorced. I was pregnant with you when we got married, and he thought you were his child until you were about three or four. That's when the Davenports started asking questions."

"I, uh . . . I don't exactly know what to say. How did all this happen? I mean, shouldn't I know?"

"Yes, you should," said Hannah, who then told him about how Clark had forced himself on her, and how she and Judah had fallen in love that fall quarter at Armstrong, and how tender Judah had been with her. After she had finished Matt again looked over at Judah, who was close to tears. Then he stood, walked over, and extended his hand. "It's good to know you, Dad."

Judah took Matt's hand and shook it. In seconds they embraced each other as they both broke into sobs.

"Where you goin'?" asked Abdul as Hassam turned his 1999 Chevrolet Impala with dark tinted windows onto Oglethorpe Avenue and headed west.

"Across the bridge," answered Hassam.

"Across the bridge?" echoed Abdul. "What for?"

"Fireworks."

"Fireworks! Fourth of July was two months ago, what do you want with fireworks?"

"Use 'em on that bomb," said Hasam confidently.

"Man, you crazy. If those two hand grenades couldn't blow that bomb open, some little firecracker sure can't do it. Turn this car 'round, man, I got no time for this kind'a bullshit."

"I'm not after firecrackers, I'm after sparklers," said Hassam as he crossed Martin Luther King Boulevard and headed for the bridge over the Savannah River.

"Sparklers! Man, you done lost your mind!"

Hassam cracked a wicked little smile. "You don't know anything, Abdul. I talked with Alphonso, who has a friend he calls The Lion. Seems The Lion knows a lot about explosives. The Lion says sparklers have magnesium in 'em. That's why they burn. Magnesium burns at four thousand degrees. We get a hundred pounds of sparklers and stack 'em in real tight around that bomb, and The Lion says it'll melt the bomb's casing. He says that when magnesium and aluminum get together, there can be some real fireworks then. That bomb casing is made of aluminum. When it starts melting and mixes with the magnesium, something real hot's gonna happen."

Hassam had to drive over to South Carolina for sparklers because fireworks were illegal in Georgia. When he got to Hardeeville, several stores lined that patch of Highway 17. He bought out those stores, then got on I-95 and found three more fireworks dealers a few miles up the road. By the time he was finished, Hassam was headed back to Savannah with almost two hundred pounds of sparklers in his trunk, and a very plausible plan to breach the casing of the Tybee Bomb.

After Gusto had rented a car at the Savannah airport, he headed directly to Isle of Hope, where he had arranged a meeting with Judah on his boat. All the way up from Miami he was thinking about making this his last job and retiring. He was also hoping he would live long enough to see Castro dead and have an opportunity to return to the island he had loved so much. It was six in the afternoon and only just starting to cool a little when he stepped aboard the *Solitude*, where Judah greeted him with a firm handshake.

"Good to see you again, my friend," said Gusto as he stepped into the salon and out of the heat and humidity.

Lloyd was sitting on one of the sofas, with Damian next to him. Judah closed the cabin door and said, "You've already met Monsignor Bryan, Gusto, but not Damian Small."

Both Lloyd and Damian had risen to their feet when Gusto entered. He approached Lloyd with his hand extended.

"Monsignor," said Gusto, "what a pleasure to be in your company again. I have to tell you that my wife has never stopped talking about that Latin Mass you celebrated on this very boat. She was in the convent, you know, and is still a very devout Catholic. That was quite a moving service for her."

Lloyd smiled. "That was a very special night for us all. I know I'll never forget it." Then he turned to Damian, put his hand on his shoulder, and said, "Mr. Camacho, this is Damian Small. He has quite a story to tell you, so let's take a seat and hear what he has to say."

As Damian recounted all he knew about the bomb in Wassaw Sound, Judah fixed a Bacardi and Coke for Gusto and a vodka and Diet Coke for himself. After giving Gusto his drink he listened quietly as Damian nervously spoke.

"I don't know much about bombs, Mr. Camacho. All I ever seen was on the TV, but this looked to me like it was one." Then Damian recounted as best he could the conversation he heard in the wheelhouse between Abdul and Hassam.

"Do you think you could take me to the place on the sandbar where this bomb is resting?" asked Gusto.

"I don't know, it's real big out there and I don't know it too good. I haven't been working on the shrimp boat very long and I'm not sure about things out there. I could try, though."

"Do you know what a GPS system is, Damian?"

"Yes, sir, I know what they do and there's one on the boat, too."

"Did you see either one of these men write down the coordinates that were on the GPS?"

"Hassam had me workin' in the hold most of the time after he got back on the boat from diggin' 'round that thing on the sandbar. I didn't see 'em write anything down, 'cause it wasn't until after we was a pretty good ways from the bar that I went to the wheelhouse."

Gusto thought for a few moments. "Would you be interested in trying to show me where that thing is?"

Damian looked at Lloyd as if asking permission. Lloyd nodded his approval.

"Yes, sir, I'll try."

At low tide the next morning, Damian, Gusto, and Judah were all in Lloyd's boat headed for the sound. There would be spring tides for the next couple of days, meaning the low tides wouldn't be as low as they were the day Hassam had spotted the bomb. There was also a brisk wind from the south whipping up waves on the sandbar which would make visual recognition of low-lying objects even more difficult. After an hour of cruising up and down the bar, Gusto decided the search was fruitless. Lloyd headed back to the dock.

Congressman McQueen ushered Gusto into the library of the Ardsley Park home where he had grown up. Gusto recognized all the signs of old money: the oil portrait over the fireplace of the congressman's father dressed in his Navy uniform, the portrait of Will's mother in an evening gown on the opposite wall, the gun case filled with the finest of hunting rifles and shotguns.

"How old is this house, Congressman?" he asked while he watched Will mix drinks at the wet bar under a stained-glass window depicting a troop of Scottish Highlanders fighting the Spanish.

"My parents built this house just before the war started. I think they moved in here in '41, only a few months before Pearl Harbor," said Will as he handed Gusto his drink.

"May I ask the significance of this window, Congressman? It's truly magnificent." Gusto was gazing up at the Scots wearing kilts and firing their muskets at other soldiers as they fled through chest-high marsh grass.

"That's the Battle of Bloody Marsh. Several of my ancestors fought in it. My father always said it was the most important battle in prerevolutionary America because it stopped the Spanish from coming into Georgia. It's called Bloody Marsh because it was quite a slaughter."

Gusto was silent for several seconds, then asked, "May we speak frankly and with complete confidence, sir?"

"Absolutely, Agent Camacho."

"Is there any possibility that we may be overheard?"

"None. My wife is out of town, and the maid left hours ago."

"Good, because what we need to talk about is quite sensitive."

"Let's sit down and relax a little, Mr. Camacho, and speak in comfort. By the way, may I call you Gusto?"

"Yes, sir, by all means," answered Gusto as he settled into one of a pair of high-back, winged leather chairs facing the fireplace. Will sat in the other.

"Excellent then, Gusto, and I insist you call me Will, okay?"

Gusto wasn't completely comfortable calling the congressman by his first name, but it sounded like an order. He always obeyed orders.

"Now then, what seems to be on your mind?"

"Well, Will, you know I've been asked to check into this lost H-bomb business."

"Yep," said Will just before he took a sip from his glass, "I serve on the committee that keeps tabs on our nonconventional operatives, so I knew you were assigned to the case. From what I've been told you were a little busy after nine-eleven."

"Yes, sir, we had a few fires to put out, and I'm one of the firefighters they call on."

"So, do we have a fire to put out in Savannah?"

"I'm not sure, sir, but I've been in this line of work for over thirty years, and sometimes you just sort'a get a hunch, you know, your gut's telling you something isn't quite right."

"I know the feeling well. I used to have it all the time in Vietnam. If I'd listened to my gut the last mission I went on, maybe I wouldn't have had my legs blown off."

The room got quiet for several seconds before Gusto continued. "Well, I've got a hunch about a couple of shrimpers who might know a little more about the location of the bomb than I'm comfortable with; and I'm just wondering what you think about me looking into their activities a little more closely, if you know what I mean."

Will took another sip from his glass, then looked directly at Gusto. "I know what you mean, and I think a closer look at these two birds would be an excellent idea."

Gusto had a stone-cold look on his face when he asked, "Am I authorized to use my discretion in dealing with these two?"

Will looked up at the portrait of his father, then at Gusto. "You are, but whatever you do, don't leave any tracks."

"I never have, congressman. You know that."

It was three in the afternoon of the next day as Gusto slipped along the side of Hassam's house. When he came to the back porch, it took him about a minute to pick the two deadbolt locks Hassam had installed in hopes of thwarting would-be burglars. Gusto was hoping he would find the hand grenades Hassam was supposed to have bought weeks ago; after a quick search of the kitchen he moved into the dining room. What he found puzzled him greatly. Cases of sparklers were stacked in a corner, and for several seconds Gusto simply stared at them as he tried to determine why Hassam would have such an absurd number of simple fireworks stacked in his dining room. After a search of the rest of the house, Gusto was gone. Hassam would have no clue that he had ever been there.

Even though Moshe knew him he still barked when Gusto stepped onto the *Solitude*'s deck. Gusto greatly admired the large, sleek dog. He had had quite a chuckle when he had first learned its name.

"Where's your master, Moshe?" he said as he stroked the dog's back, then looked up when he heard the cabin door open.

"Ah, Mr. Gusto," said Tran, "nice to see you again."

"Good to see you, too, Tran."

Anticipating the reason for Gusto's visit, Tran said, "Mr. Judah no here."

Gusto had thoroughly vetted Tran's records months ago and found nothing that would cause him to be suspicious of the graying former helicopter pilot. He decided that he could trust Tran to help him.

"Well, to be frank, I didn't come here looking for Judah. I really came here to talk with you, Tran."

"With me?"

"Uh-huh."

"'Bou what?"

Gusto looked around the dock carefully. "Can we step inside?" They did so; and Gusto immediately got to the point.

"Tran, you know I'm an agent of the U.S. government, don't you?"

Tran nodded sharply.

"You know about the H-bomb that's lost in Wassaw Sound, too, don't you?"

"I know 'bou bomb in sound."

"Well, I have reason to believe those two guys who're running Billy's old boat now might know something about where the bomb is, but I don't want to ask them about it. You understand?"

"You mean Abdul and Hassam? They no good. I think they happy when nine-eleven happen. You no want to ask them 'cause you think they bad guys, too, don't you?"

"You got it. That's why I'm here. I'm wondering if you'd be interested in helping me keep an eye on Abdul and Hassam when they're down at the docks. You know, kind of let me know when they leave and come back, what they're up to, that sort of thing."

Then Gusto reached into his pocket and pulled out five hundred dollar bills. "I'd like to compensate you for your time, if you think you can be of some help."

Tran looked at the money, then into Gusto's eyes. "You say you work for United States government?"

"That's right. I work for the U.S. government, which has a great deal of interest in where that bomb might be. We sure don't want it falling into the wrong hands."

Tran stiffened his back and proudly raised his chin. "Uncle Sam good to me and my family. I no take any money for helping my country. You tell Tran what you want, he do it!"

ꟻ ꟻ ꟻ

"You think that hurricane's gonna hit here?" asked Abdul as he stacked the sparklers in the back of his pickup.

"Looks like it could," replied Hassam, while passing Abdul another case of sparklers over the tailgate before going back into his house for the last box. "That's why I want to try and break that bomb open now rather than later. If we get that storm it'll probably bury the bomb again. Besides, if we can blow it up or at least crack it open before the hurricane gets here, then I think the storm'll help spread that radiation shit out more."

"Yeah, I think you might be right." Abdul wiped the sweat off his forehead with the tail of a dingy T-shirt that had a picture of Malcolm X on the front. "But, if we do crack that bomb and all that radiation leaks out, that's the end of the shrimpin' business around here, ain't it?"

Hassam laughed. "You'll be needin' ta find another line of work, but the brothers'll take care a you. Just remember, it ain't every day that a brother has the chance to pop a cap into the head of them honkies like we do."

Abdul savored the idea for a moment, then let out a long, low, "Yeah."

Tran Nugyen had been the first Vietnamese refugee to come to Savannah. As more followed he helped each arriving family find a home and a job; he also taught them the ropes of life in Savannah as best he could. He had been living in the area for almost thirty years, and was regarded by the Vietnamese community as their de facto leader.

With the help of the Catholic Church, Tran had been able to educate his daughter and two sons in Catholic schools. Both boys ultimately graduated from Benedictine Military School, and his daughter from St. Vincent's Academy. The older son had been accepted to the Naval Academy and was serving as an officer with the 1st Marine Division in Iraq. His wife had her own seamstress shop, where she employed several other Vietnamese women. Whenever possible Tran and Min attended daily Mass; their repeated prayer as they knelt after receiving Communion was never one of supplication, but rather of thanksgiving. Both of them were acutely aware of how lucky they had been to escape from Vietnam and to be taken in by America. When Tran told Gusto he was happy to help the country that had adopted him, he was absolutely serious and took on the mission with determination.

In certain ways many of the Vietnamese who came to Savannah followed in the footsteps of the Italians who had journeyed to the city a century earlier and taken jobs in the seafood industry. Several of the boats that sailed out of Thunderbolt were crewed and skippered by Vietnamese; Tran knew everyone of them. He was on the docks and speaking with his friends only an hour after his talk with Gusto.

"I want you to keep an eye on those two on the *St. Patrick*," said Tran in Vietnamese to the captains of the two boats tied only one dock away from Abdul and Hassam. "I want to know everything that goes on. I want to know if they're getting ready to leave, and if you can find out, I want to know where they're going. You call me tonight and give me a report and keep your mouths shut about this."

Gusto had just come in from dinner and was watching the progress of Hurricane Hannah on the Weather Channel in his room at the 17Hundred90 Inn when his cell phone rang.

"Camacho here."

"Mr. Gusto, this Tran."

"What's up?"

"My boys on dock just call and say Abdul and Hassam look like they getting ready to leave tomorrow."

"Yeah, anything else?"

"They say they bring bunch of boxes on boat."

"They know what's in 'em?"

"No can see, but soon as it get dark, I go and find out."

"You be careful. Those guys catch you, they'd probably kill you."

"Don't worry, I take pistol with me. Soon as I find out 'bou what in boxes, I call back."

It was ten when the phone rang again.

"I no understand, Mr. Gusto. Boxes full of nothing but sparklers. Same kind my wife put on birthday cakes when our children little."

"Okay Tran, good job. I've got your cell number and I'll be getting back to you, but the minute your guys see the *St. Patrick* shoving off, I want to know about it, understand?"

After saying good-bye to Tran, Gusto turned his attention back to Hurricane Hannah.

"Here's the seventy-two-hour plot on Hannah's path," said a svelte-looking young woman as she stood in front of a satellite image of the Atlantic. "If Hannah continues on her expected path, she could track up the eastern seaboard of Florida, with the eye staying between fifty and a hundred miles offshore, following the coastline and not making landfall until somewhere around the South and North Carolina border. This means that coastal cities in Florida from about Daytona and all the way up the Georgia coast can expect to see some very high winds in the range of eighty and perhaps even above a hundred miles an hour as the eye of Hurricane Hannah and her most intense winds, which are now clocked at 125 miles an hour, remain offshore. We'll know more after the hurricane-tracking plane makes its next pass through Hurricane Hannah around twelve hours from now. But as you can see the National Weather Service has issued Hurricane Warnings from Daytona, Florida, to Wilmington, North Carolina."

"If those two birds are gonna do anything before that hurricane gets here," said Gusto to himself as he turned off the TV and slipped his feet under the cool sheets, "they better get busy tomorrow."

The next morning he was about to step into the shower when Tran called.

"My boys called and say looks like *St. Patrick* getting ready to shove off."

"How long before they do that?"

"Maybe hour or so," answered Tran, "but this nothing unusual. Hurricane headed this way and all boats getting ready to sail into Wilmington and ride storm out. Maybe *St. Patrick* just doing same thing, Mr. Gusto."

"Maybe, Tran, but I'm not ready to take that chance. You call me the minute that boat leaves."

After Gusto finished talking to Tran, he sat on the side of his bed and thought for several minutes. Then he made another call.

"Hello."

"Judah?'

"Yeah."

"This is Gusto Camacho."

"Gusto, good to hear from you again. What's up?"

For the next several minutes Gusto sketched out what was going on with Abdul and Hassam, saying his greatest fear was that they'd found the Tybee Bomb and that they might try and do something with it before the hurricane hit.

"It's just a hunch, Judah. But I'm suspicious of those two."

"Sounds like a job for the Coast Guard," said Judah.

"No, I don't want to spook 'em. I want to follow them in a civilian craft and see what they're up to. Besides the Coast Guard's got its hands full with the storm, and I doubt they'd be inclined to go on some wild goose chase right now. Can you come up with a relatively small, fast boat that can take some rough seas in about two hours? Perhaps Dr. Hartman's boat?"

"I'll call him, but I don't know."

"You can tell him what I'm going to tell you."

"What's that?"

"Your country needs you."

"I'll call him right now."

"One more thing, Judah."

"Dear, God, now what?"

"I know Dr. Hartman has a rather extensive weapons collection, he told me so himself. If he can go, tell him to bring something that can hit hard and fast, and tell him to give you something, too."

Gusto had just finished shaving when his cell phone rang.

"This is Camacho."

"John-Morgan is a go," said Judah. "Hell, he's all excited about this. His boat is gassed up and at his dock. Do you know where that is?"

"Isle of Hope, just down the river from you. I'll be there in less than an hour."

Gusto paused for a moment, then asked, "Firepower?"

"The doctor assures me you'll be impressed."

Gusto made one more call before leaving his room.

"Tran, are you willing to be of further assistance to your country?"

"Anyway I can help U.S., I do."

"That's what I thought you'd say. You know where Dr. Hartman lives, don't you?"

"Been there many times, Mr. Gusto."

"Can you meet me at his dock in an hour?"

"Yes."

"One other thing, Tran."

"What that?"

"Bring your pistol with you."

When Gusto rolled into Sandfly on his way to Isle of Hope, he stopped at the CVS pharmacy, made a purchase, then headed for Driscoll House, where John-Morgan lived.

John-Morgan was known around Savannah not only as a medical doctor, but also as a well-informed historian with a particular interest in the Second World War. His father had fought in that war with the Marine Corps, and as with so many early baby boomers, World War II loomed large in his consciousness. He also had other relatives who'd fought in the war, but on the other side. Indeed he had been so inspired as a child by the epic sea story of the German pocket battleship *Graf Spee* that he had even named his boat after it.

Dr. Hartman was a man with deeply held convictions. He was patriotic and devoutly religious. When nine-eleven happened he was enraged. He sought to join the Navy as a physician, but was turned down because of his age and his old war injuries. Nevertheless, like millions of Americans he seethed with anger and wished that he could strike a blow for his country. Gusto's request for help came as a welcome gift.

When Gusto arrived at John-Morgan's dock, everyone else was already there, including General Moshe Dayan, who nervously paced the dock as if knowing something unusual was afoot. The *Graf Spee* was at idle, warming her engines; and as Gusto approached the dog and petted him, Judah called out from the bow. "I thought he might come in handy."

"Good idea," replied Gusto as he stepped aboard. After a quick round of handshakes he gave a short briefing.

"I don't know what they're up to, but I have my suspicions. They may be leaving just to anchor in the river like everybody else and this all could be for naught—but my gut tells me something else is going on. I want to see where they go, but I don't want them to see us." Gusto looked at John-Morgan, who was sitting at the helm. "Do you think they know this boat?"

"I know Abdul does, he's seen me on it. I don't know about his buddy, though."

"Everybody know this boat," said Tran with a smile.

"Well," continued Gusto, "with this storm coming, I doubt there'll be anything on the water other than shrimp boats looking for a safe anchorage, so we'll be standing out like a sore thumb."

"You're right about that," said John-Morgan.

Gusto adjusted the shoulder-holster that held a Glock 17 pistol. "If they're up to something with the bomb, then they have to go to the sound. We can't follow after them; they'd see us and think something was up. John-Morgan, this is a fast boat, right?"

"I've got two brand new Merc 250's hanging on my stern. This boat can do fifty-five miles an hour all day long," answered John-Morgan, with just a hint of pride.

Gusto nodded. "Okay, is there any way we can beat them to the sound without being seen? And once we get there, is there anywhere we can go so they can't see us?"

John-Morgan went below and returned with NOAA chart 11512, which he unfolded on the dashboard. Without looking up he asked, "What time is low tide, Tran?"

"Tide just turned, Dr. Hartman. Low tide at mouth of Savannah River supposed to be at 4:32 this afternoon."

"How long has the *St. Patrick* been gone from the dock?"

"Maybe fifteen minutes."

"How much speed can she make?"

"My boys say *St. Patrick*'s hull no scraped this year. She covered with barnacles. That slow her down a lot. I no think she make more than six knots."

"That's a tad over seven miles an hour," said John-Morgan as his eyes followed the twists and curves of the Skidaway River on the chart. "How long do you think it'll take the *St. Patrick* to reach the sound?"

"Probably about two hours," Tran replied.

"Take a look here, Gusto," said John-Morgan as he motioned to the chart. "We can leave here and head south, and follow the Skidaway into the Vernon River, and then take the Vernon all the way to the south end of Wassaw Island." As he spoke John-Morgan traced the course they would take on the map. "Then into the Odingsell River, where we turn right into Wassaw Creek. I think we'll still have enough water to get through New Cut, which dumps us out right behind Dead Man Hammock. What I can do then is run to the beach here on the northern end of the island, get as close to the beach as I can, and put you and Tran over the side. I'm thinking you and he can get on top of Battery Morgan and have a pretty good view of the sound. Judah and I then take the boat back into New Cut and hide behind the trees on Dead Man Hammock. Any boat coming down the Wilmington won't be able to see us behind there. You and Tran take the binoculars and this hand-held radio. When you're ready for us, just give a yell and we come charging out of the cut like gangbusters and pick you up off the beach. You're gonna get a little wet though, but I don't think the water will be more than waist-deep."

Gusto studied the map, then smiled. "This is a pretty good plan, Dr. Hartman, I like it—but can we get in place in time?"

"Well, they've got to cover about thirteen miles at around seven miles an hour. We've got to cover roughly twenty miles at fifty-five miles an hour. Do the math. Of course we'll need to blast through seven different no-wake zones at full speed, but what the hell, we're government workers now, aren't we agent Camacho?"

Gusto laughed, then said, "Let's roll, Doc!"

Because near-hurricane winds were due by the next morning, there wasn't any river traffic to speak of. John-Morgan tore through the Skidaway Narrows at almost full throttle, then zoomed under the Diamond Causeway Bridge, rocking the docks at Butterbean Beach with his wake. The sky was overcast, but the wind was light out of the west and the temperature was only around eighty-three. The birds had sensed foul weather was afoot, so all the herons and egrets were gone from the marsh; the gulls were headed inland. The tide was on the way out, and with little wind the waters were calm, the only ripples being caused by the sharp bends in the rivers that forced the water to pile up on the outsides of the curves. All in all John-Morgan considered the weather and the river perfect for a very fast run to the sound. When the *Graf Spee* reached Green Island Sound, he shouted over the roar of his engines to Gusto and pointed to the sound's namesake island. "There's a Confederate fort on that island. It's really something. When this whole thing is over, I'll take you there." Gusto gave John-Morgan a thumbs-up and shouted back, "I'm looking forward to it."

The *Graf Spee* was traveling with the tide and had the wind at her back as she sped into Ossabaw Sound at better than sixty miles an hour. In the sound the swells were gentle and rolling. The rise and fall of the boat reminded Gusto of the merry-go-round wooden horses he rode as a child at an amusement park back in Havana. In a few minutes the southern tip of Wassaw Island came into view; a little while later the *Graf Spee* was streaking through the Odingsell River headed for Wassaw Creek, where the twists and turns really started. When they got to New Cut the turns were so sharp that John-Morgan was forced to throttle back. The engine noise wasn't as bad at half throttle, so Gusto didn't have to shout when he asked, "What kind of firepower did you bring with you, Dr. Hartman?"

"M-1A, the civilian version of the M-14. You familiar with it?"

"I know the weapon quite well. I've fired the M-14 at Quantico while training."

John-Morgan kept his eyes on the river as he nodded. "Yeah, I trained with the M-14 when I was in boot camp at Parris Island. Had it when I got deployed to Nam, but only a few months after I was there, they took it back and gave us M-16's. The M-14 was heavy as hell, but that .308 round was a bear, that's why I brought it today. I guarantee you that round will penetrate the hull of the *St. Patrick* and whiz right through the wheelhouse like it's a paper bag. I brought three magazines, one filled with tracers. If we have to get down and dirty, I always found that cutting loose with tracers intimidated the hell out of the bad guys."

"And Judah," asked Gusto, "what did you arm him with?"

"Didn't have to. He had his own. It's a stainless steel Colt .45. Billy willed it to him. It was a pistol he used to carry on his boat."

Gusto shook his head at the irony. The last time he had seen that pistol was during the Mariel boat lift. "Never thought I'd see it again," he said.

"I couldn't hear you," said John-Morgan as he guided his boat through the last curve and pointed it toward the straight section of New Cut, where the trees on Dead Man Hammock came into view.

"It was nothing, Dr. Hartman. I was just thinking out loud."

John-Morgan pushed his throttles forward, and the *Graf Spee* once again was at full speed heading for Dead Man Hammock.

"Tran," yelled John-Morgan, "when we get to the hammock, I'm gonna peek the bow to the west side of it. I want you to take the binoculars, get up top, and see if you can spot the *St. Patrick*, okay?"

"You got it, boss," replied Tran. He hung the binoculars around his neck.

The tide was half out when the *Graf Spee* came to a stop behind Dead Man Hammock. Tran climbed onto the hardtop that covered the boat's cockpit. With the binoculars to his eyes, he slowly swept the Wilmington River.

"I no see anything, boss."

"Okay," said John-Morgan, "come on down and I'll shoot you and Gusto to the battery. Then I'll come back here and hide while we wait for the *St. Patrick*."

It was about a two-mile run from where New Cut emptied into the sound to the old concrete fort on Wassaw beach. When John-Morgan got to the beach in front of the fort, he took his boat in as close as he could. When his engines started kicking up sand, he tilted them up and drove in a little further.

"You're gonna get a little wet, boys. So hold your weapons over your heads."

When Gusto and Tran slipped over the side, they landed in three feet of water and waded through the surf to Battery Morgan. Once there they took up perches on top of the bombproof shelter, from which they had an elevated and unobstructed view of the entire sound, up the Wilmington River almost to Priest Landing.

Before pulling away, John-Morgan tuned to channel 22 on his marine radio, a channel he knew was seldom monitored by fishing vessels. He depressed the mike button.

"You read me, G-man?"

"Loud and clear, Doc."

"Roger that, I'm headed for the bushes." John-Morgan pushed the throttles all the way down, and the *Graf Spee* lurched onto a plane with surprising speed. He took her back behind Dead Man Hammock. Then the waiting started.

Judah, standing on the top of the boat, scanning the river with his expensive binoculars, was the first to catch sight of the *St. Patrick* over the top of the marsh as she sailed down the Wilmington River, apparently headed for the sound.

"John-Morgan, get up here! I think I see 'em."

John-Morgan raised the binoculars. It took him only seconds to recognize the unique paint job of his old friend's boat.

"G-man, come in," he said into the mike.

"This is G-man, Doc, over."

"We got company."

Gusto and Tran slipped down and hid behind the bombproof as the *St. Patrick* drew near. She was only a hundred yards away as she passed directly in front of the battery, and Gusto had to resist the urge to sneak a closer look. When the boat was about a quarter of a mile away, the two of them climbed back to the top of the battery and trained their glasses on the *St. Patrick*.

The sandbar where the bomb lay was now not only fully visible but getting bigger as the tide continued to flow out. For at least ten minutes Gusto watched the *St. Patrick*'s stern grow smaller as she continued on her course away from them. When he saw the boat make an abrupt turn to the south, he stood up.

"I think they're gonna ground the boat on that sandbar, Tran. Take a look."

"You right, Mr. Gusto, that just what they're doing."

From atop Battery Morgan they took turns watching as the *St. Patrick* approached the sandbar, then grounded herself. They saw Hassam go over the side, cross the bar, and return to the boat.

"Doc, this is G-man."

"I read you, G-man."

"They've grounded themselves on the bar."

"What's going on, G-man?"

"Don't know yet, but stand by. As a matter of fact, if they can't see you, why don't you start heading this way?"

"Roger that, I'm heading out now."

While Gusto was talking to John-Morgan, Tran had been watching the activity on the sandbar. When he thought he saw something being passed over the bow of the *St. Patrick*, he instinctively pressed the glasses closer to his eyes. After a few seconds he said, "Mr. Gusto, you better take look, I think they unloading something over bow."

As Gusto watched he saw Abdul pass a box to Hassam, who then trudged with it to the middle of the bar, and returned to the boat for another.

"What in the hell are they up to?" said Gusto, the binoculars still to his eyes. Then it suddenly hit him. "Oh shit, Tran! Those are the sparklers you saw in the boat last night. They're gonna use 'em to blow the bomb!"

Gusto thrust the glasses into Tran's hands, pressed the radio to his mouth, and yelled urgently, "Doc, this is G-man, come in."

"This is Doc, G-man."

"I understand now, Doc. We got a situation out here. Move out now and get here fast, Doc!"

"Roger, I'm on the way."

"What's he talking about, John-Morgan?" asked Judah with a concerned look on his face.

"Damned if I know, but we're fixin' to find out real soon." Again John-Morgan jammed the throttles forward as far as they would go.

When Gusto and Tran saw the *Graf Spee* headed toward them, they waded chest-high into the water and were ready to climb aboard the moment the boat arrived. Judah was at the swim platform on the stern to lend a hand.

"What in the hell are you talking about?" he asked as he grasped Gusto's hand and pulled him up.

"It's the sparklers. I saw them when I searched that Hassam bastard's house." Gusto was panting; he had to take a moment to catch his breath. "Tran saw them stacked on their boat last night. They're putting them under the bomb right now. I counted twelve cases at his house."

Judah reached down to Tran, who weighed a fraction of what Gusto did; and helped him onto the swim platform. Gusto climbed up to the cockpit and flopped into the portside chair.

"They must have a couple of hundred pounds of sparklers packed around the bomb, Doc. There's not a doubt in my mind they're gonna light them and hope it melts the bomb casing and sets off the initiating charge."

"Sparklers?"

"Yes, sir. They're made out of magnesium and burn hot as hell. I think there's a good chance they could melt the casing. We gotta do something right now." Gusto took his Glock from its holster and checked to make sure a round was in the chamber.

"The only thing we can do is run up on 'em and stop 'em at gunpoint. There isn't enough time to call the law and then wait for 'em to get here." John-Morgan looked through his binoculars at what was happening on the sandbar. All four men were now standing in the *Graf Spee*'s cockpit and looking at the *St. Patrick* in the distance.

"Any suggestions on how we stop these guys, Dr. Hartman?" Gusto asked.

John-Morgan thought for a second as he watched the activity on the bar, then turned to Gusto with a slight smile on his lips. "Shock and awe, Agent Camacho. Fuckin' shock and awe!"

Without waiting for Gusto's reaction John-Morgan looked at Tran and said, "You take the wheel, Tran. Set a course like we're headed for the ocean. Keep us about a hundred feet from the bar.

When we get opposite the *St. Patrick*, you cut the wheel hard to starboard and head right for 'em. I want you to run the boat onto the bar. We should slide almost completely up on it. They'll be watching us, but they'll never suspect we'll cut right at 'em at full speed. Tilt the engines up as much as you can and just before we hit the sand, cut the engines and tilt 'em up all the way. Got me?"

"You bet, boss," replied Tran, who relished the idea of bringing some hurt down on Abdul and Hassam.

"Then get your pistol, go over the side, and listen to what I tell you to do once you're on the sand."

"Got it."

John-Morgan turned his attention to Judah. "Once we hit, get the general over the side as fast as you can, then you go with your pistol ready. Ever shot anybody before?"

Judah's eyes were wide open now. All he could do was shake his head and spit out, "Good God, no."

"What am I thinking? Of course you haven't—but if it comes to them or you, you'll know what to do. Just keep your weapon trained on them, and if they don't want to play nice, sic Moshe on 'em. They'll be more afraid of him than they will of us."

Without missing a beat John-Morgan turned to Gusto. "I don't have to tell you what to do, do I?"

Gusto let out a quick snort and said, "No, señor, this is not my first rodeo."

"Good." John-Morgan went below and quickly reemerged with his M-1A and three magazines that each held twenty rounds. While he inverted the rifle and inserted the magazine with the tracers, he continued explaining his plan.

"Just before we make the turn for our run to the beach, I'm going to the bow with this little honey. When Tran gets us lined up right, I'm cuttin' loose. I won't be aiming to hit 'em, but I'm gonna light up the real estate in their immediate proximity, if you know what I'm talkin' about."

After he had snapped the magazine into the rifle, he looked up at Tran and said with a sly grin, "Nothing can get your attention like tracers coming your way, can it, Tran?"

"Nothing, boss." Tran also grinned. "Nothing in the world like tracers coming at you."

Judah stared at John-Morgan in amazement. Right before his eyes the man he had never seen even lose his temper had been transformed. It was an astonishing thing to witness. It seemed that everything about him had taken on a different aura. His eyes were fast and keen, his jawline set hard; the veins in his neck stood out like blue cords, and his movements were all quick and purposeful. Everything about him seemed dangerous and menacing. Gusto wasn't the least surprised. He, too, had seen the instant change that had overtaken John-Morgan—but he had also seen his war record and recognized the man's metamorphosis for what it was. He had become a warrior again.

"All right," said John-Morgan after he had pulled back the bolt on his rifle and let it go, instantly forcing a round into the firing chamber. "Does everybody understand what's coming down?"

"We got it," said Gusto, answering for the group.

"Okay," John-Morgan said as he moved aside to let Tran take the helm, "battle stations. It's show time on Wassaw Sound!"

Abdul and Hassam had finished digging sand from under the exposed portion of the bomb and had placed all of the sparklers under and around it. They had just placed a liter-size vodka bottle filled with gasoline on top of the sparklers when they first noticed the *Graf Spee* approaching Battery Morgan.

"What's that boat doin' out here?" asked Hassam as he taped another homemade firecracker to the vodka bottle.

"That's that doctor's boat," said Abdul. "You know, Dr. Hartman. He's friends with that stinkin' little Jew Benjamin. I've seen him on the Jew's big boat at Isle of Hope."

Hassam glanced over his shoulder at the *Graf Spee* as he reeled out thirty feet of green fuse down the length of the bar. He watched for another moment as the *Graf Spee* quickly rose to a plane and sped parallel along the length of the sandbar. Then he yelled to Abdul, "You all set to get back on the boat?"

"Yeah, I'm ready," shouted back Abdul.

As he fished around in his pocket for his lighter, Hassam could see the *Graf Spee* from the corner of his eye running at high speed toward the ocean, a little blue flag with a single white star in its center snapping in the wind. "Dumb motherfuck'a," he said under his breath, "don't even know not to go out when a storm's comin'."

Hassam finally found his lighter. He was shouting for Abdul to climb aboard the *St. Patrick* when all of a sudden the doctor's boat took a sharp turn and started heading right for the sandbar. And somebody was sitting on the bow pointing a rifle at him.

"What the!" was all Hassam could manage to get out before an eruption of noise and flame came spewing from the bow of the *Graf Spee.* Bolts of orange fire came at him so quickly that all he could do was drop the lighter and turn to run. Five feet in front of him the sand exploded, as rounds from John-Morgan's rifle hit, but he kept running.

John-Morgan then trained his rifle in Abdul's direction and unleashed a fury of fire that plowed the sand all around him. Abdul was more scared than he had ever been in his life. At once he threw up his hands with a scream: "Don't shoot! Don't shoot!"

Seconds before the *Graf Spee* slammed into the sandbar, John-Morgan squeezed off his last round, then braced himself for the sudden stop. The boat came to rest completely out of the water on top of the bar. Tran had carried out his orders to the letter; and no damage had been done to the engines—which now were silent. Gusto jumped to the beach from the portside; Judah hoisted Moshe over the starboard gunnels and dropped him onto the sand. He could see Hassam running down the bar toward Wassaw Island. Still standing in the boat, he pointed in his direction and yelled "Get 'em" to his dog.

Judah had taken Moshe to Quantico and had him trained as an attack and guard dog by experts: this was a perk he fully enjoyed. He was almost smiling as he watched his animal chasing Hassam, and he scrambled over the side almost leisurely and ran after them, pistol in hand. Judah could see the sand flying up from Moshe's feet as he ran: It reminded him of the way racehorses threw track dirt behind them in a race.

Hassam was about a hundred and fifty feet down the bar from where the *Graf Spee* lay; it took Moshe about five seconds from the time he hit the sand to catch up with him. He latched on to his prey's ankle and pulled him down with ease; then he proceeded to tear at his pants, ripping off gaping pieces of cloth in the process. Hassam was absolutely terrified: He rolled into a ball, covered his head with his hands, and screamed at the uncomprehending animal to stop. Moshe continued his merciless attack, working his way up Hassam's left leg to his buttocks, all the while growling, snarling, and biting. Finally, from fifty feet away, Judah yelled, "Heel, Moshe, heel." Instantly the dog ceased his attack, then sat next to Hassam and waited for his master.

Gusto and Tran had Abdul surrounded at gunpoint; and when John-Morgan determined the situation was well in hand, he stood on the bow of his boat, calmly removed the spent magazine from his weapon, and recharged it with a full one. Then he slung the rifle over his shoulder, climbed over the bow railing, and jumped to the sand with a thud.

"Hold him there," he said to his teammates, "I'm gonna help Judah." He turned and trotted down the beach to where Judah and Moshe had Hassam—who was still curled in the fetal position when John-Morgan put the muzzle of his rifle to his back. "Get up," he said, with a nudge. Hassam neither moved nor spoke, so John-Morgan poked harder and shouted, "I said get the fuck up!" Still nothing. Then John-Morgan looked at Judah—and Moshe—and smiled wryly. "If you don't get to your feet right now, I'm gonna sic this dog on your ass again, you read me motherfucka'?"

"No, no, don't do that!" screamed Hassam. "I'm getting up, just keep that dog away from me!"

Slowly he uncurled, rolled to his knees, and then stood—never once taking his eyes off Moshe, who obediently sat next to his master, ready to go to work again if so ordered. John-Morgan stood a few feet behind him, aiming his rifle from his hip at Hassam's midsection.

"Put your hands on top of your head and get moving to the boats," he ordered. "And if you so much as cut a fart, I'll blow you in half. Understand?"

"I got'cha, I got'cha, I ain't gonna cause no trouble," shouted Hassam.

When John-Morgan and Judah got to the boats with their prisoner, Judah sensed that the dynamics of the situation were changing. No word was spoken—but it was Gusto who was now giving the orders.

"Face down and spread 'em," he yelled to Abdul, who slavishly obeyed. Gusto's English had always had just a hint of a Cuban accent, but now it was heavily and deliberately accented when he put his face close to Abdul's left ear and said, "If chu move a muscle, chu piece a chit, I'm gonna blow your fuckin' brains out, chu hear me, chu stinkin' piece a chit?" Then he looked at Hassam and screamed, "Assume the position, chu piece a chit!"

Without a word Hassam dropped to his knees, then went spread-eagle face-down in the sand. Judah had always thought that Gusto bore a slight resemblance to Al Pacino, and when he heard him call Abdul "a piece a chit," he immediately saw visions from the movie *Scarface.*

Gusto walked over to the bomb and kicked at the sparklers piled around it. He circled it several times, then took the bottle of gasoline from the top of the stack and pulled the fuse from the big firecracker taped to it.

"Looks like our two friends here were planning on setting off these fireworks with a gasoline bomb," he said as he walked over to Hassam and set the vodka bottle next to him in the sand. "Just what are you two clowns up to out here?" There was no reply. "Well," he continued conversationally, "looks to me like you wanted to make that bomb melt and break open."

Hassam had somehow regained a little of his courage and bravado, so he lifted his head and snarled. "I want to see your badge, motherfucka, 'cause if you a cop, then arrest me, an' I want my lawyer, too 'cause I ain't sayin' nothin' else."

Gusto went down on one knee next to him, pressed the muzzle of his Glock against Hassam's right temple, and said, "Here's my badge." With sarcastic emphasis he added, "motherfucka." Then he stood; the Al Pacino accent was gone. "You're going to be seeing so many lawyers you'll never even want to hear the word again. Then, when the lawyers have finished with you, you're going to take a nice long vacation at Club Gitmo or some other equally delightful resort courtesy of Uncle Sam."

"Tide's coming back in," said John-Morgan. "In thirty minutes this place will be underwater again. We need to get moving, Gusto."

"I understand," answered Gusto as he unsnapped a cell phone from his belt. "I have to make a quick call, then we can load these two pieces a chit into the boat and head for town." He pressed a speed-dial key and walked well down the beach, where his conversation couldn't be overheard.

Tran had his eyes and pistol fixed on the two captives; John-Morgan and Judah traded looks as they watched Gusto with his cell phone. He spoke rapidly, then nodded his head several times as if acknowledging instructions. Judah assumed that this unknown was high up in the Department of Defense. Gusto had been on the phone for only a couple of minutes when he snapped the cover shut, turned, and walked back to them.

"Here's the deal. Tran, you tie their hands behind their backs. Then we all help to load them onto the shrimp boat. Tran will take the *St. Patrick*'s wheel while I stand guard. John-Morgan, you will take Judah back in your boat. I have been issued a sedative for these two that I will inject them with once they're secure. It's long-lasting, and these two cowboys are going to take a nice nap, because they've got a long flight ahead of them, and we don't want to have any security issues on the plane. When we get to the dock at Thunderbolt, I have arranged for the appropriate authorities to meet us there and take these assholes into custody."

The wind was picking up from the northeast; and as Hurricane Hannah's first feeder bands pushed their way up the coast toward Savannah, it started to rain on Wassaw Sound. By the time Hassam and Abdul had been loaded onto the *St. Patrick*, the water was ankle-deep on the bar. The *St. Patrick* could back off the bar with ease, but Gusto and Tran both wanted to stay until they were sure the *Graf Spee* could get underway. By the time it was deep enough over the bar to float John-Morgan's boat, the wind had increased considerably. Waves now slammed into the *Graf Spee*'s stern, sending spray into her cockpit.

"You good to go now, boss?" asked Tran over the VHF radio.

"That's a roger, St. Pat," was John-Morgan's reply, "it looks like we're getting out of here just in time. Another hour and it would be a little too rough even for this boat."

Just after the last transmission, Gusto looked at the *St. Patrick*'s GPS, copied the coordinates, and stuffed the paper into his shirt pocket.

In the state of Georgia insulin and syringes may be purchased at pharmacies without a doctor's prescription. As Gusto watched the *Graf Spee* pull away from the *St. Patrick*, he reached into the left pocket of the cargo pants he was wearing and pulled out a vial of Humulin N insulin, the most potent form of the drug. He was standing in the head next to the cabin where Abdul and Hassam lay tied to their bunks. Gusto watched them closely as he filled one syringe, then the other, with 200 units of insulin.

"Here is the sedative I promised you," he said as he injected his two captives. "In a few minutes you'll be sound asleep."

Abdul had resigned himself to his fate; he figured he would be spending a long time in some federal prison. Hassam struggled and cursed; he vowed to have his brothers in the Nation of Islam settle the score once he had gotten the word out through the network of believers that existed in most big prisons.

Gusto didn't say a word; he just went back to the head, gathered up the insulin vial and its packaging, and tossed them overboard along with the empty syringes. Then he went to the wheelhouse and stood next to Tran. The rain was getting heavier.

"They out yet, Mr. Gusto?" asked Tran.

"Not quite, but it won't be long." Gusto was keeping his eyes on the *Graf Spee*, about a half mile ahead of them. "Don't be concerned if you hear those two yelling and screaming. Sometimes the drug I use induces hallucinations for a few minutes before it puts them under." Tran shrugged and said, "I not worried."

The *Graf Spee* was nearing Salt Pond shoal, and the *St. Patrick* was passing Battery Morgan when Gusto said, "I think I'll go back and check on our passengers."

Moderate hypoglycemia, or low blood sugar, can cause a number of symptoms ranging from sweating, dizziness, and palpations to lightheadedness and drowsiness. When Gusto entered the crew's cabin, both Abdul and Hassam were wet with perspiration. Hassam spat out, "That shit you stuck me with is making me sick."

Gusto was smiling and calm. "It won't be long now, and then you'll be getting sleepy. The next thing you know you'll be waking up in a nice jail cell, where you belong."

Hassam was still defiant. "Fuck you, motherfucka."

Gusto walked over to his bunk. "You tried to poison the entire Atlantic coastline with that bomb. If it makes you feel any better, I think you came damn close to breaching the casing and even setting off the TNT. If the plutonium trigger is there, and I think it is, you would have succeeded in destroying this environment for thousands of years to come, as well as killing and maiming God only knows how many innocent people with radiation poisoning. So I will leave you with these last words: No, it's not me who's getting fucked, it's you. And you deserve it . . . motherfucka."

Gusto returned to the wheelhouse, looked over at Tran, and said, "They're getting real sleepy now."

Signs of severe hypoglycemia usually start with disorientation. Gusto hadn't been back in the wheelhouse more than five minutes before he and Tran heard Abdul screaming about being back in jail. The next symptom is usually either a seizure or unconsciousness. The last is death. On postmortem examination and toxicology analysis, death by an overdose of insulin is almost impossible to detect.

The *St. Patrick* had just reached Cabbage Island, and the *Graf Spee* was in the Wilmington River opposite the Tybee Cut, when Gusto went back to the cabin to check on his prisoners. He was back in the wheelhouse in less than a minute.

"Something must have been wrong with the sedative I injected those two with, Tran," said Gusto as he brushed a lock of black hair from his forehead.

"What you mean, Mr. Gusto?"

"They're dead. Maybe I made a mistake in how much I gave them; or maybe the stuff I was provided with was bad; but they're dead. Both of 'em." Gusto had a pained look on his face.

Tran thought for a moment as he watched the river through rain-spattered glass. "They were trying to blow up bomb, right?"

"Do you doubt that was what they were up to, Tran?" responded Gusto as he looked directly into Tran's eyes.

"No, I no doubt at all." Tran fell silent for several seconds. "They get what they deserve, then. They try hurt America just like those bastards do on nine-eleven. I no sorry one bit they dead."

Gusto dropped his head for a moment, then looked at Tran again. "I guess I feel the same way you do, Tran. But we still have a problem on our hands."

Silence descended once more as Tran tightened his hands around the ship's wheel and looked for green channel marker nineteen, his next landmark close to Sister Island. Further up the Wilmington he could see several shrimp boats anchored in the river to ride out the storm.

"Tran, I've got an idea. Is this a good place to anchor and ride out the storm?"

"You bet."

"All right. Let's drop the anchor right here, only don't put out enough anchor line to keep the boat from dragging when the winds pick up, okay?"

Tran looked at Gusto, then smiled and nodded. "I think I know what you got in mind." He depressed the switch to the electric winch and let the *St. Patrick*'s anchor down into the turbulent river.

While Tran was setting the anchor, Gusto put the VHF mike to his mouth. "Doc, this is G-man, come in."

"This is Doc, over."

"We've got a situation here; you need to turn about and come up alongside us."

"Are you in danger, G-man?"

"No, but we've got a problem."

"What kind of problem, G-man?"

"Inappropriate to discuss over the air."

"That's a roger, we're coming about now."

John-Morgan was surprised to find the *St. Patrick* at anchor. As he got closer he could see Gusto and Tran carrying the limp bodies of Abdul and Hassam from the crew's cabin and placing them on the deck outside. Then he watched as Gusto went back to the wheelhouse. Seconds later he heard him calling over the radio.

"Come alongside, Doc. Tran and I are coming aboard your boat."

In the rough water it was tricky to get the *Graf Spee* close enough to the *St. Patrick* for Gusto and Tran to jump safely aboard. But John-Morgan had a lifetime of experience handling boats in all kinds of weather, and after some hair-raising maneuvers and one hard hit against the *St. Patrick*'s hull, his two associates were standing in the *Graf Spee*'s cockpit.

"What's going on?" asked Judah as he held tightly to a grabrail while Gusto and Tran climbed up to the control deck.

"They're dead," explained Gusto, looking first at Judah and then at John-Morgan. "Something went wrong with the sedative I injected, and they're both dead."

"Good God a'mighty," said Judah, as his eyes locked with John-Morgan's.

"What the fuck are we gonna do now?" asked John-Morgan as he fought to keep the *Graf Spee* pointed into the wind.

"We leave them and the boat here," answered Gusto.

John-Morgan and Judah both turned to look at the *St. Patrick*. Its bright anchor light on the top of the mast weaved back and forth as the old boat was rocked heavily by the wind and waves. Gusto looked steadily at the two men in turn. "Let's get going, Dr. Hartman. I'll explain the plan on the way."

Judah was way past upset and blurted out, "Shit, Gusto, we gotta call the Coast Guard and let them know about this. I mean we can't . . .

Judah was stopped in mid-sentence by Gusto, who put his face uncomfortably close to Judah's and said, "We don't call anyone. We don't say anything to anybody about any of this. Do you understand me, Mr. Benjamin?"

"But . . . "

The look on Gusto's face brought an immediate halt to all further babbling. Slowly he repeated his question. "I said, do you understand me, Mr. Benjamin?"

Judah looked at the deck, let out a long breath, then shook his head. "Yeah, I understand."

Gusto then looked squarely at John-Morgan and asked, "How about you, Dr. Hartman? Do you also understand?"

John-Morgan had stared into the face of death before. He had killed before, too, and he wasn't intimated by Gusto. He also didn't want to be an accomplice after the fact to a double homicide, but saw no other choice and with the hint of a smile on his face said, "Yeah, I understand. This is all a secret, just between the four of us." Then he looked at Tran, who quickly spoke up saying, "I no talk to anybody, Mr. Gusto know that."

"Well," John-Morgan continued, "now that we're all on the same page, I've got to get this boat to the Yacht Club. I've got to pull it out of the water before the storm gets here. Ann Marie is meeting me there with the trailer."

Savannah was almost a ghost town on the evening before Hurricane Hannah was supposed to hit. From very early in the morning, I-16 had been jammed with cars fleeing the area. All lanes of the expressway were westbound as thousands of people from all over the city sought refuge upstate. There were, however, a few hardy and determined souls who decided to stay put. John-Morgan was one of them. So was Hannah.

"This house is over a hundred and sixty years old," said John-Morgan to Gusto as they stood on his front porch, watching the wind stir the river and toss the trees around. "It's seen every hurricane that's ever hit here, and it's still standing. I'm not sure I'd leave even if a category five were on the way."

Gusto nodded in understanding and puffed on his Cohiba while John-Morgan took a sip from his Jack Daniels over ice.

"It's very kind of you to have invited me to stay with you tonight, Dr. Hartman. I wasn't looking forward to a hotel room, I can assure you."

"How 'bout you just call me John-Morgan, okay."

"Very well then, John-Morgan."

"Why don't we go get comfortable in the library? Ann Marie should have dinner ready shortly."

"An interesting painting," said Gusto as he looked above the library fireplace.

"Thanks. That's the Battle of Battery Jasper during the Civil War. My great grandfather, Captain Patrick Driscoll, was killed there, along with his servant Shadrack, defending the Lost Cause."

"You Southerners still haven't gotten over that war have you, John-Morgan?"

"It's a matter of honor, Gusto."

"Yes. I understand well the concept of honor."

A bright flash outside was followed quickly by a thunderclap. The lights in the library flickered once, then once again, and were gone for the rest of the night.

"I'm surprised we had power this long," said John-Morgan as he stood to light the two hurricane lamps on the mantle. With only candlelight the room seemed to shrink a little. It became more intimate as shadows fell across the room.

During an elegant, candlelit meal in the main dining room of Driscoll House, Gusto took notice of how John-Morgan looked at his wife. It was clear that he was still very much in love with her. After dinner the two men returned to the library. Gusto was nursing another rum and Coke and had an unlit cigar between his fingers as the wind began to howl louder.

"I would like to tell you how impressed I was with your actions today, John-Morgan," he said as he sat back in his chair. "You really knew exactly what to do."

"I had a lot of practice once upon a time. Besides they weren't shooting back."

"Still impressive. And your weapon selection was perfect."

"Thanks." John-Morgan seemed to hesitate for a moment before asking, "Would you like to see the rest of the collection?"

"Indeed, what an honor."

John-Morgan stood and walked over to a wall lined with bookshelves, opened a small drawer, and pulled a latch on the inside. Instantly the bookshelf opened, revealing a concealed room. He glanced back at Gusto and said, "Come on in."

The room was twenty-by-twenty; its walls were lined with gun racks, all of which held a wide assortment of rifles, pistols, and cases with military memorabilia of every kind. John-Morgan lifted a Heckler and Koch model 91 from its rack. In the fully automatic version, the all-black weapon, designated the G-3, was Germany's main battle rifle. No wood was employed in the shoulder stock or the handgrip, only black high-tech plastic. While John-Morgan's M1-A still had a handsome full wood stock and bore a resemblance to military rifles of the past, the HK-91 had a very modern look about it. Handing the rifle to Gusto, John-Morgan said, "I thought about bringing this one with me today, but decided against it because I'd been trained with the M-14 and knew how to handle it well."

Gusto hefted the rifle, opened the breech, and looked at the bolt.

"H and K have a unique roller-block action," said Gusto. "It's in all of their automatic rifles. That's what makes them so good."

"You know your stuff," replied John-Morgan as he racked the rifle and moved down the line. He had all the examples of the Heckler and Koch line of weapons, including pistols. As Gusto passed by several different styles of Colt AR-15's, then three immaculate M-1 Garands, John-Morgan asked, "What do you think went wrong today, Gusto?"

Gusto was standing in front of a cabinet filled with WWII-era handguns. He stopped to pick up a nickel-plated Walther P-38 complete with Nazi markings. After carefully inspecting the pistol he noted, "All parts have matching serial numbers, a valuable piece."

"I know. You didn't answer my question. What went wrong today. Why did those guys die?"

Gusto carefully replaced the Walther in the cabinet, then turned to face his host, who had placed the old oil lamp he had been holding on one of the gun racks.

"As I said, John-Morgan, something must have been wrong with the medication I had been provided with by my employers."

"I don't understand."

"Have you ever seen the bumper sticker that says, 'Shit happens?'"

"Yeah" answered John-Morgan. "I've seen it."

"Well, it does."

The wind, picking up, made a ghostly moaning sound as it swirled around the angles of Driscoll House. Inside the secret gun room the dim light of the oil lamp revealed scores of killing machines all neatly lining the walls. In one corner of the room stood a mannequin dressed in a Marine uniform just like the one John-Morgan's father had worn at the invasion of Guadalcanal. John-Morgan didn't say anything for several seconds as he studied the expression on Gusto's face.

"You know what I wonder about, Gusto?"

Gusto could see by the look on his face that John-Morgan hadn't bought into his explanation of how Abdul and Hassam had died. He never really believed he would.

"No, John-Morgan, what are you wondering?"

"I wonder why we haven't been hit again by the terrorists in this country."

"Perhaps because of our increased diligence, John-Morgan."

"I'll tell you something else I wonder about," continued John-Morgan, with a hint of sarcasm in his voice. "I wonder if there are government agents who are authorized to take somebody out right on the spot, if they're deemed to be a real threat to this nation's security. You know, no arrest, no imprisonment, no trial, none of that; just a bullet or a knife or maybe just a little Jim Jones Kool-Aid, if you know what I mean."

Gusto knew exactly what John-Morgan meant. "You mean they disappear into the *Nacht und Nebel*, the night and fog?"

"Yeah. That's exactly what I mean."

"That wouldn't happen here," answered Gusto calmly. "We're a country of laws that grant certain rights to everyone, even to our worst enemies."

"I'm not so sure about that, Gusto. I'm not so sure at all."

There was another heavy pause; then Gusto said, "For your kindness and hospitality, I'd like to give you a small gift." He reached into his back pocket to produce his wallet, and pulled out a yellowing, laminated card. In the upper left corner of the card was a photo of a much younger Gusto Camacho. Running diagonally across the card was a yellow band with two red stripes. The top of the card read: "Republic of Vietnam Armed Forces, Quyet

Thang." Below that was printed: "The bearer of this card, SSgt. Augusto Camacho, whose picture appears above, is assigned to a special mission. All military and civilian agencies are required to cooperate in the accomplishment of assigned duties. The bearer of this card is authorized to wear military or civilian clothing and is authorized to carry a concealed weapon." Then there were the signatures of the senior U.S. adviser and the commanding officer.

As Gusto handed the card to John-Morgan, he explained, "This was my 'get out of jail free card,' also known as a 'walk on water card.' They're fairly rare. They were issued to a few Special Forces people. It entitled the bearer almost total access to everything on military installations. If I got into a fight in a bar and the M.P.'s came, all I had to do was flash this card and I was good to go. It could get me into and out of anything. I want you to have it for your collection."

John-Morgan took the card, looked at it, then at Gusto, and back at the card again saying, "These are Republic of Vietnam colors across this card. Were you Special Forces in Vietnam? How could that be? Billy didn't pick you up from Cuba until 1980. We were out of Nam by '75. How could you be Special Forces then? It doesn't add up."

"My good friend," said Gusto with a smile on his face, "ask me no questions, I'll tell you no lies. Just accept this gift as a small token of my appreciation, and let's not speak of these things again."

John-Morgan nodded slightly, then said, "Let's go fix another drink. It's going to be a long night."

They returned to the library; and after both had settled into their chairs, John-Morgan looked at Gusto and said, "I've got a question, but it's not about your past, it's about the bomb."

"I'll try to answer, if I can."

"The real rub about this bomb is whether or not the plutonium trigger is present, right?"

"That is correct."

"From all I've read you'd almost have to ingest some of the uranium in the thing for it to kill you, right?"

"Right again."

"The government claims the plutonium not only was never inserted into the bomb, it was never even on the plane in the first place."

"That is also correct."

"So why were you so scared of Abdul and Hassam blowing the thing up? What was so urgent?"

Gusto shifted in his chair, took a sip of his drink, and said, "I think the bomb does indeed have the plutonium trigger inside of it. I'm not the only one who thinks that." He allowed a pause for that to sink in, and then continued. "When that bomb was dropped into the sound, we were at the height of the cold war. Curtis LeMay was Air Force Chief of Staff. I don't believe he would send up one of his birds and not have it ready to strike at Russia without landing again and taking on the plutonium trigger. But there's another reason I think the trigger is in it. It may seem like the most incredible coincidence, but on March 11, 1958, only five weeks after the bomb was jettisoned in Wassaw Sound, another B-47 flying from right here at Hunter Air Force Base dropped a Mark-6 thermonuclear device near Florence, South Carolina. It happened when the bombardier climbed into the bomb bay because something was wrong with the suspension system holding the bomb in place. He pulled the wrong lever and the bomb was dropped. When it hit the ground the TNT inside it used to initiate the nuclear reaction went off and tore a big crater behind a pig farmer's house. The reason I'm telling you this is that this particular bomb, a Mark-6, was a much earlier model than the Mark-15 dropped into Wassaw Sound. When it hit the ground it didn't have the plutonium trigger inside it because it was still on the plane. You see, back then, when a B-47 got an order to go hot, the bombardier had to climb into the bomb bay and manually insert the plutonium into the bomb. It was kept in the bomb bay in a metal container they called the bird cage. Now fast-forward from the time the Mark-6 was produced to the time the Mark-15 was made. Not many people know this, but Colonel Paul Tibbits, the man who dropped the big one on Hiroshima, was a wing commander at Hunter. While he was at Hunter he and some others developed an arming device that didn't require the bombardier to climb into the bomb bay to arm the bomb. The plutonium trigger was already in the bomb itself, and a lever next to the bombardier's seat was used to arm the bomb. The best way I can explain it is to compare that mechanism to a pump shotgun. The gun is harmless as long as the shell is in the tube beneath the firing chamber. But when you work the pump, a shell is introduced into the firing chamber and the gun is armed and ready to fire. That was the mechanism present in the Mark-15. That's why I think the plutonium is in the bomb, and that's the reason I'm still concerned about it."

"Holy shit," was all John-Morgan said.

The power stayed on a little longer in Kensington Park, but it was raining just as hard as it was on the bluff at Isle of Hope. Hannah and Judah were in the den watching the Weather Channel as it plotted the passage of Hurricane Hannah. Jim Cantori was reporting from St. Simon's Island at Brunswick, where the wind was blowing the rain in horizontally.

"Wherever they put Cantori," said Judah, "that's where they think the storm will hit."

"The eye of Hurricane Hannah passed fifty miles due east of Jacksonville just three hours ago, headed in a north-northwesterly direction. Top sustained winds are at 125 miles an hour. If we go by the latest track from NOAA, we can expect Hannah to make landfall somewhere along the Georgia coast from Sapelo Island up to perhaps as far north as Ossabaw Island, not far from Savannah. Winds of hurricane proportion reach out from the eye for almost a hundred miles. The coastline of Georgia takes a decided curve back to the east, which means that those above where Hannah strikes will be taking a pounding from the highest winds, which are always in the right upper quadrant of a hurricane. From the Weather Channel, I'm Jim Cantori on the Georgia coast at St. Simon's Island."

"It's after eleven," said Hannah. "Hurricane or not I'm getting sleepy."

"So am I, but I think I'll stay up a little longer, I'm not ready for bed yet."

Even though they had been dating regularly for the last several weeks, Judah and Hannah had not been intimate. For him it just didn't seem right: He thought it much too soon after Billy's death. Although they'd never discussed it, Hannah knew what was bothering him; she decided to simply let time apply its healing balm. After Hannah had said good night and gone to her room, Judah fixed himself another strong vodka and diet Coke. He had just settled down to watch Jay Leno when the lights went out. For a few minutes he sat in the dark thinking, then rose and went to Hannah's room. Standing at the door he whispered, "Are you awake?"

"Yes, Judah, what is it?"

"The power is out now."

"Why don't you come in and lie next to me? Maybe you'll get sleepy."

Judah sat on the side of the bed and kicked off his Bass Weejuns. They were still his favorite shoes.

"It's funny," he said. "I'm still wearing the same style clothes I was wearing when we were dating back in '65. I've got my Bass Weejun loafers, my Corbin khaki slacks with an alligator belt, and a button-down Gant shirt. Nothing's really changed. Not even in my life. I'm back in Savannah and I'm in bed with you. How strange can that be?"

Hannah ran her hand across Judah's back. She felt him stiffen a little.

"Judah, Billy's dead. He'll never be back. You and I are alive, and we have to go on. He'd want it that way. We've got a child together, and maybe a life together, too."

She could see that his back was heaving in the darkness, and she knew that tears were rolling from his eyes when she sat up and pulled him to her. She put her arms around him and said, "Lie next to me, my darling. I want to hold you."

Judah fell back on the bed, rolled over to Hannah, and buried his head in her chest. For many long minutes he wept as hard as he had when he had first discovered that she was going to marry Clark. He wasn't sure why he was crying, but thought it must be a release of emotions long repressed. It felt good to let go with Hannah; and as he did so he began to be aroused. Judah breathed in her scent and instantly remembered how wonderful and perfect her aroma was that first kiss. Hannah lifted his head and kissed him deeply, and Judah also remembered the taste of her kiss. It had not changed; there had never been another who smelled or tasted like her. These were visceral sensations, sensations that couldn't be faked. The lightning came with increasing frequency and Hannah watched in flashes as Judah removed his clothes. She pulled him to her and sighed as their bodies touched. Their pleasure lasted for hours; and they hardly noticed the storm swirling around them.

The eye of Hurricane Hannah crossed St. Catherine's Sound at four the next morning with sustained wind speeds of 105 miles an hour. McIntosh County took the brunt of the storm before it moved in a northeasterly direction across the state. Hannah dumped more than eight inches of rain from Darien to Augusta before it finally blew itself out over central South Carolina. Although the eye passed well south of Wassaw Sound, the upper-right-quadrant winds of ninety to one hundred miles an hour thrashed every island and sound from Ossabaw to Tybee. For four hours hundred-mile-an-hour winds from the northeast whipped the Atlantic into a cauldron of huge waves and fast-running currents. Like Hurricane Debbie before her, Hannah tore apart existing underwater sandbars and shifted millions of cubic yards of sand in front of the barrier islands. The erosion on the north end of Wassaw Island was profound. Before Hannah, Battery Morgan was almost completely out of the water at high tide. After the storm so much beach erosion had taken place that the battery was now almost covered at high tide. The City of Savannah suffered mostly from downed trees, which clotted the streets, fell across power lines, and blocked traffic. Structural damage was moderate on Tybee and Hilton Head and light in the city. Hannah's house lost a few roof shingles, and her favorite oak was blown over. Across the street at Judah's old house, the sweet gum where his tree house used to be was resting on top of the house. Driscoll House had weathered another storm with no serious damage, but John-Morgan's lawn was covered with tree limbs, leaves, and pine cones. Once Hannah made landfall she traveled quickly across the state. By mid-afternoon the skies over Savannah had cleared, but the city was still deserted and littered with the detritus of Hannah's fury.

Two days before the storm Judah and Tran had anchored the *Solitude* in the Skidaway River just in front of Modena Island. When it was clear that the storm was long past, Judah called John-Morgan and asked if he could take him out to his boat on the *Graf Spee.*

"Of course I can. As a matter of fact Gusto and I were just talking about going out to the sound and checking on things. We'll put it back in the water at the Yacht Club tomorrow, because I don't think the roads are passable yet. You and Tran meet us there and we'll all ride out to the sound together. After that we'll drop you off at the *Solitude* on the way back."

It was hot, sticky, and windless when John-Morgan maneuvered the *Graf Spee* away from the docks at the Savannah Yacht Club and into the middle of the Wilmington River. The Wilmington and Skidaway rivers were dotted by anchored shrimp boats and large pleasure craft. Judah had counted twenty-eight boats by the time they rounded the bend of the Wilmington in front of Priest Landing. None of the vessels they had passed had dragged anchor; all seemed to have weathered the storm well. The *Graf Spee* was about half a mile from Joe's Cut, and Judah was wondering what had happened to the *St. Patrick*, when he caught sight of a shrimp boat's mast lying off-kilter on the edge of the marsh. As they got closer they could see the *St. Patrick* resting on her starboard side at a forty-five degree angle, her stern to the river. The roof of the wheelhouse was gone, and wind against her nets had bent one of the outriggers. The boat was close enough to the river's edge that she could be boarded from the stern, so John-Morgan eased the *Graf Spee* up to her, and Tran scrambled over the *St. Patrick*'s stern to have a look around. He wasn't gone five minutes before he appeared back at the stern and shouted, "Nothing, nobody, all gone."

John-Morgan cut a quick glance at Gusto, then shouted back, "Okay, Tran, get back aboard."

"It appears," said Gusto coolly, "that the unfortunate shrimpers aboard this equally unfortunate boat were washed overboard and drowned during the hurricane."

"Son of a bitch," Judah muttered, "I can't believe I'm involved in this damn thing. Shit, Gusto, we could all wind up in jail for what happened out here."

"As I said, Judah, all signs point to a most unfortunate accident. It's quite apparent that this boat dragged its anchor during the storm and wound up in this position. It looks to me like the men who were on her were probably swept overboard, especially with the angle of the deck. Perhaps their bodies will wash up at a later date. But, whatever happens, you have nothing to fear."

"That's easy for you to say," said John-Morgan as he backed the *Graf Spee* away from the *St. Patrick*'s corpse, "but how can you be so sure?"

A slight smile thinned Gusto's lips. "I can walk on water, remember?"

"Oh, brother, that's just great, now he thinks he's Jesus Christ," said Judah as he looked at John-Morgan in desperation.

John-Morgan let out a breath, looked into Gusto's eyes, and said, "Yeah, I remember, now." He looked back at Judah with a nod. "Everything's gonna be all right. Just keep your cool, you're with a professional. If Gusto says everything is cool, believe me it's cool, okay?" John-Morgan then reached up to his GPS and punched in the coordinates of the bomb. When the *Graf Spee* arrived at the proper location, the tide was low and still going out. "This is the spot, Gusto. See for yourself." John-Morgan pointed to the numbers on the GPS. "There's nothing here now. No bomb, no sandbar, nothing but water."

"I'm not surprised," said Gusto as he looked across the water at the long beach on Wassaw Island. "The wind and water current were moving from north to south. I'll bet that bomb was just rolled along the bottom on its side like an empty beer can being rolled down the beach by the wind." He pointed south across the water in front of Wassaw Island. "It's out there somewhere. It can't have rolled that far or have that much sand piled on top of it by the storm. Hell, it might just be resting naked out there on the bottom. We'll find it sooner or later. Now we know where to look."

A day later the front page headline in the *Savannah Morning News* read, "HARD-HEARTED HANNAH DROWNS SHRIMPERS." Beneath the headline was a picture of the *St. Patrick* resting at an angle on the edge of Romerly Marshes. The caption read, "Local shrimp boat *St. Patrick* was wrecked by Hurricane Hannah. The two crew members who were on board during the storm are missing and believed to be lost."

Saturday afternoon Gusto attended Mass at the Cathedral of St. John the Baptist with John-Morgan and Ann Marie. They arrived early so Gusto could go to confession before Mass.

Gusto was a conservative, old-school Catholic who had been educated by the Christian Brothers in Cuba before the revolution. He didn't like folk Masses, the sign of peace during the Mass, or face-to-face confessions with a priest. Instead he liked the confessional box. It was dark, secretive, and anonymous; the priest never saw his face, and he whispered his sins through a screen partition. At the cathedral the penitent could have it either way.

Monsignor Bryan was hearing confessions that Saturday. As he heard someone enter the confessional box and kneel, he opened the little door to the confessional window. When Gusto began Lloyd recognized his voice.

"Bless me, Father, for I have sinned. It's been a month since my last confession." There was a pause before he continued. "I have committed the sin of gluttony by drinking too much lately. I have lusted for women, women much younger than I. I have lost my temper twice when trying to discuss things with my wife. I stole a newspaper from my neighbor's lawn when mine didn't get delivered. I lied to my wife about what I was doing because I didn't feel like coming home right then. I missed Mass once when I could have easily attended because I was too lazy to get up and get dressed. I have taken the Lord's name in vain more times than I can count. I lost my temper in traffic and made an obscene gesture to a person who cut me off."

After that he became silent for several seconds. Lloyd was prompted to ask, "Is there anything else on your conscience?"

"Well, Father, I really have a question to ask about Church law."

"Please feel free to ask whatever you want. I'll try to answer."

"I know the Church doesn't consider justifiable homicide a sin, but what if there's an element of pleasure in it, Father? I mean what if a person kills someone justifiably and derives satisfaction from the act itself. Is that sinful?"

Lloyd thought for several seconds before answering, "If it's just a feeling, something that just happens after the act, something almost that a person can't help feeling, then no, I wouldn't consider that sinful."

"Thank you, Father. I realize that was a rather esoteric question, but it's something I'd been wondering about."

"Do you have any other sins you would like to confess?"

Gusto thought for a moment, then shook his head. "No, Father."

"Very well, then. For your penance I want you to be very generous in traffic and allow everyone to pull ahead of you for the next month. When you leave here I want you to light a candle at Our Lady's altar and say the Sorrowful Mysteries of the Rosary before her statue. Now say a good Act of Contrition and work on controlling your temper and your drinking, and be more considerate of your wife. She's a good woman."

Twice-a-Year Jew

Sh'ma Yisrael, Adanoi Elohaynu Adanoi Echad.
Hear, O Israel: The Lord our God is one Lord.
—Deuteronomy 6:4

IN THE CATHOLIC Church they're called "submarines." In the Jewish religion they're known as "TYJ's," or "twice-a-year Jews." In both religions the terms are used to describe members of the respective faiths who appear only twice a year at church or synagogue. For the Catholics it's Christmas and Easter. Less observant Jews show up at services on Rosh Hashanah, the Jewish New Year, then ten days later at Yom Kippur, The Day of Atonement.

Judah had been a TYJ ever since he had landed in Washington. It wasn't that he didn't think his Judaism important; it was just that he was so busy and distracted by his work and social life that he simply decided he didn't have time for frequent religious observance. He also didn't date many Jewish girls. None of his wives had been Jewish, so there was no like-minded female influence in his life.

Judah had secretly known that sooner or later he would have to confront the lack of spirituality in his life just as he would have to confront his excessive consumption of alcohol. But those were things he had been able to postpone. He had promised himself he would do something about them both when he got back home; but it seemed as though fate had lined up against him almost from the moment he had arrived in Savannah. He simply had not felt like dealing with anything as heavy as the meaning of life—or sobriety.

On his first night back in town, Hannah had sent him reeling when she had greeted him at Billy's front door and he had discovered that they were an item. Then Billy had told him about the bomb. Then Billy had gotten sick, and Judah had watched him wither away and die. Then Hannah had told him about his son Matt; and to cap matters off, Gusto up and recruits him into a scheme that ultimately results in two deaths. It was enough to drive a man to drink.

"Would you like to go to church with me tomorrow morning?" Hannah asked him as they sat in the Driftaway Café Saturday night eating dinner. "Lloyd will be saying the eleven-thirty Mass, and we can all go out for lunch afterward."

"Sure, why not? I'd like to hear the Monsignor give a good rip-snortin' sermon."

The oppressive heat of August was gone, and a hint of Autumn punctuated the latter days of September in Savannah as Judah parked his Jaguar in front of the cathedral. The church bells began to toll just as he and Hannah started climbing the steps, and Judah instinctively looked up. Soft clouds drifted across the blue between double-slate-roofed spires trimmed with copper rising toward the heavens like hands lifted up to God in prayer.

To Judah the cool interior of the church seemed cancelled by the explosion of color that filled its walls and vaulted ceilings. Everywhere he looked religious images were arrayed in stained glass, statuary, and giant murals. Whenever he had been in the cathedral he had always felt comfortable. Perhaps it was because this interior was so similar in design to that of his own house of worship, Congregation Mickve Israel.

Sitting in the pew next to Hannah, Judah scanned the murals above the side altars. On the right were the Old Testament prophets led by Moses; on the left were the Twelve Apostles led by St. Peter. As his eyes wandered they came across statues of Jesus and Mary rendered from white Italian marble, then the stained glass images above the main altar depicting the life of St. John the Baptist. Judah smiled inwardly as he realized that everyone portrayed in all this glass, marble, and oils was Jewish. It seemed ironic.

As Lloyd circled the main altar with an incense burner, Judah recalled how the ancient Hebrew priests would do the same thing before they slaughtered an unblemished lamb and placed it on a pyre as a sacrifice to God. Lloyd's sermon had been an excellent one on the parable of the prodigal son. It made Judah think about how long he had been gone from his own religion.

Over the next few weeks, he went to the cathedral with Hannah regularly, not because he was drawn to the Catholic Church, but because he was drawn to the idea of God. As he watched Lloyd perform the rituals of the Mass, he would think about his childhood and try to sort out where his heart was.

When Rosh Hashanah rolled around, Judah was seated in Congregation Mickve Israel. Hannah sat next to him. He listened for the trumpeting of the shofar, announcing the coming of the new year and a call for repentance. When the sound of the ram's horn echoed across the temple, it stirred something deep inside him.

Over the next ten days Judah immersed himself in the rituals leading up to Yom Kippur, when he would fast all day and stay in the temple to beg God's forgiveness for his past transgressions. The next day, with Lloyd on board, he headed the *Solitude* south for the Odingsell River, where they would spend the night.

"How are you and Hannah doing?" asked Lloyd while he and Judah sat atop the fly bridge and watched the sun slip behind the trees on Flora Hammock.

Judah took a sip from his vodka, then said, "Fine. I just don't know where all this is going, though."

"What do you mean? I thought this was what you'd always dreamed of. It's a little late, but you finally got the girl you just couldn't shake out of your head. I assumed you two would be talking about marriage."

The western sky glowed hot orange. In the distance, probably somewhere over Beaulieu or Rose Dhu, a deep purple thunderhead edged in gold with bolts of lightning flashing inside drifted toward them. Judah thought about what to say.

"We've discussed it, Lloyd, but there's no rush. We're just kind of enjoying the moment. Anyway, the election is close and I promised the head of the RNC that I'd go back to Washington if the real shooting started and they needed me. After that I think we'll start looking at our futures and decide what to do."

Lloyd leaned back in his chair. He let his eyes wander across the marsh, which was just starting to lose some of its lively green color, and then to the stillness of the river reflecting the last bits of daylight. Then he said, "It's been quite a summer for us, hasn't it?"

"Not exactly what I was expecting when I decided to come back home."

"Billy's death really hit you hard." Lloyd casually peeled back the label from his empty bottle of Moosehead.

"I felt like I'd been blindsided by a Mack truck." Then Judah noticed that Lloyd's bottle was empty. "Want another?"

"Yeah, I've always liked Moosehead."

While Judah opened the cooler next to his chair and dug through the ice, Lloyd said, "Seems like you've been coming to Mass with Hannah on a regular basis. Are you thinking about converting?"

Judah smiled and handed Lloyd his bottle. "I've always thought you could tell good imported beer without looking at the label or tasting it because the caps aren't the twist-off kind. You've got to use an old fashioned opener, a 'church key.' Know what I mean?"

"I know exactly what you mean." Lloyd placed his left hand over the bottle cap and, using his Notre Dame class ring as an opener, popped the cap off his Moosehead.

"Neat trick," said Judah.

"Thanks. I learned it from Will McQueen. He uses his Citadel ring to do the same thing."

"Sort of a macho-man thing." Judah grinned. "Kind of appropriate for a Citadel man."

Both laughed, and after their laughter faded, Judah said, "Yeah, I've been doing the church thing with Hannah right regular."

"Are you telling me you're interested in converting to Catholicism?"

"I don't know what I'm interested in right now other than growing more spiritual. I'm no teenager anymore, and Billy's dying just sort'a started me thinking about what comes after death. I've done that before, but I always had plenty of time back then and didn't really think about that much because in my youth I didn't have to. Now I've lived more than two-thirds of my normal life expectancy, I can see there isn't that much sand left in the old hourglass and I'm searching for answers, for meaning, for whatever it is that's gnawing at me from the inside."

"Look, if you want to know more about the Catholic Church or just Christianity in general, you know my number. But my advice to you is to return to your roots, go back to the beginning for the answers. The God of Abraham, the same God I believe in, is waiting for you."

Sometimes Judah felt as if Philip Roth had written his life story. Roth is the Jewish author of *Goodbye, Columbus, Portnoy's Complaint*, and more than a dozen other books that chronicled the problems, torments, and struggles that face Jewish-American men in the conflict between their heritage and their attraction to Christian-orientated American culture. Maybe it was that cultural conflict that had kept Judah from practicing his religion. Maybe he had just been lazy. Judah wasn't yet sure, but he had decided to find out.

It was a rainy Wednesday afternoon in mid-October when he took a seat in Rabbi Belzer's office at Congregation Mickve Israel. The rabbi was wearing a white shirt that had no conventional collar and was buttoned at the neck. To Judah it almost looked like something a priest would wear. He had grayed a little since Judah had first met him almost ten years ago, but he still had that very pleasing smile and approachable personality.

"So good to see you again, Judah," said Rabbi Belzer. "I've noticed you at shul, but we haven't had the opportunity to actually sit down and have a decent conversation."

"I agree, Rabbi."

"Well, tell me what's on your mind, Judah."

Judah looked down at his hands for a second, then out through the window at the driving rain, before he answered.

"I want to feel different inside."

"What do you mean?"

"I want to feel like I'm well fed, like I've just had a satisfying meal, only it's not food I'm talking about. It's how I feel about life."

"That's an admirable ambition, Judah. I wish more people had that hunger. If they did, it would be a better world."

"You know," said Judah hesitantly, "it's funny how I wound up sitting here."

"What do you mean."

"I got sent here by Lloyd Bryan, a Catholic priest."

"I know Monsignor Bryan well. I wish I had his oratorical skills," responded Rabbi Belzer. "What did he tell you?"

"He said I should start my spiritual quest at the beginning, at my roots."

"He's a very bright man."

"Can you help me, Rabbi?"

"I can help you help yourself." Rabbi Belzer leaned back in his chair and thought for a moment. "Why don't we take a little stroll through our new museum? Have you seen it yet?"

"No, I haven't. I'd love to."

Mickve Israel is the third oldest Jewish congregation in the United States; and the rich saga of its people in Savannah is tightly woven into the fabric of the city's culture and history. When Judah lived in the North, he was always annoyed by the comments of some who were actually surprised to discover that Jews were alive and living well in the Deep South and had been doing so for centuries. When engaged in such conversations he would occasionally go nuclear just for the fun of it by asserting that his ancestors on both sides of the family had been staunch Confederates both in and out of uniform. He referred to it as his intellectual whoopee cushion.

The second floor of the new temple annex contained a small museum made up of artifacts that documented the congregation's founding in 1736 up to modern times. As Judah and Rabbi Belzer stood before a glass case, the rabbi pointed to the two scrolls inside. "These are the two oldest Torah Scrolls in the United States."

"I knew they were here, but I'd never seen them before."

"Over here, are three Torah Scrolls that were rescued from the Nazis. During the Holocaust the Nazis confiscated every Torah Scroll in occupied Europe. They put them in a warehouse, but for some reason they didn't destroy them. There were about fifteen hundred in all. After the war the scrolls were distributed to different Jewish congregations throughout the world. We got three of them."

As Judah looked at the scrolls, he thought about the people who had once cherished and studied them. He wondered how many had gone to their deaths at Auschwitz or Bergen-Belsen or the hundreds of other death camps that had dotted the landscape of Poland and Germany. He hadn't thought about things like that in a long time.

Moving from display to display, Rabbi Belzer explained what they were and how they related to his congregation, the family in which Judah had been raised. When they'd finished in the museum, the rabbi took Judah downstairs into the temple's sanctuary.

Judah and the rabbi were on the dais, and Judah was standing behind the same pulpit where he had read from the Torah at his Bar Mitzvah. Tears filled his eyes as he looked out over the empty pews and remembered sitting only two pews away with his brother Jacob and his parents.

"It's been a long time since I stood here," he said, without looking at the rabbi.

The interior of Congregation Mickve Israel is done in warm earth tones. Stained-glass windows, which fill the walls on both sides, complement those tones in shades of yellow and brown. For several minutes Judah stood at the pulpit and gazed across the room. Rabbi Belzer could see he was lost in thought and memory.

Judah looked at the tall window to his left. Along its margin were the words, "In sweet remembrance of the just—They cannot return to us—We can go to them." This also reminded him of his parents and his brother; it was comforting to allow himself to believe he would see them again. Then his eyes traveled to the window on his right, inscribed, "Good men are greater after death—The righteous walketh in integrity—God's finger touched him and he slept." Judah thought for a few more seconds, then turned to the rabbi with a strange sense of wonder. "I always felt comfortable here, Rabbi."

"That's what this place is all about, Judah, a place of welcome and friendship. It's a haven of peace and tranquility in a world that seems pretty screwed up sometimes. Here truth is not relative, it's eternal. It's something to hold on to."

"But I just don't know what I believe," said Judah pleadingly.

"Judah, Judah, it's not what you believe that's important: it's what you do that's important. For a Jew belief is secondary. How we treat our fellow man is what defines a Jew."

"But how do I know God?" asked Judah in frustration.

"You know God by studying His Holy Word with diligence. Do that and perform charitable acts with a sincere and contrite heart and He will reveal Himself to you."

A month later Judah was sitting in Rabbi Belzer's office again.

"How are you feeling now, Judah?"

"I'm beginning to bring things into focus now. Sometimes I don't want to, but I've been reading parts of the Bible every day."

"What do you think that does for you, Judah?"

"It makes me think about how everything got started. I guess you could say it makes me think about God."

"What else does it make you think about?"

"Sometimes it makes me think about dying and what comes after."

"Does the thought of dying ever frighten you?"

"Only when I doubt the existence of God."

Rabbi Belzer shifted in his chair and asked, "What else have you done in your search for God?"

"I've started doing volunteer work for Monsignor Bryan's St. Dismas Center. Three days a week, I tutor the kids who're having trouble reading."

The rabbi looked at a photograph on his desk of his grandchildren, then back at Judah. "Let me ask you: "Has God revealed himself to you yet?"

Judah was quiet for several moments before answering.

"Yes, He has."

"Where have you seen Him, Judah?"

"In the eyes of the children I teach at St. Dismas."

Epilogue

The following May.

THE *SOLITUDE* ROCKED gently at her anchorage next to Beach Hammock. The dense hot days of summer had yet to descend upon the sound, so a cool spring breeze wafted through the boat's open cabins and hatches. It was mating season for the dolphins, and close-in a pair of them cavorted in a tight circle, frequently breaking the surface. A formation of pelicans rode the air close to the river, while scores of gulls lined the water's edge on the beach at Williamson Island. To the west the sun was below the distant green line of trees. To the east an early-rising orange-colored full moon dominated a dark blue horizon sprinkled with stars.

Judah's guests were gathered in the main salon, where he and Hannah stood before Monsignor Bryan and Rabbi Belzer, who would perform their joint wedding ceremony. Matt was his father's best man, while Matt's pregnant wife Pam was the matron of honor. Congressman McQueen gave the bride away.

John-Morgan and Ann Marie were present, as were Tran and his wife and several other close friends. Damian was there, too; he had recently been adopted by Lloyd and was finishing his sophomore year at Benedictine.

After the ceremony a buffet dinner prepared by Tran and Min was served. When it came time for toasting, Judah held his glass of champagne up to Hannah and said, "Forty years ago I yearned for this, and for a while I dreamed it could happen. Then life interfered and my dream was broken; and as I look back over my life since then, I think I was lost and wandering, just looking for a way back home. I'm back home now; and that same dream I had wished for so hard and so long ago has actually come true. I love you, Hannah, with all my heart." Then Judah took a drink of his champagne. What was in his glass would be all the alcohol he would consume. He had defeated his demon.

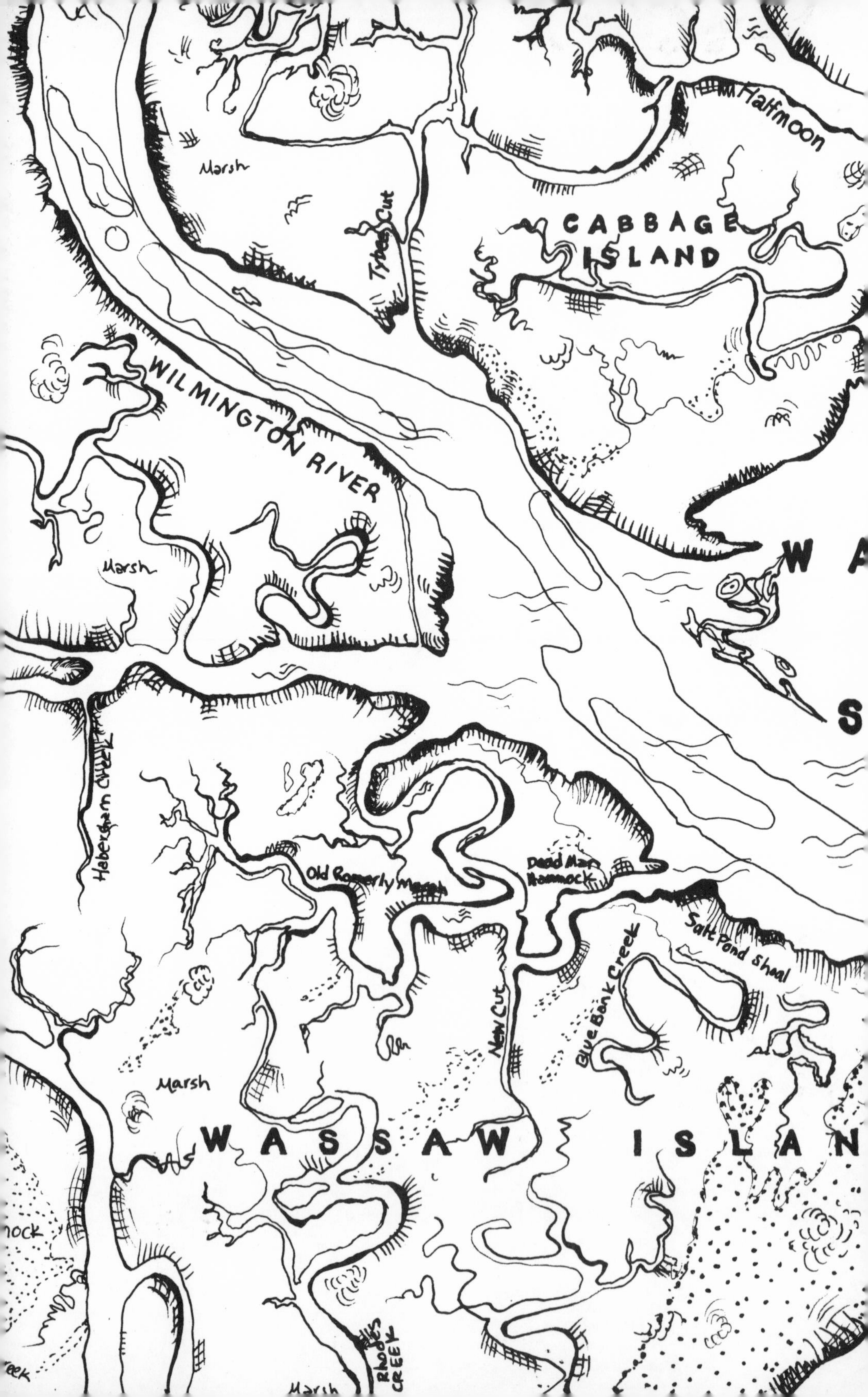

Halfmoon
Marsh
Tybee Cut
CABBAGE ISLAND
WILMINGTON RIVER
Marsh
W A
S
Habersham Creek
Old Romerly Marsh
Dead Man Hammock
Salt Pond Shoal
Blue Bank Creek
New Cut
Marsh
WASSAW ISLAN
Rhodes Creek
Marsh